"Hey, where are you? Come on out and show yourself."

The words drifted up the stairs, penetrating the brick wall in front of the closet.

"I know you're up here somewhere. Come on out and let me see you. I just want to talk."

Talk! Hah! As if she had anything to say to a MacPherson. Shuddering with anger, she held herself still.

"Spirit, come on. I'm not afraid of you. You don't have to be frightened of me either. If we're going to live here together, we need to come to an understanding, don't you think?"

Live together? Here! Cassandra's chest seized with fury. Did the great hulking bonehead actually expect them to inhabit the house in harmony? Impossible!

"Judi McCoy offers a bubble bath-reading comic romance, featuring a perfectly crafted magical world in which love is the best magic of all."

—*Romantic Times* on I DREAM OF YOU

BOOK YOUR PLACE ON OUR WEBSITE AND MAKE THE READING CONNECTION!

We've created a customized website just for our very special readers, where you can get the inside scoop on everything that's going on with Zebra, Pinnacle and Kensington books.

When you come online, you'll have the exciting opportunity to:

- View covers of upcoming books
- Read sample chapters
- Learn about our future publishing schedule (listed by publication month *and author*)
- Find out when your favorite authors will be visiting a city near you
- Search for and order backlist books from our online catalog
- Check out author bios and background information
- Send e-mail to your favorite authors
- Meet the Kensington staff online
- Join us in weekly chats with authors, readers and other guests
- Get writing guidelines
- AND MUCH MORE!

**Visit our website at
http://www.kensingtonbooks.com**

YOU'RE THE ONE

Judi McCoy

ZEBRA BOOKS
KENSINGTON PUBLISHING CORP.

http://www.kensingtonbooks.com

*For my sister Nancy, one of the true
heroines of the world.
Someday, Nan, you will find your Duke.*

*To the Women's Gymnastic Judges of North Texas.
You know who you are.
Thank you for your love and constant support.*

*As always, to Helen Breitwieser.
There aren't enough words to say thank you.*

The Curse of Cassandra Kinross

Come fire and water and air and earth, and curse this man who'd see me hurt. My trust he took, my life he stole, 'tis only just he pay a toll. For the price of his folly he shall walk alone, his male kin for his sins atone. No love shall they find in this mortal world, until I find my true love first. Then must we both with all our hearts, proclaim our love to break the curse.

Chapter One

Autumn 2001
Basking Ridge, New Jersey

Rand unfolded his six-foot frame from the body of his Jeep Sahara. Inhaling a heady breath, he stared at the nearly decrepit Victorian manor like a kid waiting to open a present on Christmas morning. This was the day he'd been hoping for since adolescence. The one-hundred-year trust had run its course. Finally, the legacy his great-great-uncle Colin had hoarded in death had come back to life. He had inherited the trust, and with it, this house. For all the mystery surrounding it, it was *his* lock, stock, and—he cast his green-eyed gaze to the sagging front porch—rotting wood.

Three stories tall, with graying cedar shakes and a black shingled roof, the mansion was surrounded on all sides by a wide porch flanked with huge columns made dingy by peeling white paint. Arched windows, most boarded up for a century to deter prying eyes, ringed the lower level, while the second- and third-story windows were coated in grime. Surrounding the front porch, overgrown rhododendrons and ungainly rosebushes commingled with waist-high weeds and thorny vines, adding a feeling of desperation to the pathetic picture.

But to Randall Colin MacPherson, it was the most beautiful house he had ever seen.

As a young boy, he'd often delved into flights of fancy, positive the house had a life of its own. Drawn here for no reason he could put into words, he sometimes swore that if he stared long enough, he could actually see the windows beckoning and the front door grinning invitingly. Though he was a child no longer, his fascination with the house triggered an itch deep in his heart, taunting him to defy the past and make a success of his dreams.

He could still hear his sister Nancy's dismissive words when he'd told her the good news. "Rand MacPherson, don't tell me you're still intent on renovating that run-down behemoth. My God, the house is on its last legs. I agree the land is prime, but you might as well take a bulldozer to the thing instead of remodeling it. Better to build a fifty-unit tract of luxury homes around that pond and make MacPherson Development a fortune."

"This family already has a fortune, Nan," he'd reminded her. "Enough for two lifetimes. And money isn't everything."

But Nancy was a realist, as was her husband, Warren. They'd even raised their kids that way—a boy and a girl spaced exactly three years apart because the experts had said it was the optimal age for siblings—and expected the rest of the world to fall in line as well.

Rand, on the other hand, was a dreamer and proud of it. He'd always been positive nothing original or exciting would ever have appeared on the planet unless someone had first envisioned it in their mind. The harnessing of electricity, the gasoline engine, even the lowly paper clip had started as a mere glimmer of an idea. Men flew in airplanes, rode rockets to the moon and scoured the ocean floor all because someone had a dream.

And this house was his.

Folding his arms, he propped his khaki-clad thighs against the fender of the Jeep and allowed the reality of owning the magnificent home to sink in. Through every high school vacation he'd wielded a hammer, trowel or wrench, done any job his father had ordered just so he could learn the building business from the bottom up. He and his dad hadn't always seen eye to eye, but he was grateful for those summers, and not only for the income.

His parents had been divorced for years when his father died of a heart attack eight years earlier. It had been a natural progression for him to assume the helm of MacPherson Construction and Development. At the time, Nancy had been newly married to an up-and-coming plastic surgeon and his mother was on husband number three. There'd been no one left to grab the reins but Rand, the only son, fresh out of grad school with a shiny, brand-new MBA.

The time he'd spent working construction had taught him two important virtues. He'd learned discipline from old-time artisans who had helped him to refine the art of planing and polishing wood, how to lay tile and hang a perfectly aligned roll of wallpaper. As time went on, they also taught him patience. Anything worth having was worth waiting for, they had lectured as he refined his sanding and leveling. When he'd heard at the reading of his father's will the house would come to him as soon as the trust had run its course, he'd breathed a sigh of contentment and remembered those sage words of advice.

MacPherson Development had always been a leader in the new housing market. During Rand's tenure as CEO, it had become one of the most respected names in the burgeoning restoration industry as well. It took extra diligence and a fine hand to modernize an old jewel while keeping the detail and beauty of its era intact. And that was exactly what he'd always thought of his uncle's mansion. The tattered Victorian was a diamond in the rough, just waiting to be polished to brilliance.

Removing the black-and-red New Jersey Devils cap from his head, he wiped a bead of sweat from his brow. He'd come here with the keys, straight from the attorney's office in Morristown. This time he would enter proudly through the front door instead of through a broken window in the basement, as he'd been forced to do as a kid. It would be the very first time he'd see the place not as a trespasser, but as its owner.

Stepping gingerly on the bottom riser, he avoided the sagging wood and did a sprightly zigzag step onto the porch. Pacing across fifteen feet of peeling floorboard, he stood in stark admiration of the double mahogany doors his father had once bragged were a solid two inches thick. They don't make doors like this anymore, Rand reminded himself as he put the key in the rusty lock. Studying the boarded-up space in the center of each panel, he envisioned an insert of delicately etched glass, maybe a bouquet of lilies or an intricately woven pattern of light and dark. If he checked the original plans, he might even be able to recreate the glass's exact design.

Turning the key, he jiggled until he heard a *click,* then he pushed. The door creaked loudly, not a great surprise since it hadn't been opened in more than one hundred years. While growing up, he'd been forbidden to enter the house, but he had managed to find a way inside every summer from the time he was twelve until he went away to college. After that, the days simply got away from him while he continued to do the normal things young men do. For the past ten years he'd been too wrapped up in making a success of MacPherson C&D to take the time to visit.

Today, after he'd been given the title and the keys,

he'd transferred the balance of the trust into his already healthy bank account. The money belonged to the house and he was going to use every penny to give it all back.

Cassandra heard the dull *snick* of the lock. Cool autumn air wafted gently up the stairs and swirled around her ankles. As if blowing away the dark stale stench of a century, the eerie wind made it feel like the house had just taken a huge cleansing breath. Filled with a strange excitement, she stood statue still, thinking how the breeze had imbued the house and everything in it with a vibrant rush of life.

Unwilling to believe someone was actually entering the house after all these years, she waited impatiently on the third-floor landing. A few minutes earlier, the rumble of an automobile engine had brought her to attention, but she never thought anyone would ever again come inside her home.

In the beginning, people had walked up the half-mile drive and stared, unable to comprehend that a house this grand was doomed to rot like a perfect shiny apple left too long in the sun. She'd watched them shake their heads, had heard their amazed whispers, and felt gladdened to know they thought Colin MacPherson a madman. Crazy as a bedbug, they'd muttered, for boarding up such a fine place simply because his fiancée had run back to her homeland.

If only they had known the truth . . .

But it no longer mattered what people thought, she reminded herself. Right now someone was in her house. After all this time, she would have the opportunity to interact with a human close up instead of studying one from the third-story window.

She drifted down the stairway and lingered in the upper hall, waiting to see if the visitor would have the audacity to climb the stairs. When she heard a noise in the foyer, she made her way to the balcony. From there she could survey the first floor and see the interloper.

The front doors stood open, letting in a shaft of late-afternoon sunlight so pure it would have made her eyes sting had she been alive. Narrowing her gaze, she scanned the foyer, noting the outline of footprints as they tracked their way over the dusty marble-tiled floor. She could tell from their size and shape the intruder was a man. And he had definitely used a key, because it was still stuck in the door's tarnished brass lock.

Cassandra set a hand on her chest, over the hollow place that would have held her heart, as she realized what the fact could signify. If someone used a key, it was unlikely they were a thief or a child looking to explore. Whoever the person was, she had to assume he was here for a legitimate reason.

Carefully, she made her way down the curving staircase. Caressing the crumbling banister that had once been waxed to a mirror shine, she let the questions tumble through her mind. Who had come into the house and what did they want? After all these years, had the MacPherson family sold *her home*?

The idea was too impossible to comprehend.

Colin had sworn he'd built the place for her. On the day she'd been entombed, after he had knocked her backward with one swipe of his powerful hand, he'd tossed the deed with which he had tried to bribe her at her feet. Who would dare to take from her the only home she had known for the last one hundred years? How dare a descendant of Colin's, for only a MacPherson would be so despicable as to try to sell her home out from under her, have the nerve to begin living here again!

Growing annoyed, she floated erratically above the smudged footprints as she followed them to the library. Her lips drew into a satisfied line at the thought that whoever was in the room would be trapped there. Slightly mollified, she tried to decide if she should confront her guest and find out what he wanted, or simply scare the intruder's socks off and then toss him out as quick as shaking dirt from a rug.

She came to the edge of the open pocket doors and stopped to take in the figure standing in a far corner of the spacious room. Arms hanging at his sides, the stranger was staring upward at the drooping mahogany molding that rimmed the walls. Her gaze was drawn to the graceful hand-carved bookshelves, empty of course but still quite impressive. The books had been taken away shortly after her death, but she still remembered fondly the wonder of those fine leather-bound volumes, many first editions from the very best writers of the time.

Casting her gaze back to the intruder, she assessed him more carefully. She'd been correct in thinking he would be tall, as he stood at least a half-foot above her own five feet six inches. With a crisp white shirt stretched across broad shoulders and neatly pressed tan trousers hugging his finely molded backside, he looked to be a braw figure of a man. Not that it mattered one whit to her, of course. Colin had been tall and nicely formed and he had repulsed her completely.

Without warning, the stranger took his hat from his head and raised a bronze forearm to his brow. The pale downy hair gilding his arm matched the sun-streaked locks that curved around his head and well-shaped ears. When hard-corded muscles flexed beneath his tanned, smooth skin, Cassandra found herself overcome with a strange and disturbing shiver of awareness.

He reseated his cap and she jumped at the motion. Snapped from her reverie, she held her breath—if a spirit could actually do such a thing—and waited for him to turn so she could see his face. Something about him niggled like a burr in her shoe, a wisp of a memory to which she couldn't quite put a name.

Almost as if he knew she was there, the man spun on his heel, causing her to gasp in silence. *He was back!* The sweet-faced boy who had invaded her space a lifetime ago had returned. He'd been younger, of course, hardly old enough to hold a job the last time she'd seen him, with piercing emerald eyes and lovely golden curls. For a while he had come so frequently, she'd actually begun to watch for him, had almost made up her mind to meet him. Then, after what seemed a lifetime ago, his random visits had stopped and she had returned to her singular existence. She had forgotten about him until this moment.

Stirring herself, Cassandra straightened her shoulders. No matter how handsome his face or admirable his form, his presence was raising her temper to the boiling point. It hadn't been clear why he'd come in the past and, since he'd already spent more time here than usual, this visit was just as murky. Surely a bad sign.

Gliding closer, she thought of all the things she could do to send him packing. A howling wind to tousle his sun-kissed curls, or maybe a dangle of chains—she'd become quite adept at rattling chains since her imprisonment—should do the trick. Better still, a laugh—soft at first but growing in intensity, until it rocked the fixtures and caused the plaster to tumble down around his leonine-like head.

With her mind intent on so many delicious choices, she didn't feel him pass through her until he actually did it. And while the sensation merely caused a tremor to ripple up from the tips of her toes to the top of her head, it brought him to a stiff and sudden standstill.

She gave what she hoped was a ferocious grin as she watched him spin around. His green eyes glittered as he slowly lifted a hand to search her invisible form. Raising a finger, he probed tentatively in the vicinity of her stomach, then went higher until he poked at a breast.

Hey, watch yourself, Cassandra thought, projecting the sentiment outward.

Quick as a wink the hand jerked back. His handsome face flushed scarlet. Emerald eyes widened as his tawny brows rose into question marks. Bold as brass, he took the hat from his head and waved it through her face, or where he must have supposed her face to be.

"Who's there?" he demanded, his eyes narrowing in a squint.

Grrrr, she growled like an angry alley cat. Let him chew on that for a while.

The man took a step backward. "Who ... what are you? What do you want?"

He had cheek, she'd give him that. *To be left in peace, you great bonehead,* she tossed out smartly. *Now go away.*

Glaring, he tugged the cap onto his head. Cassandra saw the small, leering devil's face and frowned. The intruder was wearing a self-likeness, though his face and form were much more pleasant. Still, that didn't make her want him here, in her house, a moment longer.

Pirate-like, he folded his arms across his broad, muscled chest and peered, trying to focus his gaze. "Who are you?" He lifted a hand and waved it toward her face. "What are you?"

Shoo! Scat! Be off with you! she ordered. Jerking backward, she waggled her fingers as if chasing a naughty puppy.

Dropping back another step, he hesitantly surveyed the room, looking, she thought, for some kind of trickery.

Fisting her hands on her hips, Cassandra blew a springy corkscrew curl from her forehead. She'd spent time perfecting only the simplest of spells, mostly for her own amusement. If her visitor was going to come around more often, perhaps now would be the time to start practicing in earnest. Thinking on it, she watched him back out of the room with a surprisingly silly grin on his perfectly molded mouth.

If she didn't know better, she'd think he was laughing . . . at her!

Before she could wish him into a moth, or maybe a wee, tiny flea, he left the house the way he entered and locked the door behind him.

Rand gave a thoroughly delighted chuckle, the kind he always managed when his mother sent him one of her outrageous presents. The chuckle blossomed into a chortle, which turned into a bark that quickly climbed to a full-fledged belly laugh.

Thumping the Jeep's leather-wrapped steering wheel with the heel of one hand, he shook his head in amazement. He wouldn't have believed it if he hadn't experienced it for himself. The family legend hinted at years before had been right on the money. Though it was pretty hard to believe, someone or something was inhabiting his house.

His father had always told him that no one had ever really believed his great-uncle Colin when he'd started to tell the outrageous tale. Why would anyone take the ravings of an angry, miserly coot for the truth? Uncle Colin had died at the ripe old age of eighty-four, and the rumor that a ghost inhabited the mansion had died with him. During all the times Rand had sneaked inside, he'd never been privileged to meet the spirit, so he'd never given the crazy story a thought. Until today.

Hot damn! He couldn't wait to tell his sister and his mother. Nancy would be skeptical, of course, and would need convincing, but it was a sure bet his mother would believe him. Truth be told, Irene Kline MacPherson Harding Johnston would probably arrange a séance before the next full moon. And it would be a doozy of a spirit hunt too. His mother knew dozens of people who dabbled in the occult. She'd even confessed to Rand that she consulted a psychic regularly and spent time reading tarot cards. More than likely, his mother would take up residence and—

He slammed on the brakes in order to avoid running a red light. What was he thinking? He had to be a fruitcake to even entertain the idea of telling anyone—especially his ditzy mother—that he had a ghost.

Did he really want his nosy, interfering relatives camped on his doorstep before he had a chance to make friends with the spirit itself? He certainly didn't need Irene and her dingbat acquaintances stopping by to perform exorcisms and incantations every time he turned around.

This ghost belonged to him. It went with the house, and the house was his, goddammit. No one was going to have the pleasure of sending it packing until he had the chance first.

Then again, he might decide he liked living with a spirit. It was obvious from family history he would never live with a woman, so why not a ghost? Everyone knew MacPherson men had rotten luck with women. Ever since Uncle Colin's unwilling fiancée had run back to the Scottish Highlands, the MacPherson males had put up with unhappy marriages and unfaithful wives. It was a family trait he'd come to figure was linked to their testosterone level or maybe implanted on their DNA—especially once the defect had been explained to him in detail.

MacPherson men were unlucky in love, as Robbie MacPherson had warned his only son when Rand was a freshman in high school. Rand hadn't believed it at first, because he'd always had plenty of dates. Of course, he knew he could chalk up some of his good fortune with the babes to being a football jock and track star, but dating women wasn't exactly what his dad had meant.

He didn't find out until he'd gone to college the true magnitude of the MacPherson men's lousy luck. It had been the summer between his junior and senior years and Marianne Crisswell had just dumped him like a batch of stale cookie dough. He'd come home to lick his wounds and his father had taken the time to explain the problem in detail.

It had all started with his great-great-uncle. After his fiancée had deserted him on their wedding day, Colin had turned meaner than a rattlesnake and crazier than a two-headed goat. Claiming he'd been cursed by his runaway bride, it had been all he could do to hang on to his sanity and continue to run his newly formed construction company. Colin's second marriage hadn't fared much better, as that wife had left him for one of Teddy Roosevelt's Rough Riders immediately after their victorious charge up San Juan Hill. He'd died childless, with no one to take over the family business but his younger brother, Edgar.

Edgar married a woman who'd deserted him after six months of miserably wedded bliss. His second wife had given him a son, then died of a mysterious illness no one had ever been able to name.

Grandpa Tom, Edgar's son, went through three women before he found one who could tolerate him for longer than a minute. And even then Grandma Elvira didn't fare well, dying in childbirth with Rand's father, Robert.

Irene Kline had divorced Robbie when Rand was ten and Nancy was eight. Though he'd never been told the entire story of their breakup, Rand knew there'd been a lot of fighting about the long hours his father spent making MacPherson Construction and Development a success.

So, if his father were to be believed, and Rand didn't see any reason to doubt him, the MacPherson men were lousy at love. Since their last discussion about the problem, when he'd been twenty, Rand hadn't yet found a woman who wanted to spend a long weekend with him, never mind share a life. Over the past eight years he'd drifted in and out of relationships almost as often as he changed socks. Susan Stovall had thought him self-absorbed. Julie Henderson said he had a problem with commitment. Lisa Faraday dumped him for a computer geek with adhesive-taped eyeglasses and a pocket protector full of leaky pens.

And those were just the more promising women he'd had the pleasure of dating. Though none of them ever complained of his skill between the sheets, there were dozens who, for one reason or another, had found him lacking.

If he could find a way to have a child without involving a woman, he would do it. In fact, he'd given serious thought to hiring a surrogate, but he'd yet to figure a way to explain a baby to his interfering mother and bossy sister without having to go into detail about the entire complicated ordeal. Maybe someday, when he was older, he would consider it.

The driver in the car behind him honked a rapid staccato, and Rand realized he'd been daydreaming. Hell, he'd let a full sixty seconds go by while he moped over his failings instead of concentrating on the problem at hand. All the thinking in the world wouldn't erase the fact that he owned a ghost.

He turned into the parking lot of his apartment building and climbed out of the Jeep. Whistling a fairly accurate rendition of the title song from *Ghostbusters*, he made his way up the stairs, straight to the small bedroom he'd turned into an office. Sitting at his drafting table, he unrolled the old-fashioned drawings of Colin's house he'd coaxed his father into having laminated, and began to assess the plans.

But his mind kept drifting to the unexplainable mass he had felt, rather than seen, that afternoon. By the time he burrowed under the covers of his king-size bed, he'd relived a hundred times the eerie sensation of walking through an electric field of protoplasm, or whatever kind of invisible energy it had been.

The vibes that pummeled him had been full of gentle anger, almost as if he'd bumped against an annoyed kitten who'd thought it was a full-grown cat. What, he wondered, had made the entity so furious?

Was the spirit going to stay angry, or would it come to accept his presence? Worse, did it plan to turn his life into a roller-coaster ride from hell?

The last thoughts that crossed his mind before he fell into a restless sleep were the ones he considered most important. Who had the being been when it was alive, and how had it come to be residing in his house?

Chapter Two

"Yoo-hoo! Randall darling, are you up? Mommy's here, sweetie, and I brought a surprise."

Rand stuffed his head under the pillows and groaned, but it didn't muffle the ring of his mother's too-cheery voice or the tapping of her four-inch heels as she made her way across his hardwood floors. The last time she'd brought him a surprise, he'd been eight years old and sick with the measles. Whatever it was his mother wanted must be really important.

Peeking out from under the sheets, he saw that it was after ten. High time he was up and moving. He had a twelve o'clock meeting with a fixture supplier of antique replicas and a late-afternoon appointment with a marble salesman. In between, he planned to stay at the house to see if he could scare up—he smiled at his clever pun—his houseguest.

"Randall dear, it's late. Are you ill?" Like a clipper ship heading to port, Irene coasted into the bedroom under full sail. "I've already loaded the dishwasher and made a pot of coffee. When was the last time you had a visit from your cleaning woman?"

Tossing the covers aside, Rand sat up and glared. "Good morning, Mother. How did you get in?"

Irene's green eyes twinkled mischievously. "The front door was unlocked, thank you very much. And I've come bearing gifts."

He ran a hand through his bed head and held back a snarl. He must have been in a big hurry last night if he'd forgotten something as basic as locking his door. Of course, his mind had been on other things.

"I said I brought you a present." His mother stared as if he'd grown horns and a goatee. "Are you all right, dear?"

"My birthday was last month, Mother—and you forgot it."

"Yes, well . . ." She tossed him a dimpled smile. "I decided it was high time I made up for my faulty memory. Breakfast is in the kitchen, and I'm going to clean your apartment."

Rand ran his palms over his face to stifle a moan. Last time he'd checked, his mother didn't know how to operate a Dustbuster, never mind clean an entire apartment. He could only imagine what the inside of his dishwasher looked like . . . and what his stern, efficient housekeeper would say when she found out she had to redo his mother's amateurish attempts.

"Lydia's here every Tuesday like clockwork, and she does an excellent job. Go somewhere else and let me get ready for work. Please?" he asked politely when he saw her lower lip jut out two inches above her chin.

"You need to eat, dear. As your mother, it's my duty to see you stay healthy."

The urge to remind her he'd learned to use a microwave by the time he was six in order not to starve flickered briefly through Rand's mind. Not one to pick at old wounds, he said simply, "Look, Mom, I have a lot of things to do today. Just leave the goodies and go visit

Nancy and the kids. And whatever you do, don't try to clean.''

The pout grew, forcing him to stifle a laugh when she said, "You never seem to have time for me anymore. We used to be so close."

This from a woman who'd spent two weeks at a new-age health and meditation spa in the Catskills instead of attending his high school graduation.

"And I've already talked to your sister. That's the reason I'm here." Irene walked to the window seat, tucked one spandex-clad leg underneath her and sat with a graceful plop.

Only his mother could get away with spandex and stilettos, Rand decided, raising a brow. And on her, they actually looked good. "It won't work, Mother. I'm going to restore Uncle Colin's house—make that *my* house—and there's not a thing you can say to change my mind."

Standing, he stretched to the ceiling, then remembered he wore nothing but the heart-covered boxers she'd given him for Valentine's Day a few years earlier. Showing his back, he thanked the gods his mother's unscheduled visit had kept Mr. Happy from rearing his handsome head this morning and totally embarrassing him. Grabbing his robe from the foot of the bed, he shrugged into it and faced her a second time.

Irene gave a little *tsk*. "I'm not going to try to talk you out of restoring the house. I merely want to keep you from living in it. That place always gave me the creeps."

At this, Rand snickered loudly. "The creeps? For some-one who claims to have a direct line to the afterlife, that's pretty hard to believe. Besides, I thought no one had been inside since Uncle Colin boarded it up back in nineteen hundred. What makes you so certain there's something creepy about it?"

His mother swung a dainty foot. Except for the heels,

she was dressed as if she'd just come from an aerobics class, which she probably had. With a full head of artfully arranged blond curls and a perfectly applied layer of cosmetics, Irene Johnston looked about fifteen years younger than her sixty-two years. If nothing else, Rand figured he owed her for letting him swim in her excellent gene pool.

"To my knowledge, nothing. But I heard the stories your great-uncle used to spout. Even at the end he still insisted the house was haunted. Since he was on his deathbed, I saw no reason to doubt him. That's why no one's set foot inside that white elephant for close to a century. Colin always said there was a problem—"

"Yeah, right." Digging through his underwear drawer, Rand snagged a clean pair of shorts, then grabbed his jeans and a fresh shirt.

"I really think you need to listen, dear. According to Colin—"

He sighed. "I don't have the time to hear it this morning, Mother. And I've told you before, I don't believe the stories. Now, if you'll excuse me, I have to get moving."

He walked to the window seat and kissed her on the forehead like a dutiful son, then stalked into the bathroom and closed the door before she could read the look on his face. If his mother knew the truth, that he believed the rumors because he'd already found a spirit living in the house, she would never give him any peace.

Feeling suddenly invigorated, he ran a razor over his stubbled jaw, took a quick shower and dressed. When he walked back into the bedroom, he found his bed made and the dirty clothes he'd dropped on the floor the previous night piled neatly on a chair. Shaking his head, he couldn't hide a smile. Most of the time he'd grown up, his mother had acted like the Peg Bundy of mommydom, but every once in a while she managed to surprise him with a healthy dose of caring.

He'd always known that in her own way Irene loved him. It was just different from the warm, fuzzy motherly love she showered on Nancy and the grandchildren. And it was a whole lot nicer than the kind she'd shared with his father. He'd never understood why his parents had gotten married in the first place. True, opposites tended to attract, but his mom and dad had been like planets at the farthest ends of the solar system.

He never liked to dwell on his parents' past difficulties because the memory always reminded him of the Mac-Pherson men's bad luck with women. Plenty of couples had problems, some even managed to go to a marriage counselor *before* they got divorced. But the MacPherson men all seemed to go straight to hell the second they said "I do." It was as if they had three strikes against them before they even came to the plate.

Rand tugged on his sneakers and stood, pushing the marriage-is-like-a-baseball-game analogy from his mind. Today was the day he was going to start renovating his house. He had things to do, people to see, all kinds of important stuff to handle.

Sauntering into the kitchen, he sniffed the air. There in his coffee carafe sat a pale brown liquid that smelled faintly like Columbian roast but looked suspiciously like tea. His dad had always complained that Irene had never learned to make a decent cup of coffee. Obviously the man had been right.

The sight of a bakery bag sitting in the center of his antique oak table cheered him considerably. A nice cold glass of milk would go great with a couple of jelly-filled doughnuts, or maybe a few of the sticky-sweet glazed ones he really craved.

Opening the bag, he poked at the three chocolate-covered crullers crammed into the sack. It figured, he thought with a sad-sounding chuckle. His mother hadn't even remembered he was allergic to chocolate.

* * *

The rumble of engines and the slamming of car doors startled Cassandra from her reverie. Then, just like yesterday, the front door groaned, announcing an intruder. But this time there were voices to go along with the sound of shuffling feet, which meant there had to be more than one human here in her house.

She heard a loud thudding on the stairs and puffed out her chest. From the sound of the hearty deep voices, she could tell the interlopers were men. And they were on their way to the second floor, one level closer to her private domain.

Fury spiraled inside her like a newly formed tornado. How dare he come back! she thought, knowing instinctively one of the intruders was her visitor from yesterday. How dare he return when she'd made it perfectly clear he wasn't welcome?

Floating silently down from the third floor, she hovered at the foot of the stairs to look for the visitors. She couldn't see them, but she could hear their masculine mumblings and knew they were somewhere in the north wing. Almost shaking with the force of her anger, she was incensed he would have the nerve to bring a stranger with him into her home.

"Say, Rand, you sure you want to convert that pretty little parlor into a bathroom? With a galvanized tub and everything? I mean, having a fireplace in a bathroom is going to be enough of an oddity. Installing a clawfoot tub and those fancy brass fixtures will prob'ly more than double the cost. You're gonna have to run pipe down and across and drop the ceiling in the first floor to cover your tracks. And clawfoot tubs are out of style right now. What everybody wants are those streamlined Swedish shower/Jacuzzi models with the jet nozzles and—"

Cassandra peeked around the corner of the stairwell

and watched two men walk out of the small sitting room situated between the two bedrooms to her right. The older man, dressed in white coveralls and a weighted-down tool belt that held a ruler, level and hammer, also carried a clipboard and pencil in one hand, while in the other he held a measuring tape. With his thinning gray hair standing on end and an additional pencil tucked behind each of his jug-sized ears, he reminded her of an overloaded rolltop desk with feet . . . very large feet.

The younger man, whom she now knew was named Rand, stopped almost in front of her and began ticking off items from his own clipboard before answering. "It's exactly what I want, Sam. All the plumbing needs to be replaced anyway, so it won't add much more to the job. We'll have to drop some of the downstairs ceilings, but they're over the hall, library, butler's pantry and garden room, so I doubt anyone will notice. Besides, I need another bathroom in this wing if the house is going to be habitable, and I'm going to convert a third of the room into a walk-through closet."

"Can't say as I blame you. You'll have a mighty nice guest suite with two full baths and four bedrooms in that wing. Or are you planning on having a half dozen kids to fill 'em up someday?"

Rand shot the older man a quelling look. "I already have a mother, Sam. Just keep in mind I want the best. MacPherson Construction has given Rudman Supply enough business over the years that you can cut me some slack. Now sharpen your pencil and keep writing."

Laughing mulishly, Sam Rudman nodded as he began to scribble. "Irene's right. You're just like Robbie— stubborn, closemouthed and frugal. Your old man always did know how to rub the bull off a nickel."

"Yeah, well, that's where you're wrong. When it comes to renovating this place, I plan to spare no expense. I just want to make sure I'm getting the most for my money is all. Like any levelheaded MacPherson would want.''

MacPherson! Cassandra let herself spin in a swirl of anger. So she'd been correct when she'd decided only a MacPherson male would have the audacity to show his face inside her house. Oh, he was a handsome devil, all right, but she knew from experience that evil could come in many attractive forms. Her father had been a fine-looking man. He was supposed to have loved and protected her, and instead he'd disowned her, sold her to the highest bidder and sent her to her death.

Colin had been attractive, too, and just look what he had done to her!

The men were standing directly at the foot of the stairs now, pointing at color photographs in a booklet. From her position on the steps, Cassandra could see pictures of lamps, chandeliers and all manner of lovely furnishings. Colin had showed her a similar book once, filled with fancy furniture and housewares, and had promised she could order anything she wanted from it once she said "I do," which, of course, she had never done.

"And I want five-globe crystal ceiling lights in each bathroom and doubles over the pedestal sinks. But I want these oversized porcelain pedestals, the ones with the built-in towel bars on the sides and maybe—"

"Hang on a second, son. I'm writing as fast as I can." Sam juggled the clipboard with one hand while he slipped the tape measure into a free loop on his tool belt. "Now, how about these oval mirrors? That flower pattern etched around the perimeter would look real nice against those rose-colored tiles you were thinking of putting in."

Cassandra couldn't stand it a second longer. They were talking about her house. What if she didn't want to live with rose-colored tiles or etched glass? Shouldn't she have a say as to whether or not the tubs had claw feet or the lights had five globes?

Fuming, she raised her arms to the ceiling and concentrated on the chant she'd been working on for just this purpose. *Come, wind, to me, your help I need. Rise to my call, blow down the hall* . . .

Gently, the air ruffled around her, waiting to do her bidding.

"Feel that breeze? We must have left the front door open downstairs." Sam walked to the balcony rail and gazed into the foyer. "Nope, door's closed up tight. You leave a window open somewhere? 'Cause if you did, you need to be careful. One good bout of rain and it could ruin all the hardwood flooring."

Rand only grinned as he put his hands on his hips. Slowly, he turned in a circle, until he stopped and peered at the stairs. Raising a tawny brow, he kept his gaze on the steps as he spoke to Sam. "It's nothing. I'll take care of the problem a little later."

Problem! Problem? He dared to call her a problem?

Cassandra mimicked his stance as she blew the curls from her forehead with a ghostly breath. Pushing her leg-of-mutton sleeves to her elbows, she lifted her arms again, opened her fingers and commanded the wind to whirl.

In a flash, Sam's papers flew from the clipboard and swirled around the hall. Frantically, the older man chased the pages, flapping his arms as he grabbed and gathered at a dazzling pace.

Cassandra nodded solemnly. Take that, she thought with no small amount of pride. Glancing at Rand, she was forced to frown. Instead of being awed by her impressive show of strength, he was still staring at the third riser, but this time his grin ran from ear to ear.

"That's not very nice," he whispered, shaking his head.

"You can say that again," muttered Sam, who had finally collected all the papers. "I think it best you find out where that breeze is coming from and stop it up before you have a real problem on your hands.''

"Oh, I know where it's coming from," Rand said, still gazing at the stairs. "Don't worry. I can handle it."

With that, he laid a palm on Sam's shoulder. "Let's go into the master bath. That one needs a complete overhaul as well. I want the same theme carried through in there, except I want—''

Cassandra snapped her hands to her sides, then slowly folded her arms across her chest as she wrinkled her nose. The man had gall, she'd give him that. She wasn't finished, not by a long shot. So he thought he was smart and fearless, acting like he knew where she was and what she was doing, did he?

And *handle* her? Well, she'd show him a thing or two. She'd spent some time practicing her craft since yesterday. And today she'd succeeded at getting the wind to obey. If she could rule the wind, she could rule the other elements as well, now, couldn't she?

Tossing her head, she glided regally up the stairs. With a sense of purpose she hadn't felt in over a century, Cassandra decided she needed privacy to sharpen her skills. She'd been a mere novice witch in Scotland, dabbling under her grandmother's watchful eyes, when her father had found them both out and sent her away. Now that she was in the spirit world, as she liked to call it, she was certain she could accomplish much of what had eluded her in her earthly life.

First her father, then Colin, had underestimated her. This time she would be the one in charge and damn the consequences. No man would ever rule over her again.

Rand followed Sam into the master suite, a huge room with arched windows, high ceilings and a sunny alcove that cried out for a pair of cozy wingback chairs. Sam nodded his approval at the spacious, high-ceilinged room and made his way to the master bath while Rand held himself a step behind. He needed time to digest what had happened in the hall a few seconds ago and play it back in his mind.

It had taken all his composure to hold his laughter in check, but it wouldn't have been polite to chuckle out loud at the way the older man had run after those fluttering sheets of paper. Besides, Sam would never have believed him if he'd been told the truth. Yes, the wind had been responsible for his frantic machinations, but only in a very roundabout way.

Rand's ghost had returned, and it was in rare form.

He'd felt a familiar presence prickle the hair at the nape of his neck the second he and Sam had stepped onto the balcony. Once he sensed the entity hovering on the stairs, his heart had just about jumped out of his chest. And as soon as the breeze began to whistle down the hall, he knew they were in for it. His angry kitten was back in full force.

But if he'd done what he wanted and started to hold a conversation with the thing, Sam would have thought him crazy. Then Rand would have had to explain. Knowing Sam, the older man would have gone straight to Irene, who in turn would have settled on Rand like a fly on a cow flop. Nope, if he valued his privacy, he had to keep the ghostly presence a secret, at least for a little while longer.

Once he had a chance to communicate with it, find out who it was and what it wanted, well, maybe then he could let a few other people in on his discovery. But not until then.

"Hey, Rand? You coming in here or what?" Sam called from the bowels of the master bath. "I've got to be in Livingston in an hour to cost out another job."

"I'm on my way," Rand answered, walking through the sliding pocket doors. He couldn't wait for Sam to leave so he could begin his investigation.

* * *

Hell's bells, he's a persistent man!

Cassandra muttered all manner of angry words as she
paced her tomb. Of course, because she wasn't a living
being with solid human legs, it wasn't exactly pacing she
was doing, but more an up-and-down bobbing, as if she
were a small boat cresting a stormy sea. Still, the furious
movement made her feel slightly better than if she simply
hovered in place.

After so many years, the closet in which she'd been
entombed had become a haven, the safest place in the
house for her to hide, or think, or simply be. Sometimes
she slept there in a kind of suspended dream-state, where
she had fond but sad thoughts of her homeland and the
sister and brothers she'd left behind. Other times, she
roamed the house while she imagined what was happening in the outside world. Often, she simply stared through
the upper-floor windows, wishing she could find a way
to walk the little rise that led to the pond situated at the
back of the house.

It had always puzzled her that while she had no problem
passing through the walls and doors on the inside of the
house, she could never press farther, through the exterior
walls and into the outside world. It had been so long
since she'd been in the fresh clean air, her heart sometimes
ached for the smell of pine and heather, or the sweet
summer breezes that scuttled the clouds across the bright
blue sky.

Unfortunately, her ability to maneuver was the least
of her worries. As of yesterday afternoon, her home was
in jeopardy. Like something from her worst nightmare,
a MacPherson man had come to claim her house and,
from the sound of it, make it his own.

Initially, the threat had thrown her into a panic. Today,
when she'd heard the men talk and plan, it made her

furious. After one hundred years of relative solitude, what was to become of her? Why did the one called Rand feel the need to make changes in her house? What did it all mean?

She thought back to the first time she'd realized she was dead but still resided on earth. Almost trancelike, she'd awakened to the sound of pounding. The noise had penetrated the wall of bricks and the closet door, echoing in her mind like a hammer to an anvil. Thinking she was still alive, she'd raced to the door, only to fall right through it and the bricks, out into the hall. Shocked, but not so surprised she couldn't think, she'd floated quickly down two flights of stairs to locate the source of the noise.

Wooden crates filled the foyer. The first-floor windows were covered with wood, the library bookshelves bare. All the furniture had been removed as well, leaving the entire house as hollow as a mausoleum. And she'd found Colin, hammer in hand, walking the empty rooms.

The moment Colin had first felt her presence would live in her memory forever, warming the remains of her embittered heart. His reaction had been nothing like the smug Rand MacPherson's. Instead of smiling, Colin had stared wildly, then dropped the hammer on his foot and backed into a wall. She'd hovered close and reached out to him with clawed fingers, and he'd shrieked like a terrified woman.

Her own grin had been evil, she knew, and as threatening as she could muster. She hadn't needed to shout, or even speak. The mere sight of her had thrown him into a terrified panic. He'd run from the house as if she'd set his trousers on fire, screamed his way through the door and across the porch, tripped down the stairs and righted himself, then raced to his fancy buggy and driven down the lane at breakneck speed.

Days later, when she'd awakened with a bit more

awareness of her surroundings and realized what she'd become, she roamed the house again. It was then she noticed that someone had removed the crates of books and boarded up the front door.

Other than those few visits she'd had from Rand Mac-Pherson as a boy, it had been the last time anyone was in the house until yesterday, when he'd again shown his handsome face.

For Cassandra, the passage of time had not gone unnoticed. From the very topmost windows she'd been able to see a highway ribboning in the distance. She knew the horse and buggy had been replaced by the automobile, something she'd seen briefly on the streets of New York when she'd first stepped off the steamer from London. And great silver, birdlike machines flew the skies, carrying, she imagined, all manner of things. She could only assume that over the past century mankind had made hundreds of discoveries and come up with thousands of inventions to enrich and simplify their lives.

And, thanks to a MacPherson, instead of being a part of it, she'd been dead, or as good as dead, imprisoned in the house in this state of nonbeing, forced to watch the world pass her by.

She sighed, a huge rattling tremor that made her quiver. She had feelings; sadness sometimes overwhelmed her. And she could certainly show anger and fear. But she hadn't been able to do the one thing she knew would take away a bit of the pain and make her feel better. In all this time, she hadn't been able to cry.

"Hey, where are you? Come on out and show yourself."

The words drifted up the stairs, penetrating the brick wall in front of the closet.

"I know you're up here somewhere. Come on out and let me see you. I just want to talk."

Talk! Hah! As if she had anything to say to a MacPherson. Shuddering with anger, she held herself still.

"Spirit, come on. I'm not afraid of you. You don't have to be frightened of me either. If we're going to live here together, we need to come to an understanding, don't you think?"

Live together? Here! Cassandra's chest seized with fury. Did the great hulking bonehead actually expect them to inhabit the house in harmony? Impossible!

Footsteps sounded softly on the stair treads. Panic shimmered in her brain, then died just as quickly. She was safe in her tomb. This closet had originally been storage for the two large rooms flanking the stairway which, according to Colin, would have been the nursery for their children and a bedroom for the nanny. But that hadn't materialized. Though she would have loved having children, she hadn't been able to bring herself to agree to have his. And she had never, in all these years, regretted her decision not to marry him.

From the hall, the brick wall Colin had erected resembled a clever design made to enhance a dull upper landing. In his fury, he had arranged it so that no one would know of the closet unless they studied the original plans and seen it drawn in.

No, the MacPherson would never find her here.

And if she had anything to say about it, he wouldn't live here either.

Disheartened, Rand decided to stop searching once he'd combed the second floor. He'd been positive if he looked hard enough he would find his houseguest, but he'd come up empty. No matter where he looked or what he said, the contrary glob of protoplasm had remained stubbornly in hiding. Darn, but the thing was clever, showing up whenever and creating mischief, then whisking itself away before he could think straight.

Peering back up the center stairway from the foyer, he

wrinkled his brow. There had to be a way to coax the thing into view. He just hadn't been smart enough to figure out how. Was there, he wondered, a book that explained how one would handle a ghost? Considering all the how-to books on the shelves these days, someone must have written *Ghost Hunting for Dummies* by now.

Running a hand down the back of his neck, he shook his head. His mother had dozens of books on séances, spirits, and the afterlife, but he sure couldn't go to her with his problem. Of course, if he could finagle his way into the house when she was away, he might be able to smuggle out a book or two without her knowledge, but it would be tricky. Paloma, his mother's diligent house-keeper for the past twenty years, was worse than a guard dog when it came to protecting Irene. He'd have to use the old MacPherson charm just to get inside his own family's home.

But if he found what he was looking for, it would be worth it. Hell, it would be worth a hill of gold bullion if he could verify the fact that he had a house with a genuine ghost in residence.

Even if he was the only one who would ever know it.

Chapter Three

"Come on, big brother, you haven't been over in more than a month. Robbie and Melissa are dying to see their favorite uncle. How about Saturday at five for a game of Scrabble, then dinner—after that maybe a rousing game of Monopoly? It's been too long since we've seen you."

Nancy sat on the other side of Rand's huge mahogany desk at MacPherson Construction and Development's corporate office. Her classically oval face seemed pale, but her voice was laced with enthusiasm. With her tall frame clad in a tasteful cream-and-rust-colored suit, her precision-cut chin-length dark-brown hair and subdued makeup, she looked as if she'd just come from a charity luncheon for the Junior League.

If Rand didn't know better, he'd suspect she'd been crying. But that was impossible. His feisty, ever-cheerful, always perfect sister never cried. Even when they'd been kids and he'd accidentally on purpose run his bike over her favorite Barbie doll, all she'd done was kick him in the shin and curse him out.

Still, he couldn't dismiss the idea that something was troubling her. "What about *Doctor* Warren? I thought the two of you always had a dinner meeting or medical function to go to on the weekend?''

Nan's generous lips thinned into a smile that didn't quite reach her eyes. ''Warren's on call. I'll be—the children and I—will be alone.''

''Uh-huh.'' He raised a wary brow. ''Mother won't be there, will she? Because if she's coming, you can count me out.''

Sighing soulfully, his sister focused on the fluffy white clouds scuttling by his office window. ''Irene and Harry are visiting on Friday. On Saturday they plan to go with friends to New York to see a play and have dinner. You'll be safe.''

''And you promise not to invite anyone else? Not that Ashley woman you tried to fix me up with on the Fourth of July, or that female golfer who was at your Labor Day picnic? What was her name? Melinda, Yolanda—''

''Her name is Belinda. She's a tennis pro at our country club and a very nice girl—they both were. If you could have seen past my pathetic attempt at matchmaking and viewed them with an impartial eye, you might even have found them attractive.''

''Get real, sis. Ashley was so thin, I could have sucked her up through a straw.''

''She models for a living. And thin is in these days, in case you haven't noticed.''

Rand sat forward in his chair. ''I'm partial to women who have a few curves, Nan, not the ones who look like rulers turned sideways.''

''And Belinda?'' she asked, wrinkling her turned-up nose.

''Belinda brayed like a donkey at every word that came out of my mouth. I like to think I'm as witty as the next guy, but by the end of the night I felt like Jerry Seinfeld doing standup at the Comedy Club. And she smelled like that stuff they keep trying to spray me with every time

I walk through the Mall at Short Hills. Stinks worse than cat urine.''

"She wears Obsession. And no salesclerk in her right mind would try to spray perfume on a macho guy like yourself, so you can stop exaggerating. Besides, whether you think so or not, either one of them would have been perfect for you.''

"Yeah, well, that's your opinion.'' He tapped the eraser end of his pencil onto the desk blotter. "Tell me something. Why have you and Mother suddenly found it so important to see me married? If I'm fine with my bachelorhood why can't the two of you just leave it be?''

She shot him a look that seemed sad yet set in steel. "Why is it so many men think their lives would be better without a woman in it? What is it we do, exactly, that's so darned terrible? And why is it that once you do decide to grant us the *big* favor and marry us, we're expected to keep your life running smoothly, yet you freeze us out when we do a capable job? We cook, we clean, we bear your children, and then we get all the grief. I swear, I'd like to—''

"Hey, this is big brother you're talking to, not your husband. You got a problem with your marriage, go to Warren. Don't yell at me.'' As soon as the words were out of his mouth, Rand wanted to stuff them back inside. It was obvious from the pained expression on Nancy's face he'd said something to hurt her.

She stood and hoisted her brown leather tote over her shoulder, then slid a pair of designer sunglasses on her lightly freckled nose. Grabbing the straps of the bag with both hands, she stared at a spot somewhere over his head. "Sorry. I didn't mean to go off like that. It's been a busy morning and I have to get things ready for Melissa's birthday party. She's turning four on Thursday.''

Aw, crap. He'd hit a sibling sore spot again. He'd been so wrapped up in taking care of loose ends within the company so he could get started on the remodeling of his house, he'd almost forgotten his own godchild's birthday. Feeling smaller than a worm and twice as slimy, he walked around the desk and enfolded her in his arms. "Hey, I'm the one who should be sorry for ignoring you and the kids. I'll be over on Saturday at five, with bells on. I promise."

Surprisingly, Nancy seemed to deflate as she rested against his chest, pressing home his initial idea that something wasn't quite right. His sister had always been on the substantial side, but when Rand felt the sharpness of her shoulder blades against his hands, he realized she'd dropped quite a bit of weight since he'd seen her last. When would he learn to keep his big mouth shut?

For a brief moment she huddled against him. Then, not meeting his gaze, she pulled away and headed for the door. "That would be great. I'll tell the kids so they'll have something to look forward to. We'll have birthday cake and I'll fix lasagna. I know you and Robbie love it."

Watching her walk briskly out the door, it took a few seconds before the gist of what she'd said earlier in the conversation registered. Warren was a plastic surgeon with a successful private practice. Since when was that kind of doctor required to be on call?

Before he could get a handle on what it was exactly about Nancy that disturbed him so much, his mobile phone rang. Picking it up, he went back to his comfy leather chair and propped his feet on his desk. "MacPherson here."

"Hey, boss. It's me. I've got some good news . . . and some bad news. Which do you want first?"

Oh, boy, he thought, raising his gaze to the ceiling. He really hated conversations that started like this one. Especially when they were with a competent guy like Bill Dukovsky, one of his best foremen and the man he'd put second in command at the mansion. "I'm an optimist. Hit me with the good stuff first."

"Okay, great. I'm at the house with the engineers and they've just finished a top-to-bottom inspection. According to them, this place is built like Fort Knox. Your uncle didn't skimp on a thing, so there's no dry rot, no structural damage that can't be handled, and very little work that needs to be done except for the obvious cosmetic upgrades. They were more than a little impressed that a house this old had weathered the way it did. You'll have the report on your desk in a day or two, but I thought you'd want to know."

Rand resisted the urge to jump to his feet, dance around the office and high-five the air. Grinning like a fool, he released a breath. "I appreciate it. And thanks for doing the walk-through. I had some business here that couldn't be put off."

"No problem. Umm ..." The phone line hummed with Duke's hesitation. "You ready for the bad part?"

Nothing, thought Rand, could be bad after what he'd just learned. "Sure, let me have it."

"Remember that order of roofing shingles Phil said he had delivered here yesterday?"

"Yeah. Phil told me he sent the truck out himself."

"Well, they're gone." Duke sounded as disbelieving as Rand felt. "I'm at the house right now and I've searched the whole yard. There's not a shingle to be found."

Sitting up straight, Rand set his feet on the floor and furrowed his fingers through his hair. "What do you mean, they're gone? I spoke to Phil myself and he said—"

"I know what he said. I hung up with him a minute ago, and he's as mystified as we are. According to him, they were dropped in the yard on the north side of the house at ten A.M. yesterday morning. I just walked the property a third time and I can't even find the pallets they were delivered on. And the guys are here to start work.''

''Crap.'' Rand had promised the crew on this site a bonus if they finished the roof in double time. He'd have to pay the men for today, whether or not they started the job. ''Okay, have Phil deliver another load this afternoon and tell the boys to come back tomorrow. Let them know they'll be compensated and tell them to have a beer on me, got that?''

''Got it. You want me to do anything else while I'm here, like call the police or contact the insurance company? Materials go missing from construction sites every day, but who'd figure thieves would come to a house as isolated as this one to look for them? How would they even know there were shingles to steal unless they were casing the place?''

Still wondering what the heck had happened, Rand stood and began to pace. ''How about you go to the local authorities and see if you can talk them into having a car patrol the house a couple of times a night? But hold off informing the insurance company, since it seems like every time we put in a claim, our rates go up. Do you have a problem driving to the police station, then hanging around the house until the second delivery shows?''

Duke's frustrated sigh came across loud and clear. ''Not a good idea, boss. I have two other sites to visit today, and they're about fifty miles apart. If I stay here, it'll put us a day behind on the development in Panther Valley and about a week behind at the apartment complex in Morristown. That job's already on overtime because of that appliance screwup, remember?''

Double crap, thought Rand. ''Yeah, I remember. Okay, give me an hour. In the meantime, scout around again and make sure you haven't missed anything. I'll be there as soon as I can.''

* * *

Rand drove slowly up the winding lane. Lined with spring-blooming forsythias and stately maples now turned red and gold, the private road was pitted with ruts under a thin layer of gravel. But the driveway could be tackled last, after the house was renovated and he was finished with the heavy machinery. By saving the paving until the end, he could use the fresh macadam as an excuse to deter visitors for a few more days.

Once the phone and power lines were installed and the electricity turned on, he would set up his computer, modem and printer and isolate himself inside without interruption. No one knew it yet, but he planned to work from the house as often as was practical. He'd have a magnificent view of the surrounding ten acres, total privacy and a chance, finally, to spend some time with his intriguing houseguest.

After parking the Jeep, he sat behind the wheel for a few minutes and simply gazed at his unpolished jewel. A flutter punch hit his gut and he grinned. He had season tickets to the Devils games, seats on the forty-yard line at Giants Stadium, and more money than he knew what to do with, yet nothing he'd ever owned thrilled him like the sight of this house.

Just as he'd felt twenty years ago, he knew he'd finally arrived at the one place he was meant to be . . . and, strangely, the one *thing* he was meant to be with.

His ghost.

On the off chance Duke had been mistaken about the shingles, he decided to make another inspection. Grabbing his clipboard, he climbed from the Jeep and began a tour of the outside of the house, this time concentrating on the foundation and exterior of the century old manor. He would need top-notch masons to repair the three crumbling corners of the basement, a painting crew to scrape, prime and repaint the exterior, and a landscaping service to reseed the lawn and prune back the roses and other bushes ringing the house.

Glancing toward the back of the property, he knew he would also have to find a company proficient in handling polluted lakes and other water problems to take care of the algae-covered pond.

After the house was made livable, he could turn the rickety barn where his great-uncle had kept his horses and buggy into a four-car garage. In the meantime, he could drive his Jeep right inside the double doors and onto the packed earth floor. He had plenty of time, the rest of his life in fact, to restore the house, and he meant to do it right.

Circling the perimeter, he came back to the front porch and took another good look around. Duke had been right, there was no sign of the missing shingles. He'd been in the business long enough to know construction-site theft was one of the downsides of the trade. But the thieves usually took appliances or lumber, not something like roofing shingles. If things started to go missing, he'd be forced to hire a watchman full-time to keep people away—an idea he found unappealing.

He didn't want a stranger living here, guarding what was his. More important, he didn't want to risk the chance that *his* ghost might show itself to someone else.

Climbing onto the porch, he heard a rumbling in the distance. Shading his eyes, he waited as a company delivery van heaved to a stop and Phil Donlevy, his roofing supervisor, jumped from the cab of the truck.

"Hey, boss. Glad to see you're here. Sorry about the first batch of shingles."

Rand walked to meet him and shook the older man's hand. "Thanks for getting another load out here so quickly. Guess it might be a good idea if we started to store the exterior supplies in the barn."

Phil raised his gaze to the falling-down building and gave a snort. "No offense, but any thief worth his salt could break down that door with one swift kick. And it would be a total pain in the butt if the crew had to shuttle the supplies down here every morning and put them away every night. I think you should bring in a trailer or set up a temporary shed . . . something with a good, strong lock. Or maybe a guard dog?"

Rand stared at the decrepit, weather-beaten barn and had to admit Phil was right. "Okay, how about a trailer set at an angle across the front to block the way of anyone who got the clever idea of pulling a truck up to the porch and driving away with the materials?"

"I'll get right on it. You need me here for anything else?"

"Nope. Just have the men drop the new pallets round back so they're out of sight. And ask Ray Covington to get the window samples here by tomorrow morning, say eleven. Tell him I'll meet him and we can decide how to best do the change outs."

"You got it. Talk to you tomorrow."

Fifteen minutes later, the delivery van was gone. Rand waited on the porch until it sped down the lane before he entered the house, almost as if he was afraid Phil would expect to be asked inside. Shaking his head, he realized he was being paranoid. In order to get the house in shape, dozens of people would have to traipse through it over the next couple of months. It couldn't be helped. He was just going to have to stop being so proprietary about his ghost.

Once he lived in the house full-time, he'd have plenty of opportunity to get to know the entity and learn the who and why of its existence. He had to get a grip. And right now, with the early October sun streaming down and a cool breeze blowing the leaves off the trees, might be the perfect time to start.

He unlocked the door and pocketed the key, whistling as he walked into the spacious foyer. Dust swirled at his feet; dried leaves tumbled in from the front porch and settled against the foot of the stairs. Taking a deep breath, he decided fresh air was just what this place needed, along with a thorough sweeping. Tomorrow he'd bring in a push broom, dustpan and trash can and get started. He'd also contact the electric company to install the power lines and start his service and get the electricians to start installing the wiring.

Sitting on the second step from the bottom, he rested the clipboard on his knees. He'd spent so much time mulling over the incredible idea he actually had a ghost living in the house, he'd yet to compile a detailed list of the things needed to make the place habitable. The conversion of the second-floor sitting room into a full bath and the installation of a new roof had been as far as he'd gotten.

Besides major changes like a new heating and central air-conditioning system, the house needed a completely new kitchen and a total remodeling of the two baths already installed. All the cracked tiles needed to be replaced. Brittle, yellowed dining room wallpaper had to be stripped, then he had to choose paint colors for each room. Finally, the hardwood floors needed to be refinished and made ready for thick-piled area rugs.

Then he planned to commandeer the company's best interior decorator to help choose wallpaper and fabrics for the draperies and furniture. He needed sofas, tables, lamps and comfortable chairs, a dining room set . . .

Several minutes passed as he lost himself in his wish list. It wasn't until a subtle shiver tickled from somewhere inside his gut that he felt it—the whisper of a presence behind him on the stairs.

He held his breath as goose bumps did a prickly little dance up his arms and forced him to keep scribbling. But the markings were nonsense, done purposely to give the illusion he was immune to the unsettling sensations. The last thing he wanted was to frighten the spirit away when it was standing close enough to set his hair on end.

Resting his elbows nonchalantly on the step behind him, he stretched out his legs. Then he straightened, casually placed his hands on his knees and stood, as if getting ready to leave. Out of the corner of his eye he saw something—a ripple in the atmosphere—a wavery bubble of air moving on the stairs.

"Hi." He spoke softly as he scanned upward. "Glad you finally decided to join me."

Cassandra whooshed back so quickly, she ruffled the sun-streaked curls on his head. She'd been quiet as a mouse, or so she thought. How had the MacPherson heard her?

Running his hand through his hair, he gave a rakish smile while his emerald gaze continued to search the staircase. "Sorry, I didn't mean to startle you."

Well, fine, she thought with a little *humph* of annoyance. So the blackguard had an uncanny knack for detecting her presence. She would have to be more careful in the future. The last thing she wanted was to have him anticipating her every move. If that happened, she would lose the upper hand.

"Where did you go yesterday? I looked everywhere, but you'd disappeared."

Of course I did, you ninny-headed goat. I'm a spirit! She shot the thought straight into the space between them.

His tawny brows rose as his eyes grew round. Was she imagining it, or were his finely chiseled lips now turned up in a smug grin? Had he actually heard her in his mind?

"Yeah. You are a spirit, aren't you?"

Well, that answered that question, now, didn't it? He *could* read her ghostly musings. But she'd felt the last thought quite forcefully. What about the ones she gave less importance to?

What are you doing here? she asked quietly in her head.

"Me? I own this place. It belongs to me now."

Deflated, Cassandra inched up the stairs until she hovered on the balcony. Maybe if she was farther away, he would have less success.

Yes, but why are you here?

His puzzled gaze followed her as his eyes tried to focus. "What are you doing way up there? Come on back down so I can see you better."

Well, that experiment was a small success. At least if she kept her distance, he wouldn't be able to read her thoughts or sense her so easily. She remained on the balcony, waiting for him to make the next move.

He climbed onto the bottom step, then put a foot on the next stair. "My name is Rand MacPherson. Who are you?"

The hated name battered her senses. Though she'd known it all along, he'd finally admitted he was a Mac-Pherson. And proud of it, too, from the way he stood there, staring boldly.

She sighed. It would be so much more fun . . . so much safer if he feared her, as Colin had.

Uncertain how to proceed, she folded her arms under her breasts. Even using witchcraft, it had taken quite a bit of energy to move those pallets of roofing shingles, so much so, she wasn't sure she was capable of another successful spell this soon.

Glancing down, she found he'd made his way up several more stairs, until he was close enough to reach out and touch her. Which is exactly what he did.

Determined to stand her ground, Cassandra allowed his long, tanned fingers to brush against, then through, her forearm. The tingle that rippled up her spine was not unpleasant. In fact, it was quite thrilling.

"Hey. You're really there, aren't you? I mean, I feel something. It's kind of like sticking my hand in unset Jell-O."

Jell-O? Unfamiliar with the word, she repeated it in her mind.

"You know, the flavored, powdery stuff you dissolve in boiling water, then let harden in the refrigerator. I ate a ton of it when I was a kid, mostly because it was easy to make and my mom wasn't much of a— Well, anyway, you feel pretty much like it. Jell-O, I mean."

The tenor of his voice, like that of a father soothing his child on a fright-filled and stormy night, held her spellbound. Gentle and soft as a summer breeze, yet deep and dark as a loch, it touched a forgotten place inside her mind, a place she'd thought had died when she'd met her earthly demise.

He pulled his hand away. "What's your name? What am I supposed to call you?"

Cassandra, she answered before her mind had a chance to work rationally.

"Cassandra? That's a beautiful name. Musical, even. I like it."

Her name on his lips echoed softly in the stairwell, waking her from her reverie. Coming to her senses, she realized she had just made known a part of herself that hadn't been revealed to a living soul for over a hundred years.

She'd done the most stupid thing she possibly could. She'd revealed it to a MacPherson.

The handsome demon had to be a witch himself if he could so easily trick her into letting him get near enough to touch her—on both the outside and within.

Appalled she'd fallen for his courtly manners and hypnotic voice, she willed herself to disappear. Whisking away in a shimmer of heated air, she fled to the one place she felt safe, the one place she knew he would never find her.

She needed time to come up with a plan to get Rand MacPherson out of her house and out of her existence forever.

The next morning Rand stopped on his way inside the house and spoke with a few of the men working on the masonry. After giving instructions to the electricians on setting up the generator, he met with Ray Covington and talked windows for over an hour. Now, whistling to himself, he carried the plastic-coated plans and his clipboard up the stairs to the second floor. Except for the fact that he had yet to find Cassandra, today was turning into a very good day.

No one had stolen anything from the premises overnight. The roofers had arrived bright and early and were hammering to their hearts' content. An oversized Dumpster had been delivered so they had a place to toss all the trash and damaged materials, and a storage trailer, complete with a heavy-duty padlock, now sat crossways in the drive. Add that to the fact Ray had promised the new windows would be delivered inside of a week, and all in all things were humming along at a fairly incredible pace.

He stepped into the soon-to-be-converted sitting room, propped his thighs against the door frame, and began to sketch a layout for the new bathroom on graph paper. Sliding to the floor, he pulled out his ruler and penciled in the closet, fixtures, privacy room that would hold the toilet, and the area where he planned to install the tub, right in front of the quaint little Victorian fireplace with its marble mantel and hearth.

Pretty snazzy, he decided when he finished the diagram.

He'd done the same kind of sketch for the other bathrooms, positive Sam would appreciate an idea of exactly what Rand expected the rooms to look like at completion. Now it was time to climb to the third floor and decide where he wanted his computer, fax machine and printer. After the phone installers and the electric company arrived to run the cables, he would be ready to show the guy where he wanted to place the phone jacks and outlets.

He stood on the second-floor landing and gazed pensively up the narrow stairs. In all the times he'd been in the house, this would be his first trip to the third floor. Since it was the only place he had yet to search for his ghost, he suspected this was where Cassandra disappeared to. Since he'd been in just about every room of the house today and had yet to run into her, it was a good bet she was up there right now, doing whatever it was a ghost did to get through its day.

Tucking his pencil behind his ear, he thought about what had transpired yesterday afternoon. He'd felt a true sense of accomplishment at the way they'd conversed on a mental level. Once he told her his name and she had revealed hers, he'd thought they were well on their way to having an intelligent exchange. In fact, he'd been filled with an invigorating jolt of awareness at the idea he was actually having a discussion with a ghost.

Then *poof!* she was gone in a shimmer of warm, wavering air.

When her flashy escape hit home, he'd been overcome with annoyance, but that frustrating emotion had been quickly followed by an almost palpable wave of disappointment. Stranger still, he felt hot all over, yet he'd always heard ghosts made a room feel frigid and clammy. Though he'd often been in awe or perplexed by her presence, never once had he felt cold or damp, or even frightened.

Now that he knew his ghost was a woman, he figured

things would go a whole lot easier. In his experience, most women were peaceloving creatures at heart. Unless they were looking to dump a guy, they weren't into fighting or making people afraid. Though he sensed she had a quick temper, his female houseguest was probably the same. As long as he kept things quiet and clean and stayed in his own part of the house, they would probably get along just fine.

Ignoring the racket the roofers were making, he stopped at the top of the stairs and gave a passing glance to the unsightly brick facade that finished the wall in front of him. On either side of the landing was an arched doorway—entries to the rooms on this floor. After inspecting each of the rooms, he decided they were identical. Both had a pleasant view of the pond and the woods at the back of the property. Both had good light and ceilings high enough to comfortably accommodate his height. And both were large enough to hold everything needed to run his office.

As far as he could tell, there was only one small problem. Neither room had a closet. And if he remembered correctly, there was supposed to be one at the top of the stairs.

Unrolling the third-floor diagram, he perused the faded drawing with a trained eye. There it was, built right into the wall at the top of the stairs, a room that looked large enough to store copy paper, drafting equipment and cleaning supplies. In fact, it looked like he might even be able to convert a section of it into a half-bath.

He walked into the hall and better inspected the unsightly brick wall that should have housed the closet. Why would someone purposely have laid a pile of choppy brick over the door to the room? Whoever had done the job hadn't even been neat about it. The bricks were out of alignment, the mortar job sloppy. Besides the fact that he needed the storage space, he'd take down the stupid thing just because it looked so out of place and poorly done.

Glancing at his watch, Rand saw that he had a good hour before the phone rep was scheduled to show. If he put his back into it, he could probably take down the wall by late afternoon.

It would be, he thought, a perfect way to end his day.

Chapter Four

Sweet Jesus and all the saints, the pounding was making her crazy. Cassandra paced the confines of her tomb, bobbing like a cork in a bottle while she willed the noise to stop. But it was no use. The relentless banging came from all around her, as if the very walls were going to explode.

At first, she'd traveled from room to room, trying to hide from the ringing, but nothing had helped. Finally, she'd looked out a back window and gotten an angled view of the workmen laying a new roof. Since then, the continual pounding had ruined her concentration and made it impossible for her to call up a single sane thought, never mind a spell or incantation, to get the din to stop.

After a time, she realized this morning's noise was more intense than the hammering she'd heard that fateful day Colin had taken away the books and boarded up the house. Because underneath the pounding dwelled an elusive feeling of doom, even stronger than the knowledge a MacPherson would be living here. Something terrible was going to happen, if not today, then very soon, and there was little she could do to prevent it.

And through her bobbing and flashes of concern she'd had random glimpses of the MacPherson sneaking around while he dealt with all manner of things to help claim the house as his own.

First, men had come to talk with him about the electrical service and the running of lines from the main road. Then workmen had settled a huge, cumbersome box across the front lawn and delivery trucks began traveling the drive, dropping crate upon crate of what she could only assume were building materials for the house.

More bloody things to make *her* home livable for her dastardly nemesis, and nothing for which she had ever given her approval. Sadder still, there was simply too much of it to send to the bottom of the pond or make disappear.

Thankfully, she'd had a brief respite in the middle of the day. She'd made her way to the windows on the second floor and observed the roofers stretched on the lawn, joking with one another while eating their noon meal. Standing in their midst had been Rand MacPherson, talking and laughing like the impossible bonehead she knew him to be.

Taller than most, with great wide shoulders tapering to a trim waist and narrow hips, his legs encased in some kind of pale blue, snug-as-skin material, he was a hard man to miss. Cassandra recognized his sun-kissed curls and tanned, sinewy arms so well, she felt certain she'd be able to pick him out even if there had been a thousand men milling about the yard.

Like a king greeting subjects, he'd pounded the delivery men on their broad backs and shaken their hands. Then he'd gone from pallet to pallet, inspecting the deliveries and writing on the clipboard he kept constantly at his fingertips. But after lunch the hammering had started again, making her wish to heaven she had somewhere to hide.

Unfortunately, *he* had been everywhere she'd wanted to go, talking into a device that when not in use was attached to the waistband of his trousers. When she heard him ask someone to return the call on his cell phone, she could only assume the small rectangle was a modern version of the larger boxes she'd seen long ago on her one trip through New York—telephones on which people separated by great distances spoke with one another. Colin had boasted they would have one installed as soon as the lines could be strung into the country, but she hadn't cared. Her father had disowned her. She would never have the need to speak with anyone living far away again.

In the morning, the pounding had been intense. Now, it was simply a constant racket, slowly driving her mad. Worst of all, the MacPherson had paid her no heed the entire day. It was as if he were so intent on his duties, he'd no time to bother searching for her, as he'd done on his last visit. Which made her even more angry.

How dare he ignore her when she was suffering! Didn't he know the noise was driving her insane? Didn't he care that she had no place to go for solace? Was this the way it would be for the remainder of her cursed existence, with him doing as he pleased and her having no say about it?

Finally at the end of her wits, she'd whisked her way back to the closet. The din was still a pulsating ringing in her ears, but no worse than it sounded anywhere else. So, in a stab at self-preservation, she'd shrunk into a small, quivering ball of despair and huddled in a corner for the remainder of the afternoon. It was only in the past few minutes, when she'd sensed *his* presence on the third floor, that she'd begun to pace again.

Why was the MacPherson up here, so close to her only refuge? Why was he walking the nursery and the nanny's room?

Suddenly, the answer hit her like a knock to the head.

In fact, she felt as if the roofers had shaken a rafter loose and it had smacked her squarely on her noggin.

He had all but admitted he would be the one to live here. There could be only one reason. He was getting this house ready for a family. A wife and children. *His* wife and children.

The shocking pain of it slammed her chest and seized her heart in an icy grip of sorrow. Rand MacPherson was married. He loved a woman. And he was bringing her here to share their . . . her home.

As if a cloud had been lifted, Cassandra suddenly knew one true thing. She would not be able to abide living in the house if she had to hear the joyous ring of children's laughter or the muted sounds of the MacPhersons as they talked tenderly to each other or made sweet, passionate love. The pain of watching while not really being part of life would be too much to bear. She would waste away somewhere in the house, shrinking into herself until there would be nothing left but a minuscule blob of misery to define her existence.

Before she could dwell on the disheartening idea any further, she heard a different kind of pounding. The noise was heavier, louder, with a strange kind of ringing to it, as if steel were striking rock instead of iron on nails or wood. Darting to the door, she reached out and found it vibrating.

Holy Mother of God! Someone was smashing down the bricks!

Rand stopped to wipe a rivulet of sweat from his brow. He'd taken off his denim work shirt a while ago and now, dressed in a T-shirt and tattered jeans, with a bandanna tied around his forehead to keep the hair from his eyes, was thoroughly beat.

Whatever idiot had erected the wall, and he figured it could only have been his uncle, had done a damn good job. Though the trowel work was unprofessional, the mortar was tight and chink-free. Even more confusing, there wasn't just one layer of brick. There were two.

He needed to sledgehammer his way through two walls to get to the closet!

At first the discovery had startled him. Then he decided the rumors surrounding Colin MacPherson had been right on the money. The man had been nuttier than a pecan tree. Right now, after an hour of swinging a twenty-pound hammer, Rand was about ready to dig up the old goat and whack him on the head, just for the fun of it.

Setting the hammer down, he reached for his bottled water and took a long drink as he stared at the double wall of bricks. "Okay, Uncle Colin. We're finally going to find out what you've been hiding all these years," he muttered. "And it had better be good."

He was exhausted, but his father had taught him that an honorable man always finished what he started. It was a weekday night and he had nowhere important to go. Though he was losing the light, he could break through within the hour if he kept at it. Tomorrow he'd have the men cart away the bricks and take a good look inside.

He'd spent the day organizing teams of workmen and making more lists, but through it all he hadn't once met his ghost. Of course, that had probably been a good thing, since it was a rare few minutes they would have had to be alone. For whatever reason, Cassandra hadn't wanted to show herself when anyone else was around and, he realized with a jolt of clarity, the fact pleased him greatly.

After all, they had just learned each other's names and had experienced a meeting of the minds—so to speak. They needed time to find out more about each other and draw up some guidelines for coexistence. In time, he was positive they would be able to live peaceably, side by side.

Sometimes, like right then, he simply couldn't stop thinking about her, wondering where she was or what she did all day . . . or what she really looked like behind all that unset Jell-O. He was embarrassed to admit it, but in a way the amount of time he spent dwelling on his ghost was more than he'd ever spent daydreaming about a real, live, flesh-and-blood woman.

Maybe Nan was right. He did need to date more, maybe let her introduce him to another round of single friends. His dad might have been all wet when he'd talked about the MacPherson curse and how it attached itself to every man in the line. Surely he should be able to find a good woman, settle down and raise a family. He just needed to get a grip.

"Hey, boss. You up there?" Duke's hearty voice carried up the stairs.

Rand picked his way over the rubble and peered down into the second floor. "Yeah. What do you need?"

"Just wondered if you were okay. It's quitting time and it's getting dark. Want me to bring up a few of those battery-powered lanterns? New Jersey Power and Light isn't finished laying the cable yet, and the generator lines won't reach this far."

"Sure," Rand agreed quickly. "That would be great."

He waited while Duke carried up two lanterns, then used his feet to move a few of the bricks. "What the heck are you doing up here anyway?" Duke asked, staring at the battered half-wall and pile of trash littering the landing.

"Just a pain-in-the-butt job I decided needed to be done." He took another swig from his water bottle.

"You want some help?"

Rand considered then rejected the offer. He'd started this job; he would be the one to finish it. "Nope, thanks. I'm just going to take down enough to get the door open. Tomorrow maybe a couple of guys can haul away the junk. The rest should be easy."

Duke rubbed the back of his neck with a blue workman's handkerchief. "You know, I never wanted to believe the stories circulating about your uncle, but from the looks of this . . ."

Laughing, Rand picked up the hammer. "Yeah, I know. Dad used to tell me insanity ran in the MacPherson family, at least on the male side. According to my mother, the rumor is absolutely true. Now, go on home so I can finish."

Duke's grin stretched from ear to ear. "Will do. Oh, and if I were you, first thing I'd do tonight is drive myself to a massage parlor and let some curvy cutie with fingers of steel give me a good, stiff . . . uh . . . rubdown. You're going to need it."

"Yeah, I guess so," Rand answered good-naturedly. "Now, get the heck out of here. I'll see you tomorrow."

Half listening to the pounding of Duke's feet and the closing of the front door, he carefully studied the wall. Setting his hands on his hips, he had a fleeting desire to take his foreman's advice and go home for the evening. He didn't know of a massage parlor and he wasn't dating anyone who could give him a good stiff anything, but right about now a long soak in a steaming tub would be a fine way to end the day.

Shrugging, he picked up the sledgehammer and hoisted it over his shoulder. Raising his arms, he took one more hearty whack, then another and another, until finally he saw the door to the closet.

Aiming more precisely, he managed to clear an opening that revealed the entire door, which looked to be solid mahogany with an antique cut-crystal knob, just like the ones in the rest of the house.

Bending down, he turned the knob, but the darn thing wouldn't budge. The door was locked tighter than a drum full of toxic waste.

Rand took a step back and scratched his head. It would be a damn shame to ruin the door or the crystal knob by whacking it with a hammer or kicking the thing down. Besides, he'd accomplished his goal for the day. He'd taken down the wall and found the closet. The lanterns were helping, but the landing was gloomy and the closet was probably as empty as his uncle's mind had been when he'd laid the brick. What the heck. Tomorrow was soon enough to either find the key or get a screwdriver and take off the doorknob.

After setting the hammer in the corner, he picked up the lanterns and made his way down the stairs.

The next morning, clipboard in hand, Rand concentrated on his first task: ordering tile for the foyer. It took a full thirty seconds for him to acknowledge one of the workmen's anxious calls.

"Hey, boss. You might want to come up here."

Rand stopped in the middle of counting the number of tiles that needed to be replaced. Sunshine streamed in from the recently unboarded windows, filling the entryway with cool autumn light. Unfortunately, the brightness reflected off the cracked marble like a magnifying glass, confirming just how much work needed to be done.

Since he'd sent the guys upstairs to take care of removing the brick only a few minutes earlier, he couldn't imagine what was wrong. "Is there a problem, Frank?"

He heard footsteps and figured Frank was on his way down, so he waited. Every muscle in Rand's back, legs and arms throbbed. It had been a while since he'd done any true manual labor, and he'd pushed himself to the limit yesterday by taking down that wall. A near-scalding bath last night and an equally hot shower that morning had done little to ease his aches. Right now he felt like he'd been pulled through a knothole backward.

But it was good to be back working with his hands, flexing muscles he'd last used ten years ago. At thirty-

two, he was fit, still able to bench-press twice his weight
and turn female heads on the beach. Fixing up this house
and doing most of the inside work himself would get him
in top shape again.

"Tell me once more where it was you said we'd find
that brick?" he heard Frank call as the workman made
his way down from the third floor.

Rand walked to the bottom of the stairway. "On the
top landing, between those two big rooms. And I think
you're going to need something to help carry the rubble
down, or maybe you could take the bricks to a window
in one of those bedrooms and heave them—"

Frank arrived on the balcony and gave him a deadpan
gaze. "That landing is clean as a whistle, Rand. There's
nothing up there but some dust and mouse droppings."

Leaning against the stair newel, Rand grinned. He knew
when the guys were taking him for a ride. Like his father
before him, he'd always prided himself on being "one
of the boys." The tactic had gotten MacPherson C&D a
loyal crew, willing to do whatever it took to get a job
done. "Look, if you think that's going to get me to climb
those stairs, you're dreaming. My legs feel like I've run
a marathon. Now, get back up there and—"

The young construction worker tugged at his chin, then
called up to his partner. "Hey, Pete, come on down here,
would you? I need you to talk some sense into the boss."

Rand set his clipboard on the bottom step with a groan.
Straightening, he pushed past the pain. "If you fellas
think this is funny, you're dead wrong."

"Did you tell him?" Pete alighted on the balcony next
to Frank and tucked his hands into the back pockets of
his jeans.

"Tried to. Rand here thinks we're joking."

"You're not joking?" Rand folded his arms across his
chest.

"No, sir," Frank said.

"Not us, Rand. Honest," Pete added. "If you don't believe us, come upstairs and see for yourself."

Crap, thought Rand, stepping doggedly on the stairs. Every lift of his legs hurt. If he'd remembered to pop three aspirin before he left the apartment that morning, he wouldn't be in so much misery right now.

By the time he reached the balcony, he was ready to chew nails. "Lead on, you two, but if I get up there and find out this is some kind of practical joke . . ."

Pete and Frank gave each other cockeyed looks and headed up the stairs. When Rand arrived at the top of the third-floor landing, his gaze settled on the spotless floor, and he immediately thought the two bozos had gone to the ultimate trouble of hiding all the rubble. Then he raised his eyes to the wall and blinked, not once, but twice.

"Who in the hell did that?" he asked aloud, his eyes wide.

"Did what?" This from Pete.

"This is the way we found it," Frank answered quickly. Pete was right behind him with a "he's got that right."

"Well, hell," Rand spat out as he rubbed his face with the palm of his hand. Aches and pains forgotten, he walked closer to the brick, reached out hesitantly and touched it. Cool, solid and rough under his fingertips, it made him see fireworks.

"You two are telling me this was what you found when you got up here a few minutes ago?"

"Uh . . . yes, sir," Frank muttered, staring at Rand as if he'd grown a second head. "It looked just like this."

"Pete?"

"Rand?"

"Don't Rand me. Is Frank telling the truth?"

Pete glanced at Frank, his eyes crinkling. "Well, not always, he's not. But in this case, yes, sir. This is just the way we found it. You want us to tear it down?"

It already was torn down, you assholes! Rand wanted to shout. But there was no use being rude. They hadn't been there yesterday while he'd sweat blood doing all the grunt work. He needed Duke and he needed him fast.

"Where's Dukovsky?"

"Panther Valley. Told us he'd be here by lunchtime. Want me to call him?" asked Frank, sounding just a little condescending.

Rand reached out and touched the very solid wall again. Poking a finger into one of the crevices, he found the mortar to be still damp. Impossible. Why would some addlepated idiot of a thief come into the house and *rebrick* the wall?

But there was no other explanation for it. First the shingles, now the brick—only instead of stealing, this time the thief had put stuff back.

He ran his fingers through his hair, knowing full well his employees were staring as if he were one Bud short of a six-pack. "No, I don't want you to call him. I want you to dismantle the damned thing brick by brick. Then I want you to see to it each brick is stacked in a pile in the side yard with a bright red ribbon tied on top. You understand that?"

Frank and Pete rolled their eyes but kept their objections to themselves. "Yes, sir, we understand."

Rand placed both hands against the brick a final time just to make sure he wasn't hallucinating. Then he turned and tromped down the stairs at breakneck speed.

Cassandra listened raptly, holding back a giggle. She'd done it. It had taken most of the night, but she'd managed to set every brick back in place and neaten the landing as well. The work had been exhausting, as harnessing the elements had proven difficult. Fire, water, air and earth hadn't been as eager to help with this task as they had been at transporting the shingles.

She hadn't seen the look on his face, but the surprise and annoyance in the MacPherson's voice was enough to tell her the result of her handiwork had thoroughly frustrated him. He was furious, shocked and completely confused. Just hearing his questioning tone had sent a delightful tremor skittering up her spine. She'd gotten him but good.

Unfortunately, he wasn't the kind of man to simply let things be. As soon as he'd found his head, he ordered the workmen to start disassembling the bloody wall a second time, and they had obeyed. She could hear them now, tapping at the mortar and separating the brick, more than likely setting it all in a neat pile to be taken down to the side lawn. At this rate, they would finish the job in a few hours. And this time she would be too weak to stop them.

If only she'd had the good sense to be more diligent in practicing her skills these past one hundred years, she might have grown stronger and been able to conjure something outrageous, like turning the men into toads, or sending them to a mountaintop. But she'd never thought anyone would want to live in the house again. And doing something nasty to the workmen wouldn't have been fair, since they were only following orders. No, it wasn't the workmen she had to contend with. It was the MacPherson.

Bobbing in a circle, Cassandra racked her brain. All right, she acknowledged with a shimmer of practicality, so Rand would eventually find her hiding place. So what? The house was enormous. She remembered telling Colin it was much too big, too grand and too overblown for her taste. It had five bedrooms, two parlors, a library, a dining room, a breakfast room, a garden room and a kitchen, plus the two rooms on the top floor. Surely she could lose herself in fourteen rooms?

You're down but not defeated, she told herself firmly. Not yet anyway. And if she managed to make enough mischief, who knew what could happen? Maybe when Mrs. MacPherson moved in and Cassandra showed herself, the woman would run screaming, as Colin had done. With luck, Rand's wife would be the one to refuse to live here and the family would be forced to move out. It wouldn't be proper to frighten his children, of course, but it might be fun to scare his wife.

She broke from her reverie at the sound of scraping, aware the men were having an easy task taking apart the damp mortar. Soon the wall would be gone and the door again revealed.

Cassandra wrinkled her brow as she blew away a curl. Now, what was it he'd thought last night when he'd seen the cut-crystal doorknob? Something about needing a screwdriver to take the knob apart?

Workmen's tools weren't exactly her forte, but surely she had enough energy to find the thing he called a screwdriver and get rid of it? Better still, she might be able to hide all the tools in the same place where she'd deposited the shingles, or bury them in the cellar. It might take days for the owners to replace them, and by then she would think of something else to deter them from their job.

Tapping a finger onto her chin, she slipped through the door and wall of crumbling bricks. Whistling past the workmen, she headed down the stairs to begin her search.

"You feel that?" remarked Pete, his hammer poised in midair.

"Yeah. I mean no. I didn't feel nothin'." Frank continued to scratch at the mortar while he diligently separated the bricks.

"It was a breeze, but kinda like a thick breeze, if you know what I mean."

"A thick breeze?" Frank wiped his forehead with the back of his hand.

"Yeah, you know. Heavy, as if something invisible just flew right past us."

"Okay, I'll admit I felt a little shot of air, but so what? I don't know anything about a *thick* breeze, and nothing that's real is invisible ... except germs maybe. Now, let's get back to work."

"The boss was really cheesed off about this wall. From the sound of it, he thought it had already been taken down."

"That's what it sounded like to me. I haven't seen him so heated up since that delivery of kitchen appliances went to the wrong job site and the apartment complex in Montclair had to go empty for a month. Remember?"

Pete snorted as he removed a brick and set it carefully on the landing. "I'd say he was madder. And a whole lot more unreasonable. But I have to admit, from the feel of it, this brick was laid less that twelve hours ago." Glancing at the stairway, he asked, "You believe that stuff everybody says about this place?"

Frank continued to peck at the mortar and loosen the bricks. "What stuff?"

"You know. The talk about his great-uncle being crazy. That Colin MacPherson was cursed, and that he thought this place was haunted."

"Haunted?" Frank asked, unsuccessful at holding back a derisive chuckle. "Now who's the crazy one? And seein' as I never met the uncle, I wouldn't dare to pass judgment on the old guy. Now, let's get cracking. We've got a lot of work to do."

Chapter Five

Two hours later, Frank and Pete escorted Rand to the pile of crumbling brick stacked in the side yard. Like kindergartners expecting kudos from the teacher, they grinned as he inspected the pallet, complete with a wilted red-velour bow on top, exactly as he'd requested.

"Clever. Very clever." He flicked a finger at the floppy ribbon, which looked suspiciously like a Christmas wreath castoff. "Okay, you guys did good. Now one of you drive the forklift over here and cart the stuff to the Dumpster. I never want to see it again."

Duke was due to arrive in an hour. Rand had been debating whether or not to tell the foreman what had transpired with the wall, as well as another nasty development. But how could he explain to his foreman that while they had a polite and very helpful thief, they had been robbed again. After he'd come to grips with the fact some burglar who possessed a skewed sense of humor had reconstructed the wall, he found out there *had* been another theft.

Entering the storage trailer a little while ago, he'd discovered every drill, sander, router and plane in the place gone . . . disappeared into thin air. He didn't just have a thief on his hands, he had a gang, and they were bold as brass and twice as stupid if they thought they were going to get away with any more MacPherson equipment.

He needed someone to help set his head straight on this one. Did he get the insurance company involved as well as the local authorities, or buy that guard dog Phil had suggested? Maybe if he simply hired a night watchman and kept his fingers crossed, it would be enough to deter further thefts.

But if he did hire a security guard, how would Cassandra take to the idea of an overnight companion? A stranger with no investment in the house other than a paycheck, wandering around and invading her space at all hours? And what would happen if she did decide to show herself to whomever he hired?

If, after seeing her, the guy lasted more than one night, he would probably blab to the whole world about the unbelievable paranormal phenomenon he'd seen, and that would be the kiss of death to Rand's private time with his ghost. Cassandra might even decide he'd insulted her and find another house to haunt. Something he didn't even want to think about.

He hadn't seen her, felt her presence, or talked to her in more than a day, and already he missed her. In between racking his brain over the thefts, something nagged at him. Could the closet and its contents hold the key not only to where Cassandra was and how she'd come to be in the house, but also to the crazy shenanigans with the wall and the tools? Now, eager to sate his curiosity, all he wanted was to get to the third floor and open that damned door once and for all.

Walking onto the front porch, he patted at his leather tool belt for a screwdriver but came up empty. Searching the belt, he realized all of his tools, from his awl to his hammer to his measuring tape, were missing. He ran a palm across his jaw to hold back a curse. He must have been so distracted this morning, he'd left bits and pieces of himself in every room of the house.

Ambling into the library, he approached one of his best woodworkers, Jack Mulvaney, who was busy stripping the bookcases. "Let me borrow a screwdriver, would you, Mulvaney? I seem to have misplaced mine."

Jack set down a brush thick with some foul-smelling chemical and stood, checked his own belt and found it empty. Squatting, he opened the rusty metal box he carried religiously to every job. Slack-jawed, he stared at the box, now as empty as a school yard on Sunday.

"Hey, what the heck . . . ?" He gazed up at Rand with a totally confused look. "Sorry, boss. I don't know how, but . . . all my tools are gone."

Rand walked over and hunkered down to see for himself. Aside from a few bent nails, a pair of work gloves and a tin of Altoids, the battered box was clean as a whistle.

"What did you do, leave everything home today?"

"Shit, no." Jack beetled his brow in a frown. Standing, he placed fists the size of canned hams on his hips. "But I'd bet my last dollar somebody around here thinks they're being cute. Come on."

Curious to see what the woodworker had in mind, Rand followed him into the foyer, where several of the crew were pulling up cracked and broken tiles. Jack Mulvaney stood six foot six, with a shock of red hair and a grimace that frightened small children. Rand knew no man in his employ would have the balls to mess with the man or his tools.

"All right. So who's the wise guy with the death wish who decided to get smart and steal my stuff?" Mulvaney demanded, towering over everyone in the foyer.

"Stuff? What stuff?" Frank asked, unsure whether or not this was a joke.

"You know damn well what stuff," Jack growled, his face a knot of impatience. "My tools are missing."

"What's a-matter, Jack, you getting Alzheimer's or somethin', forgetting where you put your own tools?" Pete quipped, apparently proud of his clever comeback.

"I ain't gettin' anything, except my tools back." Mulvaney's cheeks had grown as red as his hair. "Now, give over or I give out."

Frank, a peacemaker at heart, reached down to his own box. "Nobody took your tools, Jack, but you can use mine until they turn up. Here." Hoisting the box, he made to swing it at his coworker, then blinked. "Hey, what the hell?"

Thrusting the box at Pete's chest, he unsnapped the lid. Together they gazed into the box, until Frank turned it upside down. Two pennies, a nickel and a small, rusted spool of wire fell to the tiles with a clatter.

In a heartbeat, chaos reigned. Every workman in the foyer scrambled through their belts and boxes, searching for their tools. Except for the crowbars or hammers each of them already held in his hand, there wasn't a wrench, screwdriver, or set of pliers to be found.

And through it all, Rand watched with a raised brow and an eerie niggling in the back of his mind he was coming to know all too well.

"Okay, okay." He glanced at his watch. "Everybody take a lunch break. A long lunch break. After you finish, go to the company warehouse and see what you can pick up. Tell them I said you could sign out whatever tools you need to do your jobs, then get back here. Your own stuff has to be around somewhere."

Flying up the stairs to her hidey-hole, Cassandra set her hands over her mouth to stifle another round of giggles. Though it had required all of her talents, so far she'd managed to thoroughly confuse everyone, including the

MacPherson, and get her task done without being detected.

The workmen had been so busy concentrating on their various projects, not one of them had noticed when their tools had become invisible so she could spirit them from the belts and boxes and whisk them out of the house. Breaking into the trailer had been a more difficult task, since it had to be done from the second-floor window. In the end, all she'd been able to do was cast a simple spell over the contents, so that anyone who inspected the cavernous box would think it as empty as her own hope chest.

But the spell wouldn't last for long; maybe another hour or two before things would start to reappear. Not the best solution to her problem, but it would do in a pinch, and buy her a wee bit more time to come up with another answer.

Whisking quickly through the closet door, she settled into a corner to think. She'd given the MacPherson enough to worry about for one day, making him ruminate over the lunacy of his men and what he thought was another round of thefts. But what about tomorrow and the next day . . . and the next?

What more could she do to keep herself and her home safe?

"All right, I know you're up here. Come on out before I do something we'll both be sorry for."

Cassandra laid a palm on her throat. It was him—the MacPherson—charging up the stairs to search for her. And he sounded more than annoyed.

Rap, rap, rap! She jumped when the force of something hard—Rand's head perhaps?—suddenly hit the door.

"Cassandra? Are you in there?"

No! I've gone back to the Scottish Highlands and the home I loved so well, she wanted to shout. Unfortunately, none of that was true. Thanks to Colin MacPherson, she would never be free to see her beloved homeland again.

The thought brought up a tremor of sadness so severe, she almost didn't hear his next request, words of sweetness murmured in a much nicer tone.

"Cassandra, where have you been? I've missed you. Come on out and talk to me."

He was a silver-tongued devil, she'd give him that. So much more persuasive than his nasty ancestor. And it was clear from his honeyed words he thought her an idiot, just as Colin had. Resolutely, she held herself still.

"Cassandra, I know you had something to do with the missing tools. Now, why don't you show yourself so we can talk about it rationally? Come on, open this door."

She heard the knob rattle, gently at first, then with the force of an earthquake. Shooting to her feet, she willed the cut crystal to tighten farther.

"Damned -fool woman . . . ghost . . . whatever she is."

Seconds passed while she hovered at the door, listening as he paced the foyer.

"Hello, Duke? Is that you? Yeah, well, I'm glad you're on your way, but I need a favor."

Cassandra rested her forehead against the closet wall. Sweet Mother of God, she'd forgotten he had one of those newfangled telephone machines at his beck and call.

"No, not lunch, though a roast beef on rye sounds darned good right about now. I need to know if you still have your tools."

The place inside Cassandra that would have held her heart gave a painful lurch.

"There's been some crazy stuff going on around here and I— Just make sure you have them in the truck. And the second you get here, come find me. Don't stop to speak to anyone and don't pass Go. And hurry."

* * *

Rand paced the front porch like a man possessed. For the last half hour, since he'd hung up with Duke, he hadn't been able to concentrate on anything but Cassandra and that damned closet door.

She'd been up there all right, listening when he begged her to let him in. He'd felt her presence as surely as he now knew she had something to do with the missing tools. But all his pleading hadn't meant a thing to the woman—spirit, he quickly amended. She had ignored him completely.

Grimly, he turned the corner and paced the side of the porch that ran along the library. His ghost had nerve, he'd give her that, but what had made her do such a childish thing as steal the men's equipment? Could she be the one responsible for rebricking that wall?

Then again, maybe she *was* a child . . . a little girl who'd run away from home, taken shelter in the house, and died or, worse, been abducted and killed here. Hadn't his mother once said spirits haunted because they were looking for closure? Or for a way to bring to light whatever dastardly deed had been perpetrated upon them here on earth?

Why hadn't he paid more attention to Irene's wacky ramblings about the spirit world when he'd had the chance? Come hell or high water, first thing he was going to do this weekend was find a way inside his mother's library to hunt up a book on the supernatural. There had to be a way to get Cassandra to stay put long enough for him to figure out what was bothering her.

Stopping at the back railing, he gazed over the rise to where the reeds rimming the pond were just visible on the horizon. In the distance a bird cried, then a pair of pheasants took flight. Sighing, he inhaled a deep breath. God, but he loved it here. No wonder his uncle had coveted this land. After a century of development in the closer cities of Bernardsville, Mendham, and Peapack Gladstone, these ten acres were worth millions on the open market. Nancy had been right. If he sold it or chose to turn it into a tract of luxury homes, he would make the family a fortune.

But that wasn't what he wanted. No matter the cost, this place was his. He was going to live here in tranquility if it killed him. And he was going to find a way to do it *with* his ghost. He just needed to convince Cassandra he meant her no harm. That he wanted her here, in the house with him. He wanted her—

"Hey, where the heck is everybody?" Duke's footsteps hit the porch with a resounding thud. "I thought you said this was an emergency? You ready for me or not?"

Rand spun around, hoping Duke wouldn't notice his boss had been daydreaming. "Thanks for getting here so fast."

Duke joined him at the back porch railing. "Can't say as I blame you for dawdling. That view is something else."

Two white-tailed deer, a buck and a doe, wandered hesitantly from the trees and picked their way to the pond. The buck raised his massive head, perused the countryside with watchful eyes, and sniffed the air, while the doe lowered her dainty muzzle and began to drink.

"Lord, that's a beautiful sight," Duke muttered. "And mighty unusual. I didn't think deer came out in broad daylight."

"Neither did I," admitted Rand. "They must feel safe here, though I can't imagine why. We haven't exactly been quiet for the past week."

"Not with the utility companies tearing up the property, we haven't, but they're done now, so it should be a lot quieter. Has the generator been working okay?"

Rand kept his gaze on the pond. "Well enough to keep the power tools going." If there were any left in the trailer, he silently reminded himself.

"So." Duke propped himself against the porch railing. "What the heck's the problem?"

"Follow me," Rand snapped, hating the nasty way he sounded. He led them to the front of the house and down the stairs to the storage trailer. "Take a look at this." He swung the door wide and stood back, waiting for the string of curse words he was sure Duke would utter.

The foreman peered inside, then glanced back over his shoulder through contrition-filled eyes. "It's a mess, isn't it? Guess I'd better have a few of the boys neaten it up at the end of the day."

Neaten it up! Rand climbed the top stair, stomped into the trailer, and felt as if he'd been catapulted straight into a Salvador Dali painting. Every sander, every drill, every router and hand saw had been replaced exactly as he remembered, right down to the bucket of threepenny nails left behind by the roofing crew.

"Sorry the guys let it get so messy. I know how much you like an orderly construction site."

Rand rubbed his face with both palms, then ran his fingers through his hair. "Duke, tell me something."

"Shoot."

Stepping slowly to the trailer door, he gave the inside a final sweeping gaze, then jumped down onto the grass. "Last night, when you said good-bye to me in the house, what was I doing?"

"Doing?"

"Yeah. Where was I? Do you remember?"

Duke leaned a broad shoulder against the trailer. "Is this a test? Because if it is—"

"No test," Rand assured him, searching for a thread of sanity to tie the past twenty-four hours together. "Where was I when you left me last night?"

"Well, let's see." The foreman drew his heavy black brows together over his hawklike nose. "You were standing on the third-floor landing, taking apart a wall of bricks—two walls, if I remember correctly—and sweating like a pig while doing it. Why? Did something happen I should know about?''

Okay, so he wasn't going crazy. He'd taken down that wall and he had a witness to prove it. But what about the trailer? Just two hours ago, he'd swear it had been as empty as Al Capone's vault, the one Geraldo Rivera had made such a stink about a few years back. And now every tool was set in place, exactly the way they'd been yesterday.

''Rand? I brought my tools, like you asked. Did you want something special?''

''Huh? Oh, I need a screwdriver, maybe pliers. I have to get that closet door open right away.''

''Oo-kay. But what happened to your own stuff, or the boys' tools, for that matter? And like I asked before, where the heck is everybody?'' Duke glanced around the front yard, empty of its usual flotilla of trucks, Jeeps and SUVs. ''What did you say to get them all gone from here at the same time?''

Rand realized how foolish he must have looked when he'd taken his latest gander at the inside of that trailer, probably like he'd just been slapped in the face with a day-old flounder. So how dumb was his story about everyone's tools disappearing at once going to sound?

Could this all really be Cassandra's fault? Did ghosts really have the power to make things appear and disappear at will? Worse, did she have some ulterior motive for making him look as nutty as his uncle? If so, it was time he got to the bottom of the mystery, whether or not Duke was here.

Better still, maybe his foreman should be around when he opened the closet. It could only help his case to have someone sensible testify at his sanity hearing when his practical, down-to-earth sister tried to have him committed.

"Don't worry about the crew. They'll be back later. You ready to come upstairs with me?"

"Sure. Let's get to it. I have to admit, I'm as curious as you are about what old Colin decided to hide up there. You think maybe he squirreled away a treasure or something?"

Oh, yeah. They were going to find a treasure ... or something.

Rand hurried up the stairs, his determination growing with every step. Whatever Colin and Cassandra—let's not forget his troublemaking, tool-stealing ghost—had hidden away was his now. He owned the house and all that was in it.

Slightly out of breath, they arrived on the landing. Rand stared hard at the door, willing Cassandra to show herself, yet not really believing she would with Duke standing at his side. Resolutely, he held out his hand like a surgeon preparing to operate. "Screwdriver."

Duke slapped the tool, handle first, into his palm.

Rand bent and unscrewed the bolts holding the brass plate in place and handed them one at a time to his foreman. When finished, he took off the plate and carefully separated the knob from the locking mechanism. Setting a finger into the hole, he pulled the door toward him until it swung fully outward.

"Holy hell, it's dark as a tomb in there. Here, let me light one of these babies." Duke stepped back and picked up one of the battery-powered lanterns he'd brought upstairs last night. After turning it on, he held it out to Rand. "Seeing as I'm claustrophobic, maybe you should go first?"

A feeling not unlike the one he'd experienced when he'd jumped from the high dive as a sophomore in high school rippled through Rand's gut. He raised the lantern and peered inside.

"Jesus, Mary and Joseph," whispered the foreman. "Do you see what I see?"

"Yeah, I see it." Rand exhaled a breath. "Do me a favor and call the police."

"Randall Colin MacPherson, I'm coming up there right now. And I want you to tell these ... these gentlemen to let me pass. Do you understand me, Rand? I'm your mother. Whatever is going on up there, I have a right to know about it."

Rand heard the contrite voice of a police officer, then the sound of stilettos hitting wood. Aw, crap, could things get any worse? This mess was going to be right up Irene's convoluted alley. Just what he needed to keep things on a completely uneven keel.

But he knew from years of experience that if he didn't let her up now, there'd be hell to pay later. "It's okay. You can let her pass."

The officer standing guard in the doorway called down to his colleague on the lower landing. Scuffling noises drifted upward, then the rapid staccato tapped again.

"Darling, are you all right?" Irene's demanding voice filled the stairway. "Randall, I asked if you were well?"

"I'm fine, Mother. But I have to warn you. Proceed at your own risk."

Shouldering her way through the men gathered on the landing, Irene stopped at his side. "Proceed at my— Why, for heaven's sake, what's going on up here? I stopped by to see how you were doing with the remodeling and couldn't believe what was blocking the drive. Two police cars and a coroner's vehicle? My God, Rand. Who died?"

Rand firmly grabbed her elbows and glanced down. "That's what these men are trying to figure out, Mother. And if you promise not to scream or faint or touch anything, I'll let you take a look."

She craned her neck, then tried to dart around him, but

Rand held her fast. "Mom, please. This is serious. Promise me, no hysterics."

Settling back with an indignant huff, Irene pulled an elbow from his grip and patted at her hair. "I'm not the kind of woman who resorts to hysterics. You should know that by now."

"Promise me, Mother."

In typical Irene style, she stuck out her lower lip. "Oh, very well. But I'm warning you, if this is something trivial—"

The county coroner stood, continuing to block her view. His no-nonsense look telegraphed the fact that he would toss her out in a heartbeat if she dared to disobey. "On the contrary, Mrs. MacPherson—"

"It's Johnston, now, Mrs. Harry Johnston. But you may call me . . . Mrs. Johnston," she said smartly. "Now, I demand to know what's going on up here."

As one, Rand and the coroner stepped apart, allowing Irene an unimpeded view of the body stretched out on the floor.

"Oh, my Lord." She tried to take a step forward, but Rand kept her in place. "Who is she?"

Rand stared down, again taking in the figure on the closet floor. Lying on her back, hands crossed at her waist, was the body of a woman looking so serene that at first glance he had thought she was merely napping. "That's one of the reasons I decided to let you up here. I thought maybe you would have a clue."

Irene's emerald-green eyes filled with amazement. "Me? Why would I know anything about this?"

Rand finally let go and she sagged against his chest. "We thought maybe you'd remember something Uncle Colin said when he talked about the house. Anything that would give us help in identifying her."

"Uncle Colin? Why would this concern him?"

"Your son's told us a little of the house's history, Mrs.

Johnston, and a bit about his great-great-uncle. Unless someone else has had access to the house in the last hundred years, we're fairly certain Colin MacPherson had something to do with this," replied the coroner dourly.

Irene fastened her round-eyed gaze on the body. "But . . . but . . . look at her. She looks so fresh, so alive— almost as if she were asleep. Are you sure she's dead?"

Rand folded his arms across his chest. "Be sensible, Mother. She's dressed in a gown that's practically falling apart at the seams. And the style is what? A hundred years out of date?"

"A hundred years?" Irene leaned closer to inspect the heavy satin dress. Though yellowed with age and weakened at the seams, it was clear the old-fashioned gown had been beautifully made and in its day had probably cost a fortune. The coroner tugged a bit of fabric at the elbow and the sleeve separated from the shoulder, throwing up a small puff of dust.

"Oh, my. I see what you mean." Tapping a finger to her chin, Irene squatted closer. Tentatively, she reached out and touched one long lock of hair, still a lustrous russet color and softly curled. "She looks so real."

"She was real at one time," the coroner remarked in a clinical-sounding voice. Standing, he helped Irene to her feet. "We'll have to take her out of here, Mr. Mac-Pherson. I'll need to call in county authorities, then perform an autopsy. That'll help us better determine the date of death and tell us how it happened."

He looked around the closet, then let his gaze wander to the ceiling. "I don't know, maybe it's the way this house was built or something, but even now, with the sun overhead, there's not a crack of light coming through the joints or beams. And you said this room was bricked up tight?"

Rand only half heard the coroner's question. He couldn't take his eyes off the woman, girl really, lying

peacefully at his feet. Her heart-shaped face and perfect
upturned nose held him mesmerized. Strangely, her wide,
full lips looked to be smiling, almost as if she'd been
happy when she died.

"Mr. MacPherson? You said there was a brick wall in
front of the door? And the closet was locked? Do you
think the room was near to airtight?" the coroner persisted.

"That's not physically possible, but it was pitch dark.
I couldn't find a key, so like I told the police, I had to
use a screwdriver to remove the lock. I doubt anyone's
been inside here for the past century."

"Hmm. Can't argue with you there." He took a final
look around the closet. "Okay, if you'd all step back
onto the landing, I'm going to cordon off the area. We
need to get this done quickly, while the flesh is still pliant.
Now that it's been exposed to the light . . . well, I don't
know how long it will be before decay sets in."

Suddenly, Rand felt as if he'd stepped off a cliff. His
heart dropped to his stomach at the idea of losing the
girl. He owned the house and its contents . . . didn't he
own this body as well? How could anyone take her away
from here . . . from him?

"Look, Doc, do you have to do all that stuff to her?
I mean, whoever was responsible has to be long dead
themselves. There can't possibly be anyone to arrest.
Couldn't you just . . . let me take care of things?"

"What a wonderful idea. We could have a service for
the poor dear, maybe give her a proper burial in the family
vault?" Irene patted his hand.

The coroner scratched his face with one latex-gloved
finger. "Sorry, there are procedures that need to be followed in a case like this. A town this small doesn't have
a real forensics team, but whoever the county sends is
going to be mad as hell that we've trooped in here and
contaminated a crime scene. Best I can do is see to it the

body's released to you after the autopsy and hoo-ha is over. That is, if you're willing to sign a paper taking full responsibility for the costs and all.''

''Sure, yes. No problem,'' said Rand. Still staring at the body, he took his mother's arm and guided her to the landing. The coroner squatted and gave the corpse a final poke, causing the girl's hands to separate.

''Holy Jehosophat,'' he chortled, jumping to his feet. ''That about scared ten years off my life.'' Reaching down, he picked up the yellowed piece of paper the woman had clutched between her fingers and gave it to Rand. ''Here you go, son. Maybe this will shed some light on her identity.''

Though the paper felt like parchment, it held together when Rand unfolded it.

''What is it, dear?'' whispered Irene, still in awe of the proceedings.

Almost unable to believe his eyes, Rand held the paper up to the light seeping in from the bedrooms on either side of the landing. ''It looks like a deed to this house. And it's made out to Cassandra Kinross MacPherson.''

''My God,'' Irene breathed. ''It *is* her.''

''Her? Who her?''

''Uncle Colin's runaway bride,'' she answered, holding her hands to her chest.

''But I thought the woman left town without a trace? At least, that's what Uncle Colin told everyone . . . didn't he?''

Irene nodded. ''He did, but that was her name. I remember Colin's murmuring it several times when we last visited him in the nursing home. But Cassandra never left, did she?'' His mother sniffed loudly as she dug through her handbag and pulled out a tissue.

''The poor girl never left.''

Chapter Six

Cassandra watched the MacPherson from the rear window of a third-floor bedroom. Dressed in form-fitting blue trousers and a bright white shirt, he stood under a cluster of pine trees, gazing at her grave as if he were in mourning. At least he had chosen a pleasant spot for her mortal remains, she thought with a tremor of sadness—just a few yards away from the pond but still sheltered from the brilliance of the punishing summer sun.

Two weeks had passed since the fateful day he'd opened the closet and found her body. And during that time, they hadn't spoken to each other once. Police investigators had spent hours in the house and on the third floor doing whatever it was officers of the law did to handle a murder, while renovations continued. The MacPherson had shown himself only to speak with the investigators or give orders to the workmen. Then he disappeared without setting foot inside or seeking her out.

And every time she'd seen him standing in the yard, a stab of pity had taken hold in her chest. Never in all her life had anyone cared for her so much, they had looked that forlorn.

But Cassandra knew better. Knew he had to be pleased he'd found her, even more thankful to have laid her to rest. To the MacPherson family, removing her body and seeing to its disposal had closed the final chapter on the story of both her and Colin's lives.

So she'd spent her time surreptitiously surveying the workmen or focusing on the small box with moving pictures—a television, she'd learned—someone had set up in the kitchen. When the men left for the day, she would command the box to start, then hover in front of it, enthralled with everything it had to offer. Over the past few days, the incredible machine had taken her mind off the absence of the MacPherson and become her window of clarity on the twenty-first century.

She'd learned of the inventive wonders of the modern world, the progress humans had made in medicine, science and building, and all of the clever educational devices that had been created for children. Though she had her choice of fashion, education and entertainment, the programs described as talk shows fascinated her the most. It was almost impossible to comprehend how people could appear on a nationally broadcast program and speak so easily about all manner of personal things. Incest, divorce, rape, sexual dysfunction and fantasies, dreams and desires . . . it seemed there was no limit to what they were willing to discuss.

But one evening, after she'd watched a particular show, she began to view the world in a different light. The program featured a woman named Dr. Rachel, a physician who dealt with the inner workings of a person's mind, if one could believe it. Her specialty was counseling those who had difficulty accepting the unfortunate things that had befallen them. Her goal was to teach people how to come to terms with their grief, and then forgive.

After listening to only one episode, Cassandra felt as if a stone had been lifted. Dr. Rachel's kind yet incisive words began to free her of all the old aches, until she was finally able to admit her body was at rest. From that day forward, she came to accept the idea Rand would be moving here with his family.

She had harbored hate for a century. It was time to heal her heart.

One of the hardest things she had to do was to admit she missed Rand MacPherson. Missed his mischievous grin and his laughing eyes, or the way he ran his long, tanned fingers through his hair whenever she gave him a good trouncing. The too-handsome and completely frustrating man made her smile, something she hadn't done since her brother Fergus had kissed her good-bye when she'd left for America.

And he'd shown himself to be fearless as well. She couldn't imagine many people willing to hold a reasonable conversation with a floating mound of *unset Jell-O,* whatever that was.

The piercing sound of children's laughter snapped Cassandra from her reverie. After a few seconds, she saw them clearly, a boy with golden curls, just like his father, and a girl with thick, dark brown braids, two small but sturdy bodies running straight to Rand like eager puppies looking for a tumble. And following them was a woman, tall and a bit on the thin side, but dark-haired like the girl, marching purposefully up the rise.

Rand scooped up the little girl and gave her a hug, and the child giggled with delight. Placing her rosebud mouth on his cheek, she planted a round of kisses, then squeezed his neck in her sweater-clad arms. The boy said something and Rand tossed out a booming laugh, then tousled the lad's sun-kissed hair. Dropping the girl to her feet, he held out his hand to the woman and she took it. Together, they trekked slowly back to the house.

As if jabbed by a fist, pain rocked Cassandra's chest. Besides the fact she still wasn't able to leave this place, she had made a promise to herself and she would keep it. The MacPherson had a family, a wife and children he obviously adored. She would try to live here among them in harmony. Somehow she would find a way.

Voices sounded in the foyer. Overcome with curiosity, she drifted to the balcony, determined to spy from above. Peering down, she watched the woman turn slowly on the marble tiles, her face set in a bright smile of approval.

"It's beautiful, Rand. I never dreamed you could craft something so perfect inside this dilapidated old shell."

"Do you really like it? I was afraid ... after what happened here ... you wouldn't want the kids to come inside."

"Don't be silly. It was tragic, I'll admit, finding Uncle Colin's fiancée that way, but at least she was put to rest. I still can't believe he would have been so cruel."

Just then, the children raced off to explore. Rand drew the woman to the bottom step and helped her to sit. "Yeah, but it sure explains a lot. Now we know the real reason the old reprobate boarded up the house and put it in trust for a century. It was the perfect way to hide his crime. We'll probably never know why he bricked Cassandra in that room, but at least we know why he was so crazy when he died. Can you imagine the guilt he must have felt, knowing he'd done what he'd done to his own ... to another human being?"

"I couldn't conceive of living with such a monstrous thing hanging over my head." She sighed as she laid a hand on his shoulder. "From the sight of that heavy-duty padlock and brand-new gate at the foot of the driveway, I'm guessing you've had your share of gawkers and newspaper reporters?"

Propping an elbow on his knee, he rested his forehead in his palm. "You don't know the half of it. The coroner was fairly reasonable when I asked him to keep things quiet, as were the police, but *The Daily Record* still found out and ran that article. Ever since they reported we'd unearthed a hundred-year-old corpse, I've been inundated with phone calls. Some rag even offered fifty thousand bucks if I'd let them come in and photograph the closet and tell them what I knew. As if I'd ever do that to—''

''Did they know about the family rumors or insinuate the house was haunted?''

''They'd already picked up a few tidbits about Colin from old newspaper stories, especially the one that ran the article on his canceled wedding. As to the question of ghosts—'' Rand ducked his head and sighed. ''It was just too much, so I had Duke install the gates. I'm hoping the fuss will die down after a few weeks and things will get back to normal around here.''

Nancy folded her hands in her lap. ''And what do you believe? Could the rumors be true? Is the house haunted, or do you think it was just the guilt making Uncle Colin rave like a madman most of his life?''

To Cassandra's wary ears, Rand waited a half second too long before answering, but when he did, his voice was flat and even. ''Ghosts are figments of a weak mind, Nan. Look at Mother and her wacky ideas on the spirit world. After listening to her this past week, I would have thought you'd be a lot more practical than to believe in ghosts. They don't exist.''

''So you're not going to allow Irene to hold that séance she's been pestering you about?''

''Hell, no,'' he snapped. ''The woman's gone. And nothing anyone says or does will bring her back.''

''Woman? What woman?''

''Cassandra, of course. I mean . . . she doesn't live here anymore. She's dead, her body's buried, and the police are satisfied Colin was responsible. There's nothing left to investigate, is there?''

''Rand, I think you need to take a step back from all this. It was generous of you to obtain that permit to have her buried here on the property, but you spent a fortune on the details, a minister, an elaborate casket—''

''It was the least I could do after what this family—one of our ancestors—did to the girl.''

''But you've been talking about this Cassandra woman as if you knew her personally.''

Hunching his shoulders, he rested both elbows on his knees. ''That's not true. I just think we should all share some of the blame. Colin was our uncle and ... and I don't want anyone to hold a séance in my house,'' he said harshly.

''Okay. That's your right, but I'd be surprised if Mother gave up so easily. She's asked me to try to convince you to let her bring a psychic here to clear the place of negative energy.''

''Great. That's all the tabloids need to hear.''

''I'll let her know how you feel.'' Sighing, Nan stood and scanned the foyer. ''It's getting late. Where do you suppose those kids ran off to?''

Figment of a weak mind! Inane thoughts! Don't exist?

Cassandra had so focused on Rand's opinion of ghosts, which she automatically assumed defined his opinion of her, she barely acknowledged the rest of the couple's conversation. Had she heard the arrogant man correctly? After she'd let him poke at her as if she were a loaf of day-old bread? After all that had transpired between them, was the MacPherson actually saying he didn't believe in her?

Anger burst like fireworks inside her belly, filling her with fury. Who did the great cabbagehead think he was, burying her, then denying her existence! Well, he could be in denial all he wanted—she would just have to remind him of the truth. Pushing all thoughts of Dr. Rachel and inner peace to the back of her mind, she raised her hands to the heavens.

Come, air, to me, thy help I need. Blow down these walls and pay me heed!

The front doors shot open with a bang. A gust of wind so fierce it rattled the crystal globes hanging in the foyer blew through the downstairs. In a flash, the children came running, screaming giddily as they raced to the adults.

"Wow." The boy clung to Rand's hand, jumping up and down. "Did you feel that? Was it a tornado, do you think? I thought we didn't get tornadoes in New Jersey."

Rand stood and encircled Robbie and Melissa in his arms. Eyes narrowed, he scanned the stairs. "Come on, let's go outside. It'll be calmer there."

"But isn't that where this breeze is coming from?" Nancy shouted above the still-whistling wind.

"I'm not too sure about that. Come on, everybody outside. It's time you went home so I can get some work done around here."

Cassandra knew the second the MacPherson saw her. Grinning, he looked back over his shoulder. Suddenly, his smile grew wide, showing flashing white teeth and the slightest hint of a dimple. Their gazes collided and he gave a hearty chuckle as he herded his family out the door.

Sucking in a gust of swirling air, she shot him a mighty growl, then whisked backward up the stairs.

Working to contain his excitement, Rand waved good-bye to his sister and the kids. As soon as their SUV's taillights faded in the distance, he raised a palm and high-fived the air. One of the workmen gave him a wary uh-oh-the-boss-is-acting-crazy-again look, and Rand nonchalantly stuffed his hand into his pocket.

Inhaling a breath, he relived the exact moment he'd seen Cassandra. An instant before the eerie wind started to blow, every hair on his head had stood on end. His heart had just about leapt from his chest when he'd focused upward and caught the faint outline of a woman with her hands on her hips, glaring from the balcony. And he knew she'd been glaring, because the eye contact had been electrical, an instantaneous sizzle that raced through him like the current from a live wire.

What an idiot he'd been, moping around all week because he'd thought that once Cassandra's body had been laid to rest she would be gone forever. Her magical reappearance only proved how little he knew about the spirit world.

Calm. He had to stay calm and act as if nothing had changed. It was important that everyone believed he was still brooding over the disturbing events or they would think he'd shorted out a few brain cells.

He nodded at Pete, who was busy installing the downstairs front windows. "Great job. How many more units do you think you can get in before quitting time?"

Pete shrugged his shoulders in response. "Maybe one more if I stay an extra fifteen minutes. Why?"

Rand flicked a gaze at his watch. "It's Friday. No sense working overtime for one window. Why don't you and the guys clock out now? I'll see to it you're paid for the full day. Go on, tell everybody they can leave a half hour early."

"No shit? I mean, thanks. I'll get right on it." Like Paul Revere spreading the news, Pete raced around the rear of the house to the masons. Rand figured he'd come in through the kitchen to tell the cabinet installers, because Pete ended up facing him on the front porch two minutes later.

"Thanks again, Rand," said Pete. "You're one hell of a boss," said another. "Have a good weekend, boss man," voiced a third. Amid pats on the back and hearty farewells, Rand held himself in check until the last pickup truck bumped its way down the drive.

Striding into the foyer, he closed and locked the front door. Dusk had settled over the house like a blanket of awareness, leaving him bursting with the feeling he was about to embark on a thrilling adventure. Thudding up the stairs, he kept silent, knowing full well Cassandra could sense him just the way he could sense her.

Before he started up to the third floor, he slowed and took several deep breaths. The landing, shrouded in near darkness, only added to the tingling suspense. "Cassandra? Where are you? It's me. Rand MacPherson."

He breathed in the silence. Oo-kay. So she was angry. But what had he done to deserve it?

"Um . . . I missed you. I wondered where you'd gone that day, after I . . . we found the body."

Still no response. Not the faintest ruffling of air.

"That was you, wasn't it? You are the spirit of the girl whose body we found, right? You told me your name was Cassandra, so I automatically assumed—"

Aye, it was me, you great idiot. What other Cassandra did you expect would be living here?

Overcome with relief, Rand slid down the wall across from the closet and squinted hard into the shadows. "Thank you, God," he murmured, his voice just above a whisper.

Unless you mean to risk your mortal soul, I'd ask you not to be thanking the good Lord, Mr. MacPherson. I find it hard to believe He had anything to do with my futile state of being.

"Sorry. It's just that I was so . . . um . . . relieved. I thought you'd left. I'm not very knowledgeable on paranormal phenomena, and I figured after you were laid to rest your spirit . . . that is, *you,* would go to wherever spirits go . . . when they're laid to rest, I mean."

Humph! Fat chance of that ever happening.

Rand narrowed his gaze, uneasy with the idea he could hear Cassandra in his mind yet not have a good fix on her location. He fumbled for one of the battery-powered lanterns still sitting on the landing and switched it on. "Are you close by? Because I'd feel a lot better if you'd show yourself, like you did last week."

You mean you enjoy looking at a blob of unset Jell-O?

Her teasing lilt had him biting the inside of his cheek. "Hey, I didn't mean to offend. At the time, it was the only thing I had to compare you to. Be a sport and show yourself."

The air around him grew heavy, almost palpable. A tingling heat rose in his chest as he scoured the closet doorway. He sucked in a breath when a shimmering substance wavered into being. Her form appeared, transparent but more clearly outlined than ever before, and he scrambled to his feet. As he took a step closer, Cassandra rippled, then settled in place—a young woman dressed in a pale-colored gown who sternly met his blinking gaze.

Is this better?

Rand swallowed. "Yeah. I can almost . . . see you."

What do you mean almost? I'm standing right in front of your face, aren't I?

Hesitantly, he shuffled forward and reached out a hand. Placing it on the forearm cocked at her side, he touched lightly, noting how the tingling increased when his fingers stroked her arm. "But you feel different. More . . . substantial? Kind of like . . . pudding?"

She drew herself up and squared her shoulders, but she didn't pull away. *Humph! First I'm unset Jell-O, now pudding! Either you've missed your calling as a cook or you haven't eaten in a very long while. And I'll ask you not to be pawing at me in such a familiar manner, if you don't mind.*

Gentling his touch, Rand grinned at her feisty tone. "Sorry. I don't mean to 'paw.' It's just that, up till now, I haven't had the opportunity to touch many ghosts."

I don't doubt that holds true for most of the world's population. You're a very lucky man, Mr. MacPherson. Another spirit might not take so kindly to someone as bold as yourself.

Resisting the urge to move closer, he decided to get right to the point. "Cassandra, I think we need to talk."

She tossed her head, and he caught a glint of fire in her eyes.

Isn't that what we're doing right now?

Still not quite able to believe he was having a face-to-face confrontation with a ghost, he curtailed his grin. "Yeah, I guess we are."

She nodded, as if pleased with his answer. *So, what is it you need to know?*

Everything, he thought silently. I need to know what happened between you and my uncle a hundred years ago. I need to know where you go when we're apart, what you're thinking and feeling right now. I need to know all about you. . . .

She made an impatient tapping motion with her foot. *I'm waiting.*

"Do you mind if I ask about Colin?"

Pulling from his touch, she folded her arms across her chest. *You want to discuss the despicable man who did this to me?*

"I just want to understand, Cassandra. How . . . why did this happen? What made him wall you up in there and leave you to die?"

Sadness . . . and a wave of utter despair rippled through Rand's mind. Her faint form quivered and blurred, threatening to disappear. "Wait. Don't go. I'm sorry I asked."

Slowly, she faded from view, but Rand clearly heard her farewell in his head.

'Tis no sorrier than I'll be if I'm forced to tell you. Now, good-bye and good night. I'm tired and I haven't the energy for more of this conversation.

* * *

"Thanks again for helping out this morning, Duke. I'm sure you could have found a better way to spend your Saturday than moving me into this place. I owe you one," Rand remarked as he climbed the mansion's front porch steps.

Duke carried in one of Rand's bedside tables and set it on the foyer floor. Flexing his arms over his head, he stretched for the ceiling. "No problem. Now that you have heat, water and electricity, you're all set. Besides, you're right about having a guard in residence. It's probably the best way to deal with the jerks who've been ballsy enough to jump the fence and try to find a way inside. But are you sure this place is habitable? I mean, you barely have a working kitchen, and the phones are still kicking out."

Watching the muscular foreman, Rand tossed him a nod of gratitude. The guy ran ten miles every morning, biked on the weekends, and spent his vacations running triathlons, something which Rand, in a moment of weakness, had done once. After working out side by side with Duke for three months and coming in thirty-fifth out of a field of forty in his first race, he'd resisted any and all ideas of ever again competing in such a grueling event.

Though Duke was as tough as cured mortar on the outside, Rand knew Duke was pure putty at heart. The two men had been friends for the past ten years, ever since Duke had come on board as an apprentice journeyman. Robbie had promoted the young man to assistant foreman and Rand made him a full-fledged supervisor as soon as he'd taken over as CEO of MacPherson C&D. Men just didn't come any better than Bill Dukovsky.

"Stop clucking like a mother hen. The toilets work, I have hot and cold running water, and now I have a bed to sleep in. As far as I'm concerned, I'm set."

Duke walked to the wall and flipped a light switch on and off, raising a brow when the lights flickered like something from a horror movie. "That is not the sign of a properly wired house. The electricians swear they did the job right, but I'm calling them back for another inspection. I told them they needed to break into a few of the walls to double-check the connections. In a place this old, there might be some kind of water leak in the walls the engineers missed. Maybe you ought to—"

"Quit your worrying. I have those battery lanterns to see me through the weekend if the generator blows. The men can take care of the problem on Monday."

Duke wiped his brow on the sleeve of his spotless white T-shirt, then followed Rand up the stairs with the nightstand. "Yeah, but there's no refrigerator or stove. I mean, a guy's gotta eat sometime. And you don't have much furniture."

Rand set down the mirror that would eventually hang over his dresser and walked back out the door. "I'm eating at my sister's tonight, and I plan to go out for meals tomorrow. The microwave and refrigerator are being delivered Monday, which is all I need until the stove gets hooked up. Besides, I've become an expert at nuking just about everything. Most bachelors survive that way. Don't you?"

"Uh ... sure ... unless I can talk some babe into cooking for me. By the way, did I hear you say you were going to your sister's?" Duke asked almost as an afterthought.

"Yeah, why?"

They made their way down the porch stairs and back into the truck. "Oh, no reason. It's just that I haven't seen her since the company picnic this summer. She has two kids, right?"

Rand positioned himself at one end of his king-sized mattress and waited for Duke to grab the other side.

"Melissa and Robert, but we call him Robbie now that Dad's gone."

Together they hoisted the mattress out of the van, into the house, and up the stairs. Settling the top section in place, Rand stood back. "That ought to do it. After all this activity, I might actually get a good night's sleep for a change."

Dark blue eyes scanning the room warily, Duke shoved his hands into his pockets. "You sure about that? Because I don't know if I'd sleep too soundly knowing this house had a dead body hiding in it for the past hundred years. Kind of gives me the creeps."

Just in case the subject of their conversation was hovering in the background, Rand glanced over his shoulder. Judging by the way Cassandra scolded him for any and everything disruptive that happened in the house, he'd be the one to pay the price if she found out someone dared to consider her creepy.

"Nah, doesn't bother me a bit. In fact, it's a relief to Nan and me, finally knowing what made Colin so crazy. For a while there, we were beginning to think insanity ran in the family."

"I've been meaning to ask what the coroner said about the state of the corpse. Did he have any ideas on the reason it looked so . . . fresh?"

Squinting over Duke's shoulder, Rand tried to focus on what he thought was a shimmer of movement in the doorway. He really did need to find out where Cassandra spent her time when she wasn't in sight. Then, when they were apart, he could imagine her doing whatever it was she did.

"Hey, boss. You daydreaming again?"

"Hmm . . . oh, no. Just trying to recall the gist of the report. If I remember correctly, the official cause of death was asphyxiation, but the coroner had no way to be sure. And the only thing he could find to logically explain the near-perfect condition of the body was lack of light and air in the closet. Figured Colin had built the house like a Tupperware container and that's what helped preserve the flesh.''

"Gross," Duke said with a grimace. "The whole thing sounds like something straight out of *Tales from the Crypt* if you ask me. And you want to know the really creepy part? Even though I knew she was dead, I still thought that woman was damned fine-looking. Why the heck do you think your uncle killed her?''

Swamped by a sudden wave of jealousy, Rand bit back a nasty retort. Who did Duke think he was, making comments on the attractiveness of *his* ghost? This entire topic was getting out of hand, depressing even if he faced it squarely. He had as close to the real thing as he was ever going to get, and that was the end of it. He had to hold tight to the reality that Cassandra would never again be a living, breathing woman, or he would go stark raving mad, just like Colin had.

"I have no idea, and like I told Nan, I don't think we'll ever know. I wish everybody would just drop it. Cassandra is buried, let her rest in peace.''

The two men worked side by side for the next hour, bringing up the rest of Rand's bedroom set, then his suitcases and linens, computer, fax machine and printer. At one o'clock they broke out the lunches they'd picked up earlier in the morning and sat on the porch steps to take a break.

"So, will the husband be there tonight?'' Duke took a bite of his roast beef on rye.

"The husband?'' Rand inspected his own sandwich, chicken salad on whole wheat with lettuce and tomato. "Oh, you mean my brother-in-law, the estimable Doctor Warren. I'm not sure. Why?''

The foreman took a long drink from his water bottle.

"Just wondering. He didn't show at the picnic, and when I asked Nancy where he was, she seemed kind of vague."

Closing his eyes against the sun streaming onto the steps, Rand thought back to the company's Memorial Day picnic. And the Fourth of July pool party at his sister's house. And the Labor Day barbecue she'd thrown. Duke brought up a good point. Warren hadn't been at any of the get-togethers.

"Now that you mention it, I don't remember seeing him. I guess I was so wrapped up in avoiding the blind dates Nancy set up for me, I didn't notice." Narrowing his gaze, he gave Duke's flushed face a careful once-over. "Hey, are you trying to find out if my sister's still happily married or something?"

"Who, me?" The man concentrated on the second half of his sandwich. "Nah. I was just making small talk is all. I like Nan. When she spent those summers working in the office, we used to have lunch together every once in a while. She was just a kid."

Rand thought back to the few summers his father had strong-armed him into spending a day or two each week at company headquarters instead of letting him work on a construction site. He and Duke were only three years apart in age, which made the foreman about five years older than Rand's baby sister. Back then, Duke and Nancy's friendship wouldn't have seemed odd or out of place. Could he actually have been interested in Nan and been too shy to ask her for a date?

"Well, she's thirty now, though she'd kill me if she found out I told. Keeps talking about having her own husband give her some free face work. Women. Go figure."

"Nancy doesn't need face work. She's a looker—I mean, she's a very attractive wom—aw, hell! You know what I mean."

Rand crumpled the wrapper from his sandwich and

stuffed it in the bag, then finished his water. He'd always thought his sister was pretty, in a sisterly kind of way, of course. Lately, she'd become thinner, which he guessed would appeal to most men, but he'd always thought her best feature was her big brown eyes. And when she wasn't putting on her "Miss Perfect" act, she had a great sense of humor. At least she had until the past few months . . .

Still, it was weird hearing another guy talk about her in *that* way. "Yeah, I guess I do know. I just wish I could put my finger on what's been bothering her."

Duke's brows drew together as he narrowed his gaze. "I only met the husband once a long while ago, when they were dating and he came to pick her up at the office. He seemed like a nice enough guy."

"Warren's okay, I guess, just full of himself, like most doctors. If he's not around tonight, I might be able to find out a little more."

Duke jerked to his feet and shook his head. "Hey, I was just wondering how she was doing, that's all." After tossing his lunch bag into the Dumpster, he marched back into the house. "Come on, we still have to set up your computer and printer. I don't have all day to baby-sit, you know."

Chapter Seven

"Me! Me! Do me next, Unka Rand!" Eager, high-pitched squeals echoed through the tastefully decorated family room. Jumping up and down, Melissa held chubby arms to Rand as he swung Robbie high in the air a second time. Princess, the family's snow-white miniature poodle, barked noisily while she sprang against his leg like a deranged kangaroo.

Setting the boy gently on the floor, Rand shoved the overexcited dog aside and squatted next to his four-year-old niece. "I don't know, short-stuff. It's pretty high up there. I'm not so sure the birthday girl can handle it. What do you think, big guy?"

Robbie gave a crooked grin. "Golly, Uncle Rand. Last time you twirled her around she hurled all over your new leather jacket, remember? She's still just a baby—"

Princess growled when Melissa stomped a dainty foot and glared at her older brother. "I am not a baby, you big . . . weenie." She turned pleading eyes to her uncle and bit at her lower lip. "Please, Unka Rand. I won't get sick, I promise. I'm four now."

Puddling like a Popsicle in August, he gave the goofy

dog a quick pat, then scooped the little girl in his arms. "I know you are, punkin'. It's just that the last time we played helicopter you—''

The single glistening tear slipping down Melissa's rosy cheek was Rand's undoing. "Aw, punkin', hang on a second. Hey, sis, when was the last time this little goblin ate? Getting puked on once a year is about all I can handle."

Nancy stood in the doorway, frowning as she took in the comfortably rumpled family room. Throw pillows littered the thick sand-colored pile rug along with an upended Monopoly game board, tiny red and green plastic houses and hotels, and a scattering of colored funny-money. Someone had set a wad of bubble gum on the coffee table, where it stuck like a glob of goo.

"Princess, come." Holding a pot lid in one hand, his sister briskly straightened the ruffled yellow apron tied around her waist with the other. Looking as neat as a television chef, she snapped her fingers and pointed at the dog cowering behind Rand's legs. With a whimper, the ball of fluff scuttled to her side and sat. "Not since lunch, and we're not eating for another thirty minutes. All I ask is that you keep the destruction to a minimum," she warned in a half-teasing voice.

Rand rolled his eyes. "It's not the furniture I'm worried about." He walked to the center of the room and gave his niece a stern look. "You ready, squirt?"

"I ready," the little girl answered solemnly, her enormous brown eyes wide.

Lifting Melissa high overhead, he began to spin. More squeals and shrieks filled the air. Hysterical giggles erupted from both kids when he made a sound like Hulk Hogan attacking a WWF competitor. Flying up the stairs, he tossed the little girl onto her bed, dove on top of her and tickled her madly.

"And the Incredible Randall is victorious again. Yaaaaah!"

Unwilling to be left out of the fun, Robbie jumped on top of them. Going on the attack, the two children scrambled onto Rand's chest and began to bounce in unison, until he decided someone was going to hurl all right, and this time it wouldn't be the feisty four-year-old.

"Ow! Hey, stop! I'm calling your mother," he threatened, making a frantic grab at the Ping-Ponging bodies. Jeez, how in the heck could two mini-midgets make it feel like a herd of elephants was using his body for a trampoline?

Somehow, he managed to turn over, so the kids were on his back instead of his chest. Shoving his head under a pillow, he lay still and did the one thing he knew might get them to stop. He played dead.

Tiny fingers of steel poked and prodded his ribs, plucked at his shirt, tugged hard at his hair. Something cold and slimy invaded his ear canal, slurping wetly.

"Hey, get that darned dog off me." He bucked like a bronco, but the little demons held fast as the dog's joyful bark set his head to ringing.

More shrieks filled the air, this time directed at Princess as she grabbed the edge of the pillow Rand was hiding under and began to tug. Dragging the pillow from the bed, the crazy mutt made a mad dash out the door, both kids hot on her heels.

Basking in the utter quiet, he grinned as he took a minute to catch his breath. The pint-sized monsters had worn him out—but in a very good way.

"You really do need to grow up, you know that?" Nan scolded, breaking the peaceful silence. "And I still think a Barbie doll, her dream house and six dazzling outfits is a bit much for a four-year-old."

Rand hauled himself to a sitting position and waggled an eyebrow. "Hey, I'm a guy. When a hot-looking babe gives me a come-hither look, I turn to mush, even if she is only eleven inches tall. Besides, I thought little girls liked dressing up dolls. What should I have given her?''

"How about a *baby* doll? Maybe a stuffed animal or an educational toy? Even a tea set would have been better than that overblown, plasticized excuse for a role model sitting on the table downstairs. The idea of Melissa thinking she has to resemble one of her father's surgically enhanced creations to succeed in the world makes me mad enough to spit.''

High on their irreverent sibling banter, Rand tried for a straight face. "Uh-oh, sounds like someone's been reading Gloria Steinem again.''

In true sisterly spirit, Nan flipped him the bird.

Holding back a chuckle, he swung his legs over the side of the bed and began to fiddle with his shirt, which had become totally undone in the scuffle. "Come on, sis, I know you've missed me. And the kids needed a little roughhousing. This place was quiet as a tomb when I walked in the front door.''

One side of Nan's generous mouth turned up slyly. Ignoring his pointed remark, she focused briefly on the expanse of naked muscled chest peeking from beneath his shirtfront. "Someone's been working out, I see.''

Rand quickly did up the buttons, then turned his back and tucked the shirt into his jeans. "Just slaving at the house. It feels good to be back in the field. You know it's the part of the business I always enjoyed most.''

"I remember,'' Nan muttered, bending down to straighten her daughter's wreck of a bed. "Mom and Dad always let you do what you wanted.''

He pretended he didn't hear the almost-snotty remark as he watched Nancy right the mess. After smoothing the pale pink sheets, she fluffed the lacy eyelet duvet and rearranged a half dozen pastel-colored throw pillows. The bed's crisp, white-ruffled canopy blended perfectly with the room's antique French provincial furniture and soft blue walls, hand painted with cottony white clouds.

The bedroom, hell, the whole house, looked as if it belonged in an issue of *House Beautiful,* and Rand knew his sister had personally decorated every inch of the spacious, center-hall colonial. To his knowledge, it was the only time she'd ever used her degree in interior design.

"So, where *is* Warren tonight?" Running his fingers through his hair, he followed her into the hall. In the distance came the happy sounds of whooping children interspersed with the ring of Princess's raucous barking.

"I told you, he's on call." She led him into the restaurant-sized kitchen and handed him a corkscrew and bottle of red wine.

"Oo-kay." Rand made short work of the cork and set the Cabernet Sauvignon firmly on the tiled center island. "But since when do plastic surgeons spend time in the hospital on a Saturday night? Two weekends in a row, I might add."

"They do if there's an accident. A burn victim—"

"There are specialists who usually handle that type of emergency."

"Or a car wreck—" Nan challenged weakly.

"Yeah, right. Why not a middle-aged society matron trolling for a shot of Botox, or maybe a rescue eye lift? Come on, Nan, tell me another story about the wonderful world of emergency chin implants and lifesaving tummy tucks. Make me believe you for a change."

She removed two goblets from the cupboard and filled them to the brim with the ruby-red wine, then carefully handed Rand a glass. Instead of answering, she rested her backside against the counter and drained her drink in one long swallow.

When she started to pour herself another glass, he snatched up the wine bottle and held it out of her reach. "Okay, that's it. Game time is over. Now, just what the heck is going on between you and Warren? And don't insult my intelligence by telling me he's performing an emergency boob job.''

In a heartbeat, Nan spun around and hunched over the sink. Before he could reach her side, her shoulders began to shake with the force of her sobs.

"Aw, crap. I didn't mean to upset you. Come on, it's me, your big brother. I'm the one you came running to when that jerk Joey Briskie turned down your invitation to the junior prom, remember? You can tell me.'' Patting awkwardly at her back, he waited until the tears subsided.

"This time I'm afraid it's a lot more serious than prom-date rejection,'' Nan finally said, exhaling a shaky breath. She dabbed at her eyes with the corner of her apron. "Warren's left me. We're getting a divorce.''

Rand parked his Jeep Sahara and deftly made his way up the steps. He hoped the sight of a car in the front drive would be enough to deter any thrill seekers or thieves brazen enough to climb the fence or hack their way through the woods at the front of the property. Fumbling for his key, he wished he'd remembered to leave on a few lights. The grounds, porch and house were dark as pitch, with only a thin sliver of autumn moon to light his way.

Once inside, he flipped the foyer switch, frowning when the chandelier flickered in a perfect imitation of Dr. Frankenstein's laboratory. Even though New Jersey Power had assured him the lines from the road were perfect, Duke had been one hundred percent correct about the state of the wiring on the inside. If the electricians couldn't find the problem, he was going to seriously consider a complete reinspection. The only reason he hadn't ordered it done in the first place was because of the mess. To do it right, they'd have to break into the walls again, which would settle another coating of plaster dust over every square inch of the house. That would put a hold on most of the bigger jobs like sanding and refinishing the hardwood floors and painting the interior. Still, it would have to be done to bring the mansion up to code.

Picking his way up the stairs, he thought glumly about his discussion with Nancy. Some older brother he'd turned out to be, not suspecting his baby sister had been miserable for so long. Duke had noticed more about Nan over the past few months than he'd caught on to in years, which made him feel lower than a snake's belly. It was disheartening to admit he'd spent more time making the company a success than seeing to the well-being of his own family.

Through the years, Nan had always found the time to worry about him. From the day their parents had divorced, she had been the glue that held them together. As she'd grown to adulthood, she'd seen to it they met with their father every few weeks for dinner. Unlike their mother, Nan had been there for his high school and college graduations. And she'd made sure to celebrate the other special events in his life, taking care that Rand had a place to go for Christmas and Thanksgiving.

Thinking back on all the times he'd tried to worm his way out of one of her gatherings, he wanted to kick himself for misreading her brave front and Melissa's and Robbie's cries for attention.

The only person he was more angry at than himself was her creep of a husband. According to Nan, Warren had been the one to demand her perfection, then screw around with half the women who came to him for help ... after they were finished getting snipped, tightened and cosmetically enhanced, of course.

And, according to Nancy, when she had pointed out that he could lose his medical license for being such an imprudent idiot, good ol' Warren had been brazen enough to remind her there was nothing illegal in sleeping with those women, especially since they were no longer his patients. What a jerk!

Walking into his bedroom, Rand flipped the switch and gave a satisfied grunt when his bedside lamps brightened the room. He unbuttoned his shirt and tossed it on the foot of the bed, then kicked off his sneakers, unzipped his jeans and slid them to the floor. The aches and pains he'd experienced after taking down the wall were gone, but he still longed for a another shower to soothe his temper. He didn't know where Warren was staying, but he had an idea it would be the most expensive hotel in the area. Maybe tomorrow he would pay the bum a visit. It might be fun to find out if it was medically possible for a plastic surgeon to perform cleanup surgery on himself.

He turned on the hot water, grateful his first priority had been the remodeling of the master suite bathroom. Beige-and-apricot-veined marble tiles sparkled in the twin globes of delicately etched glass mounted over the sinks. A wall of mirrors picked up the glitter of brass fixtures and commingled with the turquoise, peach and cream-colored towels, casting the oversized room in a cool sunrise of colors. Eventually, every area in the house would look as welcoming and restful as this one. The whole house would bring comfort and a feeling of serenity to whoever chose to visit.

After turning on the taps, Rand brushed his teeth while he waited for the water to steam, then stepped inside the stall shower and closed the glass door. Lathering himself from head to toe, he let the spray sluice over his weary body. Thinking there had to be a way he could help Nancy regain her self-confidence, he shut off the water, stepped onto the floor mat, and snagged a towel off the warming rack. He'd dried off his hair, face and shoulders before he felt the hair at the back of his neck prickle.

"Hey!" Frantically, he whipped the towel around his

hips. "Don't you know you're supposed to knock before you come into a room?"

Cassandra folded her arms and shot him a grin. She'd been watching the MacPherson for a good five minutes, simply enjoying the view, and now that she'd been caught, she decided to be bold.

I can't knock. I travel through walls, remember? she snapped. *Besides, you don't have anything I didn't see when I used to happen upon my brothers swimming in the loch on a hot summer's day.*

Rand pulled the towel tighter and Cassandra resisted the urge to snicker. "You spied on your brothers? I thought young women of your day were taught to be shy and demure."

Aye, and there's the rub. I was never very adept at being shy and demure, much to my father's displeasure.

He grabbed another towel and slung it over his shoulders, hiding most of his magnificent chest from her view. "Now, why doesn't that surprise me?" Running a comb through his hair, he raised his eyes to the mirror and their gazes locked. For a second, Rand only stared before saying, "Hey, look at that. I can see your reflection."

Cassandra bobbed closer, until she hovered behind his left shoulder. Surprised to see a faint outline that revealed a blur of tumbled curls and facial features, she sucked in a gust of air and was assaulted by another, more shocking fact.

She could smell the MacPherson! Could smell his fresh lemon-and-pine scent, even the mint of his toothpaste.

By all the saints, how long had it been since she'd actually had the ability to detect any kind of odor, be it fair or foul? In awe of the sensation, she managed to say, *That you can. Seeing as there hasn't been a mirror in the house in over a century, I never gave it much thought.*

"What about the window glass? Didn't you ever see yourself in it when you looked outside?"

Wrinkling her brow, she thought back to all the time she'd spent gazing into the world. Truthfully, she was too addled to remember. *I'm not sure. Why do you ask?*

Rand turned and she skittered backward again, but not before she felt his breath feather against her cheek. ''I guess I was just wondering if you've noticed a difference in yourself. For example, at our first meeting in the library, I couldn't really see you at all. You were just this invisible field of energy taking up space. That next time on the landing, you reminded me of unset Jell-O, the other day it was pudding—''

There you go again with that unappetizing food talk. Don't you ever eat?

''Do you?'' he teased.

She fisted her hands on her hips. *I'm afraid the urge for filling my belly has long passed, as well as the yearnings of most things human.*

His eyes narrowed as he reached out a hand and brushed her arm. And this time Cassandra would have sworn that instead of a tingling, she could feel his individual fingers stroking softly.

''Tonight you feel more like . . . mashed potatoes? You know, kind of soft and sticky, but firm.''

She bolted backward until she was just outside the bathroom doorway. Unable to comprehend what the feel of his touch might signify, she gave a delicate sniff. *For heaven's sake, man, there must be a better word to describe it. I'm beginning to think you have a one-track mind.*

''Only where you and this house are concerned.'' Grinning, he closed the door in her face. ''Don't move. Just stay there till I get dressed.''

Cassandra floated into the bedroom, still overwhelmed by the emotions that stirred deep inside. Feeling another human being after so long a time had actually caused an ache in the area of her heart, the sensation was that painful.

And the wonderful smell of him, like the warm, sweet outdoors she'd not been able to walk in for these past one hundred years, sent a shaft of longing straight to her midsection.

What was the man doing to her brain, for pity's sake? Her fate had been sealed a century ago, and nothing would ever change it. The time would arrive soon enough when Rand would be living here with his wife and children. She would have no more moments of shared wonder and discovery with the MacPherson.

The door opened and he stood before her naked from the waist up. Dressed in a pair of dark blue silky-looking trousers, his pale brown chest hair picked up the glow of the lamplight, gilding his corded arms and flat, muscled stomach in a sheen of gold. A vision of his taut, trim backside and muscular thighs fluttered through her memory. To her dismay, she hadn't been able to get a good glimpse of his manly parts, but she had no doubt those would be as admirable as the rest of his invigorating presence. By all the saints, he was a fine figure of a man.

She saw the gleam in his eyes and realized he'd caught her staring. *So, MacPherson, tonight I've a mind to ask you a question instead of answering the ones you keep tossing at me,* she managed to say, finally coming to her senses.

One corner of his full lips drew up as he walked to the bed and sat down. "Okay, I guess that's only fair. What do you want to know?"

Cassandra realized she would need to be careful when she formed her question, as he'd proven himself capable of reading her mind on too many occasions. *From the look of things, I gather you've moved in for good?*

"Almost. I still have some clothes at my apartment and a few pieces of furniture. I should be pretty much settled in by next Saturday. Eventually, I'll fill the house with new stuff. Why?"

Positive his answer would sadden her, she still needed to have it, if for nothing else than to get the words said and done. Notching up her chin, she asked, *And when will the rest of your family be moving in?*

"The rest of my family?" For a half second his face was blank, then his eyes grew wide. "Why in the heck would you want my sister and her kids or, God forbid, my mother moving in?"

Your sister and her children? The space that would have held her heart gave an infinitesimal quiver of joy. *Would that be the lovely dark-haired lass and those two bonny wee ones who were visiting just yesterday?*

"That would be them. And by the way, you scared the bejeezus out of the kids with that whirling-wind thing you do. Shocked me too, for that matter. After we opened the closet and took care of . . . well, you know . . . I didn't think I'd ever see you again."

He stood and took a step toward her, but Cassandra was too choked up to telegraph a single thought, never mind remain in his presence. Had the obstinate man, in a very roundabout way, just confessed he wasn't married?

"Hey, you're not planning to disappear again, are you?"

Only when I must, she replied, still assessing what he'd just revealed. *Now good night, Mr. MacPherson, and sleep well, as I will try to do.*

Dawn had come hours ago, tugging Cassandra from her netherworld of dreamless slumber. Last night, when she'd first retired to the closet, she'd found it difficult to settle down after her disturbing confrontation with the MacPherson. His simple answer to her question about his family had struck like a thunderbolt. Once she'd come to her senses and accepted what he said, a feeling of calm had claimed her, and she'd managed to drift into a peaceful night of nonbeing.

But this morning found her still mulling over his words. The charming little girl and handsome, energetic boy she'd seen him with the other afternoon had been his niece and nephew, the attractive woman his sister. He planned to live in this place alone. He was not married.

Now, hovering at the bay window in Rand's bedroom, she found herself alternately gazing at the drizzling rain and staring at the MacPherson's sleeping form. The bed-covers had fallen to a tangle around his legs, baring his sculpted chest to the dim morning light. His sleep-tousled hair called to mind skeins of golden yarn, while his face was at rest, showing to perfection his squared jaw, Roman nose and generous lips.

Amazingly, this beautiful man who looked like one of God's own angels had not yet been claimed by another.

Once again she thought of all the reasons that made the fact almost impossible to comprehend. Could it be that he loved a woman from afar and was too shy to tell her so? Had he been married and lost the girl through death or that distasteful twentieth-century convenience— a divorce? Worse, could he possibly be the type of man she'd seen on so many of those talk shows? The ones who called themselves gay but to her way of thinking had very little to be happy about?

The first idea seemed ridiculous, as she had no doubt Rand MacPherson knew perfectly well he was a man any woman would be proud to call her own. And from what she'd heard about marriage on those shows, no modern female would divorce such a paragon. That left only the third possibility, which seemed too incredible to bear thinking about.

Sighing out a breath, she noticed for the first time that her exhalation of air clouded the windowpane. Knotting her forehead, she studied the foggy blur, not quite aware of what the display meant. Puffing out another breath, she watched the circle of fog grow wider as it settled over the glass.

"Hey, you been up long?"

The sound of Rand's sleep-filled voice had her spinning on her heels. Propped against a mound of pillows, he was grinning as if he found the sight of her there in his bedroom near to miraculous.

Only a short while. 'Tis raining, I'm afraid.

"I figured that when I heard the dripping and saw how gray the sky looked. Still, it's been a great fall. This is my favorite time of the year." He swung his legs over the side of the bed and stretched. "Got any plans for today?"

Plans? She tore her gaze from his chest and concentrated on a space somewhere over his head. *Spirits don't make plans. There's no reason for us to do so.*

Standing, he took a step toward her. "That reminds me, I've been meaning to ask what you do all day."

Do? She folded her arms at her waist. *Why nothing. We just . . . exist.*

"Sounds pretty boring if you ask me," he answered. "Hang on a second while I take a . . . ah, use the bathroom, okay?"

As if hypnotized, Cassandra merely nodded. Since he'd invaded her pithy existence, she hadn't been bored for a minute. Her days had been filled with excitement and energy and a strange kind of longing. But to tell him so, she imagined, would only go straight to his head. She'd learned from Colin that all the MacPherson men were full of themselves. It was one of the reasons she'd conjured that curse—

My God, the curse! She laid a palm to her cheek and gave herself a healthy mental slap. What a cabbage brain she'd been not to have realized it sooner. *She* was the reason the MacPherson had no one in his life! When she'd cursed Colin, she'd cursed all his male progeny, and denied the lot of them true love for the whole of their miserable existence. She had ruined each and every one of their lives.

Still, she reasoned, some of the men must have found women who could tolerate them, else the MacPherson wouldn't be standing before her today. Was it possible the curse hadn't worked? After all, she'd been only an apprentice witch, untrained in the fine art of conjuring. Maybe she wasn't responsible for the ruination of so many innocent lives. Maybe Rand MacPherson just hadn't met the right woman yet.

Overwhelmed by the thought that she could have been successful, she gave another huff. No, she would not let herself be consumed by guilt. What she'd done had been her right as a victim, the only choice she'd had at the time of her entombment. How else was she to have retaliated against the horrible man and his despicable actions?

What else was she supposed to have done?

A rhythmic tapping sounded from somewhere in the house, causing her to jump in place. Bobbing quickly to the bedroom door, she heard a woman's voice echo up the stairs.

"Rand? Are you awake, darling? Mother's here and I've brought someone I want you to meet. I'm coming up, so make yourself presentable."

By all the saints in heaven! The *mother* had come for a visit. Thinking she had enough worries to chew on for the next two millennia, Cassandra rushed into the hall and flew to the third floor just as Irene trotted up the stairs looking as happy as a cat with a fresh-killed mouse.

"Randall. It's Mother. Are you decent?"

Aw, Christ! Rand cursed to himself as he flushed the toilet. Irene was here ... and she'd brought a friend. Now, wasn't that special. Peering through the door, he gave the bedroom a quick scan, satisfied to find that while he was trapped like the proverbial rat, Cassandra had found the wherewithal to escape.

Inhaling a lungful of fortitude, he swung the bathroom door wide. "Good morning, Mother. How did you get in?" Walking calmly to the foot of his bed, he retrieved his jeans and slung them over his shoulder.

"Back door, darling. You really must learn to lock every point of entry. You never know who's going to find their way inside, now, do you?"

"And the locked gate at the foot of the drive? How'd you manage that?" He opened a dresser drawer and took out a clean pair of boxers.

"My . . . um . . . guest. She drives one of those huge vehicles that can plow their way through anything. Not that we broke the gate, of course. We just found a clearing in the trees and drove until we came onto the property."

Rand braced his hands on his hips. If anyone had *cojones* the size of bowling balls, it was his mother. "What the hell are you talking about? You'd need a Sherman tank to traverse those woods."

Irene nodded. "Exactly. I think that Schwarzenegger person owns one . . . or maybe it's Sylvester Stallone?"

"A Hummer? You have a friend who owns a Hummer?" The laughable picture of his mother climbing in and out of a Jeep on steroids aided Rand in keeping his anger in check.

"Madame Ragnar had several modes of transportation at her disposal. Sometimes she uses a chauffeured limousine, other times she manages to project herself astrally. She's a remarkable woman. She's downstairs right now, inspecting the aura on the first level. Would you like to meet her?"

Heaving a frustrated breath, he ran a hand over his stubbled jaw. "No, I would not. Now, please, take Madame Raghead and her Hummer and—"

Irene hissed out an irritated *tsk*. "It's Ragnar. Madame

Ragnar. And you needn't be so rude. This séance will be for your own good.''

''No. Absolutely not. Now, go away, before I pull a Schwarzenegger act of my own and personally remove you and Madame Ragbag. Is that understood?''

''Randall MacPherson, how dare you speak that way to me.''

Rand headed into the bathroom and slammed the door, still disbelieving of his mother's colossal nerve. Thank God Cassandra hadn't been around to hear Irene's ludicrous suggestion. If this Madame Ragweed was a true psychic, who knew what could happen at a séance?

The last thing he needed—wanted—was to risk losing Cassandra just when he'd assured himself she was there to stay.

Chapter Eight

Rand stood in the foyer, inspecting purchase orders while he waited for Nancy to finish her tour of the downstairs. Yesterday, after he'd convinced his mother and her supposedly psychic friend to leave the premises, he spent time hunting for Cassandra. Failing to find her, he'd run a few errands and returned to his sister's for dinner. After a second evening of roughhousing with the kids, he'd come home and dropped into bed, too weary to begin another search for his elusive spirit-in-residence.

His plan to seek out Cassandra that morning had fallen by the wayside when the day dawned wet and windy. With close to twenty workmen vying to begin a dozen inside projects, he knew there was no way she would show herself, even if he made it to the third floor.

Duke had been called to another site on an emergency, which forced Rand to play supervisor, but his heart hadn't been in the job. He'd spent the day alternately wishing everyone would go home so he could find Cassandra and thinking about his sister until, finally, he managed to come up with what he thought was a clever way to help Nancy regain her self-confidence. He'd called and invited

her to the house, and she'd been snooping through the
first floor for the last fifteen minutes.

"You're absolutely positive about this?" she asked in
a voice filled with amazement. Eyes bright with enthusiasm, she dodged a trio of workmen carrying cartons of
ceramic tiles as she strode back into the foyer.

"What's the matter, sis? Has turning thirty affected
your hearing?" he asked with a grin.

"Funny. Now, tell me again that you're sure you want
me to decorate this house and it's not a charity gig."

"Trust me, the request is a purely selfish one. My
guess is you'll work cheap. And if I don't like the results, I
can complain out loud and not worry about hurt feelings."

Placing her palms on her slim hips, she snorted delicately. "Don't be so smug. I haven't been out of the
business so long that I'll undercut the job. But I am going
to need a steady income if I intend to support myself and
the kids."

Rand set his hands on her shoulders and began to
massage. "I thought you'd negotiated a good settlement?
Don't tell me that pricey lawyer Harry set you up with
isn't going to make sure you get the house, child support,
alimony . . . the whole ball of wax?"

Nan held on to his wrists as if grasping a lifeline. "I
have an excellent divorce lawyer, one of the best in Morris
County, and she and I have been over this topic about a
bazillion times. I'm getting half our stock portfolio and
savings and Warren's agreed to pay monthly support for
the children. But I'm going to allow him to pay the
mortgage on the house only until I get a steady income.
I refuse to take one more dime from the jerk than is
necessary."

"Nan, that's just plain stupid."

She heaved out an impatient-sounding and decidedly
stubborn sigh. "Gee, thanks for the vote of approval."

"You know what I mean. Most women in your shoes would take the bum to the cleaners. Don't be foolish."

She walked to the staircase and sat on the bottom step, then slid over to make room for two workers carting a commode up the stairs. "I'm being independent. I have a degree from one of the best interior design schools in Manhattan and I've never used it. Right now my main goal is to reacquaint myself with the furniture and fabric wholesalers in order to establish professional connections."

Rand plopped down beside her and rested his elbows on the step behind him. "It sounds like you've thought this thing out fairly well. What did Mother and Harry have to say?"

Chuckling, she patted at his knee. "At first Harry offered to represent me, but since his specialty is immigration law, we finally agreed I needed a female shark. Mother, on the other hand, said the same as you, except in more graphic terms. I didn't realize she knew so many colorful four-letter words."

"I suspect there's a lot about Mother we're not aware of. Tell me what you know about her friend, that Ragweed woman."

Stretching her legs in front of her, Nancy imitated Rand's relaxed pose. "Her name is Edith Ragnar. I was wondering when Mom would get around to introducing the two of you."

"She didn't. But she had the nerve to bring the woman here unannounced and let her check out the *energy* in the downstairs. I had to get tough before they agreed to leave." He ran his fingers over his face. "God, Nan, Mother actually believes she's going to hold a seance in this house."

"She won't if you don't let her. You just have to stand firm, that's all. But . . ."

"But what?"

"Why won't you let her have a little fun? What's the harm in allowing Mom and a few of her eccentric friends to sit around a table holding hands for a few hours? You don't even have to be here. I'll come over and guard the house for you."

He thought about the offer for all of a half-second before deciding the idea was just too risky. Aside from the fact he'd yet to hold a conversation with Cassandra on anything more serious than the consistency of her ghostly form, he needed to find out the reason Colin had walled her in that damned closet. Then he had to figure a way to make it up to her. And there were at least a dozen more personal questions he had to ask.

The last thing he wanted was to hurt his sister's feelings at a time when she was most vulnerable, but he had to protect Cassandra. "I'll give it some thought. If I'm lucky, Mother will stumble upon another crusade and just drop the idea."

"Hey, I'm on your side on this one. It's your house, so you make the rules." Sniffling, she straightened her shoulders and gave him a tremulous grin. "And I meant what I said. Letting me sharpen my decorating skills on this place is a godsend. I don't know how to thank you."

Rand shrugged as he laced the fingers of one hand with hers. "A good job will be thanks enough. Just remember, no chi-chi balls, no velvet swags and no cherubs. I want the house to be comfortable—the kind of home a guy would look forward to at the end of a long day."

"Oh, God, please don't tell me you want me to decorate around that gold-and-green-plaid wreck of a lounge chair that belonged to Dad, because I won't do it. This house needs style, elegance and *tasteful* comfort. I already have a dozen ideas."

"Okay, so my apartment wasn't the most sophisticated place in town; what's important is that I liked it." He gave a sigh of mock disappointment. "I guess the lounger can go upstairs in my office. Just promise me I can keep the lamp.''

''The lamp?'' Nan furrowed her brow, then shot her gaze to his. ''Not *the* lamp? The one Dad gave you as an apartment-warming present?''

The foot-high table lamp had been a private joke between father and son, a garishly painted battery-powered ceramic hula dancer with a clock in her rounded belly that vibrated when it chimed the hour. Totally tasteless, it represented a gift of male bonding he would always treasure . . . and the best part was, his father had named the hula dancer Irene.

''The very one. I was thinking it might look good here in the foyer, maybe on a table near the door or—''

''You're kidding?'' Nan said with a deadpan gaze.

Both of them burst into hysterical laughter when Rand tried but failed to dredge up a frown. ''Okay, you caught me. The lamp is going in my third-floor office. Just don't remind Mother I still have it, or she'll find a way to make good on her threat to break it into smithereens.''

The foyer door shot open and Duke blew in on a gust of damp, chilly air. ''Hey, boss—'' Bushy brows rose to exclamation points as he scanned Rand and his still-giggling sister. ''You're here. I mean, here you are. Uh . . . Nancy. Hello.''

''Hello, Bill. How are you?''

''Fine. I'm fine. And you?''

Composing herself, Nan stood and straightened the lapels of her tan suede jacket. ''Thanks to big brother, I'm doing great.'' She lifted her leather tote from the floor and slung the strap over her shoulder, then glanced at her watch. ''Guess I'd better be going. I'm sure the two of you have a lot to discuss and it's time I picked up the kids from school.''

Stepping to the side, Duke cleared his throat as Nan

paced to the front door. "So . . . what do you think of the place?"

She stopped and turned, then followed his eyes to the foyer ceiling with its dome of intricately carved vines. "I love it. You're doing a wonderful job. I'm looking forward to working with you."

"Working with me?" He slid Rand a confused frown. "You're working with me?"

"You're the foreman on this job, aren't you?"

Rand watched the foreman shuffle his size-fourteen work boots and decided it was time to put the guy out of his misery. "He is." Placing a hand on his sister's back, he gave a gentle nudge. "You'd better get moving. You don't want to be late for the kids, do you?"

Not one to be shoved aside, she dug in her heels and gave her brother a quizzical glare. "I guess it slipped Rand's mind. He's hired me to do the interior design on this place. You and I will need to go over the specs on the bathrooms and kitchen. I know the master bath is finished, and I love the drawing of the conversion in the upstairs parlor, but I want to do something special with the rooms down here."

"Uh, yeah, sure," Duke stuttered, his face suddenly the color of an overripe tomato.

"Nan, the kids?" Rand reminded her as he held open the door.

"Okay, okay, I've got it. You're busy and I'm putting a dent in your day." She held out her hand and Duke hesitated before taking it in his own. "How about tomorrow morning, say ten o'clock? That'll give you time to get the work orders together. And I'll need paint and tile samples too. Is that all right with you?"

Looking about as comfortable as a rabbit in a room full of wildcats, Duke gave her hand a quick shake. "Yeah. Sure."

"Great. See you." Tossing both men a half-grin from over her shoulder, she walked onto the porch.

Rand waited a heartbeat before he closed the door and met Duke head-on. "Well, I guess that's formal notice. You and Nan will be working together."

The foreman's face had toned down to a mottled pink. "I know what you're trying to do, boss, and it's not funny."

Aware he might have been caught red-handed, Rand scrunched up his forehead. So maybe, subconsciously, matchmaking *had* been on his mind when he'd offered Nancy the job. Was that such a big deal? "Don't be so suspicious, Dukovsky. I expect the two of you to have a totally professional relationship even though she's going through a rough time right now."

"A rough time?"

"Nancy and her husband are getting a divorce. She needed something to take her mind off her problems, and this house is the perfect diversion."

Duke's frown turned upside down as the words slowly sunk in. Grinning from ear to ear, he gave Rand's shoulder a muscle-numbing whack, then trotted up the stairs.

"Cassandra! Everybody's gone home. You can come out now."

The pounding of booted feet and Rand's whiskey-deep voice echoing on the stairway caused chills to skitter up Cassandra's spine. How could the mere thought of sharing space with the man make her tremble? What in God's name was happening to her?

She'd spent another night in turmoil, her mind filled with emotions she could barely put a name to. That morning, when she saw that Rand would be busy for most of the day, she'd almost sobbed in frustration. Then again, the sobbing would have been only in her head, as she

never cried ... nay, *couldn't* cry, she reminded herself
with a stiff set to her spine.

Still, the feeling of spinning aimlessly after so many
years of forced control had her frazzled and confused.
She hadn't felt this helpless since that fateful day Colin
had set trowel to mortar and buried her behind his wall
of bricks.

"Cassandra? Are you up here?" Rand's voice was
hesitant, which caused her to smile. From the sound of
it, the MacPherson had missed being with her today, just
as she'd missed spending time with him.

She whisked to the closet door in time to see him arrive
on the landing, a battery-powered light held high in his
hand. *You were looking for me?* she asked smartly.

He raised a tawny brow. "Yeah. Where've you been
all day?"

Floating near, she hovered just beyond his reach. *Keeping a careful eye on things. The place reminded me of a
castle today, with the industrious knights and loyal vassals all busy seeing to the wishes of their king. Are you
always so bossy?*

He set the lantern on the floor and took a step closer
to her wavering form. "Me bossy? You're making a joke,
right? Just my luck to have a ghost with a sense of
humor."

Folding her arms, she met his quirked brow and silly-
looking grin with a smile of her own. *Aye, and you should
give thanks for it. How else could I have survived all
these years without my good humor? Besides, as my
sainted grandmother used to say, it's difficult to be a
grouch all of the time. And if a person canna laugh at
himself, who can he laugh at?*

Tentatively, Rand lifted a hand and she bobbed back
a foot. "Just wanted to check the food supply is all. Are
you still a mound of mashed potatoes or have you evolved
into something a little more substantial tonight?"

Knowing full well it was a foolish thing to do, Cassandra held out an arm. If she wasn't so positive of her miserable state of being, she'd swear she could actually feel her heart pounding in her chest. *See for yourself, Mr. MacPherson, and tell me what's on the menu for the evening—mashed potatoes or pudding? Or leg of lamb, perhaps?*

His long, tanned fingers stroked her skin with a butterfly caress. Closing her eyes, Cassandra let herself float on the incredible sensations swirling through her belly. The landing grew dim, the air around them thick with tension.

"Crap. The battery's dying. I thought I told Pete to load the thing with a fresh supply."

Her eyes snapped open as she wobbled backward in surprise. Grateful the big oaf had not a clue to the kind of commotion he was causing her insides, she said smoothly, *Why not flip the wall switch and call up the electricity if it's too dark for your weak human eyes. 'Tis what it's there for, is it not?*

Rand bent and jiggled the lantern. When he had no success at turning it back on, he moved to the wall and tried the switch. But the landing remained in darkness. "Yeah. Trouble is, the wiring's been the most difficult part of this job. I'm hoping the electricians will break into the walls tomorrow and try to pinpoint the problem. In the meantime, I have more lanterns downstairs. I was going to make myself a little dinner. Care to join me?"

She'd watched the trucks from the upstairs windows as they delivered a huge white box she guessed was a refrigerator and a variety of smaller appliances that closely resembled those she'd seen advertised on television—a washing machine, clothes dryer, dishwasher and stove. She had to admit that each and every one of them piqued her curiosity.

Perhaps I'd be able to take a look at a few of those

newfangled inventions I heard you talking about the other day. I think you called one of them a microwave?

In gentlemanly fashion, Rand stepped aside and swept out a hand. "A true electrical marvel, the microwave. After you, Miss Kinross."

Rand followed Cassandra's floating form, his gaze trained on the tumble of curls falling halfway down her back. The lights on the first level worked perfectly, picking up the strands of copper and bronze that wove their way through her hair. If he didn't know for certain she was a spirit, he would swear the hair was as real as his own.

Resisting the urge to sift his fingers through those wayward curls, he stuffed his hands into his pockets as they made their way through the foyer, past the butler's pantry, and into the kitchen. Propping himself against a newly tiled counter, he waited as she made her inspection, his stomach on a roller-coaster ride. Would she like what he'd done with her house so far?

Drifting to the cabinets, Cassandra lifted her hands and placed them against the fine-grained wood, then the cool ceramic tiles on the counter. Floating to the refrigerator, she simply folded her arms and stared.

"Here, let me open it so you can get a good look." Except for a few cans of beer, a quart of milk and loaf of bread, the white, side-by-side behemoth was empty. Rand whipped open the freezer compartment door, embarrassed he had nothing to show her but frozen dinners. "I haven't had time to do much shopping."

Cassandra peered inside, then stuck a hand into the freezer. *'Tis blistering cold.*

"Keeps food rock solid for months. Just about every home has one these days."

Pulling out her hand, she tucked it under her arm. *What a marvelous invention.* She bobbed around the center island. *And this box, what does it do?*

"That's the microwave you were asking about. It and the refrigerator are working off the generator. Watch." He pulled a frozen dinner from the freezer, opened it and placed it inside, then hit the timer. "See how easy it is? I'll have a hot meal in about seven minutes and I won't even have to wash a dish."

She peered through the window and watched the turntable spin, then gave Rand a look of wonder. *Truly?* she asked, her voice an amazed whisper.

"Yep. Want to see a few of the other appliances?"

He gave her a tour of the laundry room, which included a short explanation on the workings of a washer and dryer. Then the microwave beeped and he led her back to the main body of the kitchen. Deftly, he removed his lasagna, set it on the counter, and peeled back the lid. A puff of steam rose from the box, along with the delicious aroma of tomatoes and cheese.

"Hmm. I love this stuff." Opening a drawer, he took out a fork and began to eat. "Sorry to be rude, but I'm starving."

Not at all. She settled on the other side of the center island. *My brothers were hearty eaters. Grandmother used to tease they could strip a carcass of beef to the bone faster than a pack of hungry wolves.*

"You had brothers?" Rand took a drink of ice water, then continued his meal.

Cassandra's eyes grew bright with a faraway glimmer, and he guessed she was picturing her family in her mind. *Six brothers and a baby sister. Fergus was the eldest, then came meself. Michael, Ian, Douglas, Quinn, and Linus followed quickly, with Meggie born last. I miss them all.*

"I bet they were a handful. How did your mom manage all those squirming little bodies?" He set his fork in the sink and deposited the empty lasagna box in the trash.

"Irene had a hard enough time taking care of Nan and me, and she didn't even do a great job at that."

The glow left her eyes as she said, *Ma died with Meggie, the labor was that hard. I was twelve at the time and had to see to the young ones.*

Thinking it had to have been slavery to burden a girl of twelve with such a huge endeavor, Rand's mouth turned hard. "And your father let you? Were you so poor he couldn't have hired help, a nanny or a housekeeper?"

She notched up her chin when she answered. *We weren't poor exactly, just incredibly busy. My mother's mother lived with us and she helped some, though she had her own . . . passions. Father was a farmer, doing what he could to see eight young ones clothed and fed. It was my job as the eldest girl to take care of my sister and brothers, and I did a fine job of it.*

Though uncomfortable with the idea she'd taken his probing as an insult, he recognized the opportunity to unravel a bit of the mystery. "I'm sure you did. But what made you say yes to Colin and come to America?"

Cassandra pulled back her shoulders. Once again the fire returned to her eyes—eyes he just realized were the color of rain-washed violets.

I never said yes to Colin MacPherson. At least, not in so many words.

"Then how did you end up here, so far from your family?"

Her full, shapely breasts lifted and fell with impatience, tightening the knot tied low in Rand's belly. Great. He was getting a hard-on for a ghost . . . who didn't exactly look like a ghost anymore. She had color and form—a fantastic form—and it looked like she was taking long, deep breaths.

Colin contacted an elder in our village, a cousin he'd left behind years earlier when he immigrated to the States. The cousin approached my father and claimed a wealthy

countryman was looking to wed a girl from the old school.
Said the women in his new land were too modern, too
bold for his cousin's taste. He was looking for a biddable
country lass to be the man's bride, and my father thought
it was a good way to—

She put a hand to her mouth to stop the words, forcing
Rand to tear his gaze from her chest. "To what? Why
did your father let you come here alone to marry a man
you didn't know? A man he'd never even met?"

She stared stonily, her mouth set. He stomped around
the island, his hands itching to touch her, to feel her nestle
against him for comfort. Even though it had happened a
hundred years ago, it had been the beginning of the twentieth century. The outrageous idea that a responsible parent
would allow a young girl to travel across the Atlantic to
marry a total stranger stung his sense of fair play.

Reaching out, he caught her hands in his. "I'm sorry
if this is painful for you, but I have to know why. Maybe
if we talked it out, we could find the reason that made
my uncle wall you in that closet. If we got it right, you
could—"

Her fingers stiffened in his palms, and Rand realized
he could almost feel her. Though her flesh was unusually
soft, it was pliant, warm and smooth . . . and unbelievably
alive under his hands. Raising his gaze, he saw her face
clearly. Creamy skin flushed pink, her violet eyes flashed
sparks, while her wide luscious mouth pursed into an
angry frown.

I could what? Pass on to the other side, perhaps? You
want me to go to heaven or hell, or wherever it is spirits
go when they're laid to rest? You want me to leave this
place?

"Yes! No! I mean . . . I don't want you to leave." He
tried to pull her to his chest, but she scuttled backward,
her face a furious mask. "I just want to find out what
happened so that I . . . we . . . can make it up to you."

Her face bled white. She'd fisted her hands on her hips, and he could see every detail of her gown, the one they'd suspected had been her wedding dress. Made of heavy ivory satin, the pearl-encrusted bodice shone like new in the bright kitchen light, clinging to her magnificent breasts, waist and gently flared hips. Except for the out-dated style, the gown looked as if it had been purchased yesterday.

Stay out of my world, Rand MacPherson. I've lived alone in this house for over a hundred years, and I can live here a thousand more without you. 'Tis you who should be moving on, and taking your modern inventions along. Colin gave me the deed to this place on our wedding day, and it doesn't matter if we were married or not . . . this house is mine.

Cassandra swirled up the stairs in a fit of rage. Arms thrust straight at her sides, she bobbed like thistledown in the wind as she paced the landing from corner to corner. This time he had gone too far.

How dare the MacPherson be so bold and ask her those painful questions? How dare he be so arrogant in thinking he could find a way to have her removed from her home! And how dare he pretend, just as he had the other day, that he wanted her living with him, when it was obvious he only planned to get rid of her.

Facing the closet door with a sense of dread and a surge of despair, she ordered herself to be calm. This dark, empty tomb was her home. Even with her mortal remains removed, it hadn't become any brighter or more cheerful. Thank the saints that when she resided there her mind seemed to quiet and her ghostly body found a semblance of peace.

Cassandra pushed through the door, paying scant atten-tion to the way she needed to almost force herself into the wood. At the moment her temper was firmly in charge, and it wasn't prepared to notice the subtle changes in her being.

Bobbing in a frustrated arc of anger, she could think of only one thing, one person—Rand MacPherson. The arrogant idiot was exactly like all men—all MacPherson men, she amended—concerned only with himself and his own wants and needs. His goal was to find out the truth about her and Colin and find a way to absolve his uncle of the guilt. Then, when he figured a way to be rid of her, he would go on with his life.

To think she'd felt guilty believing she'd unwittingly condemned him to a lifetime of loneliness with the force of her curse. Right now it didn't matter a hen's tooth that he hadn't a woman with whom to share his life. She'd watched enough talk shows to know there was a dearth of single heterosexual males residing in the twenty-first century. A man as financially well off and good-looking as the MacPherson would have no problem attracting a gaggle of females to do his bidding ... and warm his bed. He could find one on his own. Her curse couldn't possibly apply to him.

Slumping in a corner, Cassandra hung her head. She was a dunce, a fool of the highest magnitude, to think that a man like him could care for her. She was not a real woman but merely a shell of her former self.

Pain engulfed her chest, squeezing into a huge, hard fist. She would not fall in love with the MacPherson. It was hopeless to even think it could happen, never mind wish it were so. In this despicable condition of nonbeing, all her incantations and spells were useless to aid her personally. Truth be told, she had little knowledge of how she'd survived this long with so pithy an arsenal to choose from.

Those last few weeks of living with Colin came back to her like a sepia-toned movie playing at half speed in her mind. He'd been a harsh, bitter man with no shred of charity or sense of whimsy to his name. She'd been positive she could never love him. They'd argued bitterly on the morning of their nuptials. Once he realized he couldn't change her mind, he'd dragged her to the closet, slammed her jaw with his fist and shoved her inside. Then he'd locked the door and shouted the house down, ordering the cancellation of his plans. Shortly afterward, the house had grown quiet, until the rasping of the trowel had begun.

She'd cursed him then, making up the spell from bits and pieces of the chants she could remember from her grandmother's book. Afterward, she'd laid down and thought about how clever she'd been to have punished Colin and the men of his line for all eternity. She'd breathed her last with a serene expression on her face and the hope in her heart that what she'd conjured would come true.

She had no idea why her body had been so well preserved, or how she was able to see herself in a mirror now. Worst of all, she had no idea why she was thinking and feeling the things she'd been since the day Rand MacPherson had opened the front door and walked into her life.

She was dead, and nothing could change that fact. The babies she'd dreamed of having, the life she'd hoped to share with a man she loved and who loved her in return, was nothing more than shattered. It was as painful as a knife slicing her soul to want so much yet know she would get so little . . . again.

Curling into a ball, she shut herself off to the sounds she heard coming from the second floor—water running in the master bath, stomping feet and slamming drawers as Rand readied himself for sleep. The noises seemed an angry imitation of her own inner fears, as if the MacPherson were suffering along with her.

A preposterous idea, to be sure!

Placing her hands over her ears, she prayed as she had never prayed before, even when she'd cursed Colin so many years before. *Please God, help me to find a way out of this. Let me come home to thee. I beg of you, do not let me suffer any longer in this life that isn't really living. Help me to find my rest.*

Chapter Nine

The dreary sounds of moaning wind and heavy drizzle pulled Cassandra from her netherworld existence. Floating to the balcony, she watched workmen tromp noisily through the house exactly as they had yesterday, which told her there would be little opportunity to find the MacPherson. Prepared for a day of boredom, she refused to allow herself entry to Rand's bedroom and returned to the third floor.

Disgruntled the morning was starting out as miserable as her disposition, she roamed the house, snooping in the places she found of interest. The library, her favorite room, had been transformed into a gleaming patina of mahogany, its ten-foot-high shelves ready to be filled with books. Crown molding and matching wainscoting trimmed the walls, while the hardwood floors stood waiting for a final sanding and polishing.

Her mind boggled at the idea that fully half of the spacious butler's pantry would be converted into a powder room. It meant that eventually the house would contain three full and two partial bathrooms—an amazing concept when she recalled the one tin washtub and lone two-holed privy she, her grandmother, seven siblings and father had shared in the Highlands.

The enormous kitchen sparkled with shining appliances, while bits of fancy brought in by the MacPherson's sister covered the counters. Copper pots and clever knick-knacks decorated the island, while whimsical clay animals, deftly painted birdhouses, bright china lemons and baskets of dried flowers waited to be arranged for display.

For much of the day she observed Rand's sister as the woman sat at the farm-sized oak table in the breakfast room. Unaware of Cassandra's presence, Nancy had flipped through catalogues of furniture, fabrics, wallpaper and paint samples in a confident and professional manner while she jotted notes and made copious lists. When the pleasant man known as the Duke seated himself at Nancy's side, it was all Cassandra could do not to snicker. She had always thought him rather severe-looking, until she'd witnessed his addled stare whenever the woman deigned to glance his way.

Sometime in the middle of the afternoon Nancy left and Duke moved on to supervise the installation of fixtures in the powder room. Rand, who had disappeared immediately after his sister's arrival that morning, returned with overloaded cartons, which he carried to his third-floor office. Much to Cassandra's consternation, she had followed him from a distance, just to see, she assured herself, what the arrogant ass would be up to in the way of taking over more of her home.

A short while ago Duke and Rand left together and Nancy returned, so Cassandra was now upstairs, sulking in her closet, confused by all the comings and goings. She disliked being ignored but, short of forcing a confrontation with the MacPherson and demanding a good fight, had no idea what to do about it.

A sudden echo of voices called to her, luring her onto the landing. She peered around the corner into the room

Colin had told her would belong to their servants, and spied the children she knew to be Rand's niece and nephew huddled on the window seat. The boy sat with his knees bent, a large book propped on his thighs, while the little girl cradled herself against his sweater-clad chest.

"Tell me again, Robbie. Read me another story 'bout the boo-tee-ful princess," the little girl pleaded prettily.

With a gesture of brotherly impatience, Robbie rolled his grass-green eyes. "Okay, Liss, but this is the last one. Mom's going to be lookin' for us and I'm not so sure we're supposed to be up here. Now, stop squirming and sit still."

Obediently, the child quieted, her somber brown eyes wide as she concentrated on the pages.

"Once upon a time, there was a beautiful but very sad princess. Every vassal in the land knew why she was unhappy, but none of them could do a thing about it. Even her father the king couldn't help to cheer her spirit."

"Why was she so sad, Robbie? I don't likes it when the princesses aren't happy."

"I'm getting there, squirt. Pay attention."

Tucked together like ducklings in a nest, the children made a charming picture under the room's wide bay window. Unwittingly, Cassandra drew closer as a dozen different scenes, faded yet still as alive as yesterday, sifted through her memory. Her eldest brother, Fergus, had read to her as a child. He'd been a kind boy, her protector and her king, more loving than her father . . . and much more understanding.

When she'd grown older, she'd read to her younger brothers, then to Meggie, the little sister who'd so much resembled their mother, it had made Cassandra's heart ache. She'd missed them all terribly after she sailed to America. Colin had warned she would never see them again if she refused to marry him, but she still hadn't been able to give in to his demand.

"Who are you?" Melissa asked.

"Do we know you?" This from Robbie, who had one eyebrow lifted in curious suspicion.

At the sound of the children's questions, Cassandra jumped in place, startled to find that she'd allowed herself to wander into the center of the room. She gazed around, wondering to whom they were speaking. When she realized it was her, she opened then quickly closed her mouth. *Um, no. I don't think so. How do you do?*

Melissa flashed a sunrise grin. "We do fine. Robbie's readin' me a story."

Moving closer, Cassandra nodded hesitantly. *I can see that. Please, don't let me disturb you.*

"You want to come listen? Robbie reads really good," the little girl commented, still gazing at Cassandra. "We don't care, do we, Robbie?"

Staring doubtfully, the boy closed the book. "I guess it's okay. But we're not supposed to talk to strangers."

Cassandra bobbed nearer, willing her feet to touch the ground. Though it didn't seem to bother Rand when she floated six inches from the floor, it would break her heart if she frightened these adorable children. And how substantial was her form that they could look at her and not run shrieking from the room?

'Tis true you shouldn't be speaking to unfamiliar people, but it's different with me. After all, how can I be a stranger and still be allowed in this house?

Robbie contemplated her answer, then scooted over to make room. "Yeah, I guess you wouldn't be up here if Uncle Rand didn't think it was okay."

"You talk funny," Melissa added, still grinning happily. "Are you a princess?"

Robbie gave his sister's shoulder a gentle poke. "Liss, that's not polite." He smiled contritely at Cassandra. "Sorry, she's only four. And your dress looks kind of like the one the princess is wearing in this picture. See?"

Until that moment, Cassandra thought her presence could be detected only by the MacPherson. If that wasn't puzzling enough, the idea these children could hear her as well as Rand perplexed her completely. Vowing to think on it all later, she brushed a curl from her forehead as she hovered closer to the book. *Hmm. Yes, there does seem to be a likeness.*

"Melissa! Robert! Where are you? It's time to go home."

"Uh-oh. There's Mom." Jostling his sister off the window seat, Robbie shot to his feet and began to stuff the books and toys scattered on the floor into their backpacks.

Thinking she was well and truly caught, Cassandra fluttered madly as she headed toward the door.

"Hey, where you goin'?" the little girl called, following Cassandra onto the landing.

"You two better not be in Uncle Rand's office fiddling with his computer. . . ."

Undaunted, Melissa stopped a mere foot from Cassandra's wavering form. "Are you leaving?" she asked somewhat wistfully.

I must. Maybe we can talk another time. How would that be? Footsteps thudded on the stairs. Cassandra pushed through the closet door just as Nancy's feet hit the landing.

"Melissa, I thought I told you and Robbie not to play up here?"

Melissa pulled her gaze from the closet and stared at her sneakers. "We wasn't playin', Mommy, we was readin'."

"Reading is playing, sweetie. Quiet playing. Now, where's your brother?"

"Right here." Juggling two backpacks, Robbie appeared in the doorway. More footsteps sounded on the stairs, and he trained his eyes on the floor. "We weren't making trouble, honest."

Before Nan could answer, Bill Dukovsky's six-foot-two-inch frame filled the landing. "So you found them. Hi, guys. What's shakin'?"

Robbie's lightly freckled face drew into a frown. Thrusting his lower lip into a one-inch ledge of stubbornness, he raised his gaze and stuck out his chin. "We were just looking for a place to go where we wouldn't be in anyone's way. Mom said not to get underfoot."

Duke reached out to ruffle Robbie's hair, and the boy pulled back a step. "No harm done. Just stay out of your uncle's office. He's kind of particular about who touches his stuff." Ignoring the boy's rebuff, Duke scooped Melissa in his arms and settled her against his chest. "You guys ready for pizza?"

Clearly delighted, Melissa clapped her hands. "Yeah, teet-za. Can Unka Rand and the princess come too?"

Duke raised a brow as Nan *tsked*. "Robbie, you're not filling her head with crazy ideas again, are you? Letting her think those storybook characters are real?"

Robbie shot his sister a quelling glare. "Nah. She's just playing make-believe, aren't you, squirt?"

"But, Robbie, the princess went into the—"

"Okay, then. Let's get to it." Duke turned as Nan took her son's hand and led the way down the stairs.

Rand tucked a flashlight in his back pocket, then grasped a battery-powered lantern in one hand and a screwdriver and hammer in the other. Fully armed, he climbed the stairs with a cheerful but determined whistle. After last night's frustrating argument with Cassandra, he'd had enough. He was a grown man in charge of his life. He owned this house and he had the right to get to the bottom of the mystery surrounding it. If the woman—

He stopped on the first landing and heaved a sigh. Get a grip, MacPherson. Cassandra isn't real.

If the *ghost* had a problem with him, they needed to talk about it like two sensible adults . . . er, beings.

His headstrong spirit-in-residence hadn't fooled him one iota today. He'd felt her disconcerting presence in every room as surely as he breathed. Not only had the back of his neck prickled while he'd organized the files in his office—he'd actually seen Cassandra hovering at the edge of his peripheral vision. But each time he'd turned to confront her, she disappeared on a shimmer of undulating air.

He was going to get to the bottom of the problem tonight even if he needed a gallon of patience to make it happen. Stomping to the third floor, he set the lantern in a corner and gazed at the closet door. "Cassandra? Are you in there?"

Aside from the echo of his footsteps, an eerie silence was his only answer.

"You're being childish, Ms. Kinross. There are things we need to discuss. If you refuse to talk about them, that's fine, but I'm not going to let you continue to hide."

A gust of wind slithered from under the closet door and skittered around his ankles. Grinning, Rand shook his head. This angry-tornado act was just one more bullet to add to his list. He'd heard plenty of stories about ghosts rattling chains and making scary noises, but how in the heck was she able to call up the wind at the drop of a hat?

More important, what other surprises did she have waiting for him?

"All right, I didn't want to do this, but you leave me no choice." He walked to the door, raised the hammer, and gave the top hinge pin a good whack, then did the same to the second and third hinges. After failing to loosen the pins, he set the hammer down and cursed as he began to work on the doorknob.

"Damned fool creature," he muttered, at a loss for a

better name to call her. He undid the screws in the brass plate and stuck them in the pocket of his jeans, removed the cut-crystal knob and set it down, then gave the center bolt a push. The knob on the other side hit the floor with a loud *clunk,* and he gave a satisfied snort.

Angry wind gushed through the hole in the door, pushed against his chest, and blustered around the landing.

" 'Fraid it's going to take a whole lot more creativity than that to frighten me, Ms. Kinross."

Sticking two fingers in the hole, Rand pulled. The door opened a crack before the wind snatched it away and slammed it firmly back in place. He tugged harder, but the door wouldn't budge.

"Okay, be that way." Jabbing the screwdriver sword-like toward the door, he moved to the hinges and attacked the screws, placing them in his pocket exactly as he'd done with those of the doorknob. Methodically, he removed the first hinge plate, then the other two and set them on the floor. Wind whistled as it pressed against his back, whirled around to his front and tossed him into a corner, then spun him in a tight circle.

Catching his breath, Rand shouted into the swirling gusts. "This door is coming off whether you like it or not, Cassandra, so you might as well stop wasting your time."

Within a heartbeat the bossy wind ceased its tirade. He gave a satisfied *humph,* and again stuck his fingers in the hole. This time he managed to open the door. Stretching his arms wide, he grasped the outer edges, lifted the mahogany panel and dragged it out onto the landing. With a grunt he walked to a far wall and propped it up carefully, then turned and folded his arms across his chest.

"Fair warning, Cassandra. I'm coming inside."

He picked up the lantern, and the light grew dim, until it winked out completely. Raising his gaze to the ceiling, he rolled his eyes, set the lantern back on the floor and calmly pulled out his high-powered flashlight. She was a trip all right, he thought with a wry grin. Life around here certainly wouldn't be dull or boring as long as Cassandra Kinross was in residence.

Cassandra fisted her hands and stood like a prizefighter ready to defend her title as Rand stepped across the threshold. Startled by the flashlight's golden arc of light, she gave an angry blink. *By all the saints, shut off that blasted beacon. I'll answer your intrusive questions if I've a mind, but I'll not stand here and be blinded while doing so.*

"Fair enough," Rand replied, his expression entirely too smug for her liking. "I was hoping I could persuade you to come to your senses."

I'm not coming out, she threatened, poking a finger in the air. *You can speak your piece from there.*

"Stubborn thing, aren't you?" He took another step inside the room.

She sniffed delicately. *I'm no "thing" but a spirit, and a free one at that. I can stay in here till the cows come home, and you can't force me out.*

"Last time I checked, there weren't any cows on the property. And I've got all night."

At the sight of Rand's still-twitching lips, she folded her arms under her breasts. *'Tis unfortunate I don't find the same humor as you in this situation.*

Taking a seat across from her on the floor, he peered through the dim light. "Okay, but I thought you liked spending time in the rest of the house?"

I do, when there are things of which I'm curious.

Rand set the flashlight on end so that it pointed to the ceiling. "So you're telling me nothing interested you in the house today? Funny, I thought you'd be enthralled with the purple curtains and maroon carpeting we'd laid in the living room. Or maybe the fluorescent orange tiles in the downstairs powder room?''

Randall MacPherson, you did no such thing.

"How would you know unless you'd come out of this damned closet today?'' he asked with a satisfied-sounding snort.

She aimed a glare square at his solar plexus, thumping with the jab of a kitten's paw. *Don't be so smug, MacPherson. I still have a few more tricks up my sleeve.*

Still grinning, Rand rubbed at his belly. "Is that a fact? Well, why don't you tell me what you can do and let me decide whether or not it's worth taking the risk?''

Never you mind. Her disgruntled gaze settled on his hard, flat stomach and Cassandra was shocked to realize she wished it was her hand doing the rubbing. *I've heard it's sometimes smarter to surprise the enemy,* she said prissily.

"Cassandra, I'm not your enemy. I want only what's best for both of us.''

And you think it's best I'm gone?

"I do not. And I'd like to know what gave you that ridiculous notion to begin with.''

She raised her hand and began ticking off fingers. *First of all, you keep questioning me about Colin, asking me why he did what he did, as if trying to find a way to blame me for the horrible deed.*

"I only want to—''

Secondly, you sound so certain that once the reasons are made clear, I'll find peace—or whatever you keep calling it.

"But—''

Tell me, Mr. MacPherson, what makes you so positive I'm not at rest right now? That this might be the state in which my mortal soul was always meant to be, in the exact spot it was meant to reside for all eternity.

Testily, he ran a hand through his hair and she curved

her fingers into fists, fighting the temptation to rumple his gilded curls herself. "Cassandra, I don't want you to leave."

Unsure whether or not to believe him, she narrowed her gaze. He looked so sincere . . . and so intrinsically male, propped against the wall of her domain. With a green-and-brown-plaid shirt stretched tight across his broad chest and form-fitting trousers tapering to hefty leather work boots, he reminded her of the lords of the Highlands. Her dream man and her nightmare come to life.

She sighed, fluttering the tendrils of hair on her forehead. *Oh, no. Of course you don't.*

"I don't. I just want to get to the truth of the story. When I use the word *peace,* it's more for my own state of mind than yours. I never met my uncle, but I heard from my parents he was an always-out-of-sorts crazy old guy who used to spout all kinds of nonsense about this house. After meeting you, I find it hard to believe you had anything to do with your own demise. Nan and I have always worried that the men in our family were . . . odd. If any of them were truly insane, I need to know it for my own sense of well-being."

Cassandra set her chin on her fist and propped her elbow on her knee, annoyed that this man was capable of creating such turmoil inside her. If she told him what had transpired all those years ago, he might find a way to use it against her. After all, his mother had a psychic waiting in the wings to exorcize the house, which meant the woman would exorcize her.

Right now, she wasn't able to leave the place. What if, after hearing her tale, he decided to allow the seance and she was tossed to the wind like a withered leaf to simply disappear into nothingness for all eternity? Where would she go? With whom would she live? So far, none of the talk shows she'd watched had interviewed homeless spirits. Was it possible she could be Mr. Jerry Springer's very first ghostly guest?

"Cassandra? I know my uncle hurt you, but I'm not like him. I won't lie to you. And no matter what you tell me, you're welcome to stay here."

Oh, he had a silver tongue, he did, cajoling so sweetly it made her brain start to melt. Colin had promised her lots of pretty things. Her father had told her a new life in a new land would be good for her. But in the end she'd been betrayed by them both. If she and the MacPherson did live here together, it was going to become more and more difficult with them speaking one moment and fighting like cats in a sack the next. Still, she couldn't help but wonder if any interaction with Rand MacPherson was better than living alone for the rest of her earthly existence.

I'll warn you now, the truth isn't pretty. It will show your uncle as a cowardly cur. Can ya handle such a truth?

Quirking up a brow, Rand rested his wrists on his bent knees. "Considering I already think him a murderer, cowardly cur would be a compliment."

She stretched her legs out in front of her and crossed them at the ankles. *All right, ask your questions, but no tricks or I'll be forced to call on the elements again. Could be I'd damage the house irreparably. You wouldn't want that, now, would you?*

"Nope. I definitely wouldn't want you to do that."

There it was again, she thought with an indignant snort, that cursed flicker of a grin on his rugged face, taunting her until she felt the need to explode. Reminding herself that a bluff was only as good at the intent in which it was given, she scolded as if lecturing a naughty child. *'Tis not a laughing matter. I have the power to reduce this house to rubble, and you'd best remember it.*

Pulling his lips into a thin line, Rand's face grew serious. "Sorry, I didn't mean to offend. Now can we get started?"

She shrugged. *We can.*

"Careful, you two! Robbie, don't let Princess drag you down the sidewalk. Melissa, stop punching your brother! And don't go past the corner or cross the street or . . ."

Scrambling frantically after Robbie, Melissa let out an ear-splitting screech. "Let me hold the leash, Robbie. It's my turn to walk Princess. Let me!"

Nancy covered her face with her hands and peeked from between her fingers. Great, just what she needed to end the perfect single-mom evening. Robbie had been sullen throughout dinner, picking at his food and unwilling to answer any of Bill's friendly questions. Melissa had spilled not one but two glasses of lemonade, drowning the last of their pizza. And now both children were acting like unruly ruffians.

Sifting her hands through her no-longer-perfect bob, she tucked a few scraggly strands behind each ear. "Sorry about that," she said with false brightness. "Guess they're a little wound up tonight. It's been a long time since I've worked outside the home, and they're used to my full attention."

Bill Dukovsky flashed a grin that made him look like a nervous sophomore on his first date. "Hey, that's okay. Kids will be kids. I imagine they'll get used to it."

She propped a shoulder against the door frame but kept her gaze firmly on her children and their overexcited pet as the trio picked their way down the sidewalk and onto a grassy stretch of lawn. "There was no excuse for Robbie's rudeness. I'll talk to him—"

"No, don't. He was just being a little boy. I imagine he'd act that way with any man who wasn't his father . . . or Rand. It's tough when a new guy—er, a stranger comes into their lives at the same time his parents are getting a divorce.''

Satisfied the children were within sight, she turned to him. ''That doesn't mean I should forgive his bad attitude. I raised my children to be polite and well-mannered.''

Bill gazed over her shoulder into the front hall. ''If you want, I could come in and make sure things are all right inside, check the place out and everything?''

''All right?''

''You know. Look for burglars, make sure the lights are working. That kind of thing.'' His face flushed a ruddy red, as if he'd just realized how blatantly obvious he sounded. ''Or maybe you could make me a cup of coffee?''

Nancy stifled a giggle. ''I don't think you realize what holy heck the children will be tonight. Once they get back from walking the dog, there's going to be enough chaos in this house to send a full-grown male screaming in fear.''

The big guy stared dejectedly at his work boots, and Nancy resisted the urge to give in. Bill Dukovsky had always been kind to her, even when she'd been a spoiled rich girl working a summer job for her father during college. At the time, her eyes had been filled with stars and the romantic notion of marrying a doctor and being the perfect supportive wife. It had taken a few years, but she finally realized the stars had turned to spots and she'd been stricken with a disease called reality.

Since she'd learned of Warren's infidelities, she'd made a promise to herself to be more independent. It was time she learned how to manage her life and her children on her own, without looking to a man for assistance. The house had an excellent security system; it was just one more thing she would need to start using to keep her family safe. Not that Warren had been much help with the kids or the house over the last year. But there were a lot of things she had to accomplish, and sticking to her list of rules was important, as was properly disciplining her children.

It was nice to know a man like Bill Dukovsky was willing to lend a hand, but she couldn't help wondering why he would bother. The guy had a full head of wavy black hair, navy blue eyes and a to-die-for body. She was certain he wasn't married, but how could she be sure he wasn't seeing someone? And why would he want to get involved with a woman and children in the throes of emotional meltdown?

Thinking she'd sort it out later, after she got the kids to bed and had a long, hot bath, she said, "Maybe some other time, when things aren't so ... hectic?"

Shouts and angry squeals overrode his answer. Dog, leash, kids and clumps of wet leaves all flew into the house on a gust of chilly autumn air.

"I get the television first."

"No you don't, you ... you weenie."

Nan rolled her eyes. "See what I mean?"

"Ow! Mom, the squirt hit me. She won't let me have the remote."

Within seconds, boyish shouts and little-girl sobs filled the air. Flustered and embarrassed, Nancy turned to rush inside, then remembered her manners. "We had a really nice time tonight. But next time I'll pay for dinner. Good night."

"So, I guess I'll see you tomorrow?"

"Mom! Melissa dropped the remote in the fish tank. I'll vaporize you, you little—"

Frazzled, Nan started to close the door. "Tomorrow at ten. Maybe I'll get enough done so that I won't have to bring Captain Invader and his dastardly baby sister over after school."

Bill placed a hand above her on the jamb and grinned. "I had a great time too. And I didn't mind the kids."

The squabbling escalated until Nancy suddenly felt overwhelmed. Her children were screaming the house down. Princess was cowering between her legs, and she would probably need a new remote. And this guy would not let her say good night. On top of all that, he was being just a little too nice.

Angry words spilled from her lips before she realized what she was saying. "That's good, because those kids are a part of me. We're a package, Dukovsky. A big, rowdy package any sane man would treat like a nuclear bomb. Now, good night."

She slammed the door, threw the dead bolt and headed into the family room to the sound of booming laughter echoing from the front porch.

Chapter Ten

Rand settled against the closet wall, prepared to listen carefully to Cassandra's every word. It would be a relief to finally learn why she had such an odd attitude about her past. He'd already guessed she wasn't afraid of him, but she did act reticent at the thought of what might happen if the truth about her death was revealed. If only he could figure out why she was so worried, when it was obvious she was the one who'd been victimized.

Folding his hands behind his head, he tried to keep his body language nonthreatening. To his way of thinking, Cassandra had already suffered because of two controlling males. The last thing she needed was a third one gumming up her existence. Maybe if he started small he could build to bigger questions. He could find out how her body had managed to stay so well-preserved after a century, or ask how she'd become a ghost in the first place.

And stranger still, why, after almost four weeks of spirit-to-human interaction, was she looking more like a live person? It seemed as if each moment they spent together brought her further into focus. Even now, with the darkness of the closet closing around them, he'd swear he could see the violet sparkle in her eyes, the delicate paleness of her skin . . . the way her pearl-encrusted gown hugged her shapely breasts. . . .

Rand gave himself a swift mental don't-go-there kick. The reason the woman—make that *ghost*—set his palms to sweating was simple. For the past year he'd immersed himself in the company. He hadn't been on a date in over six months. Worse, he couldn't even remember the last time he'd gotten laid. Besides, who wouldn't be nervous at the thought of conversing with a bona fide supernatural phenomenon? It had taken only one look at her perfect remains, that lovely face and curvy body, and she'd become so imprinted on his brain, he had no choice but to see her clearly.

Reminding himself to stick to the facts and only the facts, he said, "I guess I'd like to know what made you come to America in the first place. If you didn't know my uncle and you didn't have any relatives here, why did you agree to leave a home where you were content?"

With a frown that looked decidedly impatient, Cassandra tossed out a delicate *tsk. Dinna I already explain that?*

"Sort of. But why to Colin?"

She groaned a long-suffering sigh. *Are ya daft, man? It was decided by my father.*

"I got that part too. What I'm asking is why? It was the beginning of the twentieth century. I've studied enough history to know there were laws in place to keep women from being treated like chattel. The idea that someone like you—and you did say you weren't much for being shy and demure—would agree to a forced marriage is pretty unbelievable."

Steepling her fingers on her knees, she closed then slowly opened her eyes. *My father was a strong man, Mr. MacPherson, a lot like Colin in many ways. When he caught me doing something that displeased him, your uncle's offer seemed the perfect way to render discipline. He also threatened to turn my grandmother, a sweet, kind, loving woman, out of the house if I dinna obey. I was twenty-two, well past the age to be married, and no man in our village would have—was interested in me. I did what I thought best for my family.*

"What the heck did you do that was so terrible, it forced your father to sell you to the highest bidder?" And how could a parent do such an incredible thing to their own child?"

Cassandra's brows rose to question marks. *Having had a hundred years to think on it, that part is no longer relevant. My father did what he felt he had to, and I agreed for the same reason. That's all you need to know.*

Oo-kay. If this was her way of telling him to mind his own business, he'd let the point rest. There were a hell of a lot more important things to talk about at the moment. "So what happened when you got to the States? Did my uncle meet the ship? How did you get to New Jersey?"

Raising her head, Cassandra rested it against the wall. In the glow of the flashlight, her hair shimmered an earthy rainbow of bronze, copper and gold. Rand couldn't help but notice once again how much she looked like a flesh-and-blood woman.

Colin came to collect me with his housekeeper and a groom. He stayed with me while the authorities processed my papers and sent me on my way. The four of us took a ferry, then drove his buggy into Manhattan, where we stayed in a fancy hotel for two days. During that time he was a perfect gentleman. He bought me expensive clothes, took me to the finest restaurants, and treated me like a queen.

Rand ground his back molars. Getting her to tell this story was harder than squeezing water bare-handed from a rock. "And then what?" he asked in his most patient voice.

Then we drove here, where I was escorted to a lovely room. The one next to the sitting room you've converted to a bath. It was quite nice—

"Cassandra!"

Oh, all right. I'm getting to it. She sat up straighter against the wall. *It took me less than a week in Colin's company to realize I could never love him. I'd always had an inner sense about people—these days it's called ESP or some such—and I knew we were wrong for each other. After a few days I was positive we would never be happy as man and wife and told him so.*

"And?"

He took exception to my opinion and locked me in my room. Mrs. Bartleson, our housekeeper, was kind enough to smuggle me a bit of food, but I wasn't allowed out for two days. It seemed your uncle placed a high value on what people thought of him. No country lass, especially one from the wilds of the Scottish Highlands, was going to humiliate him in front of his friends and business acquaintances.

The ache of Cassandra's hurt crested through him, until Rand could actually feel her pain. She'd come here under duress and been treated like a prisoner by a member of his family. One of his own had killed her, a fact he was having a hard time coming to grips with. He started to speak, but she raised a hand.

I'll be finishing now, if you don't mind. 'Tis easier if I get all the words out before I lose the stomach for it.

"Okay," he muttered, fisting a hand on his knee. "But I still have a lot more questions."

Staring into her lap, she spoke as if talking to herself. *Colin and I played an ugly game, with him cajoling and my refusing for several weeks, until I could no longer bear it. He went merrily along, telling the servants I was being coy, that I wanted more "things" from him, as if he could buy my affection. To be certain I would acqui-*

esce, the day the vows were to be spoken he deeded me this house. He had two maids dress me in my wedding gown and do my hair while he waited downstairs for his guests to arrive.

Finally, I had no choice but to shriek the house down until he came to my room. I warned him if he forced me into this farce of a marriage I would stand before his friends, the minister, and God and deny him. Not only would I never marry him, I would embarrass him to the world.

I could tell then by the wild look in his eyes that he'd finally come to accept what I'd been saying. He locked me in my room again, and I heard him order the servants to mount horses and ride through the countryside to inform everyone the wedding had been postponed. He sent Mrs. Bartleson away, then dragged me from my room and carried me up the stairs to this closet. After tossing the deed at my feet, he punched me hard in the jaw, and I passed out.

"Cassandra. God, I'm so sorry." Rand clutched at his knees as a way to hang on to his temper. The words to comfort her wouldn't come, so he merely waited as she heaved a sigh.

Don't be, MacPherson. It was not your doing.

"He was my uncle. His blood runs through my veins. I—"

When I came to, it was all over. The closet was dark as a tomb, already leached of most of its air. I found the deed and held it to my chest as I listened to Colin lay the bricks. I begged to be set free, but he wouldn't answer me. Hours later he was gone. I met him only once after that . . . and I was already as you see me now.

Cassandra waited until the ache in her heart lessened. Instead of urging her to continue, Rand just sat there, his face a stony mask. She knew it was dishonest to omit the part about the curse, but then she would be forced to tell him the real reason her father had sent her away. Things hadn't changed much over the past century in the way people reacted to the unknown. She'd become a spirit through some kind of freakish accident; she'd been a witch by choice. She'd watched enough television to know anyone who claimed to delve in the magical arts was ridiculed or thought to be insane.

And if Rand dwelled on it long enough, he might even realize it was her fault he had no one with whom to share his life. Her fault he had no one to love.

She was in the middle of a mess of her own making, with no way out that she could see. The knowledge that Colin had forced her hand was bitter comfort. She'd done what she felt needed doing at the time, and it had served her well. Until today.

Rand cleared his throat, jarring her to the present. "So, how did you come to be a spirit?"

Cassandra forced out a smile. In all her years as a ghost she had wondered the same and could come up with only one answer—when she'd placed the curse on Colin, it had somehow affected her own immortality. When the gist of the curse was fulfilled, she assumed her own spirit would be set free. Except the chance of her finding true love was about as slim as the chance Rand MacPherson would forgive her once he learned she was the one responsible for ruining his happiness.

Believing it was too late to do anything about it now, she gave herself permission to tell the smallest of lies. *Truly, I've no idea. I remember waking one day to the sound of hammering and rushing to the closet door. It was only after I fell through it that I realized what I'd become.*

"Was that the last time you saw my uncle?"

She laughed at the memory of confronting the man. *Aye, it was a grand meeting. If I recall correctly, I was quite ferocious.*

Rand's posture relaxed as he chuckled with her. "I'll just bet you were. What did you do to him?"

Loomed up on him in the library and made myself as big as a bear, I did. Then I growled. He took off like a scalded dog, fell down the steps, and kept on running. It was a very satisfying sight to behold.

"He deserved it," countered Rand. "Funny, how his friends and relatives thought he was nuts when he claimed the house was haunted. After all these years, it's hard to believe he was telling the truth."

I often wondered, she began, hoping she didn't sound too much a heathen, *did he die a horrible and gruesome death?*

He barked out a laugh. "Bloodthirsty, aren't you? No, not really. But I was told he passed away in a nursing home with no one at his side. In the end he was just a lonely, frightened old man whom everyone thought was crazy."

Good, she said, trying to be cheerful. *It makes all of this worthwhile, then.*

Rand blinked, his face a sudden mask of sorrow, and the strength of it pierced the place that had once held her heart. "Does it, Cassandra? Does it really?"

Rising from the floor, she fluttered in place. His poignant question had taken her by surprise. Unable to answer, she bolted from the room to find a quiet spot where she could be alone with her thoughts.

Rand paced his kitchen, waiting for the coffeemaker to finish its drip cycle. Gloomy drizzle continued to pelt the windows, reminding him that fall had arrived with a vengeance. He scanned the counter with a distracted frown as he inspected the odds and ends that cluttered the room. If he didn't know better, he'd think one of those cutesy whatnot shops from downtown Basking Ridge had launched a scud missile through his door during the night and it had exploded artfully on impact.

A six-inch clay chicken with a cluster of inch-high chicks pecked at a far corner of the countertop. Herbs planted in cachepots lined the windowsill over the sink. The island was covered in brightly painted birdhouses, glazed ceramic containers filled with dried flowers, and a basket overflowing with an assortment of colorful paper vegetables, giving the spacious room the quaint appearance of a French country kitchen.

He shook his head as he laid a finger on the mother hen's outspread wing. Nancy had gone full tilt into this project, not even asking if she had a decorating budget. She'd simply taken it upon herself to purchase a truckload of *charm* and assume her brother would like it. To be honest, while all these froufrous were a bit more than he'd expected, they didn't offend him, and the kitchen was starting to look homey and appealing.

Recalling the way Nancy's eyes had sparkled when he'd helped her unload the boxes, Rand gave in to a grin. It had been a long while since he'd seen his sister so enthusiastic. She and Warren always had money to burn, but he'd never known her to be a spendthrift. In fact, she'd sometimes lectured him when he bought things she thought were frivolous or too expensive.

This time, he guessed, it was different. Interior design was her craft and she was more than competent. She knew Rand was well off financially and she knew what he wanted, so she'd made up her mind to spare no expense. If, in the process, Nancy was finding renewed purpose to her life, so be it. Since taking over the company, he hadn't done anything to get himself elected big brother of the year. To his way of thinking, it was about time he became her white knight.

He took a hunter-green mug from the cabinet, noting it matched the tasteful green-and-white-striped paper that lined the shelves. Oh, yeah ... Nancy was definitely on the road to recovery. Now, if only he could help Cassandra.

After she'd left him in the closet, he'd carried the door to the basement, then gone to bed feeling more guilty than insulted. If he'd had his way, he would have slept on the damned hardwood floor just to be able to offer a little comfort. She hadn't wanted him around, and he didn't blame her. The memory of what his uncle had done was painful enough. Cassandra didn't need his presence to remind her of his family's treachery.

But he was certain of one thing. The door was off that closet for good. Short of pulling a disappearing act every time they met, she would never be able to hide from him again.

Thudding feet and loud expletives rang out at the rear of the house. The doorbell chimed and Rand guessed it was the first of the inside crew, ready to continue their work. Coffee cup in hand, he walked to the back porch, which Nan had christened the mudroom, and let the men inside.

"Rainin' cats and cows," Pete said, as he stomped the water from his boots onto a huge plastic tarp Rand had laid to cover the enclosed back porch.

Duke shoved his way inside, followed by three more of the crew. "Hey, boss man, you look beat. Rain got you down, or what?"

"Or what," Rand answered dourly. "Do the men have a handle on their jobs today?"

Duke gave his feet a good swipe on the tarp. "Yep. They're finishing the converted bath and hooking up the washer, dryer and dishwasher. Nan and I are supposed to finalize the light fixtures in the downstairs, pick out the tile for the rest of the bathrooms, and go over paint samples. Then she's checking out wallpaper for the bedrooms upstairs." He glanced down at the mud-splattered plastic. "You want me to tell the guys to take off their shoes?"

Well, hell, thought Rand, if he didn't know better, he'd think Duke and his sister were remodeling their own house instead of his. Still, they were the two people he trusted most to look after his pet project. "Nah. The hardwood floors are pretty much a wreck until we get the sanders going. Trouble is, we can't do that until the electricians take care of the wiring, then we have to replaster and paint. To do it right, we need a week of dry, sunny days."

The men wandered into the kitchen and stared longingly at the coffeepot. "Sure smells good in here," Pete said, sniffing like a hound on the scent.

Rand propped his hip on the kitchen table. "Help yourselves, but I'm not running a cafeteria service. The guy who pours the last cup has to make a new pot—got that? And no dirty dishes."

Fifteen minutes later, a second carafe of coffee was dripping cheerfully and the workmen were scattered throughout the house, ready to begin their various tasks. Rand was still concerned about Cassandra, but from the dopey look softening Duke's granite face, he knew there might be a different problem he needed to address.

"You okay?" Rand asked. Shoving aside a chair, he moved a pile of wallpaper books and took a seat at the table.

Duke carried his cup over and sat across from Rand. "Me? Yeah, sure. Why?"

"I don't know. Maybe it's that goofy grin you're wearing. How do you know so much about my sister's plans, by the way?"

"Nan? Well, um . . . she told me last night."

"Last night? You mean when she left here with the kids?"

"Uh . . . no. When I dropped her off at her place . . ."

with the kids ... after dinner.'' Sheepishly, he ducked his head and thumbed through a stack of paint samples.

"I see.'' Rand sipped at his coffee to hide a frown. He'd played matchmaker, and now that it sounded as if he was a success, he wasn't really sure he liked the idea of his foreman and his sister dating. Nan had been hurt, was still hurt if he knew his sister. Bill Dukovsky was the top of the line as far as foremen went, but Rand knew very little of the guy's history with women. And Nancy wasn't just *any* woman.

"Before I climb on my white horse and hit you broadside with my sword, would you care to tell me what your intentions are?'' he asked, his voice a steady demand.

Duke raised his gaze and ran a hand across his jaw. "Damned if I know, because I've already been run down. I think the license plate on the truck read Nancy plus two.''

"Nancy plus—? Oh, the kids.'' Rand grinned. "Those two are a handful, aren't they? Melissa has the vocabulary of a twelve-year-old. And Robbie—''

"Doesn't like me.'' Duke finished the sentence with a harsh sigh. "The kid has a chip on his shoulder the size of Newark.''

Rand set his cup down and crossed his legs. "At his best, Warren was what you'd call an absentee father. Always had a medical conference to attend or a liposuction to perform. I tried to do guy stuff with Robbie until the business started eating up my time, so I'm fairly certain he hasn't been privy to a lot of male bonding. Nan makes it a point to go to his Little League and soccer games, even dragged Irene and Harry along some of the time, but I don't think it's the same without a father to cheer you on.''

"No offense, boss, but the idea of your mother coaching on the sidelines could be grounds for a kid to run away from home. I can hear Mrs. Johnston now—Robbie, don't dirty your clothes. Robbie, stay out of the nasty boys' way. Robbie, why did you let that young man get the ball— It makes me crazy just thinking about it, you know?''

"Yeah, it was hell growing up," Rand said, hoping he'd made it sound like a joke. "So . . . how does Nan feel about the idea?''

Duke stood and grinned. "Warming. I think she's definitely warming. Anyway, I'm not going to let her get away. Um, if that's okay with you.''

Before Rand could figure out if he approved of the idea, his mobile rang. "MacPherson here," he said into the phone. "Uh-huh. No. Yes. I don't know. Hang on a second.''

"Hey, Romeo?" He grinned at Duke's indignant glare. "You planning on spending the whole day with my sister?''

"I'd hoped to." Duke's glare turned all business. "Why? Is there a problem?''

Turning his attention back to the call, Rand sighed. "Okay. It'll be me. I'm on my way." He hung up and carried his mug to the sink. "The apartment complex in Trenton is flooding out. Miller's down with the flu and the crew doesn't have a clue. Someone has to go down there and supervise. Since you have plans, it looks like I'm elected.''

"Hey, I can go. This place is your baby. I don't mind.''

Rand pulled his jacket from the back of a chair and shrugged his arms into the sleeves. Cassandra rarely showed herself in the daylight. With Nancy and Duke in charge, he really didn't have much of a reason to hang around. Besides, who was he to stand in the way of true love?

"It's fine. Just keep nagging those electricians about the lighting problems, will you? I'm getting tired of living in Dr. Frankenstein's basement. And lock up when everyone leaves. I may have to stay the night if it keeps raining like this.''

Thunder boomed as a bolt of blue-white lightning split the darkness. Cassandra jumped in place, then bobbled from the spare third-floor bedroom onto the landing. Because the MacPherson had carted the closet door to the cellar last night, she no longer needed to worry about the difficulty she'd been having passing through wood. But she was still uncertain about no longer having a protective cave in which to dwell.

The rainy day had dragged with agonizing slowness. She'd not seen Rand at all, though she'd searched the house from top to bottom and back again, so she'd spent most of her time spying on the Duke and Rand's sister. Nancy and the foreman had whiled away their time going over the details of the renovations and sparring with each other about their evening meal. The Duke very much wanted to take Nancy and her children to a restaurant, while Nancy argued that she could just as well cook for him at her home.

Sometime in the middle of the afternoon Cassandra wished she had the nerve to simply show herself to the two adults and frighten them into playing nicely. It was obvious, even to her untrained eyes, that the man was enthralled with Nancy. And to her way of thinking, Rand's sister was just as interested. But from the conversations she'd overheard, the woman was bent on regaining her independence and self-respect. The Duke would need to move carefully if he wanted to win her hand.

In a way, the couple's playful banter helped to take Cassandra's mind off her worries. Last night, she'd lied to the MacPherson and, as her grandmother had always lectured, living a lie was never pleasant. Now she understood exactly what Gram had meant.

The last of the workmen had left several hours before. During that time, the storm had grown to mammoth proportions, pounding at the house with furious fistfuls of rain and wind. Thunder still rang out as lightning split the blackened sky, turning the evening eerie and as bleak as Cassandra's hopes for her future.

Wandering the second floor, she drifted into Rand's bedroom to find that Nancy had already put her expertise to work in the suite. Bolts of fabric in rich jewel tones of bronze, plum and gold lay on the top of his dresser alongside books of matching wallpaper. Through the glaring bursts of lightning she could tell the patterns were pleasing, several in fact were what she might have chosen herself if she'd been given the chance.

Sadly, she acknowledged, that would never happen. For as hard as she wished this house were truly hers, she knew it could never be.

The noise of a door as it opened and closed jarred her into action. *The MacPherson had returned!* She skittered down the stairs and into the foyer. It was there she realized the racket had come from the kitchen, which had her puzzled, since Rand always entered through the front of the house.

A faint drone of thunder rumbled in the distance, and she could tell the storm was moving on. Thinking it possible he'd decided not to soil the marble tiles in the foyer with spatters of mud, she made her way to the kitchen and hovered in the doorway. The lights flickered on, and she whisked into the butler's pantry just in time to avoid being seen by the two women standing in the entryway of the rear porch.

Shaking droplets of water in all directions, they walked into the room. After stopping at the table in the eating area, Rand's mother and a woman Cassandra didn't recognize began to remove their sodden coats and hang them over the back of a chair.

"Are you sure your son knows we're doing this, Irene? If I remember correctly, he made it quite clear on my first visit that I wasn't welcome. I would hate to be accused of trespassing at this stage in my career."

Cassandra bobbled backward as she stifled a cry. Rand's mother had brought Madame Ragnar back to the house. Lord have mercy, the woman was going to perform an exorcism and the MacPherson wasn't here to stop her.

"Of course I'm certain. Nancy told me Randall drove to Trenton to handle a problem. When I called him on his mobile phone, he assured me he would be staying in a hotel near the construction site. The storm is moving southward, and he wisely decided not to risk traveling through it at this hour."

"And you told him we would be out to inspect the house again?" Hesitantly, the woman stepped into the body of the kitchen and waited for Irene to answer.

Irene walked to the sink before she said innocently, "Well, not in so many words."

Madame Ragnar sighed as she folded her arms across her chest. "I don't like the sound of that. If I remember correctly, your son was quite adamant. He didn't want me within a mile of this place. If he arrives home and finds us here—"

"Oh, pooh." Irene turned on a tap. Stretching, she opened a cupboard and took down two mugs, filled them with water and set them in the microwave. "Don't just stand there. Help me find the teabags. Nancy said she bought a box of Earl Grey just yesterday."

The women nosed in the cupboards until Madame Ragnar found the tea. Cassandra watched while the microwave brought the water to a boil and Irene prepared their drinks. Carrying the mugs to the kitchen table, the women sat in the breakfast area and sipped as they decided on a course of action.

"I'm serious about this, Irene. I won't perform a ritual

unless I believe it's what your son desires. So far, we don't even have proof a spirit inhabits this house."

Irene's cherry-red lips pursed as she blew on her tea. "Of course there's a wandering spirit here. An innocent young woman was killed just two floors above us. If I'd been the one murdered, you can bet your crystal ball I'd be hanging around to take my revenge."

"Not all spirits are the same. Remember the exorcism I performed in Bayonne? That poor ghost practically begged me to let it remain on earth. If the spirit of the girl you found has lived here for over a century, she may be content. Has Rand ever mentioned sighting anything that would make you think the house is haunted?

"He didn't have to. Once I saw that body, I realized Colin had been telling the truth his entire life. I'd listened to him ramble about the woman from the time I first met Robert. We visited him in the nursing home just two days before he passed away, and I heard Colin quite clearly when he told Robert for the thousandth time about his one encounter with the ghost. He may have been physically infirm, but his mind was sharp as a tack. For some reason, Robert wanted to believe his uncle was crazy rather than admit there was a spirit."

"Still, that doesn't mean Rand—"

"That boy never did know what was best for him. I'm his mother and I simply have to be sure he's safe. Now, let's finish our tea and take a look around, shall we?"

Chapter Eleven

"Saints preserve us!" Cassandra muttered, shuddering at the woman's decisive words. Damn the MacPherson and his meddling tricks! With her closet now open to the landing, she had nowhere to hide. If she'd the brains of a flea, she would have spirited the door up from the cellar and back over her hidey-hole last night, after he'd stomped to bed. Instead, she'd let the handsome devil sweet-talk her into believing she was safe.

Thanks to his continued interference, she'd ignored the confusing changes that had taken place in her existence over the past few weeks. The subtle differences in her ghostly form, the return of her sense of smell, and seeing her breath against a windowpane were so disturbing, she hadn't known how to begin sorting it all out.

And another more frightening occurrence had begun over the last week. Some mornings just before she was fully coherent, she swore she could feel the beating of her heart.

This riot of emotions swirling in the deepest part of her being was unlike any she ever remembered, even when she'd been alive. Just as Rand had taken down that cursed door, he had somehow managed to remove a goodly part of the barricade she'd built around her world. Because of it, she'd started to dream all kinds of impossible things ... things no self-respecting spirit had any business thinking.

To make matters worse, she'd been finding it more and more difficult to become invisible. If Rand's niece and nephew could see her, was it possible these humans could too? Peering around the edge of the pantry, she shoved her anger to the back of her mind and gave in to curiosity, waiting and watching to see what the women would do next.

"I've already inspected the downstairs, remember?" Madame Ragnar rinsed her cup and set it in the sink. "And I didn't intuit even the slightest bit of psychic vibration on the entire floor."

"That only means we have to move to the second level, nearer where the girl was murdered." After setting her own mug in the sink, Irene turned and reached into the leather bag hanging from her shoulder. "I've brought a flashlight and candles. Nancy mentioned Rand was still having trouble with the electricity. Are you ready?"

Ducking backward, Cassandra scrunched up her nose and fisted her hands. Willing herself to become invisible, she stayed perfectly still.

A beam of light flooded the hallway, followed by the tapping of high heels across the kitchen tiles. The glow intensified as the women neared the pantry doorway. "Hold a moment," Madame Ragnar whispered. "Tell me what you notice."

"What is it?" Irene asked, the light bobbing with the trembling of her hand.

Madame Ragnar raised her nose and sniffed. "Can't you smell it? Lavender, I think, or perhaps verbena? Have you detected the scent here before?"

Cassandra tucked her face into the shoulder of her dress,

which she remembered had been wrapped in lavender-scented paper when it arrived from the dressmaker over a century before. Holy Mother, but she hadn't noticed the telling fragrance, even with her own sense of smell returned. Thinking the woman had to be a witch herself to have such keen insights, she made a concerted effort to shrink into a ball of nothingness. Though the feeling of being invisible eluded her, she didn't waver.

"This is only my third visit to the house, so I'm not sure," Irene said, delicately sniffing the air. "Couldn't the aroma be coming from one of those herbs Nancy set in the kitchen window?"

"Then why is the fragrance strongest right here? I wonder . . . did Colin ever lock the girl in this pantry?"

"I have no idea." Irene spun in a circle, causing the light to swing in a jagged arc. "But I do get the sense of something flowery. What do you think it means?"

Terrified of being found out, Cassandra's brain spasmed in fear. She had the distinct feeling she wasn't invisible, but there was no way to be sure. If she wasn't, the women would see her whether or not she hid. If that happened, Rand's mother would make certain the dreaded exorcism was performed. Any way she figured it, she would be evicted from her home and sent out to face the unknown world.

What was she to do?

Years of feeling hopeless, of questioning fate and finding no answers, suddenly rose up to claim her. She'd let her father rob her of everything she held dear. She'd allowed Colin to take her life. Even the MacPherson tried to impose his will. She'd been ordered about the entire time she'd been alive, and it was still happening in death.

Suddenly weary of playing the coward, she stood tall. Time seemed to stand still as she folded her arms under her bosom and waited. Invisible or no, what would be would be.

The golden circle crept across the pantry floor, hit her ivory satin pumps, and slowly inched up the hem of her wedding gown. "M-m-my goodness," Irene stuttered, the flashlight jerking erratically in her hand. "Edith, do you see what I see?"

Amid the rasp of indrawn breaths, the wobbly light continued its journey, dancing upward across Cassandra's skirt to reflect the pearlescent sheen of the gown's bodice, then float over her arms and onto her face.

Ladies. I bid you welcome to my home. She projected the greeting outward, hoping the women would hear it in their minds, as had Rand's niece and nephew.

Irene's flashlight and leather tote hit the floor with a thump. She stumbled toward the pantry wall and floundered for the light switch. When the overhead fixture flickered and winked out, Cassandra's lips turned up knowingly. *I'm afraid the electricity is in a terrible state. And I'd much prefer the softer glow of a candle, if you don't mind.*

Madame Ragnar dug frantically through the fallen bag, whipped out a candle, and thrust a book of matches into Irene's shaking hands. Cassandra waited patiently while the women got the taper to light. Rewarding them with another smile, she hovered in place. *Thank you. Now, how may I help you?*

"H-h-help us?" Irene laid a hand to her throat.

Madame Ragnar took a step closer, but Cassandra stood firm. "Are you the spirit of Cassandra Kinross?"

Gathering her courage, she dropped her arms to her sides. *Aye, that I am.*

"What did I tell you?" Irene spit out through bloodless lips.

"And I didn't disagree. I merely needed to be certain," Madame Ragnar responded in a soft but firm voice. "Now, hush and let me do my job."

Irene closed her mouth with a *humph*.

Madame Ragnar stepped farther into the pantry. "I think the correct question would be—how may we help you?"

Inexplicably, Cassandra's negative forebodings melted like butter in the sun. Instead of the harridan Rand made her out to be, Irene, with her lovely blond curls and colorful modern clothing, resembled an older version of one of those fitness instructors she'd seen on the television. And Madame Ragnar, with her bright brown eyes and delicate frame, reminded her of her grandmother, a lady of great wisdom and fairness.

More important, neither woman had a drop of MacPherson blood flowing through her veins, a point most definitely in their favor.

Thank you for your concern, but I don't need any help. I'd appreciate it if you told no one of this encounter and went on your way, while I tended to my own business. Deciding that would be all she needed to say to rid herself of the nosy pair, she made another attempt at becoming invisible.

Seconds passed before Madame Ragnar asked politely, "Excuse me, but are you in pain?"

Cassandra snapped open her eyes. What in the world gave the woman that idea? *I don't believe so. Why do you ask?*

Before Madame Ragnar could answer, Irene found her voice. "Because you look rather . . . ill. I didn't realize spirits could take sick, did you, Edith?"

The psychic took a step closer, a look of caring on her wizened face. "Maybe not in the true physical sense, but I've found they can be afflicted with an ailment of the soul, which could easily cause the girl that pained expression. Tell me, is there something we can do to assist you?"

Cassandra blinked. Instead of feeling threatened, she was overwhelmed by a blanket of warmth much like the emotion she'd felt when her grandmother had rocked her as a young girl. These women, these non-MacPherson women, actually had her well-being in mind. They wanted to see her happy. They would not send her away from here if she didn't choose to go.

I'm quite content at the moment, but thank you for asking, she replied, too choked up to comment further.

"Well then, perhaps you won't mind if we ask a few questions? It would help in my quest to understand the ways of the spirit world, you see."

Sighing, Cassandra bit at her lower lip. Her efforts at becoming invisible had failed, exactly as she feared. Backed this far into the half-bath, she felt her gown bunching against the commode. In order to get away, she would need to pass through both women, something she was fairly certain she could no longer do.

These changes taking place were confusing, sometimes frightening. Perhaps Madame Ragnar, with her kindly face and offer of assistance, was as perceptive as Cassandra's grandmother. If so, the woman might be able to help figure out what was happening to her spiritual form. After all, many modern people thought psychics to be the new century's version of witches, did they not? Discounting the MacPherson, whom she still felt could not be trusted completely, it had been too long since she'd had someone in which to confide.

I fear there's not much I can tell you about the afterlife, as I haven't left this house in over one hundred years. But I'll try to answer honestly, if you promise to do the same.

Tentatively, the two women tiptoed toward the pantry. Standing in the doorway to the bath, they wore twin grins of delight, as if being in her presence were the highlight of their existence.

"May I?" asked Madame Ragnar, holding out gently

curved fingers. Cassandra couldn't see the harm in it, so she offered her arm.

"Why, you feel almost solid, child. It's like touching a marshmallow or a freshly baked potato. What do I feel like to you?"

Thinking Americans had to be the hungriest people on the planet, she acknowledged the woman's touch was acceptable. But it didn't make her tingle, as did Rand's touch when he stroked her skin. Instead, there was just a soft, insistent pressure. *'Tis firm and not unpleasant.*

Hesitantly, Irene reached out and Cassandra allowed her the same liberty. "Oh, my. This is the most thrilling thing I've ever had the privilege to experience," the woman squeaked, her green eyes sparkling like emeralds.

"Get hold of yourself, Irene," Madame Ragnar chided. "The girl isn't day-old bakery to be prodded at will."

Hearing almost the exact words she'd used to scold Rand, Cassandra grinned. *I don't mind. It's been a long time since I've had any kind of intimate human contact.*

Irene took her hand away and held it under the flashlight beam, scrutinizing carefully. Seemingly satisfied she was still in possession of all five fingers, she placed the hand on her hip. "But you did appear to Colin MacPherson, did you not? He was always quite adamant about the fact that he'd seen you."

I did, Cassandra confessed. *Unfortunately for him, I wasn't in as pleasant a frame of mind as I am right now.*

"I always suspected he was telling the truth. No wonder he went mad. Well, good for you, frightening him out of his wits. For what he put you through, he deserved it."

Aye. That's exactly what the MacPherson told me.

"The MacPherson?" Irene's mouth dropped open. "You talked about this with my ex-husband?"

Cassandra could tell from the woman's goggle-eyed stare that she'd unleashed a fox in the henhouse. But she'd already spoken the words; it was too late to take them back. *His son.*

Irene lifted her leather tote and slipped it back on her shoulder. Raising an eyebrow, she flashed a joyous smile. "You've appeared to Randall? He knows you exist?"

Since before he discovered my earthly remains, I'm afraid.

"I knew it," Irene said, her voice atwitter. "I knew that boy was hiding something."

"Do tell us more," exclaimed Madame Ragnar. "We need to hear every tiny detail."

"So, your mom tells me you're really into all this computer stuff." Duke stood behind Robbie's chair and squinted into the brightly lit monitor, which showed a cartoon scene straight from an animated version of *Star Wars.* His older sister's boy, Paul, had a game similar to this one and he'd played it once or twice with the kid. Unfortunately, he'd lost to the ten-year-old both times.

Instead of answering, Robbie's thin shoulders jerked up and down. So far, he was still treating Duke like rain at a baseball game. Duke hoped if he admitted to a failing, the kid would take pity and talk to him one-on-one.

"I don't know a thing about them," he confessed. "I never had the time to learn."

Still no answer from Robbie. Gamely, Duke squatted next to the desk until he was eye level with the monitor. "What's that guy with the red cape and pointy hat trying to do, exactly?"

Robbie huffed out a long-suffering sigh. "He's a bad guy from the death star. He's trying to plant a bomb on the good guys' spaceship without them finding out."

Contact. Duke mentally patted himself on the back and dropped to his knees. Sometimes it was worth a white lie to gain a little trust. "And the good guys are . . . ?"

"The ones wearing the white space suits. Jeez, don't you know anything?"

"Not about computer games, I don't," Duke said, crossing his fingers behind his back. "This one looks pretty complicated. What else do you have?"

His gaze still fixed on the monitor, the boy raised a shoulder. "Lots of things. There's stuff on outer space, places I can go to get help with schoolwork, games about sports—"

"Sports games? For what kind of sports?"

"Anything you want. Hockey, baseball, football—"

"Football? No kidding? Can you let me see some football?"

Robbie shrugged again, but his fingers flew across the keyboard while he manipulated the mouse. A tray slid open and Robbie removed a CD-ROM, then hunted through a drawer and brought out a slim plastic case. Once the new program was loaded, a colorful blinking logo popped onto the screen, along with the fairly authentic sound of cheering and an aerial view of a stadium filled with screaming fans.

"Wow. Look at that. Can you teach me how to play?"

"It's set up for a single user right now. It'll take a minute to reinitialize the system and—"

"I thought I sent you up here to get ready for bed, young man? It's hours past your curfew." Nancy's stern voice rang softly from the hall.

"Aw, Mom . . . just give me a few more minutes."

She stepped across the threshold and Duke stood. Feeling like a little boy confronted by every kid's worst nightmare—super mom—he gave a half-grin. "It's my fault. He was showing me a football game and the time got away from us."

Robbie pushed from the desk and Nancy placed a hand on his head of blond curls, her face softening. "Put on your pajamas and brush your teeth. I'll shut down here. Go on, scoot.''

Robbie stamped a foot, but he didn't utter a sound as he walked out of the room. ''He'd be on this thing all night if I didn't enforce the ground rules,'' Nancy said. Taking control, she ejected the disc, gave a few clicks on the mouse to shut down the machine, and put away the game.

''Hey, how'd you learn to do that?'' Duke asked, impressed Nan was so adept at working such a complicated piece of hardware.

She walked to her son's bed and turned down the covers. ''At design school, though the system I worked on would be considered antiquated by today's standards. When Warren bought Robbie his own computer, I started playing around while Robbie was in school. I use it to e-mail college friends and research recipes; I even have a CD-ROM on interior design. Sometimes I go in and mess around.''

''I'm impressed.''

''Don't be. Fiddling on a computer is just another one of the things Warren used to tell me I did to kill time. I could never make a living at it.''

Duke almost made a comment about what a jerk her soon-to-be-ex-husband sounded like, but before he could blurt out the words, Robbie shuffled into the room. Dressed in flannel pajamas imprinted with the face of the big blue genie from Disney's *Aladdin,* he looked teary-eyed and subdued. Ignoring Duke, he climbed onto the bed and squirmed under the covers.

Nan planted a kiss on his forehead as she tucked him in. ''You need to be at the soccer field by eight. I'll drop you, then Melissa and I have her mommy-and-me gymnastic class. When we're finished, we'll be back to cheer your team to victory. How does that sound?''

''Okay, I guess. Should I say my prayers?''

Nancy sat on the edge of the bed and ruffled her fingers through his hair. "It couldn't hurt."

"I'm gonna ask God why Dad hasn't been to any of my games. Do you think he'll be there tomorrow if I pray really hard?"

When he heard the boy's pointed question, Duke side-stepped into the hallway. No one had to hit him with a brick to tell him the boy was dropping an I-already-have-a-father hint. He didn't catch Nan's answer, but he imagined it was encouraging. During the short time he'd spent in her company, he'd come to realize she was one hell of a mother. To her credit, he'd never heard her utter an unkind word about her husband either.

When she came out of the room, he let her pass, then followed her down the stairs and into the kitchen. "Do you think he'll ever like me?" Duke finally asked, break-ing the uneasy silence that pulsed between them.

"Don't be silly. Robbie likes you. It's his mother and father he's angry with just now."

He thought about her answer as he stacked the dishes still sitting on the table. Carrying the plates to the center island, he set them down and stood directly behind Nan, who was bent at the waist, loading the dishwasher. Prop-ping a hip against the counter, he grinned as he admired the view.

He'd wanted Nan MacPherson from the moment he'd met her ten years earlier, but she was the boss's daughter. College-educated and engaged to a medical resident, she'd been strictly off limits. Nancy had brought diminu-tive cups of yogurt and dainty sandwiches with the crusts cut off to the lunchroom, while he'd eaten huge subs piled high with cold cuts, mayonnaise and hot peppers. He'd felt like an overgrown moose in her presence—sometimes he still did.

Over the past week, he'd finally come to realize there was a real woman under all that finely wrought perfection.

A woman bogged down in insecurity and overcome with needs. Needs he desperately wanted to fulfill.

Nancy straightened. Unaware he'd sneaked up behind her, she turned and bumped smack into his chest. She stepped to the right and he danced in the same direction, watching while she caught her lower lip between her teeth.

"Excuse me—"

"You're excused," he answered, standing so close he could see flecks of gold in her wide-open eyes.

"I . . . um . . . need to get to the . . . sink." She ducked to the left and he continued the waltz.

"This isn't a good idea, Bill." Eyes downcast, she stared at the front of his shirt while her cheeks turned the soft shade of a flower he'd once admired in his mother's garden. "Besides not having the right to get involved with you, I'm not ready."

Cupping her chin, he slowly raised her head until their gazes locked. "While that might be true for you, it feels like I've been ready a lifetime."

He caught the flutter of her pulse as it beat under the delicate skin of her neck, and he leaned down to taste her.

"Bill." Nancy sucked in a breath. "I . . . can't be doing this."

He grasped her upper arms and drew her close, nuzzling the soft hollow just under her ear. "Baby, you don't have to do a thing. It'll be my pleasure to oversee this project."

She gasped a little half moan of laughter. "You dope. You know what I mean."

Grinning, because he knew exactly what she meant, he ran his mouth over her peony-pink cheek to the corner of her parted lips. "Yeah. But I never was very good at following directions."

Capturing her wide, tempting mouth with his, he sipped gently, savoring her sweetness. The kiss stretched into eternity until, gasping for air, they both pulled away. Reminding himself he'd already wasted too many years wondering what it would be like to have Nancy underneath him in his bed, he pulled her to his chest.

"I won't rush you, Nan, but I don't want to wait either. I know what you've been through, and I swear I won't be like Warren. You're already perfect in my eyes."

Setting her back on her feet, Duke reached for her hands and gently kissed her knuckles. "I'll see you soon. Good night."

Nancy stared at her fingers. By the time she raised her gaze to the kitchen doorway, Bill had slipped from the room. In the distance, she heard the front door open and close. For a big guy, he had really smooth moves. Maybe too smooth.

Rubbing the backs of her hands on her slacks, she ignored the racing of her heart and turned to the sink to finish her chores. Warren had charmed her into his bed before they'd solidified their engagement. He'd been her only lover, though she knew now he'd had a ton of experience. It hadn't taken long for his polished golden charm to tarnish like brass.

She'd known Bill Dukovsky for a long time, but she'd never seen him act this way before—sure of himself and just a little too cocky. Like Robbie, it was going to take a while to decide whether or not she liked what she saw.

Cassandra hovered behind a ladderback chair, afraid to fold her not-quite-real body and sit. For the first time in longer than she could remember, she felt physically weary, but the idea she was too ethereal to relax on the rattan seat was worrying her. Though more substantial than she'd been for the last hundred years, she still found it hard to admit her ghostly form was undergoing a serious change.

Once Edith Ragnar and Irene backed out of the closet, they'd encouraged her to take them into her confidence. They'd been clustered around the kitchen table for the better part of an hour, listening with rapt fascination while Cassandra recited her incredible tale. It was now close to midnight and the women were trying to come to terms with her story, as well as what appeared to be her unbelievable transformation.

Exhausted by the evening's excitement, Cassandra decided to make a final attempt at getting her point across. *But don't you see? When I included Colin's descendants in the curse, I harmed innocent people. I was the reason his nephews and their wives were so unhappy. I caused your failed marriage and I ruined your son's life. Thanks to me, the MacPherson has yet to wed. And he probably never will.*

Dropping her chin, she stared at her fingers as they rested lightly over the top rung of the chair. *I was . . . I am a terrible person.*

Wrinkling her nose, Irene pursed her lips. "Let me see if I understand this correctly. You think the curse you cast on Colin is somehow responsible for the misery of all his decendants, right to the present? And it's also got something to do with the reason you're, um, changing?

Cassandra raised her head and rubbed her burning eyes. *That's exactly what I'm saying. I want to fix it, truly I do. I just don't know how.*

Madame Ragnar notched up her chin, a look of indignation darkening her eyes. "Well, I for one don't blame you a bit for cursing the old goat. The way I understand it, he was a pompous, angry man more concerned with garnering wealth and impressing people than being happy."

As if realizing what she'd just spouted, she sent Irene a contrite smile. "Sorry, Irene, but it's the way I feel."

"I understand perfectly, at least where Colin was concerned." Irene's breasts lifted with her sigh. "But from here on out, I believe it's Cassandra, Rand, and Robbie we need to concentrate our energies on."

Robbie? Sharp as a blade, guilt knifed through Cassandra's heart. Sweet Mother Mary, but she'd forgotten about that darling little boy. Thanks to her, he was destined to live his life alone, never to know the love of a good woman, unless she could find a way to get them out of this mess.

Ignoring Cassandra's frown, Madame Ragnar drummed her fingers on the tabletop. "I'm not up on the finer points of witchcraft, but I do have a friend who might be able to help. Unfortunately, she's on sabbatical in Salem. I have no idea how to reach her or when she's scheduled to return." She gazed at Irene. "Do you have any thoughts?"

"Well, I do have that wall full of books on the occult and paranormal in the library at home. Some of the volumes are collectors' editions. If we're lucky, we might find something in one of them that will help."

Cassandra folded her arms. Irene's face, so filled with kindness and understanding, only made the dagger stab deeper into her heart. *Can you ever forgive me for ruining your marriage?*

The older woman's eyes misted with tears. "Please don't take this the wrong way, dear, but is there a possibility you're overestimating your powers?"

Cassandra thought back to the book of spells her father had tossed in the fire. The curse had been a mingling of remembered phrases as well as the emotions clamoring in her heart, not something she'd been instructed to say. Even as she'd repeated the words, she could only pray they would come true. She had never been certain of their success until she'd heard Colin's story from Rand.

I must confess I was only an apprentice to my grandmother. I never had the need to curse a soul until the

*day I was locked in the closet. I just assumed . . . because
I was a spirit . . . and from the things Rand said about his
great-uncle, that my curse was at work in the MacPherson
family.*

"Hmm, interesting," Irene murmured. "All right. How
about this? Let's suppose Colin's life took the turn it did
because he saw you as a spirit and went mad, and not
because of the curse. And let's assume the MacPherson
men and their miserable luck with women was of their
own making. If that's the case, there still has to be a
reason for what's happening to you right now, doesn't
there?"

Leaning forward, Cassandra rested her forearms on the
top of the chair. *Are you telling me you don't think I'm
the one responsible for the dissolution of your marriage?*

Irene reached out and laid a palm on Cassandra's hand.
"Believe me, Cassandra, I didn't divorce Robert because
I no longer loved him. I left him because he put the
success of his company ahead of his family. It was only
after we divorced that he realized his mistake and started
paying attention to his son and daughter. When I saw
that my children finally had their father back, I stayed in
the shadows so the three of them could find one another
again. Sometimes I wonder if I gave up too much of my
own time with them, especially in Rand's case. But I
loved Robert MacPherson until the day he died. I just
couldn't live with him."

A pall of silence fell over the trio as Irene seemed to
gather her thoughts. Finally, she tapped her forefinger
onto the tabletop. "Back to your condition. Is it possible
only a part of the curse came true? It worked on Colin
and you alone? If that's the case, there's only one thing
we need to focus on—salvaging your life."

Irene and Madame Ragnar rose from their chairs. Each
woman took one of Cassandra's hands, then joined their
own, forming a united triangle. "Irene has a point. Though

it would be a good idea if we took a look at those books she's been hoarding. If not, we can wait for my friend to return from her sabbatical. But we will find a way. Now, I think I've come up with something that might shed some light on the problem. May I ask you a question?''

Cassandra pulled free of the women and ran twitchy fingers through her hair. Could her overstuffed brain handle one more question or impossible thought before it burst? *Of course. Anything to help us get to the heart of the matter.*

Tossing Irene a wink, Madame Ragnar finally gave a full-fledged smile. ''Who have you met since Rand opened this house?''

Met? Why, no one. Except for the two of you and the MacPherson, that is. She chewed on her lower lip. *And I did show myself to the children, but that was only for a moment.*

Madame Ragnar folded her arms. ''But Randall is the only adult male, correct?''

Cassandra blinked her confusion. *Yes, but what does that have to do with anything?*

''And here I thought you were such a clever girl. I'm surprised you haven't figured it out. What was that last part of the spell again? 'No MacPherson male will find his true love until you find your own?' I have a suspicion, my dear, that the reason all this is happening to you is because you're very close to that point. Thanks to Irene's son, you're becoming human. I believe that Rand MacPherson *is* your own true love.''

Chapter Twelve

After saying good night to Irene and Madame Ragnar, Cassandra climbed the staircase and wandered the master bedroom suite. Overwhelmed by the evening, her mind was a blur. She'd just told two complete strangers her life story and survived. The women had been kind and understanding; they'd offered to return with books and ideas ... all to help her. The very thought that she'd found such wonderful friends gave her hope for her future. Surely, with the three of them working together on her problem, things would turn out for the best.

Settling into the colorful cushions lining the window seat, she stared at the moon, a perfect golden coin dangling high over the pond at the rear of the house, and tried to organize her befuddled thoughts. Madame Ragnar admitted she knew little about witchcraft. Could she be so insightful a psychic that she'd been able to interpret the curse correctly anyway? Was the spell already on its way to being broken? And when it was, would she be allowed to return to the world as a real woman?

Even more amazing—were she and Randall MacPherson destined to be together? Was he her one true love?

Not quite prepared to face such a shocking prediction, she willingly admitted to the part about becoming human—mainly because her head ached and she couldn't remember the last time she'd felt so tired.

Focusing on the window, she huffed out a gentle puff of air, fascinated when it fogged the pane. Raising her gaze, she stared at the dim reflection of her image, so much more clear now than it had been the day the Mac-Pherson caught her staring over his shoulder while he shaved. It had been so long, since the morning of her supposed wedding in fact, since she'd scrutinized herself, she'd almost forgotten what she looked like. Yet there she was, clearly reflected in the glass.

Her wide forehead and slightly pointed chin still gave her face a subtle heart shape. Her eyes were still accented by arched brows. Her nose, neither too large nor too small, sat exactly where it was supposed to, as did her full-bowed lips.

Yes, that was her face as she remembered it, not looking too worse for wear after a century of nonexistence.

Raising a hand, she ran shaking fingers through the riot of springy curls clustered around her head. The hair felt soft and resilient, like the silken skeins of yarn Gram had used to knit sweaters for Cassandra and her many siblings. She'd always been proud of her hair, considering it her finest feature. It pleased her to know it looked the same.

She turned from the window and heaved a sigh as Madame Ragnar's incredible words played over in her mind. Thinking about the past few weeks, she recalled the strange feelings, small jolts of awareness and tremors of emotion that had skittered through her veins whenever the MacPherson came near. Since she'd never been in love, she'd made herself believe those indefinable waves were because of all the changes taking place around her.

Not once in her wildest imaginings did she think he was the cause of it all.

Too exhausted to give further thought to the upsetting idea, Cassandra had no clue what to do next. Scanning the room, her gaze rested on the bed, warm and cozy-looking with a fluffy comforter and oversized pillows lined up like clouds against the finely carved headboard.

She tossed the covers aside and sat lightly on the mattress. Bouncing up and down, she was reminded of the bed she and Meggie had shared and the comfort it had given on so many cold, rainy nights. Nestling under the covers, she lay her head on a pillow and remembered what Irene had told Madame Ragnar when they'd first entered the house. Rand was gone for the night and would not be back for a while. She would have time to ponder the startling changes taking place inside her. She could figure it all out before she had to explain it to the Mac-Pherson.

Cocooned in the faint but pleasant aroma of his masculine scent, she closed her eyes and willed herself to a place where she felt safe and secure. A place where she could dream.

Soon, she slept her first real sleep in one hundred years.

Rand padlocked the iron gate behind him, climbed into his Jeep, and continued up the rut-covered drive. The Trenton complex wasn't far enough along for the inside crew to take over, so, with the prediction of more rain in South Jersey, he'd closed down the construction site and organized a few of the men to run the drainage pumps. Beside the fact that the guys couldn't perform their jobs safely in a downpour, he refused to allow shoddy workmanship on a building stamped with the MacPherson name.

He'd given up his feeble excuse of not wanting to drive

in a thunderstorm and stomped on the gas pedal, eager to be home. Compared to what he'd been experiencing lately, blinding rain was no big deal. Spending a night out of touch with Cassandra was.

He'd had plenty of time to think about her and all the other situations he needed to get a handle on during the miserable two-hour ride. Okay, so his housemate was a ghost . . . he'd come to accept that bizarre fact from the first day they'd met. It had taken some work, but he thought they'd been relating pretty well. They still had a lot of things to iron out in their relationship, but he and Cassandra were getting closer—

He whacked the heel of his hand against the steering wheel. Scratch that last sentence. People did not have relationships with spirits—they had relationships with other people. And Cassandra was definitely not *people*.

But sometimes he wished she were.

Which she wasn't!

He had to get a grip and move to the other quirky stuff cluttering his life. For one thing, what the heck was happening between Nancy and Bill Dukovsky?

At first he'd thought a little matchmaking might be the very thing his sister needed to pull her out of her funk. She hadn't dated many men before she'd settled on good ol' Warren, so what harm could there be in getting her back into the single swim? None, right? Well, now he wasn't so sure. With Duke spouting off about how great it was to be a bachelor, then hanging around with a moon-eyed stare whenever Nancy was at the house, it was almost ridiculous.

Then there'd been that call from his mother while he was down at the flooded-out construction site. The last time she'd phoned him "just to see how he was doing" she'd been scheming behind his back with people from a local secondhand store. He'd come home early from a meeting and surprised her and two moving men in the act of leaving the condo with his lounge chair, hula clock and a box of his favorite grunge clothes—including a pair of his most well-worn and comfortable work boots.

Though Irene had sounded innocent on the phone tonight, he just couldn't shake the feeling she was up to something . . . and it involved him.

After skirting the equipment trailer sitting crosswise on the lawn, he parked the Jeep. Climbing the porch stairs, Rand noted the darkened first floor. He unlocked the door and flipped the switch. After a second of furious flickering, blackness engulfed him and he blurted out a string of curse words. What the hell was wrong with the electrical crew that they couldn't take care of what should have been a simple problem? He was starting to feel as if he lived inside some kind of damned physics experiment run amok.

Stumbling through the foyer, he knocked over one of the half dozen battery-powered lanterns he'd set throughout the house, jerked it off the floor, and turned it on. Who the heck did the electrician think he was anyway? The guy solely responsible for keeping the energizer bunny in carrots?

He raised the lantern and ambled into the kitchen, prepared to do a quick check of the house. Spotting two cups in the sink, he made a second mental note to give the crew a good talking-to. He'd already warned them this wasn't a lunchroom, and he certainly wasn't their maid.

Letting out a breath, he turned on the hot water and picked up a dirty cup. Running his fingers over the rim, he squinted through the dim light, his gaze drawn to the deep red stain coloring the edge of the mug.

Since when did any of his men, or his sister for that matter, wear this shade of lipstick?

The only woman he knew who wore this dark a color

was his mother. But the last time Irene visited, he'd made it crystal-clear she wasn't to stop by again without an invitation. And he damn well hadn't invited her. Would she have had the nerve to sneak over here on her own?

The phone call! Rand stared at his reflection in the window over the sink. Could he be any more stupid? He'd bet a day's pay that was the reason for her call. He was going to strangle his sister. Or Duke. Or whoever had let Irene into the house without his permission. He was going to—

Aw, crap, who was he kidding? Sometime over the weekend he just needed to have a long talk with Nancy and remind her their mother and her psychic friends weren't allowed on the premises. Maybe the lipstick stain belonged to one of her girlfriends or another decorator she'd invited to tour the house. He'd be a jerk to insist Nan couldn't have someone over while she worked.

Lantern in hand, he climbed the stairs to the second floor, vowing to rein in his anger. But that lipstick-stained coffee mug hung in his head like a bat in a cave, ready to take off and bite him on the backside. Cassandra would never forgive him, hell, he'd never forgive himself, if he allowed his mother or any of her psychic cohorts to endanger her existence.

Right now he needed to get some sleep. The storm front had passed, the electricians were going to get the wiring straight or they were history, and he could certainly handle his mother. The only unknown was Cassandra. Once he figured out how to fit her into his life, he'd be a lot less tense.

Resisting the impulse to climb to the third floor and find her, Rand walked into his bedroom and went directly to the master bath. After a quick shower, he slipped into a pair of clean boxers, doused the lantern and found his way to bed by the light of the moon.

* * *

Half asleep, Rand stretched, rolled onto his side and peered into the darkness. The sound of twittering birds had replaced the patter of rain he'd been listening to for the past five mornings, telling him it was almost daybreak. Definitely too early to be up after the night he'd just experienced.

Smiling lazily, he took a deep breath and mentally examined the puzzling scent filling his nostrils. Neither tangy and herbal nor sweet and flowery, the light, pleasant aroma seemed to envelop the duvet and pillows. Something told him he'd smelled the scent before, but he couldn't quite place when or where. Nancy must have arranged a few of those girly-smelling candles on his nightstand, or maybe a basket filled with the stuff that looked like dried mulch, and he just hadn't noticed. Though not necessarily the most politically correct smell for a guy's bedroom, it evoked a homey touch he could live with for the time being—or until one of the workmen yanked his chain.

He burrowed under the covers, pulled the pillow lying next to him closer and willed himself back to sleep. Wrapping himself around the fluffy mound, he fondled the slippery material and grinned. Nancy had really outdone herself when she'd decorated this room. Besides the fancy-smelling froufrous, she'd found luxurious covers and soft satin pillows for his bed.

Flexing his fingers, he snuggled into the bolster with a contented sigh. He'd have slept with satin pillows sooner if he'd known they felt exactly like his idea of the perfect woman, with gently rounded hips, lush breasts and a curvaceous, sexy shape. Nuzzling nearer, he brushed against a silky mass. Long, curling stands of what felt like real hair feathered his nose and cheeks.

He froze, then slowly skimmed his hand over what

he'd swear was a taut, well-formed thigh and warm, firm calf. Holy-moly, how lucky could a guy get? Ms. Fantasy had the legs of a pampered marathon runner, muscular yet yielding and soft, and damned arousing to his fingertips.

Inching his palm back up, he came in contact with what he thought was stiff, lacy material . . . almost like a corset. Continuing his tactile inventory, he tried to pinpoint the day his dream girl had become a full-figured woman wearing lingerie from a bygone era. Was this how Cassandra would feel if he held her in his arms?

Well, hell, where had that stupid thought come from?

Besides, if Ms. Fantasy continued to fill his arms in this incredible manner, did it really matter? It had been months since he'd had a dream this sexually graphic. Mr. Happy's imagination must have been on overdrive when he'd come up, and Rand definitely meant *up,* with this bit of morning glory. And since no one was going to interrupt him on a Saturday, he was damn well going to enjoy it.

Cassandra was vividly aware of the large, capable hands that caressed her well before she came fully awake. Instead of questioning the strange sensations their gentle-yet-sensuous stroking called up, she gave in to the wondrous feelings arcing from deep inside and sighed softly with pleasure. It had been so long since she'd been touched by another human being, and never in such a personal way. How could this intimate-yet-thrilling fondling be wrong?

This was the stuff a true woman's dreams were made of, she thought with an inner burst of clarity. These hands, a man's hands, were responsible for the emotions rising from a secret place hidden in her core.

Her grandmother had explained the acts of intimacy practiced between men and women before Cassandra had left for America. She vaguely remembered experiencing these unbelievable sensations a few times in her past life, but her dream lover had always been a nameless, faceless entity who hovered just beyond the edge of her mind's eye. This morning, with the faint gray light of dawn slipping through the windows, he finally became more fully formed.

Though his true identity was still shrouded in foggy mist, she could see his broad forehead as it furrowed with anticipation, envision his eyes as they smoldered with longing. His sensually carved lips turned up in wonder, widening his cheekbones, while his nostrils flared like a stallion scenting its mate. Palms, work-roughened yet exquisitely tender, stroked and caressed all the places that had ached for so very very long.

She felt his erection grow hard and throbbing as his hips ground into her backside. His fingers wandered past her waist and onto her breasts, and another jolt of sensation shot up her spine. This man, her dream lover, was taking her to wife.

Rand groaned as his finger touched twin mounds of satin tipped with rosebuds. No, not rosebuds, he quickly decided, but nipples taut with desire.

Christ, it was amazing what the mind could manufacture. He couldn't remember the last time he'd spent himself like a horny teenager, but if this kept up, he was going to do the deed all over his new satin pillow.

Losing himself in the dream, he set thumbs and forefingers on those perfect pretend nipples and tugged. He cupped breasts that seemed formed for his hands alone and nibbled at a sweetly scented neck. Still fondling a bountiful breast in one palm, he buried his face in yards of thick, curling hair and ran his other hand to the back of the pillow. Fumbling with a long row of buttons, he grinned when a few bounced against his chest.

Ms. Fantasy made a kittenish purring sound and he tangled his hand in the corset strings, working at the laces as fast as his fingers would allow.

Deftly, he peeled the dress down to her waist, then tugged at the bony underwear until it lifted free. Tossing the imprisoning garment off the side of the bed, his smile broadened. There, that was better. Now he could feel every full, satiny inch of her.

And damn, but she felt good.

Suddenly free of her constricting corset, Cassandra let out a breathy sigh. Gloriously alive for the first time in a hundred years, she reveled in the touch of warm human hands, the melding of two souls as they sought to be one.

Sleek warm skin brushed sleek warm skin as she arched like a cat under its master's hands. Turning in his arms, she ran her palms down the front of his lightly furred chest and over his steely abdomen, until she held his life force in her hands. Lengthening in her fingers, he grew thick and rail-spike hard with the strength of his passion, filling her with a hot flowering of desire.

Setting his firm, moist lips against hers, he coaxed her to open, and she happily complied, eager to taste him on her tongue. Lightning sizzled through her breasts, down to her womb and farther, making her toes curl with longing. 'Tis wicked to feel this way, she told herself, secretly praying he would never stop.

His hands moved up to cup her throat, then her chin, and she whimpered with need. Rubbing noses like playful puppies, they giggled in unison, as if consumed with joy.

Slowly, she opened her eyes to confront the man she'd been waiting to meet for over a century. As if dashed by a bucket of icy water, she woke fully from her dream as Madame Ragnar's words came rushing back at her, swamping her with a tidal wave of conflicting emotions.

Her gaze locked with that of Rand MacPherson's, and she sucked in a huge rush of air. The face of her lover confirmed her most heartfelt desire . . . and her deepest fear. She'd finally found her one true love . . . and he was a MacPherson.

Shrieking, she rolled backward and fell off the bed.

He shouted a nasty curse and jumped to his feet.

Glaring daggers, Cassandra blew a wayward curl off her forehead and peeked over the edge of the mattress. "For the love of God, what exactly did you think you were doing?"

Red-faced, Rand folded his arms, his pose as superior as any Highland lord. "Me? Why the hell are you blaming me? In case you haven't noticed, that's my bed you're . . . you were sleeping in."

She came to her knees, dragged up the top of the gown, and hastily stuffed her arms in the sleeves. Struggling to stand, she huffed out an indignant breath. "You weren't supposed to be back for another day or two."

Fisting his hands in his hair, he practically snarled. "You didn't bother trying to find me before I left, so how would you know?"

Raising a brow, Cassandra took in the bedcovers, then his nearly nude form. Wispy flickers of fire inflamed her cheeks and sparked in her belly; her heart beat loudly in her chest. Wasn't this a fine kettle of haggis? She was practically naked in front of the man, she'd allowed him to touch her in places so private she'd forgotten they existed, and now she had less than nothing to say in her own defense.

To make matters worse—if that were possible—she'd sworn to Edith and Irene she wouldn't reveal they'd sneaked into the house. And here he was, with typical MacPherson bluster, demanding she break that promise.

Rand dropped his hands to his sides and followed her gaze. Glancing down at the bulging placket of his shorts, he snatched his trousers from the foot of the bed and hopped on one leg.

Cassandra clutched at her bodice and began to pace, but that didn't keep her from stealing a glance at his finely molded chest and other manly . . . attributes. "I assumed . . . because of the rain . . . and you didn't come home for supper . . .''

Jerking into his pants, he turned and zipped the zipper, then whirled to face her again. "Well, you assumed wrong. And even if I wasn't coming home, what business do you have taking over my bedroom?"

Fleetingly, the fairy tale about Goldilocks testing the beds of the three bears crossed her mind. Thinking it might lighten the situation, she almost blurted out Madame Ragnar's unbelievable prediction, then suddenly thought better of it. The man was a swaggering tower of muscle with a knot of stubbornness wedged firmly between his ears. The psychic had to be wrong. How could he be her one true love when he had the sensitivity of a goat?

The front of her dress drooped alarmingly, and she slapped her palms back to her chest. "Bother and damnation! Because, thanks to you, I no longer have anywhere to rest. With no space to call my own, this room was the only place I could go for privacy. I was tired, and your bed looked—"

Stomping to the window, he spun on his heel. "What are you talking about? You still have your space. The closet's open."

"Are ya daft, man? Don't you understand what that means?" she shouted.

"Hey, I just wanted you to stop running away from me. I didn't expect you to find your way to my . . . here."

Praying for patience, Cassandra looked to the ceiling. Just like a man, he was thinking only of himself. "Have ya no idea what you've done, MacPherson, opening my small bit of space to the world?"

Before she could come up with a more specific explanation, the insufferable clod was looming over her, his green eyes wide with disbelief, his hands grasping her upper arms in a viselike grip.

"Cassandra, yell at me again. Say something . . . anything."

Struggling, she glared up at him. "Oooh . . . let go of me, you . . . you cabbagehead!"

His fingers bit harder as he pulled her near. "Cassandra, I can hear you. Not in my head, but with my ears. Your mouth is moving, and I can hear you speak. It's daylight and I can touch you . . . hold you. Jeez, I can see you."

She looked at his hands, gripping her so tightly, he was indenting her flesh, then focused on his naked chest. Her throat dried up and she swallowed hard, still trying to accept what he was saying.

Finally, she met his glittering stare. "Aye, it seems that you can."

He dropped her arms as if the feel of her burned his palms, and he shuffled backward toward the door. The heels of her satin shoes thudded loudly against the bare wood floor. Rand shoved his hands into his pockets, his gaze filled with suspicion. "Is that all you have to say? What the hell is going on here?"

She stepped away and gave the gown another stiff tug, hooking it up onto one shoulder. Too confused to answer, she showed him her back and focused on the tops of her shoes. Perversely, he walked around to stand in front of her. She stared at his feet, slowly inched her gaze up his skintight jeans, past his hard-as-rock stomach, until she met his befuddled stare with one of defiance.

What was she supposed to say, when she didn't understand a bit of it herself? Somehow, some way, her world had just flipped on its axis and decided to spin in an entirely different direction.

Her gaze slid back to the floor and the toe she was tapping in frustration. Sweet Mother of God, she was standing—not floating or hovering, but standing—with both feet on the ground. Madame Ragnar had been correct.

She'd become human.

Chapter Thirteen

Rand grabbed a shirt and shoes and stormed out of the bedroom. Cassandra stood stiff as a post, listening as he tore down the stairs, crossed the foyer and slammed the front door. She raced to the windows facing the front of the house just in time to see the angry spew of gravel as his automobile plowed down the drive.

Shocked by his reaction to her situation, she stared at the barren trees and clear November sky, but all she could envision was the MacPherson as he had looked only moments before. Like a boat without a rudder, his face had traversed a river of emotion so turbulent, she would remember it always. Finally, he'd choked out something about needing time to think, and fled the room.

Heaving another sigh, she slumped onto the edge of the bed, then realized what had last taken place there and jumped to her feet. Casting the bed a threatening frown, she rubbed at her forearms and started to pace.

The MacPherson lived here now. Surely he would be back. Somehow she would find a way to explain the unexplainable. . . .

Like the sun flooding the bedroom with sweet morning

light, reality brightened her mind. Sprite as a fairy, she twirled in widening circles as she hummed a folk tune from her childhood. Elated, she waltzed into the hall, onto the second-floor balcony and back again, while her toes skimmed the wood as delicately as a dragonfly on water.

A surge of sensations swept through her system, causing her to tingle from the inside out. She was breathing air, she was warbling out loud in her usual slightly off-key soprano while her feet were planted firmly on the ground.

Singing softly, Cassandra stripped off her wedding dress, stockings and what was left of her undergarments and ran to the bathroom mirror to view herself in greater detail. After tugging at her hair and pinching her cheeks, she found a pin and pricked her finger. A drop of bright red blood welled and she broke into a loud giggle, finally convinced her current state was not just a wondrous dream but a reality.

Somehow, she'd come alive.

She found a fresh toothbrush under the sink and used it vigorously, then drank a full tumbler of water. Moving to the glass-encased shower, she fiddled with the knobs until the stall billowed with steam. Standing under the stinging spray, she soaped her body and washed her hair, letting the hot water batter away a hundred years of anger and pain.

And when at last she felt clean, she wrapped herself in a towel, knelt in the center of the bedroom and bowed her head, offering up thanks to her Creator.

God had answered her prayers and given her a miracle.

Newly fortified, she shot to her feet and began to rummage through the dresser drawers. When she found nothing remotely feminine to wear, she slipped into one of the MacPherson's flannel shirts, buttoned it and turned up the sleeves. After stepping into a pair of baggy gray trousers, she tightened the drawstring waist, rolled up the hem so she wouldn't trip and skipped barefoot into the kitchen.

Inspecting cupboards, she took down a mug and the box of teabags Irene and Madame Ragnar had used the night before. She filled the cup with water, placed it in the magical microwave, and, several attempts later, managed to start the machine. Just as she added a bag of tea to the cup, the MacPherson barged into the kitchen, growling like a bear with a sore paw.

Carrying two large sacks, he marched to the breakfast area and dropped his packages on the smooth worn oak. "I need coffee. Would you like some?"

Cassandra brought her mug to the table and sat primly. Eyeing the bags, she heard as well as felt her stomach rumble—a decidedly human reaction that thrilled her to her soul. "The tea is fine, thank you." She swept a hand in front of her. "This all smells delicious."

"Help yourself," Rand muttered as he turned and stalked to the coffeemaker.

Still uncertain of what he wanted her to say, she rifled through the sacks, pulling out a box from one and a raft of small packages wrapped in paper from the other.

"Figured out how to work the microwave, I see."

"It was quite simple." She opened a pink-and-orange box, lifted a blueberry-filled treat to her nose and inhaled. "I just remembered what you told me the other night. These muffins smell heavenly."

Before she could take a bite, he charged to the table and glared down at her. "Jeez, Cassandra. How can you sit there and be so calm? Don't you realize what's happened here?"

Deliberately, she broke the muffin in half, then quarters, and popped a piece in her mouth. Oh, she knew all right. But she had no way to tell him so without explaining the whole of it. First off, she'd have to confess to being a witch. After he finished laughing his head off, she'd have to tell him her coming back to life was connected to a curse . . . one she'd placed on *his* family. Once he heard the entire story, he would never believe they belonged together. More than likely, he'd have her committed first.

"Cassandra? I asked you a question." Rand pulled out a chair, sat and folded his arms.

Refusing to meet his probing gaze, she finished the muffin, then poked through the smallish, wrapped bundles from the bag that read McDonald's. Strange, but she'd known a family named McDonald when she'd lived in Scotland. Had they come to America and started their own restaurant?

"I'm waiting." He grabbed one of the bundles and opened it, letting out the tempting aroma of sausage and eggs.

Hoping to keep her thoughts to herself a little longer, she chose her own packet. "It's amazing, isn't it?"

Rand took a bite of his biscuit and chewed. He licked at his lips and she felt heat flood her cheeks. She'd kissed that firm-yet-pliant mouth only a short while ago, and, much to her chagrin, longed to do it again.

"Is that all you have to say? Amazing? If you ask me, it's unfuckingbelievable. Christ. Amazing."

Unwrapping the McDonald's cooking, she tossed him a frown. "Please watch your language, Mr. MacPherson. 'Tis not polite to utter such a nasty word out loud."

"Trust me, that's mild compared to what I've been thinking for the past hour. How can you sit there and eat an Egg McMuffin when something so fantastic just happened? I don't get it."

How, indeed? she continued to wonder. But the look of suspicion etched across his face told her now was not the proper time to smile with her joy. "Well, for one thing, I haven't tasted food in a very long while. I think it's the simple pleasures a body misses most. And all of this is very tasty."

"I'll just bet." Pushing from the table, he went to the counter, took down a mug and filled it with coffee. He sighed, and she almost felt pity for his confusion. But when he marched back to the table like a warrior going to battle, her pity turned to dread.

"So, you're claiming you have absolutely no idea how this . . . this unbelievable reincarnation took place?"

Cassandra bit into the biscuit and chewed. Bliss . . . pure heavenly bliss, she thought with a roll of her eyes. He cleared his throat, reminding her he was awaiting a response, and she swallowed. "It was gentlemanly of you to go out and purchase all this wonderful food."

"Cassandra—"

"No, really. I would have been more than happy to cook for the both of us. I was quite handy in the kitchen when I was a girl."

"And what are you now?" He dropped both hands to the table, rattling the salt and pepper shakers. "I know you're female, but how old are you? Twenty-two? One hundred and twenty-two? And how do you propose we explain your existence? Who do I say you are?"

Silently, she acknowledged he made a good point. It wouldn't do to tell people she'd simply popped into his life, especially when his relatives had seen what her first body looked like. And there were other, more logistical problems. How was she going to obtain a position and support herself without the proper training? More important, she'd learned from watching police dramas on television that a person needed identification to be accepted as a human being before they could exist in the modern world. She couldn't very well thrust her turn-of-the-century immigration papers at the authorities and expect them to be accepted, even if she could find them, which was highly unlikely after all these years.

"I'm not sure." Fisting her hand, she thumped it over her heart. "Inside of me, here where it counts, I know I'm Cassandra Elizabeth Kinross. I feel it as surely as I did a century ago. But up here"—she set a finger to her temple—"everything is a bit fuzzy. I'm going to need some time to sort it all out."

Okay, Rand warned himself, time to take this slow and easy. Maybe if he went over it again, things would make more sense. To begin with, he was pretty darned positive the woman sitting in front of him had been a spirit only forty-eight hours ago. Though ninety-nine point nine percent of the world's population would say she hadn't existed, he knew firsthand she'd been, at the very least, an insubstantial but viable blob of electrically charged protoplasm. To say she'd been a supernatural marvel would be a stretch.

And that definition would wash only if one believed in the supernatural in the first place.

Well, he had believed, which now forced him into going a step further. Over the past weeks, he'd watched this same shapely mound of protoplasm appear and disappear at will. He'd seen her transparent form waver in lamplight, walk through closet doors, and float six inches off the ground. Everything he knew about her was unbelievable, yet he had believed in her ghostly existence.

And now she did exist. At least she felt, looked and sounded as if she did. If he could accept the fact that she'd been a spirit, why was it so impossible to accept she'd come to life?

Inhaling a breath, he set his cup on the table and took a seat. "I didn't mean to sound like a bully. But you have to admit all this is pretty remarkable. What's been going on with you, this ghost business and everything, is not something the normal person would find easy to believe. I guess I'm just a little shell-shocked."

Cassandra sipped at her tea. Holding the mug in both

hands, she brought it to her chest and leaned into the table. "If you can understand that much, then I'd ask you to put yourself in my shoes. Try to imagine what I'm experiencing right now—see it from my point of view for just one second."

Rand settled back against the chair and ran a hand over his eyes. She certainly had him on that point. "Fair enough. And I'm sorry if I yelled at you before."

She quirked an auburn brow. "Before when? As it seems to me, you've done nothing but shout since the day began."

He rested his elbows on the table and set his chin on his hands. He'd been acting rude . . . and boorish and impatient. But no matter how hard he tried, he couldn't shake the image of what Cassandra had looked like falling out of his bed. With her hair a riot of lustrous copper, her lips swollen with his kisses, and her face a warm, glowing pink, he'd never seen a more beautiful sight. And he would never, as long as he lived, forget the feel of her in his arms.

Suddenly overcome with guilt, he nodded. "Earlier . . . when I found you in my . . . I . . . um . . . shouldn't have shouted or been so impolite." That seemed to soothe her a bit, so he forced out a smile. "You have to admit it was a surprise."

"Aye, that it was. But I also found it to be quite . . . stimulating. From the feel of it, I gather you did too."

From the feel of it? Well, crap, that answered his question about whether or not she'd been introduced to Mr. Happy. So, now what?

Rand waited while Cassandra swallowed the last of her breakfast and daintily licked her fingers. Steeling his senses against the onslaught of desire the simple action roused, he handed her a napkin and ordered himself to start thinking with his head instead of what was behind his zipper.

She dabbed at her rosy lips, then gazed at him through lowered lashes. " 'Tis starving, I was. Thank you for the food."

Before he could formulate a "you're welcome," she confronted him squarely, her violet eyes alight with mischief. "So, MacPherson, when do you think we might do it again?"

Cassandra worried the inside of her lip as she watched Rand pick his chin up off the floor. His mouth snapped shut so hard, she heard his teeth click together. Dunderhead that she was, she'd let her tongue race ahead of her brain . . . again.

His scorching gaze sent a prickle of heat shimmying up her spine. Jaw tightly clenched, he raised his grass eyes to the ceiling, as if the answer to her question would magically drop from above.

She fiddled with the wrapper from her breakfast. In between showering and changing and eating, she'd thought all morning about Madame Ragnar's shocking explanation and decided the woman had been correct. Rand MacPherson had been the only man she'd met since the house had been opened.

He had to be her one true love.

If he wasn't ready to admit they belonged together, she simply needed to convince him of the fact. She'd learned from all those daytime talk shows that modern men appreciated women who spoke their minds, rather than shy, simpering maids. Once the MacPherson realized she was willing to go to bed with him, they could finish what they'd started this morning, declare their love for each other, and that would be that. The curse would be lifted, Robbie would be safe, and she and Rand would live a long and happy life together.

Finally, he took his gaze from the ceiling. Clearing his throat, he stopped and started twice before saying, "Do it again? Sorry, I'm not quite following you."

She dredged up a smile, hoping to put him at ease. If he boomed out a laugh, she could act as if she'd made a ribald jest. There would be time to come up with a secondary plan. Time for her to wade through her emotions while she waited for the MacPherson to realize she was the woman with whom he was meant to spend his life.

"I want to know when we can do again what we did this morning. In your bed."

His face washed pale. His brow furrowed with what she hoped was contemplation. He shook his head and walked across the kitchen to refill his cup.

Her dander up, Cassandra fisted her hands around her empty mug. The one thing she hadn't expected was to be ignored. A full minute passed before she asked, "Surely it can't take that long to decide whether or not you're interested in bedding me?"

Rand sloshed coffee over the tiles, grabbed a towel and mopped up the spill. Turning, he propped his backside against the counter, a hint of amusement hovering in his eyes. "Don't you think we have a few things to talk about before we get to the part about our personal relationship?"

Hope buoyed in her chest. He wasn't laughing like a loon, merely telling her they could think on it once they untangled the rest of her predicament. And he was probably right to put their longing on hold, when there were so many more important things to discuss.

"I suppose we do. What is it you think we need to take care of first?"

He brought his cup to the breakfast area and stood staring from across the table. His heat-filled gaze warmed the bodice of her shirt until she thought it would burn a hole through the flannel. The idea that he had touched her there, in such a private place, shot a jagged tremor of fire from her hardened nipples to a spot low in her belly.

"For starters, you need clothes. Unless you want to continue wearing mine, of course."

She glanced down at her chest, encased in the soft green material that still smelled of his pleasant manly scent. Self-conscious of the fact she was not wearing underclothes, she placed a hand on the top button. Lifting her head, she raised both brows and willed her heartbeat to slow. "I dinna think you'd mind, since I had so little clothing intact after . . ."

The memory of their morning tussle filled her brain, and she knew she was blushing again. Certainly today's women no longer colored red whenever they spoke about things of a personal nature? If they did, their faces would be crimson twenty-four hours a day.

Apparently unmindful of her discomfort, he said, "I don't care if you wear them, but you need regular clothes— sweaters, jeans, some . . . um . . . girly things."

Cassandra had to admit he was correct. More lessons from the television had taught her that modern women no longer wore constricting undergarments or tightly laced boots. She'd had a devil of a time getting her slippers off; she wasn't about to pour herself into them or that damnable corset again. Besides, her old shoes needed to be fastened with a buttonhook, an outdated necessity that surely had gone the way of the butter churn and outdoor privy.

"I would be deeply grateful if you could find me something more suitable. I'll repay you, of course, if you'll have the patience to wait until I have a means of support."

Frowning again, he rested his hands on the table and leaned in close. "Don't be ridiculous. It's the least I can do for you after what happened with Colin. The MacPhersons owe you a lot more than a new wardrobe, Cassandra. As head of the family, it's my job to see you're taken care of."

Taken care of? Did he think she was owed his kindness, as if she were some kind of debt or obligation?

So there it was, she thought with a rush of sadness. He thought what had happened between them was an accident of time and place, and he didn't have the cruelty in his heart to tell her so. She'd been misinterpreting his thoughtful glances as those of remembered pleasure, when it was clear he regarded her only as a burden.

She's been a dead woman, a fact he was well aware of. He would never accept her as his one true love.

She thrust up her chin just to show him she didn't plan on being a slacker. "Women of today have jobs outside the home. I'm strong and I'm clever. I can find work . . . once I'm properly taught. You don't have to worry about me, MacPherson. I'll be taking care of myself soon enough."

His mouth lifted into a smile, and her stomach gave a funny little flipflop. "Don't you think it's about time you called me Rand?"

All thoughts of fighting her cursed blushing fell by the wayside as another wave of warmth rose from her belly. "Rand." She tested the word on her tongue. "All right. Rand."

"That's better. Now, let's get going."

She sat back in the chair. "Going?"

"Well, since I'm not experienced at buying women's clothing, it might be a good idea if you came along. Otherwise, I can't be held responsible for what I bring back from the mall."

The mall? Did he mean a group of shops that sold clothing and other sundry? and could she actually go?

After being a prisoner for so long, venturing into the sweet fresh air would be a true test of her humanity. Though she hadn't been able to leave the house as a spirit, she was now human. It would be wonderful to feel a cool breeze caress her cheeks again.

"I'm thinking that's a grand idea. When can we leave?" She pushed away from the table and jumped to her feet.

Rand's gaze settled on her naked toes, then traveled up her legs to rest on her chest and the baggy flannel shirt drooping from her shoulders. "Hang on. You don't have a jacket or shoes. It's about forty degrees outside. You'll freeze without something on your feet."

The force of his stare had her wondering if he could see straight through to her bare skin. "I've a strong constitution. Besides, it's been forever since I've felt the grass between my toes. The cold will hardly bother me—"

"Look, forget what I said for a minute." He spun on his heel as if his boots had just caught fire. "I wasn't thinking straight. You can't go out of the house without shoes; they won't let you into a mall without them. And you need a bed. There's this place I know in Newark, open twenty-four/seven. They even promise same-day delivery. I'll go take care of it."

He backed up a few steps. "All of this has probably knocked your socks off . . . if you were wearing socks, that is. Maybe you should put your feet up . . . down . . . and turn on the television, get acquainted with the world."

Sticklike, he walked to a drawer, pulled out a notepad and pencil, and tossed them on the table. "Here. If you see or think of anything you want, just write it down and I'll make sure to get it. I'll be back later, and we'll talk some more." Grabbing his jacket, he raced out the door.

Cassandra sighed as she watched him leave the kitchen. Could the man have been in any more of a hurry to get away from her? Only if she had the plague.

She carried their cups to the sink and cleared breakfast from the table. Now what was she supposed to do? She'd had a bath and eaten her fill. The house wasn't ready for a good cleaning, except in the MacPherson's room, and

she wasn't overjoyed at the idea of visiting there again—
unless, of course, Rand would be with her.

Shoulders slumped, she leaned forward and rested her
elbows on the counter. Closing her eyes, she thought back
on the morning. She'd been a Jezebel to suggest he take
her to bed a second time, but the words had tumbled
from her lips as quickly as she'd fallen off his mattress.
It was too late to take them back now. Her feelings were
out in the open, a sad counterpoint to his own.

How could he accept her as his one true love, when
he thought of her as a duty, an obligation he needed to
repay, and nothing more?

Dejected, she walked to the back of the house and
stared through the glass pane of the door. The outside
air looked crystal-clear. The sun shone golden against a
cloudless blue sky, and she could see birds swooping
down onto the pond, a huge green-gray pebble that rose
in the distance, swollen from the past week of rain.

So what if she froze her feet off? It would be worth
a chill just to dance on real grass, inhale fresh air, hear
the birds sing once more. Being part of the world was
what she had longed for ever since the house had come
to life again.

Hesitantly, she opened the door and inhaled. Growing
brave, she lifted a hand and moved it outward through
the doorway.

She closed then opened her eyes as despair filled her
heart. Her hand, which she could still feel at the end of
her arm, had disappeared right up to her wrist. Her worst
nightmare was a reality.

If she left the house, she would turn into nothingness.

Rand sat in his Jeep and gazed at his sister's neat white
colonial. Thumping his forehead against the steering
wheel, he asked himself why in the heck he hadn't had

the guts to finish what he'd started. He'd gone to the mattress wholesaler in Newark and ordered the most expensive queen-sized bed and brass head- and footboard the store carried. Then he'd driven to the nearest mall, where, instead of going to a department store that sold normal clothing, he'd found himself drawn to a Victoria's Secret. Once he'd worked up the courage to go inside, he'd lurked between the displays for so long, he thought the salesclerks were going to call security and have him arrested.

Finally, he'd scraped up the nerve to ask for help. He'd left the store with two shopping bags full of lacy briefs, two satin sleepshirts, and a raft of bras in a variety of cup sizes he was positive would never fit Cassandra's voluptuous figure.

And the entire time he shopped he'd felt twisted inside, thinking how all he wanted was to return to the house, carry the maddening woman upstairs, and make love to her like some chest-thumping Neanderthal.

He'd been so distracted, he'd forgotten totally about the important stuff—jeans and sweaters, maybe some warm socks and a jacket . . . and shoes. The woman needed shoes, for cripessakes.

It was all Cassandra's fault, he suddenly decided. As if it hadn't been enough of a shock to find her in his bed, he'd been dumbfounded to learn that she'd turned into a living, breathing woman. Then she'd thrown him a doozy of a curve and asked if the two of them could get up-close and personal again.

Didn't Cassandra realize she was a gosh-darned walking, talking miracle? Didn't she care about what had just happened to her? Didn't she see that she'd made history, even if there was no one to document it for the record books?

And instead of discussing the outrageous event, he'd made those stupid shopping excuses and hightailed it out of the house like a wide receiver sprinting for the goal line. He'd been a total jerk.

Heaving a sigh, he got out of the Jeep and headed up the walk. Drumming his fingers, he rang the doorbell and waited for someone to answer, then thought better of it. If he was smart, he'd just turn around and do what he'd promised—buy Cassandra a shelf of heavy sweaters, voluminous pants and thick wool socks—clothes that covered her from her delicious-looking toes to her adorably blushing cheeks—and go back home.

He stepped onto the top stair, ready to cut a path to his car. The woman needed clothes, and he was the only one who could take care of it. What was she supposed to do—walk around in his shirt and sweat pants for the rest of her life?

And why did he like the sound of that stupid idea so much?

"Rand? Is that you?"

He turned to Nan, who had opened the front door and stepped onto the porch, and slapped a grin on his face. "Hey, sis. How you doing?"

"Come on in. Unless you really don't want to be here." Bright-eyed, Nancy walked into the house and he followed, hoping to hide his frustration.

Before he could answer, Melissa ran from the living room and catapulted into his arms. He swung her up and she gave him a loud smacking kiss on the cheek. "Unka Rand! I did gymnastics this morning an' I walked on the high beam all by myself. I told Mommy not to hold my hand, didn't I, Mommy?"

"That you did, big girl," Nan said, patting her daughter on the back.

"Robbie's soccer team tied. He tried to make the last kick, but it didn't go in the net. He's really mad." Melissa pulled her head from the crook of Rand's shoulder and drew her eyebrows high. "Daddy wasn't there to see. He got stucked at the hospital again."

Rand gently set Melissa on the ground. "Gee, that's too bad about the game. Where's your brother right now, squirt?"

The little girl did a cartwheel on the tiled foyer. Raising her hands in a gymnastic salute, she marched to her mother's side. "In his room. Want me to go get him?"

Rand could only imagine how miserable his nephew felt at that moment. Robbie had blown the winning goal and his dad hadn't even had the decency to see him play . . . again. Staying here to spend time with the kid wasn't cowardly. Robbie needed a little manly moral support. Cassandra would be there when he got home; where in the heck did she have to go?

"Sure. Tell him I'm here and ask him if he wants to play catch in the backyard, okay?"

With a wince, Nan watched as Melissa charged up the stairs, shouting for her brother with Princess barking at her heels.

"You don't have to do that, you know. He'll be fine after he's worked out his disappointment on a few computer games."

Ignoring her comment, Rand followed her into the kitchen. "What was the absentee father's excuse this time?"

She poured two cups of coffee, carried them to the glass-topped breakfast table and settled into a chair. "No excuse. When the big moron didn't bother to show, I just used the standard Daddy-must-have-been-called-to-the-hospital line, like I always do." She ran her fingers through her curly hair and sighed. "But I'm getting so tired of lying to them. I keep wondering if it's worth polishing Warren's super-dad image just to let the kids think they have a father who really cares."

Rand took a quick swallow of coffee to douse his temper. "Warren's a bum, but I know what you mean. That's one thing I have to give Mother credit for. No matter what happened between her and Dad, she never bad-mouthed him. Would it help if I went with you to Robbie's games the next few Saturdays?"

Nan stared into her cup, her cheeks a wash of color. "Um . . . maybe next week? After that, someone else might want to come."

Mildly annoyed that he'd been usurped, Rand took a wild guess at the name of his rival. "Wait, don't tell me. Bill Dukovsky's offered to tag along."

She raised eyelids, her own annoyance clear. "It sounds like you have a problem with that."

"Not really. I just hope you know what you're doing. Bill's a nice guy, but I'm your older brother."

Nancy rested her chin in her hand and gave him a brittle smile. "In case you haven't noticed, I'm all grown up. And I'm definitely being careful. Now, what brings you here at noon on a Saturday? I thought you were staying overnight in Trenton?"

"Who told you that?"

She shrugged. "Bill mentioned it when I got to the house yesterday. Did something happen that made you come home?"

"Not really. I put the crew on pump duty and decided that was all I could do. By the way, did Mother stop by while you were there?"

"Not while I was working. Why?"

Princess trotted through the kitchen doorway with what looked to be a dirty sock in her mouth. Scampering toward Rand, she gave a doggie bow, taunting him to play tug-of-war. "I found a coffee mug in the sink I swear had her color of lipstick on it. And she called my mobile to see if I was going to be home last night. I got this gut feeling that she'd been in the house."

Nan rolled her eyes as she scolded. "Darn that dog. She's been digging under the beds again. Princess! Give me that."

Rand snapped the sock from the dog's mouth and tossed it at Nan. "What's the matter, sis? Didn't the maid show this week?"

"Very funny. It just so happens that because of all the work I'm doing on *your* house, I haven't had a spare minute to take care of mine."

She set the sock on the counter and shook her finger at Princess. "Let's get back to Mom. Why do you think she'd do something like that?"

"Because I told her I didn't want her or any of her loopy friends messing there, that's why."

Raucous screams sounded from overhead, and Nan's chestnut-brown eyes narrowed. On cue, Princess bounded from the room, yapping like a puppy on speed. "I agree that Irene will never win an award for Mother of the Year, but she's not that bad. The way I remember it, she always wanted to investigate Uncle Colin's ghost stories, but Dad forbade her to set foot in the mansion, just like you're doing. I think it was his way of punishing her for divorcing him."

"I'm not trying to punish her. I just want her to stay away until she's invited. I'm serious about this, Nan, and I expect you to honor my wishes."

"Oh, all right, but it'll be tough. Mom always seems to find a way to get what she wants."

Not interested in pursuing the idea, Rand glanced around the kitchen and spied a pile of boxes sitting near the back door. "Don't tell me you've finally gotten smart and decided to donate Warren's leftover wardrobe to Goodwill?"

Nan followed his gaze. "Those are just some old clothes the kids and I have outgrown. I was going to take the stuff to the woman's shelter. I've lost a little weight—"

"I've been meaning to talk to you about that."

"Yeah, well, thanks for the concern, but I don't plan on gaining it back. I thought the shelter could use the clothes. Some of them are practically new."

"Hey, Uncle Rand." Eyes shining and faces flushed, Robbie and Melissa ran into the kitchen with Princess at their heels. "You really want to play some catch? The gloves and stuff are on the back porch."

"That's what I'm here for." He stood and eyed the cartons, then flashed Robbie a grin. *Sometimes the answer to a problem just fell into your lap.*

"But first, how about you help me carry those boxes to the Jeep? I'm going to deliver them for your Mom."

"Rand, that's not necessary." Nancy stood and began bundling Melissa into a jacket. "I was going to do it Monday morning before I came to the house."

He gave Robbie a wink, then hoisted the largest box. "No problem. I can do it on my way home today, right, sport?"

"Right," Robbie mimicked. Picking up a smaller box, the boy followed Rand, Melissa and their crazy, bounding dog to the car.

The phone rang and Nan grabbed it on her way out the door. "Mom, hi. What's up? No, Robbie's team tied, and Melissa walked on the high beam by herself this morning. Other than that, it's been pretty quiet. . . . Rand's here. . . . No, I'm not sure for how long, but I'll probably talk him into staying for lunch. . . . I'll see you and Harry for dinner tomorrow night, right? Take care."

She hung up the phone, then walked to the closet and pulled on an old sweatshirt. She had a ton of housework to do, but the sun was shining for the first time in a week, and it had been too long since she'd cut loose and had a good tussle with her kids. Hefting the final box of clothes, she shouldered her way through the back door and headed for Rand's Jeep.

The last thing she wanted was to spoil her brother's morning by telling him about their mother's phone call.

Chapter Fourteen

Her cellular phone in one hand, Irene grabbed the strap dangling over the passenger side window with the other as Madame Ragnar steered the Hummer into the woods north of Rand's house. At the sound of Melissa's cheery voice, she jolted upright in her seat.

"Hi, sweetheart. It's Grandmother. Aren't you a clever girl, answering the phone like a grown-up. Is it true you walked on the high beam all by yourself this morning? That's very good. Is Uncle Rand still there? No, **no**, don't get him. Just finish your drink of water and go back outside to play. You don't even have to tell Mommy I called. I love you too, sweetie. See you tomorrow night."

Barely able to contain her excitement, she began to babble as she clicked off her phone for the second time in an hour. "It's the luck of the universe, I tell you. It was no accident when I got that urge to call Nancy this morning and learned Rand was visiting. Now that I'm sure the boy will be busy for a while, let's just hope Cassandra is around, so we can show her what we've brought."

Edith Ragnar nodded sagely as the Hummer roared

past the pond and lumbered to a stop near the mansion's back porch. "I couldn't agree more. And I'm thrilled with all the books we've discovered. I'm certain she'll feel the same."

"Do you need help with that bag?" asked Edith as she climbed from the oversized ATV and walked around to the passenger side.

Irene hefted a shopping bag from the floor of the backseat with a muffled grunt. "I can manage, thank you."

Once on the porch, she set the bag down and faced her friend. "Do you think we'll be able to locate her? It is broad daylight, you know. Don't most spirits hide until it gets dark?"

Edith placed a hand on the doorknob, turned and pushed. "If last night is any indication, my guess is she's almost through the transition. A truly incredible paranormal event, though I certainly have no idea how it took place." She *tsked* to herself. "One would think that after all these years, I'd have the expertise needed to decipher such a remarkable occurrence."

Irene picked up her precious cargo and led the way inside. "I don't think you should blame yourself for being inexperienced with something I imagine is extraordinary, even for the spirit world. I only wish we'd had the time to do a bit more research before we came back here. But with that stubborn son of mine out of the house and Harry at the office with a new client, we have a chance to get some real work done. Even so, it will take hours to go through these books."

Edith followed her inside and shut the door. "Thank you for the words of encouragement. I agree we need to take advantage of every opportunity to be alone with the girl. With the three of us searching, we'll find the answer that much sooner."

The women stepped through the mudroom, swept past the eating area and strolled into the kitchen. Irene set the bag on the tile-topped island and looked around. "Should we call out or just check the house? I wouldn't want to frighten the poor thing after all she's been through."

Edith set down her huge leather carryall and put her hands on her hips. "Why don't we start by warning Cassandra we're here? If we don't get an answer, we can hunt for her on the second floor. And it's my turn to tote that bag," she added. Hoisting the shopping bag, she headed for the foyer. "Really, Irene, how did you manage to accumulate so many volumes on the art of witchcraft?"

"I found most of them when I toured England and Scotland with Robert on our honeymoon. Used bookstores in the United Kingdom are so much more interesting than those here in the States. There were some real treasures in Edinburgh, books I believe were actually calling to me from the shelves and bins where they'd been gathering dust for years."

They stood at the bottom of the stairs and peered onto the upper landing. "Hel-lo-ooo!" Edith called, cupping a hand around her mouth. "Cassandra. Are you up there?"

Greeted by silence, the women looked at each other and shrugged. Edith picked up the bag, and they climbed the stairs to the balcony.

"Cassandra," Irene said in a more moderate tone. "We're coming up. Don't be afraid, dear. We need to speak with you."

They scoured the second level, but it was obvious Rand's empty suite was the only habitable room. "Where could the girl be?" she wondered out loud.

Just then, she spotted a frilly bit of lace peeking from a bottom drawer. Falling to her knees, she slid open the drawer and pulled out an old-fashioned corset and worn cream-colored stockings. After handing them to Edith, she dragged out a bounty of yellowed linen petticoats and a pair of silk pantaloons. Finally, she found a worn and dusty pearl-encrusted wedding gown.

"Oh, my," she whispered, her green eyes twinkling. "I do believe the girl is hiding somewhere. And who could blame her? By the looks of it, she's as naked as the day she was born."

After she'd straightened Rand's suite and put away her old clothes, Cassandra climbed the stairs to the third floor. She'd already decided to commandeer the large attic room across from his office, since she hadn't the heart to spend any more time in the bedroom the two of them had shared overnight.

She could be content, she decided, if he allowed her this space nestled in the top of the house. The room was airy and bright, the window seat framed a wonderful view of the rear of the property, and no one came to this floor unless invited.

She could make a home in this room, out of the way of noisy workmen and surprise visitors, yet close to Rand's private place . . . close to him.

Since settling on the window seat, she'd spent her time pondering everything that had occurred over the last few weeks. She hardly recognized herself as the same lonely, bitter-spirited woman she'd been on the first day Rand MacPherson barreled into her existence. Through their open and occasionally boisterous discussions she'd learned to forgive. He had convinced her the MacPherson family were not a bad lot. They'd merely had the misfortune of growing a mutant branch on the family tree. Now that the branch had been properly pruned, she could find no reason to hold any of them accountable for her past or present condition.

Cassandra had no cause to disagree with Madame Ragnar either. As far as she could tell, if Rand hadn't taken charge of this house, she would still be a ghost with no hope of a normal life. He had wakened her from her

uneventful spirit world and in the course of a heartbeat
had made her feel anger, then misery, then excitement
. . . more excitement than she'd ever experienced in her
other lifetime.

With him, she'd found the humanity to quiver in rage,
to dream with longing, and, finally, to ache with desire.
He was the one directly responsible for the return of her
life.

He was her own true love.

She heaved a sigh when she heard footsteps on the
balcony. For the past few minutes, she'd been aware that
Edith Ragnar and Rand's mother were in the house. She'd
watched their huge vehicle roll into the backyard, seen
the women climb from the body of the beast. Irene carried
a bag that Cassandra assumed held the books they'd
promised. Unfortunately, she simply wasn't prepared to
read them. She was certain no book would contain the
answer to her problem.

No book could force Rand MacPherson to love her.
And without his love, the curse would never be broken.
She would never be able to leave the house.

She could never be fully human.

She peered onto the landing in time to see the women
trundle into Rand's bedroom. Madame Ragnar, dressed
in a long, colorful skirt and matching sweater, and Irene,
in her usual high-heeled shoes and flamboyant fitness
outfit, chattered loudly, and Cassandra knew they were
searching the house. Soon they would climb to the third
floor and discover her sulking like a child.

Instead of hiding, she decided it would be better to
meet them on her terms. Cowardice had no place in her
life now, nor had it ever. In facing them, she would
bravely face this latest disappointment.

Grasping the banister, she walked to the balcony. She
stopped in the bedroom doorway when she saw what
Irene held in her hands. " 'Twas a beautiful dress when

it was new," Cassandra said out loud, remembering how wonderful the luxurious ivory-colored satin had felt when it first brushed her skin. Never in her life had she owned a dress so fine. "Colin made a point of telling me he'd spared no expense when he'd had it made."

Madame Ragnar and Irene jostled to face her. As if embarrassed to be caught with the dress in her hands, Irene thrust the gown behind her back. "We didn't mean to pry, dear. We just—"

Her guilt-ridden gaze took Cassandra in from head to toe. "Well, it looks like you found something to wear after all."

Cassandra glanced at her bare feet, grabbed the baggy sweat pants between her fingertips and held the material away from her thighs. "I know this looks strange, but the MacPherson said I was welcome to his clothing, until he could purchase some things of my own."

"Randall has seen you as you are now? He said he would buy you clothes?" Her gaze suddenly merry, Irene draped the dress over her arm and took a step closer. "When?"

For once, Cassandra decided to think before she spoke. Though she hated lying to the women, some measure of common sense warned her it wouldn't do to let Irene know her son had shared a bed with a newly transformed spirit. "Um . . . this morning. He came home and found me this way. He was a bit surprised at first, but I thought he took the sight of my reincarnation rather well."

Never mind that he'd run from the house like a scalded dog.

"He said buying me a few bits of clothing was the least he could do after what Colin . . . what happened to me."

"I see." Irene walked to the bed, laid the dress down and folded it neatly. When finished, she put it back in the bottom drawer and stacked the other items on top.

"How are you feeling this morning? I must admit you look very . . . human." Madame Ragnar began sorting through the bag on top of the dresser. "Doesn't she look human, Irene?"

"Amazingly so," Irene concurred, her smile wide. "Have you been able to go back to your ghostly form, or has this remarkable condition persisted since last night?"

Cassandra sighed. How could she explain that while she might look human when she was on the inside of the house, outside of it she simply didn't exist. "I canna go back, it seems. I'm unable to disappear or pass through walls, or do any of the magical things I did as a ghost. I'm flesh and blood, or close to it."

"Close to it? Whatever do you mean? Everything you've just said is more than enough to convince me you're human again," said Madame Ragnar. "Did you sleep? Do you feel like your old self this morning, the way you did before . . . when you first came to the States?"

"I slept—" *In the seductive circle of Rand's arms,* she almost blurted out. "And I woke up hungry as a bear. The MacPherson was kind enough to provide breakfast from a restaurant. I also used the privy and washed. I must confess, feeling my heart beat after so long a time is very disconcerting."

Madame Ragnar's brown eyes crinkled. "I would imagine so, but isn't it wonderful? A true miracle, if you want my opinion. Why do you look so miserable?"

Cassandra heaved a sigh. Though she might not be able to explain her inability to leave the house to Rand, an inner voice reminded her these women would understand. They didn't pity her or think of her as an obligation, but more as a work in progress. They knew about things otherworldly, and they accepted the curse and its ugly implications even though the bloody thing had damaged people Irene loved.

"There's a wee bit of a problem, ladies. I've not told

the MacPherson, because I didn't find out about it until after he'd left to go shopping. I think, rather than explain, it might be easier if I show you."

"But we have the books. It's possible the answer to this latest difficulty rests in one of them. Why don't we—"

Cassandra stepped toward the door. "Please, just come downstairs with me. Once you see what's wrong, we can discuss the books."

Madame Ragnar began repacking the shopping bag, but it was obvious she did so with reluctance. "We need to listen to the girl, Irene. After all, who better than she to know her own fragile condition?" She gestured to the door. "Go on, follow her down. I'll be with you as soon as I'm through here."

"Lord in heaven, is that the doorbell?" Irene's mug of tea hit the table with a thump. Glancing at her watch, she drummed her fingers. "Who in the world could it be? Randall isn't due for another hour, and the gate at the end of the drive is padlocked."

Cassandra stared at the books scattered across the table. It had taken them almost two hours to get halfway through the contents of the shopping bag, but they'd found nothing remotely related to her amazing transformation, or her perplexing slip into nothingness. Which only confirmed Cassandra's immediate suspicion—until the MacPherson recognized the fact that she was his true love, the curse would stay in force and the house would hold her prisoner.

Her gaze darted from the books to Irene and then Edith. "I'm fairly certain no one but you and the MacPherson should know of my existence yet. Madame Ragnar, perhaps you could go to the door and see who it is?"

The bell chimed again, this time more insistently. "This is as good a time as any for us to stop our investigation. I'll get rid of whoever's out there, but you two should probably pack up these books. Since Rand doesn't know you're a witch, it would be quite a shock for him to find them, don't you think?''

"That's an excellent observation," Irene said. Closing the leather-bound volume she'd been studying, she set it back in the bag and started stacking the rest of the books.

A few seconds later, Edith returned. ''I thought it best not to open the door, in case whoever it was told Rand a woman answered, but I peeked through one of the side panels. The man ringing the bell is wearing coveralls embroidered with the name of that mattress place—you know, the one that offers same-day delivery. He must have walked all the way down the drive from the main road because of that padlock on the gate. What do you think we should do?''

''Well, I certainly don't have a key to the gate. That's the reason we've been offroading onto the property. Cassandra, do you know where my son keeps a key?''

The doorbell rang again, along with the rattle of the deliveryman's impatient pounding. Cassandra furrowed her brow. If she had no bed, the MacPherson would probably insist she sleep in his. While he slept . . . where?

Irene continued to pile books in the bag. ''Edith, go back to the foyer, open the door a crack, and ask him to wait. Cassandra, check out those drawers for a key.''

Before Cassandra and Madame Ragnar could do as Irene suggested, they heard a murmur of male voices coming from the front of the house.

Irene stopped clearing the table.

Madame Ragnar's eyes grew wide.

Cassandra rested a hand on her throat. Good God, there was no mistaking that voice. The MacPherson was back. And he was inside, talking with the deliveryman. ''Quick, out the mudroom door,'' she ordered. Scuttling around the island, she set their teacups in the sink. ''More than likely he'll come tell me about the delivery. Someone is probably driving the van to the house right now. If you hurry, you can escape before anyone notices your automobile is out back."

The women scurried like rabbits sprung from a trap. If Cassandra hadn't been so worried about what Rand might do if he saw his mother and the psychic in his kitchen, she would have laughed at the way the older women raced around the room.

"Hide those books," Irene ordered, heading for the door.

"We'll be back when the coast is clear," hissed Edith.

Rand walked into the kitchen just as Cassandra closed the door of the cupboard under the center island.

"Hey, your bed's here. Lucky I came home early and found the van parked at the top of the drive. The guy who was ringing the bell is waiting for the truck right now." His wary gaze searched the kitchen, then settled on her face. "Are you all right? Nothing else weird happened since this morning, did it?"

From the corner of her eye, Cassandra caught a flash of sunlight hitting metal through the breakfast-nook window. The weight of discovery lifted when she realized Edith and Irene didn't have to worry about Rand spotting them. Deftly, she stepped in front of the glare. "I'm fine. But don't you need to do something to help?"

Rand grinned. "Nah. The guy at the door will handle it. The truck followed me down the lane, but the driver has to take it slow. We just need to decide where to put the bed."

Suddenly, a loud rumbling fairly shook the house. "That would be the van, I assume?"

"Should be," Rand agreed, walking into the hallway. "Have you decided which room you'd like?"

"Oh. Um . . . the one on the third floor, across from your office? It would put me out of sight of the workmen, since most of the remodeling up there is finished, and I'd have my privacy.''

''Sounds good to me. Wait here while I take care of it.''

Rand strode to the foyer, his brain working on overdrive. Well, there went his pipe dream of taking Cassandra up on her earlier offer. Instead of declaring she didn't care where he put the friggin' bed—because she planned on joining him in his for the next fifty years or so—she was acting happy as a clam that she'd be sleeping in a room of her own.

Cool it, stud boy. The last thing you need is that kind of problem, he warned himself as he opened the front door. The woman had been in shock that morning, just as he had. No way did she realize what she'd been saying.

He waited while the driver jockeyed the truck into position and raised the van's rear sliding panel. After the men deposited the framework and brass head- and footboard on the front porch, they brought up the box spring and mattress.

''Where do you want everything?'' the driver asked.

''Go straight to the balcony and take the staircase to the third floor. It'll be the room on the right.''

He caught the men's mild grumbling and decided to lend a hand. Picking up the disassembled bed frame, he followed them as they brought the mattress and other hardware upstairs, then supervised while they put the bed together and situated it on the wall opposite the window seat.

At the front door he handed them each a twenty-dollar bill. ''Thanks. Just close the gate when you leave the drive. I'll go down later to lock it.''

Shoving his hands in his pockets, Rand walked slowly from the foyer into the back hall. Now what? Cassandra had her bed and she'd made it pretty clear she wanted her privacy. But who could blame her? He hadn't exactly been Mr. Sensitivity since they'd surprised each other in bed that morning. Was it any wonder she'd had the good sense to rethink her offer of spending some personal time with him?

He heard water running and found her at the sink, washing dishes and setting them aside to dry. Propping himself in the doorway, he folded his arms and automatically assessed the woman he'd begun to think of as his own private miracle. His gut somersaulted when he realized she wasn't wearing a stitch under his clothing. The soft flannel of his shirt molded to her back, waist and hips, while his sweat pants hung loosely over her shapely bottom in a way they'd never fit him.

Cassandra was taller than Nan, but with those lush curves, she looked a hundred times more alluring, even up to her elbows in soapsuds and hot water.

How in the hell could she be so calm, so matter-of-fact about what had happened to her? Then again, being sold into virtual slavery by her father, sailing halfway around the world to marry a stranger, and getting entombed in a closet had gone above and beyond what most people suffered. She'd been a ghost for a century when he'd shown up and invaded her world. From her point of view, this remarkable metamorphosis was probably just another bump in the road. Instead of barking at her like a rabid dog, it was time he tried to make her transition easier.

All of a sudden it dawned on Rand that Cassandra could use a whole lot more stuff to make her new life livable. She didn't need just a bed—she needed sheets, blankets, pillows, bedroom furniture. And new clothes. And makeup. All the things it took to make living life as a woman comfortable.

Later, once he got her acclimated, he could teach her how to drive, maybe buy her a car, give her all the bells and whistles she needed to function in the modern world.

After what his uncle had put her through, it was up to him to see to her well-being and help ease her way into the twenty-first century. He could introduce her to everything she'd never had the chance to experience—movies, concerts, the theater, exotic food and drink. They could even take a vacation together, see some of the sights, maybe go to Scotland to visit her old home.

The idea of seeing the world through Cassandra's shining violet eyes made him smile. He'd never been on vacation with a woman before, simply because he'd never met a woman with whom he wanted to spend that much time. It was different with Cassandra. *She* was different . . .

He ran nervous fingers through his hair. Talk about letting his train of thought veer off track! The woman had made it perfectly clear she wanted to be on her own. She'd already told him she planned to get a job and support herself, which was fine. Women should have a career, do whatever they needed to feel fulfilled, just like men. But until she was out from under his roof, Cassandra was his responsibility. And he damned well took care of what was his.

"Hey, you don't have to do that," Rand said, pushing from the doorway. "We have a dishwasher and other conveniences to make housework easier."

She spun around to face him, her cheeks rosy from the steam rising off the water. "I know. But this is simpler. Besides, I'm going to need a few lessons before I'm ready to tackle any of the wondrous machines you own. And won't the electricity be difficult if we start using too many of the appliances at the same time?"

"Not after Monday. I had Duke order a second generator so I could run the office and household items separately from the construction equipment. Once the men figure out what's wrong with the wiring, we shouldn't have any more problems. The new furnace and air-conditioning units should be installed on Monday too. After that, the only inside work will be the wallpaper, paint and floors. Then we start on the outside while Nan finishes the decorating."

"I think everything is very nice right now," she answered. Resting her lower back against the counter, she reached out and touched one of the baby chicks clustered around the larger mother hen. "The house already has warmth and a more homey appeal than it did when I lived here with Colin. I can tell it will be beautiful when it's finished."

A ripple of pride surged through Rand at the thought that she approved. "You really think so? I know what I like, but my taste runs to what's comfortable, not what's in fashion. That's why I hired Nancy. She's the expert."

The setting autumn sun flooded the window over the sink, turning Cassandra's hair a dozen shades of gold. She smiled and he felt the hammering of his heart kick up a notch.

"I approve of quite a few of the things your sister did," she said in a quiet voice. "Were the house mine, I would probably have done much of the same."

Aw, crap, Rand cursed silently. He'd been so bowled over by the idea of his ghost becoming human, he'd forgotten about the house. Technically, his uncle had given it to Cassandra on their wedding day. Never mind that the ceremony hadn't taken place and the deed hadn't been recorded. She had suffered the ultimate injury at Colin MacPherson's hands. Legally, the house belonged to him. Morally, it was hers.

"I wouldn't mind if you wanted some input on the rest of the decorating. There must be a way to express your likes and dislikes without calling attention to . . . telling Nan . . . uh, you know what I mean," he stammered. "At least, until we figure a way to explain your existence."

"Ah," she said with a weary-sounding sigh, "but

there's the rub—informing people the house had a ghost
and it somehow came to life.'' She ran a finger over one
of the brightly painted birdhouses, then picked up a paper
artichoke from the basket of fake vegetables and tossed
it in the air. ''I've been wondering how you were going
to tell people about me.''

''How am I going to tell people about you?'' Great,
now he sounded like a parrot. But how *was* he planning
on introducing Cassandra to the world? ''I hadn't really
given it much thought. I guess I was hoping things would
just sort of fall into place.''

She set the artichoke back in the basket, walked to the
table and fixed him with a questioning gaze. ''I fear
there's quite a bit we need to discuss, but I'm just not
up to it right now. I was hoping you had some ideas as
to where we'd go from here.''

He grinned. ''It's almost time for dinner, and there's
a great Chinese place in Bernardsville I sometimes go
to. After I run a few errands, how about I bring us something to eat?''

''Chinese? Really?'' The way she pressed her hands
together and held them to her shirtfront reminded him of
Melissa when he'd given her that Barbie paraphernalia
for her birthday. ''I can't imagine ... I've never eaten
anything so exotic-sounding before.''

''Chinese it is, then. And if you're very good, I'll treat
you to Italian tomorrow. In the meantime, you can have
some fun with the things I unloaded from the car.''

''Things? For me?''

God, but her smile lit up the room. If he could figure
a way to harness her happiness, he might not even need
a second generator. ''Yes, for you. I went shopping,
remember?''

He waited until Cassandra scampered to his side, then
turned and walked to the foyer with her practically skip-
ping to keep up. After handing her the two bags from

Victoria's Secret, he hefted one of the boxes he'd pilfered
from his sister.

"Nan was donating clothes to a local charity, but she
told me the stuff was practically like new, so I didn't
think you'd mind. The best I could do about shoes was
to buy an assortment of sneakers for you to try on. Once
we know your size, we can go to the store and get whatever you want. I promise."

She glanced down at her chest and quickly crossed her
arms. "Your sister? She looks to be a bit thinner than
me. Are you sure anything of hers will fit?"

"I don't see why not. You're almost the same height.
Nan used to have a really great ... uh ... she's lost a
little—" Feeling red in the face, he shifted the box in
his arms. "Just try them on, okay?"

Looking overwhelmed by his generosity, Cassandra
nodded and followed him up the stairs.

Chapter Fifteen

Cassandra sat on her new bed amid piles of clothes and a heap of silky, shimmering unmentionables. Lingerie, she quickly corrected herself. In twenty-first-century jargon, ladies undergarments were referred to as lingerie. But most of the time the stuff was simply called underwear. And men's personal clothing was known by the same.

The confusing terms were attributed to something Rand called the sexual revolution. But enabling women to dress with more comfort and daring was only a small part of this revolution, as the socially significant event had also given them the right to smoke and drink in public and vote in elections, plus take part in the myriad radical activities Cassandra had viewed on the television.

As far as she could figure, women were also free to wear garments that had at one time been sold exclusively to men. They could purchase gentlemen's sweaters, shirts, jackets, even shoes if they chose.

Before he'd left, the MacPherson had given her a sketchy lesson on her new wardrobe. She'd gotten the gist of his instructions, and even managed to hide a smile

when he turned red-faced while describing the items in
the pretty pink bags. Then he'd promised to return with
linens for her bed and their Chinese dinner. In the meantime, she was supposed to sort through everything and
choose whatever appealed to her.

Eagerly sifting her fingers through the gossamer-like
unmentionables, Cassandra heaved a blissful sigh. The
tiny scraps of material felt positively sinful to the touch.
She couldn't wait to get them next to her skin and experience their full effect. Standing, she slipped out of Rand's
oversized sweat pants and shirt and stepped into a pair
of lacy black panties. After pulling them around her hips,
she set her palms on her face to cool the rush of heat
that shot to her cheeks.

Sweet Mother, she'd seen that the garment was small,
but this was ... was scandalous. The back half barely
covered her bottom and the front didn't even reach her
navel. But the satiny material felt wonderful resting
against her body, and walking in the scanty bit of lace
was much easier than walking in her bulky pantaloons.
It was obvious why women of today enjoyed this less-
constricting lingerie, even if the filmy stuff made her feel
naked as a newborn lamb.

The next article of apparel looked a lot more convoluted. After a few seconds of hemming and hawing, Rand
had explained that the stretchy straps, lace and wire were
made to go around her arms and chest in order to support
her bosom. But she was skeptical, as the brassiere—
bra—didn't look substantial enough to hold a pair of
good-sized dinner rolls, never mind the breasts of an
amply-endowed woman.

Once she'd examined the delicate yet daunting-looking
garment from all sides, she thrust her arms through the
straps and settled herself into the rounded pockets. Oops,
she thought with a giggle, this couldn't be right. Not only
was she barely able to get the plastic pieces at the front

to join—there was no way she was going to squeeze herself inside these paltry cuplike sacks.

Several tries later, she slipped into a beautiful ice-blue contraption that fit the way she supposed it should. The tag read 36C, so she guessed she'd found her size, and made a mental note to inform Rand.

Digging through the pile of minuscule pantaloons, she grabbed a pair in the same pretty blue and exchanged them for the black ones. After she sorted out all the properly sized garments and set them aside, she placed the rest of the underwear back in the bag so Rand could return the articles to the store.

Now it was time to go through the clothing. First she separated the jackets, sweaters and blouses, then the trousers from the skirts and dresses. Reminding herself she had to forget about modesty if she planned to dress like a modern woman, she determinedly tugged a pair of dark blue pants up her legs. Struggling with the sliding metal tab and button, she stooped and bent until the trousers—jeans—gloved her calves, thighs and hips in the same way she'd seen them fit women on the television.

After a bit more stretching, she decided the jeans were actually comfortable and set aside the other three pair. Fifteen minutes later, she'd accumulated a stack of sweaters in a variety of colors, two blouses, a jacket made of supple tan leather and a skirt. The remainder of the clothes were too small across her bosom, and two of the skirts were so short, she was positive that if she bent over she would expose herself to all so bold as to bother looking.

She pulled one of the sweaters over her head, a lovely gray wool that felt like the softest of lamb's wool, and returned everything she didn't want to the box. Then she placed the bag of lingerie on top, hoisted the carton in her arms and made her way to the foyer. Setting the box near the door, she peered through the darkness to see if Rand was coming up the drive.

Disappointment washed through her when she realized he still wasn't home. It had been reassuring to talk with Edith and Irene, even if they had yet to find a way to assist with her problems. Their warm camaraderie and pointed observations had enlightened and comforted her, giving her a sense of belonging in this strange new world.

But it was different with the MacPherson. Rand's easy banter and sometimes frustrating commentaries, coupled with his warm-eyed gazes and casual touches, made her feel truly alive for the first time in a century.

And the things he'd done to her in his bed . . . well, there were no words adequate to describe how that had made her feel.

She turned on a battery-powered lamp and carried it to the staircase. Sitting on the bottom step, she glared deliberately at the door and willed his footsteps to sound on the porch. Someday, she vowed, he would see her not as a freak of nature or a debt to be repaid, but a woman. The woman he was destined to spend the rest of his life with.

The woman who was his own true love.

Her stomach rumbled and she suppressed another giggle. Human for only a day, and she was already taking for granted the normal cravings that made a body real. So far this afternoon she'd fiddled with the telephone, turned on all the kitchen appliances, inspected the washer and dryer, and drunk an ice-cold container of some sweet, fizzy concoction she'd found in the refrigerator. She'd even stood at the back door and inhaled huge breaths of crisp outside air.

But sadly, when she made another attempt at crossing the threshold, she'd found that nothing had changed. She still disappeared. She was still a victim of the curse.

Walking to the kitchen, she took the shopping bag full of books from the cupboard under the island and carried it and the lantern to her room. Without a closet or some kind of cabinet to hide them in, the only place she thought they might be safe was under the bed. So she got on her hands and knees and pushed the bag to the very center, back toward the headboard. Then she walked around the room and scrutinized from all angles until satisfied that unless Rand got down on all fours, it would be impossible for him to see the books.

Before she could decide on her next step, a deep voice pulled her from her reverie. "Cassandra! I'm home."

She raced down the stairs onto the balcony and watched Rand struggle with the door. A half-minute later, she took a sack from his hand and toted it to the kitchen while he followed, his arms filled with additional packages.

After setting the parcels on the table, he shrugged out of his jacket and hung it on the back of a chair. Finally, he flashed straight white teeth. "Hey, turn around."

She spun in a circle, almost afraid to hear his opinion. But Rand's bright-eyed gaze caused her heart to hammer hard in her chest. Did his look of blatant approval mean she resembled a woman of today, or did it hide other, more intimate thoughts? Hands at her sides, she did another quick pirouette, then waited for his verdict.

"Very nice. Nancy will be happy to know her clothes are being put to good use."

"Oh, but they didn't all fit," she answered, secretly thrilled by his words. "I left the rest in a box by the front door, as well as the under ... um ... other things that need returning."

"No problem. There's plenty of time to shop." He walked to the island and began unpacking a half dozen containers.

"All of this is for one dinner?" she asked, thinking of the difficulty she'd had pulling up the metal tab on her jeans. "Do you eat like this at every meal?"

"Hardly, but I wanted you to try a little of everything. Kung Pao chicken, moo shoo pork, hot and sour soup, shrimp toast, spareribs, egg rolls, fried and white rice. If you think this is too much, just wait until you see what a grocery store has to offer.''

He opened the cartons while she brought silverware and plates to the table, then picked up a serving spoon. ''I don't know about you, but I'm starving.''

Overwhelmed by the meal laid before her, Cassandra chose to ignore his remark about visiting the grocery store and his promise to take her shopping. She'd cross that bridge when she had to. Right now the open containers were sending a wonderful aroma into the room, making her mouth water and her stomach growl. ''There's enough here to feed an army. Why did you go to all the expense? I could have made—''

''Not tonight, you couldn't. We're celebrating. It's not every day a ghost becomes human, you know. Grab a plate and dig in before it gets cold. We need to get you settled. Tomorrow I'm taking you to see the sights.''

Cassandra stood on the far side of her bed, unsure what was expected of her. Though it didn't seem to bother the MacPherson to be tackling such a menial task as making up her bed, the intimate act had her insides churning and her face hot as an oven. Fairly certain it wasn't polite for her to stand immobile while the man acted as her personal maid, she grabbed a section of the stretchy white coverlet.

''What's this bit of linen called again?'' she asked, trying to sound all business. Briskly, she tucked the cover tight under a corner of the bed.

''A mattress pad. Years ago, when I first moved into my own apartment, both my mother and Nancy told me I had to have one, so I figured you should too.''

Rand unfolded a set of white satin sheets and snapped open the one that fit directly onto the mattress. The sheets looked so cool and silky, they made Cassandra yearn to flop on the bed and float for the next hundred years. "Gram would have been thrilled to sleep on something this fine," she confided, running a hand over the beautiful fabric. " 'Twill be like sleeping on a cloud."

"I ... um ... like the feel of them myself," Rand muttered as they finished their task. Then he tossed a blanket the color of freshly churned butter over the sheets and tucked the bottom tight. "I ... um ... I read somewhere women liked this kind of thing. Once you get to a department store and see your choices, you might want something different. A person's sleeping space is their own private domain, if you know what I mean."

Finally, he unzipped a large clear bag, pulled out a fluffy comforter embellished with a dainty pattern of yellow, creamy white and pale orange tulips, and let it fall gently onto the blanket.

"These linens must have cost a fortune," she said, sliding a matching cover over one of her new pillows. After setting the puffy bolster at the head of the bed, she stepped back to admire their handiwork. "I expect you to keep a tab, MacPherson. I don't plan on being a charity case forever."

"Cassandra." His outthrust jaw reminded her of the way her younger brother Linus used to hold himself when he set his mind on solving a problem. "I thought I made myself clear. You're welcome to live here until ... well, for as long as you want. But you're not going to find a job until I figure a way to get you a social security card. Let's just take this one step at a time."

Disgruntled, she folded her arms. "I'm only reminding you that I'll be taking care of myself as soon as I'm able, that's all. Now, if you don't mind, I have to ... I need to use the—oh, bother," she sputtered. "I have to change my clothes and take care of things in your privy."

Rand couldn't help but grin at her embarrassment. Until

he understood what she meant. Hell, there wasn't a working bathroom in the place, except for the one off his
bedroom. Even the men used the port-o-potty at the back
of the house. And he sure couldn't ask her to do her
business out there, now, could he? What was the woman
supposed to do, wash up in the kitchen sink?

Nope, they'd have to share the bathroom in the master
suite like two grown-ups. One male and one very *female*
grown-up, he reminded himself.

He threw her a curt nod. "No problem. I have stuff I
can do in the kitchen. Feel free to bring your things into
my room. I'll find a drawer you can use until you choose
your own furniture."

Shoulders thrust back, Cassandra seemed to stiffen at
the offer. Without answering, she walked to a corner of
the room, bent down, and rifled through the bag from
Victoria's Secret. Rand's tongue stuck to the roof of his
mouth as he took in her perfectly shaped rear and long,
coltish legs. God, the woman was built. How in the hell
was he supposed to keep his hands to himself, never mind
control Mr. Happy, while the two of them were practically
cohabiting?

Crap! He'd rank lower than pond scum on the food
chain if he acted on any of the thoughts simmering in
his brain at this moment. After a century of nonexistence,
Cassandra had just found her humanity. The last thing
she needed was a descendant of the guy who'd murdered
her pawing at her like a sex-obsessed caveman. The least
he could do was let her get used to her situation and learn
how to function in the twenty-first century before he clued
her in to the fact he was attracted to her in *that* way.

And God help him, he was attracted to her. Every time
he recalled the way she'd jump-started his morning, he
realized she set his libido to humming like no other
woman before. Problem was, he had no idea how the

heck he was supposed to tell her so and hold himself in check at the same time.

He shoved his hands into his back pockets and made for the door, determined to give her a little space. "I'll be in the kitchen. If you need anything—towels, soap, shampoo, just holler."

Clutching one of the satin sleepshirts to her remarkable breasts, she turned to him. "I think I'm capable of finding what I need, thank you."

"Yeah, well, just remember, if there's something you want that I don't have, we'll get it tomorrow. I meant what I said, Cassandra. I'll see to it you're taken care of."

Quick as a speed skater, she crossed the room. Skidding on the wool socks he'd given her, she stopped a mere inch from his chest. "And I told you I don't need your charity."

As if she'd just realized she was in his face, she took a small step backward. "Besides, we don't even know if I'll be capable of traipsing through department and grocery stores tomorrow. Use your head, man. For all we know, I might wake up to find I've returned to my ghostly self. I don't think you should be making plans until we're certain this transformation is permanent."

Not permanent!

The compulsion to reach out and drive away Cassandra's fears hit Rand like a tidal wave. She was his, goddammit, and nothing was going to take her away from him. Before he knew it, his fingers were wrapped around her upper arms, the nightshirt a crush of satin between them.

Cassandra's eyes, dark as pansies in the dim lantern light, grew huge. Aware he might be frightening her, he loosened his grip and ran his palms to her shoulders. She sighed, soft as a summer breeze and twice as sweet, and he felt the ache inside of her arrow straight to his gut.

Why didn't he have the sense to see that she was terrified? How else could she possibly feel after everything she'd been through over the past few weeks?

Exercising control he didn't realize he possessed, he shuffled closer and moved his arms to her back, determined to offer comfort. She stood rigid, until he whispered in her ear. "I'm not going to make you do anything you aren't one hundred percent happy doing, Cassandra. I promise."

She seemed to wilt at the sound of his words, melting into his chest on a ragged sigh. Awkwardly, he patted her as if he were comforting Melissa. Only she didn't feel a thing like his four-year-old niece. Breasts, round and firm and warm, branded him with the reality of her presence. Her pelvis rested almost level with his zipper while their bodies touched, but not close enough. Her legs parted and he settled against her, unable to resist the lure of showing her where he wanted to be.

She shuddered and he stepped farther into her heat, nestling against the juncture of her thighs. Somehow, he'd managed to maneuver her into the wall. He thought about backing off. He knew he should leave her be, but his body acted as if it had disconnected from his brain.

"Cassandra, I don't want to frighten you, but you have to know that I . . . I'm attracted to you."

Her chin shot up a notch as her long-lashed eyes locked with his. Their deep purple hue softened to violet as understanding slowly sunk in. She smiled, showing small, even teeth. "I can tell that you are, MacPherson. So how do you propose we proceed from here?"

Rand sucked in a breath. God, she was perfect in his arms. He leaned forward an inch, then another, until his lips covered her sassy mouth. Incredibly, she opened to him, offering herself like a flower to a honeybee. And he drank his fill, taking small sips at first, then longer, deeper, more desperate gulps.

Dizzy with the taste of her, he rested his palms against the wall and caged her between his forearms as his lips continued to plunder hers. Memories of their morning encounter inched into his consciousness and reminded him of how fantastic it had been to hold her, touch her in all the right places. . . .

"Take me to bed, MacPherson," Cassandra murmured as she threaded her fingers through his hair. " 'Tis time to make me your own."

Make me your own?

Rand froze in place. Staring into her dreamy eyes and kiss-swollen lips, he was tempted to toss aside his scruples and do just that. Then common sense took hold and he jumped back a foot. What the heck were they . . . was *he* doing?

"Um . . . look, I know you think . . . that is . . . I do want you. I mean, what guy in his right mind wouldn't? But this just isn't right."

Cassandra blew a curl off her forehead, her gaze as sharp as a dagger. "Isn't right? That wasn't the way it felt to me."

"Cassandra, don't get me wrong. Any guy would—"

"Any guy?" she spat out as she placed her hands on her hips. "You think I would act like this . . . offer myself to just any man?"

"Well, no. Of course not," he stammered. "I only meant you don't want to jump into bed with the first man who tells you he's attracted to you . . . do you?"

She bent to retrieve her clothes, and he took another step back, fearful she'd draw blood with the sharpness of her stare. Why couldn't she see that he was only trying to think of what was best for her?

"Look, you don't understand. It's not right for me to take advantage when you can't possibly know what you want, not really. Once you're out in the world, you're going to meet lots of guys. I . . . we shouldn't be doing this until you're sure of things.''

''Is that the way you see me? You think I'm such an addlepated innocent I'd jump into bed with the first man who waggled a finger in my direction?'' She lifted her chin and he had the good sense to let her pass.

''Yes . . . no . . . I mean, that's my point. You haven't met anyone else. It's not right for me to come on to you like this.''

Spinning on her heel, she faced him squarely. ''See here, MacPherson. My body may have been incapacitated for the past one hundred years, but my mind's been working just fine . . . and it knows what it wants. I've asked you to take me to bed twice now, and both times you've refused. I'm thinking the next time you're feeling amorous, it's you who'll need to do the askin'. And don't be so certain I'll be willin' to say yes.''

Rand tossed and turned on the bed, unable to settle down for the night. The sound of Cassandra pacing overhead, her muffled footsteps counting out a muted rhythm, had him wide awake, frustrated, and . . . edgy?

Yep, edgy was definitely the word for his condition, he decided with a groan of disgust. What else could he call it when his fingers itched to touch the satin of her skin and his mouth still tingled at the memory of her lips? Or, worse, when he could still feel Mr. Happy semi-awake and throbbing against his thigh?

Christ, was there any single bigger idiot on the planet? Here he was, living in a house with a beautiful, exciting woman who had offered herself to him not once, but twice, and he had turned her down *both* times. No doubt about it, he was a grade-A noble-to-the-point-of-lunacy fool.

Sitting up on the side of the bed, he swiped both hands across his face. Okay, so he and Cassandra had a few problems they needed to iron out. None of them was insurmountable. Except, of course, for the fact that she'd been a ghost less than twenty-four hours ago. And as far as he could see, that glitch had already taken care of itself.

All he had to do was come up with a logical way to introduce her to his family and ease her into the world. After that, the rest would be a piece of cake. Cassandra could become a part of society, find a career and make a new life. She'd be free of her past, and so would he. Then, maybe, if she still wanted to take a chance on building a relationship with him . . .

Uh-uh-ah . . . Let's not forget the part about the men in your family being unlucky in love, a rude voice sing-songed from inside his head.

Oh. Yeah. Somewhere along the line he'd managed to forget that pesky sticking point. And although he had only his father's word on it, and it might not even be true, did he really want to take the chance of getting involved with Cassandra, maybe have her fall in love with him and then blow it, like all the rest of the men in his family had done? If that happened, her life would be a mess all over again, and he'd be the second MacPherson male to see her hurt.

Trouble was, he couldn't imagine himself helping her put her life in order and then standing idly by and watching her go out with other men.

Coming to his feet, Rand walked in an impatient circle as he pushed his feelings aside. Right now he had to find a way to give Cassandra a normal life. His stepfather was an attorney. Maybe he could ask Harry, in a vague sort of way of course, about the ins and outs of coming up with an identity for a person who didn't exist. If that didn't work, he'd talk to Duke, who often joked about the fact he had a broad range of family connections, most of whom lived in Jersey City. Rand had always heard it said that for a price you could find someone willing to do just about anything in Jersey City.

All they needed was a way to make Cassandra legal and the rest of their problems would take care of themselves. She was human now, and he was pretty certain nothing could change that. And if something did happen to threaten her existence, he'd damn well find a way to take care of it.

Tomorrow morning he'd sit down with her and discuss things rationally, explain why they needed to take one step at a time. Communication and understanding were the tools to a successful friendship, which is what he hoped they could have. After what his uncle had done, he refused to take the chance of seeing her hurt again.

Feeling a world better about the scenario, he headed for the bathroom. A long, hot shower would take the edge off and get him to sleep in no time. It was just what he needed to end his day.

Cassandra wore a path in her bedroom floor, too frustrated to settle down and sleep. The absolute gall of the man, to think she was so naive she didn't know her own desires. Who did Rand think he was, making that kind of decision for her? She was a grown woman. She'd been on her own for a century, longer if one counted the time spent on the ship when she'd traveled to America. She certainly knew her own mind by now.

And his perplexing speech about wanting her to meet other men—well, that was just so much sheep dip. His kisses had been demanding, his tongue as clever as Cupid's own arrow. He admitted he was attracted to her. She'd felt the impressive proof of his arousal through both their trousers. According to the television, any man who was that taken with a woman wanted her in his bed. At least, it always seemed to be that simple when she'd watched those daily stories called soap operas.

Instead, Rand had let her humiliate herself by practically begging him to have his way with her. Then he'd left her flapping in the wind like yesterday's wash. At this rate, it would be years before she could convince the man they belonged together ... years before they were free of the curse.

She plopped onto the window seat and rested her elbows on the ledge. The moon, a smiling crescent of white, hung over the pond, shedding little light on her quandary. The sigh she heaved fogged the windowpane, reminding her she had other problems to consider.

She was human, but not quite. She loved a man who pitied her for her predicament and was too noble, or was it too bullheaded, to take her to his bed. And if he found out the truth—that she'd placed a curse on his male ancestors that had proven true for the past century—he would never accept her as his own true love.

How could he, when she'd been the one responsible for his parents' divorce and Rand's own inability to find someone willing to share his life?

Oh, but this business of being human was a terrible state of affairs. Things had been so much simpler when she was a ghost. Aimless existence had been easy. The aches were less sharp, the loneliness and longing more bearable. After one hundred years, she'd forgotten how painful it could be to love and not be loved in return.

Sniffing, she swiped a hand under her nose, thinking a long, hard cry would do her a world of good. But when the tears refused to flow, she realized she didn't even have that small bit of humanity for comfort.

Tea. She needed a cup of tea with a splash of milk and a bit of honey. The drink always made her sleepy when she'd been a child. If nothing else, it would soothe her nerves and calm her heaving stomach.

Wearing nothing but wool socks and a satin sleepshirt that came to the tops of her thighs, Cassandra crept down the stairs. When she arrived on the balcony and heard the shower running, she stood and gazed in the direction of Rand's bedroom. How nice, she thought as she glared a hole through the door, that the pompous ass felt relaxed enough to go about his business and shower, while she'd done nothing but pace for the past hour.

She should have coshed him on the head when he'd turned down her offer. Better yet, she should have given him the hives or turned him into a flea or ... Well, she could have done all those things—if she still had her powers.

And who said she didn't? she wondered, tapping a finger to her chin. As a ghost, she'd been fairly successful at creating a few diversions with the workmen and the MacPherson too. Even though Madame Ragnar and Irene didn't think her powers were intact, she had hopes they still were.

And wasn't the heart of casting a spell the belief that it would come true?

If the man wanted a shower, who was she to begrudge him one? Of course, a good washing didn't have to soothe or warm. Sometimes an ice-cold dunking could give a body fortitude. And didn't her gram always say cold water cleared a muddled head?

Smiling slyly, Cassandra fisted her hands at her sides and pictured the shower stall in her mind. Concentrating, she imagined the knobs turning ... slowly turning ...

"Yeeooowww! Holy Mother of—"

Rand's curse-filled shout rang from the bath, tore through the bedroom and echoed into the hall. Slapping her hands over her mouth, Cassandra skipped down the stairs and into the kitchen, her conscience only slightly tweaked.

After all, if ever a man needed to have his head cleared, it was the MacPherson.

Chapter Sixteen

Singing softly to herself, Cassandra took a mug from the cupboard, filled it with water and set it in the microwave. While the machine hummed, she found a box of tea to her liking and chose a bag. The sound of the upstairs water pipes went quiet, which brought a fleeting grin to her lips.

Right now the MacPherson was probably shivering into his pajamas and hopping under the bedcovers to keep warm. Which was exactly what he deserved after making her so angry.

Drat the man's noble ways and handsome good looks. Why did he have to be so engaging, so ... so caring? Why couldn't he be like the rest of the men she'd seen on the television, the ones on those afternoon stories who damned propriety and simply took what they wanted from their women?

Why did *he* have to be her own true love?

She fisted her hands on the edge of the sink and gazed out at the back of the house. The same sliver of moon she'd stared at earlier hung in the star-studded sky, leering as if it had a secret to guard, or maybe knew something about her predicament. Though it heartened her to find that her powers were still in force, the idea she'd let herself use them in anger shamed her.

The last time she'd been so reckless, she'd caused the ruin of a half dozen innocent lives. But without the curse she would probably not have turned into a spirit, which meant she wouldn't have met Rand MacPherson—surely the best and the worst thing that had happened to her in her one hundred years plus of existence.

Still, she had to keep in mind that one of her goals was to fit into the twenty-first century as a modern woman, as well as remember she was supposed to keep the fact that she was a witch hidden. Practicing the magical arts definitely marked her as different. If Rand found out she was a witch, he might begin to suspect other things. Things that would lead him to Colin, then to the curse and, finally, his own sorry situation. Once he put all the pieces together, his noble caring would change quickly enough. He might even go so far as to banish her from the house, and then where would she be?

So, as did the moon, she had to keep her secrets. She had to be careful and not let her frustration take her down a road from which she could never return. She had to find a way to make Rand say the words out loud, to tell her he loved her, without using witchcraft or subterfuge. Somehow, he had to recognize the fact he was her own true love.

The microwave rang and she snapped to attention. Opening the door, she dropped the teabag into the water and set the timer for another thirty seconds. She walked to the refrigerator, took out the milk and set it on the island, then pressed her fingers to her temples. Since coming to the kitchen, she'd begun to experience one of the more distasteful sides of being human—a headache. If she could find a bit of honey, it might help to soothe the niggling ache . . . and her temper.

Ignoring the timer's second ring, she searched the upper cupboards for a jar of the golden syrup, then decided to explore the lower cabinets. Hands on hips, she bent and peered into the shelves under the sink. As if on a mission, she moved to the next cupboard, then the next. Earlier, the MacPherson had given her paper and pen to write down what she wanted. Obviously, honey needed to be at the very top of the list.

Criminy, thought Rand. Now the friggin' plumbing was going haywire on him. Until then, the pipes were the one thing in the house that hadn't given him a problem. His uncle had used top-grade copper tubing and done a good job with the connections and joints. If the plumbing needed to be replaced, he'd really have a situation on his hands.

Fighting goose bumps, he stepped into a pair of cotton pajama bottoms and grabbed a lantern. Everything was quiet on the top floor, so Cassandra must finally have fallen asleep. Poor kid, she was probably exhausted. Today had been a regular roller-coaster ride. He'd been a jerk to take advantage of her and get them both worked up, then encourage her to walk away as if she hadn't mattered.

But if she knew how much she *did* matter to him, she never would have left. And he wouldn't have been able to resist another assault to his senses. One more look from her pansy-purple eyes, one more stroke of her fingers through his hair or kiss from those full tempting lips, and he would have gone straight over the edge.

Just thinking about Cassandra had him itchy all over for the second time that night. Between her and the quirky plumbing, he needed something to warm him up and calm him down at the same time. He didn't have any decaf coffee, but maybe a shot of whiskey would help.

He tiptoed into the hall and down the stairs. Outside, the wind whistled an eerie moan, reminding him winter weather was definitely on its way. The triple-hung windows were doing a decent job of keeping the wind out. If they could get the electricity to cooperate, the rest of the remodeling would be a piece of cake.

All of a sudden he remembered this coming Thursday was Thanksgiving, a time for family get-togethers and the making of holiday plans. Cassandra wouldn't be ready to eat turkey with his family, but with a little luck and some help from his stepfather, she might be able to join them for Christmas. He needed to make an appointment with Harry to discuss her situation, but first he had to come up with the solution to his most puzzling problem: a plausible story about who Cassandra was and how she'd arrived here.

Working through a jumble of thoughts, he strode past the butler's pantry and into the kitchen, where he was surprised to see the glow from another lantern lighting his way. Ready to curse out loud at the fact he'd already spent a fortune on batteries for the darned things, he came to an abrupt stop in the doorway when he found the reason for the light.

He blinked as he sucked in a breath. There was Cassandra, bent at the waist and bathed in a soft shadow of gold, rustling through his cupboards. And from what he could tell, she wasn't wearing a stitch under her peach-colored sleepshirt. All he could see were his wool socks scrunched down around her ankles, the backs of her long, shapely legs and her bottom, bare and beckoning in the lantern's dim glow.

Wow, he thought, swallowing a whistle of admiration. Just—wow. He cleared his throat and she spun around to face him, taking away the dynamite view.

"Lord in heaven, you scared the life out of me," she sputtered, placing a hand over her heart. "Where did you learn to sneak up on a body like that? One would think you were a bloody *buachailleen.*''

Rand crossed to the island and set his lantern next to hers, banishing the memory of what he'd just been privileged to see. ''A what?''

''A *buachailleen,*'' she said with a grin. ''Fey creatures we Scots look upon as totally lacking in manners. When they set their minds to it, the wee beasties are known to hide the biscuits and make the cows go dry. And they're very quiet. Once, when Ian was tending our sheep in a faraway field, a *buachailleen* sneaked up on him and stole his jam and buttered bread right from under his nose. Then the rude creature soured his milk and left him with no lunch a'tall. 'Twas a terrible afternoon for the poor lad.''

''Mythical beasties.'' Rand shook his head. ''And I suppose you believe in alien abductions? Or maybe hob-goblins and witches? Don't you know so much of that stuff is just plain crap?''

She straightened her shoulders and quickly looked away. ''I'm simply saying there are things that exist in the world, magical things if you will, that most of us find difficult to understand. And those who are blessed with a ready imagination and an insightful mind are more able to accept them.''

''Ready imagination? Insightful mind!'' Hell, he had an imagination, and there wasn't anything dull about his mind either. His gray matter might be a little foggy right now, but he'd believed in *her,* hadn't he? Of course, the fact that he'd grown up listening to his mother ramble for hours about all kinds of paranormal hoo-ha had probably helped. His mother had always—

Rand huffed out a breath. Unh-unh. No way was he going to acknowledge the fact he had Irene and her goofy ideas to thank for his immediate acceptance of Cassandra's ghostly form. If he had his way, the two of them would never even meet.

"Hey, I resent those words. I don't know about the rest of the world, but I conceded you were real from the moment I knew you were around, remember? So don't try to lump me in with everybody else."

Cassandra sighed, a sound so pitiful it made him ache to enfold her in his arms. Definitely not a good idea.

"If you will remember, I didn't exactly give you a choice. But I do think we need more people who believe in things unknown. Without the power of belief, we may lose everything whimsical we have left in the world. Thank goodness for your mother and her friend."

"My mother?" Now Cassandra was being downright spooky. If he didn't know better, he'd think the woman could read his mind. "How do you know what my mother or her loony friends think?"

Rand thought he heard her gasp, but her face was shrouded in shadow. She sidled to the refrigerator and opened the door. "I ... um ... overheard you talking about her to your sister and the Duke. And I saw her the afternoon she brought that psychic for a surprise visit. It was quite obvious she believes in things otherworldly. Now, let's change the subject, shall we, seeing as this is a topic I don't think we'll agree on."

As she passed, he caught her delicate scent, the same herbal fragrance he always seemed to experience when in her presence. Since the last thing he wanted to think about was his mother or that Ragweed woman, he let the pleasing aroma carry him back to the up-close and personal conversation he and Cassandra had shared in her room just a few hours ago. Coupled with the memory of this morning's encounter, he was beginning to get hot and bothered all over again.

She bent down to search the fridge, rewarding him with the outline of a taut, naked thigh and the curve of one bountiful breast. "What are you looking for?" he asked as he felt himself grow hard and heavy.

"Honey."

"Honey." He gave himself a mental kick at the way he'd made the word sound like an endearment.

She shut the door and threw him a scalding glare. "For my tea, MacPherson. It needs sweetening and I thought it might make the sleeping more bearable."

Rand's mind wandered into dangerous territory, and he roped it back with a jerk of his head. "That's why I'm down here. I . . . um . . . couldn't fall asleep either. I don't think I have any honey. How about I find us some whiskey instead?"

She placed a hand on her hip. "Are you trying to tell me you have a bit of the Highland's finest about?"

"You mean scotch? Yeah, I'm pretty sure I have a bottle. Hang on a second." He skirted the island in the hope she wouldn't see his awkward condition. Opening a cabinet over the microwave, he took down a bottle of his best single malt. "Here you go. And if you don't mind, I'll join you."

Cassandra came toward him slowly, as if she were having second thoughts. "I don't need much, just a wee drop or two," she said in a hushed voice. "It's been a long while since I've had anything in the way of spirits. Oops." She giggled. "That sounded a bit strange, didn't it?"

He poured a splash into her upraised cup, then filled his tumbler halfway. "A little. It's still mind-boggling, when I think about it. I can only guess how you've been feeling."

Settling back against the counter, she sipped slowly at her tea. "Ah, but that's tasty," she murmured, still not giving him a straight answer.

"Cassandra. How are you feeling? Really?"

She shifted her gaze from the teacup to the kitchen

window. "I'm not certain. Confused mostly, but sometimes when I dwell on it, I'm simply terrified. The idea I could wake tomorrow morning and find myself a ghost again— When I get those thoughts, I'm so frightened, I want to crawl back into my closet and never come out."

She gave a half-smile. "Still, I'm happy to have this small bit of humanity for however long the Good Lord chooses to grant it to me."

Rand shuddered inside when he saw her hesitant grin and trembling lower lip. There had to be something he could do to comfort her, to show her he understood. Instead of acting on the thought, he swallowed half of his drink in one desperate gulp, welcoming the line of fire that arrowed to his gut. "I'm sure you're going to stay this way. I mean, why would you change back? What would make that happen?"

She took another sip of tea before she answered. "How can I know? I haven't the slightest idea how I came to be a spirit in the first place, except for the dying, of course, and there's pitiful little I remember of that." She bowed her head and concentrated on her mug. "Since I have no idea what brought me back to life, there's no way to tell what might change me back again."

Blindsided with the idea Cassandra could be right about her mortality, Rand's palms began to sweat. What if her worst fear did come true? What if she changed back into a spirit and he never got a second chance to hold her? Could he live with the knowledge he would never feel the satin of her skin or the taste of her lips for the rest of his life?

Like a tidal wave, the urge to bury himself inside of her, to take her right there on the kitchen table, washed away every one of his nice-guy promises. He didn't want to be noble. And he didn't give two nickels about his family's so-called run of bad luck. Cassandra had already suffered at the hands of one unscrupulous MacPherson male. He wasn't like his uncle; he never would be. More important, if he had straight the facts of her life, she was a virgin. No matter how much the idea of a fast tumble appealed to him, she deserved better than mindless sex on a kitchen table.

He smacked his glass down hard on the counter. The sharp *thwack* startled her, and she clutched the mug to her chest with an intake of breath. "What is it? What's wrong?"

Gently, he took the cup from her hands and set it on the tiles. Drawing closer, he traced the delicate curve of her jaw with his fingers. He owed it to her to give each of them one night of passion, one night they both could look back on and remember, just in case reality crashed down around their heads.

Gently, he stroked her lower lip with his thumb.

With an eyebrow raised in suspicion, she stood statue still and allowed him to run his hands to the nape of her neck. "I don't like the looks of this, MacPherson. Dinna I tell you the next time, you would have to ask?"

"You did." He bent down and brushed her mouth with his. "And I'm asking. Please, Cassandra, let me give you what you . . . what we both want."

Rand kissed her again, long and slow and sweet. She melted into him, and a sigh escaped her, then a desolate whimper when he pulled back and studied her face.

"So, you've finally decided to have your way with me?"

The look in her eyes, so eager and filled with hope, set his heart to hammering. Hell, it made him think he could conquer the world. Reaching down, he placed one arm around her back and the other under her thighs and lifted her against his chest. "I have."

* * *

Cassandra lay atop the MacPherson's oversized bed, basking in the fire that glowed from Rand's eyes. The incorrigible man had just carried her up the staircase and set her on his mattress as if she weighed no more than a bag of feathers. Incredibly, he wasn't even winded. And he was staring at her so intensely, she thought she might burst into flames.

"You're a surprise, Randall MacPherson," she teased, raising her arms over her head. "I dinna think you had it in you."

His face filled with pride and a kind of gentle amusement as he knelt to lie beside her. "I lift weights, Ms. Kinross. And you're a tidy package, for all your height and impressive . . . charms."

She grinned as she laid a palm against his cheek. "You're an admirable package yourself. And one I've been waiting to unwrap for quite a while now," she answered honestly. "I'm not ashamed to admit I'm eager to learn what happens next."

Stretching out alongside of her, Rand placed a hand on her waist, then moved it over her rib cage to rest under her breast. "This," he whispered, nibbling a trail of fiery kisses along the crest of her cheek. "And this." Pressing his lips to hers, he cupped the sensitive mound and caressed slowly through the silky fabric.

Cassandra tasted the whiskey on his tongue, so much more potent because it was a part of him, and opened to his sensuous onslaught. Her nipples grew hard and aching as his fingers tugged and released. He moved his hand to a shirt button and deepened the kiss, filling her with a strong, slow burning.

Cool air danced over her collarbone, then her chest and her belly as, one by one, she felt the buttons separate and the nightshirt fall open to his seeking hand. His mouth captured a breast and sucked slowly, drawing her into him until she thought she would faint from the pleasure spiraling through her body.

Lovely, she thought as she made a purring noise in the back of her throat. If she had her way, she'd see the man canonized as the world's first living saint.

With each slide of the satiny material, his mouth moved downward to place a heated kiss on her sensitized skin, until finally, inch by inch, he branded a trail to the juncture of her thighs.

"You are so beautiful," she heard him murmur as he ran a hand from her hip to her calf and back again. Slowly, he plied his coaxing fingers, until he'd parted her thighs and . . .

Cassandra stiffened from head to toe. My God, what was the man thinking! Digging her heels into the mattress, she snapped her knees together so hard they cracked. A tickle of warmth brushed her belly. Then she heard a muffled rumble of laughter.

"I'm not sure this is a'tall what the Good Lord intended," she gasped. "And I don't find it a bit funny."

His hand cupped her woman's mound, sending a delicious tingling through her veins. "Cassandra, this is exactly what the Good Lord intended," he said in a voice filled with patience. "Men and women who are attracted to each other take pleasure in each other's bodies . . . and they want to give pleasure as well, trust me."

What he was saying might very well be true, but it dinna make what he was doing any less shocking. Resisting the urge to open to him in every way possible, she couldn't help asking what she deemed the big question. "So tell me, MacPherson, how many others have you done this with?"

Rand grew quiet, his breathing slow and soft against her thigh. Seconds passed before he answered. "Right now I wish to God I could give you another answer,

Cassandra, but I have to be honest. I've been intimate with quite a few women, but not in a very long while.''

His response was a small comfort she would ponder later. At the moment, all she could manage was to swear a silent oath: Once the man realized they belonged together, he would never have the need to take another woman to his bed.

Her silence made him bold. She felt his clever fingers move lower, until one was right inside of her, rubbing and circling and turning her bones to water. As if they had a mind of their own, her legs fell open. Frantically, she grabbed at the comforter with both hands. ''I'm still not certain this is something I—''

''Let me take care of you, Cassandra.'' His breath feathered her hip. ''You said yourself you feared waking one morning and finding you'd become a spirit again. Let me show you how wonderful it can be to feel and act like a human, even if it's for only one night.''

Carefully, Rand moved to lie between her knees. When he slid his palms under her bottom, she gave an involuntary moan. Still unsure of the idea, she bucked when he lifted her to his mouth. His tongue touched her and she fisted her fingers in his hair. Though what he was doing made not a bit of sense, what he'd just said made all the sense in the world.

His tongue continued its swirling assault, and she sobbed out a cry. Warmed by the quivering waves of sensation coiling and unfurling from somewhere deep inside, she decided it just might be time to put herself in his hands and show a little faith. If the morning would be her undoing, she would have this night to remember forever.

A whimper escaped her as he laved a spot she'd only dreamed might exist. The colors of her beloved Highlands swirled before her eyes, all purple and gold and green, as she gave herself up to the incredible sensations. Seconds later, a brilliant tremor tripped wildly through her veins, and she arched from the bed with a ragged scream of fulfillment.

Floating back to the mattress on a breathy sigh, she opened her eyes to find Rand grinning with boyish satisfaction. Somehow, he'd escaped from his pajama bottom and was kneeling between her thighs. Tentatively, she reached out and grasped the shaft of steely velvet rising from between his hips.

" 'Tis my turn," she murmured, shocked by her boldness, "to do a bit of the same. I want to learn how to pleasure you as well."

He groaned as he dropped to his hands. Lifting her arms, she pressed him to her breasts. Mouth to mouth again, their tongues mated as she spread her legs farther and welcomed him inside. With sure but gentle strokes, he found his way to the opening of her womb, filling her with a piercing ache and a different kind of wanting.

Cassandra hissed out a breath and hugged him tighter when he mumbled a curse. "I didn't mean to hurt you, baby. I'm sorry. It won't happen again."

Blissfully happy and more content than she'd ever thought she could be, she wrapped her legs around his backside and whispered the words she'd waited to utter for a century. "You could never hurt me, MacPherson, for you are my one true love."

Somewhere in a far corner of his mind, Rand heard the murmur of Cassandra's voice, but his body had skyrocketed light-years beyond the boundaries of reason. If she was going to be taken from him, this would be their moment in time. Their one chance to be together in every possible way. And maybe, if he held on long enough, wished for it hard enough, God would take pity and let her stay.

Resting his weight on his elbows, he slid his hands under her back and pulled her up as he fused his mouth to hers. He'd hurt her, dammit, just as he feared he might. Now it was up to him to see to it nothing and no one ever hurt her again.

Determinedly, he moved inside of her, stroking until he felt the breath catch in her throat. Raising his head, he gazed into her softly flushed face. "Easy, sweetheart," he managed to say, holding himself in check. "Tell me if I'm hurting you, and I'll stop."

Her amethyst eyes flew open as she gave a fierce-sounding growl. "Stop now, MacPherson, and I swear I'll send you to the bottom of the pond."

He chuckled through gritted teeth when he felt her hot, slick channel squeeze his throbbing flesh. She raised up to meet his lips and he forgot to breathe. She shuddered and he pumped harder, until he saw pinpoints of light behind his closed eyelids and thought his body would shatter.

Thrusting faster, deeper, longer, he began a rhythm as old as time and twice as sweet. Cassandra cried out her release, and he gave up all control as he fell over the precipice and flew them to the stars.

Cassandra snuggled deeper under the covers and turned her face into the pillow at her side. Dawn light was just starting to brighten the room. The weight of a man's lightly callused hand tugged her against a wall of muscle and she let herself smile . . . again. This time when she'd slept in the circle of Rand's arms, it had been perfect.

Nestling her bottom into his front, she felt his arousal, hard and pulsing at her lower back. His palm settled over her breast and fondled a nipple, causing waves of longing to rise from low in her belly. Sweet Mother, but the man had stamina, she thought as she gave a serious wiggle of encouragement. First he'd carried her, a woman of no small stature, up the stairs like a wee kitten, then he'd loved her so thoroughly they'd fallen into an exhausted sleep.

Here it was, barely morning and he was ready to start all over again. What a lucky woman she was. What a fine life they would have together. And, oh, the beautiful bairns they would make! The lads would be tall and strong, with emerald eyes and softly curling hair. And the lassies would be sweet-natured with her love of family and hope for the future.

She said a silent prayer of thanks to the Creator for her wondrous good fortune. It didn't matter that she'd had to wait a century to find the man who would break the curse, because find him she had. And she loved him with all her heart.

At that thought, a tiny flag of worry fluttered in her brain. Last night Rand had been demanding yet tender, insistent yet solicitous of her feelings. He'd murmured compliments on the color of her eyes, the perfection of her breasts and the length of her legs. But not once had he said the words.

Not once had he said "I love you."

His hand moved on her belly to trace a circle around her navel, and she couldn't help but recall something she'd heard on one of Dr. Rachel's television shows: Modern males had trouble voicing their feelings. At the time, she remembered thinking that nothing had changed since she'd been a young girl. She'd never heard her father give her mother those words either. Love and commitment, it seemed, were still emotions most men found difficult to discuss out loud.

But surely this morning, after the night they'd spent together, Rand would say the words, especially when she told him one more time how she felt.

Slowly, his hands returned to her nipples. Tugging them to hardness, he brought her breasts to a throbbing ache. She rolled to face him, and his smile grew smug.

" 'Morning, beautiful. Did you get enough sleep?''

His lips grasped a turgid peak and drew the bud into his mouth. Her hands roamed to his chest, then lower, and she wrapped a palm around his shaft. "Aye, Mac-Pherson, I did," she managed to moan. "But I'm awake now and so, it seems, are all your bodily parts as well."

Growling playfully, he nuzzled against her chest until he found her other nipple and paid it the same careful attention. Waves of longing settled near her heart, overtaking the words she wanted to say. Sweet Jesus, but the man's mouth should be declared a lethal weapon, she thought, riding a crest so huge, it threatened to toss her under.

His lips burned a path back to hers and she opened for him, eagerly giving in to his demands. Crying out, she trembled at the force of his passion. He entered her and they began to rock in unison with the now-familiar rhythm. Rand clutched her to his chest, holding her so tightly she could feel the wild beating of his heart against her breast. Joined in body and soul, they shuddered as one being when they reached the pinnacle of their desire.

Minutes later, Cassandra sighed as they snuggled into each other and fell back to sleep.

Chapter Seventeen

Rand raised his head a few inches off the pillow and squinted through the sunlight streaming from the bedroom windows. He could just make out the alarm clock on the nightstand at the opposite side of the bed. Holy-moly, it was past two o'clock. He'd practically slept the day away.

Well, not slept, exactly. He lifted a handful of coppery curls and nuzzled the back of Cassandra's perfectly shaped ear. When he cupped a palm under one full breast, her bottom wiggled enticingly, and he fought the urge to laugh out loud. She was in his arms, as real and responsive as any female he'd ever had in his bed. Except sex with this woman had been a thousand times better. He'd never felt with anyone what he'd experienced with Ms. Cassandra Elizabeth Kinross.

As clear as the afternoon sunlight, he knew absolutely that he'd done the right thing last night when he'd talked her, talked both of them, into taking a chance. Everything was going to be fine. Cassandra was his, and she was here to stay.

Inhaling her flowery scent, he kissed the sweet spot at the nape of her neck. Damn, if the woman didn't smell good enough to eat. He chuckled softly at the witty but ribald double entendre.

"I'm awake, if you'd care to share the jest," Cassandra muttered, snuggling her back into his chest.

"Not on a bet. A guy has to have a few secrets, or he'll lose all credibility."

She rolled to face him, the shadow of a smile playing on her rosy lips. "Oh, so you think you have credibility, do you?"

Scrunching up her nose, she gave a look that said she was deep in thought. "Hmm, let's see ... Well, I do admit you're a credible builder. The restoration of this house is a fine example of your work."

"And ... ?" Rand nipped at her mouth, hoping for a more personal accounting of his talents.

"And? There is no *and,* MacPherson, as it seems to me building is the one thing you do best," she said wryly.

"How about telling me I'm an incredible lover?" he persisted. "If I recall, last night, in between all your moans of delight, you had plenty of compliments for my bedroom skills."

Her face flushed a becoming pink as her grin broadened to a full-fledged smile. "Truly? I don't remember."

Trying his best to look wounded, he raised a brow. "Sounds like I need to walk you through my complete list of talents one more time, just to jog your memory."

He worked his hands under the covers and palmed both of her breasts, pulling at her nipples until her eyes clouded over with desire. Nibbling kisses up her throat, he reached his final destination, her slightly open mouth. Feeling honor bound to demonstrate his other more interesting skills, he plundered slowly.

Like a train whistle shattering the quiet of the night, Rand's mobile phone rang. Cassandra stiffened in his arms. Pulling back, she bit at her lower lip. "Perhaps you should find out who's disturbing you on a Sunday afternoon?''

He shrugged as he dived at her delectable throat like a starving vampire. ''They *vill* call back if they need me.''

A few seconds later, the intrusive ringing began again. Cassandra giggled as she placed her hands on his chest and firmly drew away. ''I need to use the privy, so you might as well answer it. I'll be back in a minute.''

She rose from the bed, and he had all of two seconds to admire her bountiful curves before she tugged on one of his flannel shirts and scampered into the bathroom. Grabbing the phone off his night table, he cleared his throat. ''Whoever this is, it had better be good.''

Rewarded with a dial tone, he swung his legs over the side of the bed. Amazingly, the doorbell rang, echoing up the stairs like a cannon shot. ''Aw, for— What the hell's going on around here!''

Cassandra poked her head from behind the bathroom door. ''Go see who the blackguard is. I should take a shower.''

Rand stood and waggled his eyebrows. Since entertaining company was the last thing on his to-do list, he threw her his best bad-boy leer and stalked around the foot of the bed. ''Me too. How 'bout I join you?''

The chime of the doorbell changed to an insistent pounding. Cassandra flashed a teasing grin and ducked back into the bathroom. ''You'd better answer it, MacPherson. It sounds important.''

Well, crap. He plowed his fingers through his hair, then stumbled into his jeans. It dawned on him that in his hurry to bring home dinner last night, he must have been careless and forgotten to padlock the gate. Vowing to pay better attention to that type of detail in the future, he stomped from the bedroom, stubbed his toe on the doorjamb and limped down the stairs just in time to hear the house line ring.

Mad enough to gnaw on a roofing nail, he threw open the front door. "Whatever you're selling, we don't want any."

"Hey, Rand." Duke shuffled his size-fourteen feet. Dressed in a fleece-lined leather coat over worn jeans, a black turtleneck sweater and hiking boots, he took in his boss from head to toe. "Did I wake you?"

Rand leaned against the door and shot his foreman a grim smile. Why was it the guy always looked as if he'd just been backpacking, or rappelling or participating in some other manly sport? Didn't he know most people relaxed on their weekends off? "Nah, I always spend my Sunday afternoons naked from the waist up. What the heck have you been doing?"

Red-faced, Duke opened then closed his mouth. "Took a drive up to Vernon Valley this morning and hiked one of the old ski trails. I . . . um . . . needed time to think. It's freezing out." A gust of frigid air blew through the foyer, and he shouldered his way inside. "Aren't you going to ask me in?"

Rand folded his arms. "It's Sunday, bud. Some people like to sleep late on the weekend." If he could tell anyone about the fantastic night he'd spent with the woman waiting for him upstairs, it would be Duke, but that simply wasn't possible. Not yet anyway.

"Sorry. I was hoping you could spare a cup of coffee for a friend, or maybe a beer," he persisted, heading toward the rear of the house.

Rand spotted a rumpled sweatshirt hanging off the stair newel and dragged it over his head. The sound of water flooding the upstairs pipes started, and he cringed. If he could keep Duke distracted, maybe he wouldn't notice the noise. Dodging the cans of varnish and stacks of building materials that lined the hallway, he walked into the kitchen and straight to the sink. "I haven't made any coffee, but you can help yourself to a soda."

Duke opened the refrigerator and pulled out a Coke. Without a glance in Rand's direction, he popped the tab, took a long swallow, and set the can on the island. Stuffing his hands into his back pockets, he cut an impatient path to the eating area and back again.

Rand's gaze followed the nervous pacing until he swore he was watching an Agassi-Sampras match. The guy was making him seasick, for cripessake. "Think you could stand still long enough to tell me what the hell is bothering you?" he finally demanded, leaning his backside against the counter.

Duke stopped in his tracks, took his hands from his pockets, and ran a palm over his unshaven jaw. "Sorry. I'm just . . . Oh, hell. Nancy invited me to have dinner with the kids and her—*your* mother tonight."

"With or without Harry?"

"I'm not sure." He hung his arms at his sides. "Would it make a difference?"

"Damn straight it would." Rand nodded. "Harry usually does a good job of keeping Irene in line."

He grinned shamelessly. Though he didn't envy Duke, the idea boded well for his side. If Irene got wrapped up in her daughter's love life, maybe she'd be too busy to involve herself in his. "Okay. You're eating at Nan's and my mother will be there, with or without my stepfather. So what?"

Duke dropped his jaw. "So what? Jeez, cut me a break. I can't just sit down at a dinner table with your mother."

Rand crossed to the fridge and snagged his own can of soda. Better you than me, good buddy, he thought with a silent smirk. He turned to face the guy. "And why not?"

The foreman shuddered visibly. "Mrs. Johnston is kind of, you know, formidable."

As far as Rand was concerned, calling his mother formidable was akin to calling the Rocky Mountains a bump in the road. Suddenly, he felt sorry for the poor slob. Duke must really have it bad for Nancy if he'd felt the need to traipse through Vernon Valley at the crack of dawn, never mind that he'd agreed to put himself through an evening of chitchat with Irene.

But he couldn't resist another jab. "Are you trying to tell me you're afraid of a one-hundred-pound, five-foot-two-inch woman with a spine of tempered steel? Come on, she never bites unless she's provoked. After all these years, you ought to know that."

Duke's massive shoulders rose up and down on a sigh. "Real funny. Look, she's Robbie's ex-wife. She's my employer, for gosh sakes."

"No," Rand said firmly. "I'm your employer. Irene is just a stockholder in MacPherson C&D, as is my sister. And that hasn't stopped you from dating Nancy, has it?"

Duke gave a lost-puppy grin. "It's not like that with Nan. I've known her for years, and she's never acted like a part of the company. Mrs. Johnston is . . . different."

"Well, that's one way to describe her." Rand shook his head. "I'm sure it'll be fine. Nancy is a smart girl. She wouldn't put you in a situation unless she was sure you could handle it."

Suddenly looking a bit green, Duke picked up his soda and finished it in one long swallow. The house line rang again and Rand picked up the receiver.

"Thank God, I thought you'd never answer," Nancy said, her voice just a little too cheerful.

"Hey, how you doin'?" He turned his back on Duke. At least he knew now who'd been ringing his phone all morning.

"Not too good," his sister responded hesitantly. "I did something really stupid, and I need your help."

Fairly certain of what she was going to ask, Rand leaned into the counter, prepared to say no. "Yeah?"

"Come to dinner tonight? Please."

Rolling his eyes, he sneaked a sideways glance at Duke, who was sitting at the table with his head in his hands. "I'm busy. Maybe some other time."

Nancy's sigh was so loud, it almost hurt his ears. "You've got to come. I invited Mother, Harry, and . . . someone else."

"Sounds to me like there won't be any room at the table."

"This isn't a joking matter, Rand. Bill Dukovsky said he'd come. The kids and I went to the movies with him last night and I guess I wasn't thinking. The words just kind of popped out. Between Robbie's miserable attitude and Mom's third degree, the poor man will run screaming after half an hour. At least, if you're here, Mother will have to *try* to behave."

Rand hunkered lower over the counter, thinking of all the interesting things he'd planned to do with Cassandra that afternoon . . . and evening. How in the hell could he leave her after the night they'd just spent?

"Look, I can't talk right now."

Nan sucked in a breath. "Oh, my gosh, Bill's there, isn't he? And he's asked you to help him find a way out of this mess. He doesn't want to come and he's too polite to tell me."

"Uh . . . no. I'm busy is all." Rand drummed his fingers on the counter. "Is this really important? Like life and death or something?"

Seconds passed before Nan finally answered in her best I-will-not-cry voice. "Life and death would be easier."

She sniffled and Rand frowned into the receiver. "Aw, crap."

"Thanks, big brother. I knew I could count on you. Get here by five for drinks, all right?"

"Yeah, fine, but you owe me."

Rand hung up the phone, gathered his composure, and turned to Duke. "Looks like you've been granted a stay of execution. That was Nan, and it seems I'm invited to dinner too."

The man shot him an elated smile. Slapping both palms on the table, he stood. "Great! I have to go home and get cleaned up, but I'll meet you there. I offered to bring the wine, and I guess I'd better find a florist. Nancy deserves roses. . . ." He pumped Rand's hand once, then headed out the kitchen, mumbling under his breath.

Cassandra walked from the bathroom into Rand's bedroom. A short while ago, she'd stood at the door and heard a murmur of male voices coming from the kitchen, so she'd wrapped herself in a towel, secured her hair turban-style under another, and raced up the stairs to her room. After dressing in jeans and one of Nancy's castoff sweaters, she'd returned to complete her toilette and straighten the suite.

Now, with time to ponder all that had transpired, she sat on the window seat and stared wistfully at the jewel-toned coverlet lying neatly across Rand's massive bed. Had she really allowed the MacPherson to take such scandalous yet thrilling liberties with her person last night on that very mattress? And had she truly reciprocated in kind, kissing and fondling as aggressively as the wanton women Gram had once warned her about?

Had she truly given herself to him as if they'd been wed?

A wave of heat rushed to her cheeks. Yes, she had. And she'd done so without the blessing of a priest, or even the plighting of her troth. Surely they . . . she . . . would be damned for all eternity if the man decided he didn't want her for his wife. Worse, without his declaration of love, she might never have the opportunity to seek out a priest and beg forgiveness for her sin. She would be stuck in a netherworld between life and death, not quite alive but not able to pass to her eternal rest.

Huffing a breath, she viewed the problem from another, even more hopeless angle. If she did end up locked in some kind of damning half-world as a prisoner of the curse, she would be forced to live in this house and love Rand MacPherson forever, without being loved by him in return.

The dilemma pounded in her brain. She'd been raised a good girl. Father MacTavish, her parish priest, had spent hours advising her and the other young women of their church on the proper conduct of a lady. Gram, too, had instructed her on the difference between right and wrong. Young women of her day didn't give themselves to a man without the benefit of marriage. If her father or grandmother ever found out—

Cassandra set her palms to her burning face. She was being a goose to think of such things. Her father was dead, may he rest in peace, as were Father MacTavish and all her relatives. She was a woman of the twenty-first century now. Even if the worst happened and she returned to the spirit world, she could never go back to her homeland or her family. Her place was with the MacPherson, even if he didn't know it yet.

The slamming of the front door echoed in the distance. Footsteps sounded on the stairs and she stood, waiting to meet Rand head-on. There was no more time to waste. She needed to tell the MacPherson one more time that she loved him. Then, when he said he loved her in return, all of her problems would be solved. She would escape the curse, become fully human and marry the man. They and little Robbie, along with the future generations of MacPherson males, would be saved.

"Hey, beautiful." Rand sauntered into the room, a wide

smile etched on his impossibly handsome face. "Sorry I took so long. That was Duke at the door."

Twisting her fingers into a knot, Cassandra stepped to the foot of the bed, almost close enough to touch him. "I see. Is there some kind of emergency with the company?"

"Not exactly. It's more of a personal problem." He strode to meet her and enfolded her in the circle of his arms. "I have to go out for the night. I don't want to leave you alone, but my sister needs me. And so does Duke."

Cassandra settled her head against his chest. The sound of his heart beating loud and strong under her ear made her feel protected and safe . . . and loved. "I see."

Rand kissed the top of her head. "It's not a big deal. It's just that the poor guy is in a panic at the thought of having dinner with my mother. Then Nan called. She sounded more upset than Duke and asked me to be there for moral support. Seeing as I haven't been the most caring brother of late, I couldn't say no."

"I see," Cassandra said a bit more fervently. And she did see. If one of her brothers or Meggie needed her, she would have been on the first boat back to Scotland, damn Colin or any person who stood in her way.

"You'll understand better once you meet my mother, though I'm hoping to put off that debacle for as long as possible." He sighed into her hair. "Everybody is going to have to meet you eventually. They're going to want to know how we met and where you came from, so get prepared for a hell of a lot of questions. It's something we really need to talk about."

Cassandra stiffened. "Meet your mother? You're going to introduce me to her . . . and your sister? When?"

He pulled back and lifted her chin with his forefinger. "I don't know. As soon as I come up with a plausible story, I guess. Right now I don't want to leave you, Cassandra. Last night was . . . incredible."

Tell him, a small voice blathered at the back of her brain. Tell the man how much you love him. That you will always love him. Make him say the words.

"Aye, it was." She wrapped her arms tighter around his waist. "I want you to know that I—"

Leaning forward, Rand interrupted her confession with a breath-stealing kiss. The touch of his lips had her jelly-legged, while the taste of his tongue curled her toes. Melting into him, she marveled at the way the man made her feel, all warm and mushy inside, as if she'd just downed an entire kettle of oatmeal. Putting her whole heart into returning the kiss, she hoped he could read her thoughts and intuit what she'd been trying to say.

Finally, gasping for air, he pulled away and gazed into her eyes. "I know we have a lot to discuss." He walked to the dresser and took out clean clothes. "But I don't have much time. Nancy wants me there before Irene and Harry arrive, so I have to get going."

He stopped at the bathroom door. "There's leftover Chinese in the fridge along with a few muffins from yesterday's breakfast you can microwave. If that's not okay, I can get you something else to eat before I leave."

Too dazed to answer, Cassandra watched the bathroom door close. She heard the toilet flush, the water run in the sink, the sound of the shower. She sat on the side of the bed with a plop and breathed deeply as she struggled to take this latest delay in stride.

Rand was distracted, she reminded herself, and worried about his sister and his best friend. He'd told her last night had been incredible, a phrase that to her mind was tantamount to a declaration of love. And the way he'd kissed her just now, so thoroughly and with such utter abandon, was surely proof of his feelings.

She remembered the books hidden under the bed and decided today would be the perfect time to finish reading them. If she was lucky, she might find a reversal of the curse, some small chant or clue that would make her task easier.

Later tonight, after he'd taken care of Nancy and the Duke's problem, Rand would come home to her. They would spend another night of passion, and she would make her feelings known. Once they were together in the bed, she would force him to listen and give him the opportunity to tell her how he felt.

"The table looks really nice, sis." Rand eyed the bouquet of yellow roses mixed with an assortment of colorful autumn flowers. He maneuvered his nephew into a chair on one side of Duke and sat Melissa in the other, then waited to take his place at the head of the table while everyone else got seated.

"Thanks. Bill brought the flowers." Nancy telegraphed a thin but grateful smile toward Duke, set down a bowl mounded high with mashed potatoes, and headed back into the kitchen.

Since Rand had arrived, things had moved along fairly well. Harry, just back from his latest business trip, had spent the afternoon playing old maid with Melissa, while Nancy and Irene popped in and out of the family room with drinks and assorted snacks. Rand, Duke, and Robbie had watched the second half of the Giants-Patriots game, with the foreman holding his own when Robbie refused to sit anywhere near him.

Rand had to give the guy credit. Instead of acting annoyed, Duke had politely answered the many personal questions Irene tossed at him while he continued his commentary on the game as if nothing were amiss.

Once in his seat, Rand passed the platter of freshly carved meat Duke's way. "The roast beef smells great, Nan."

"It sure does," Duke responded. He stabbed a hefty

slab and set the platter down. "Hey, Robbie, your mom's a terrific cook, isn't she?" He placed his hand on the boy's shoulder and Robbie shrugged just sharply enough to let everyone know the touch was not appreciated.

"So, Bill." Irene's green eyes narrowed as she buttered a dinner roll. "How come a good-looking young man like you has never married?"

"Mother." Rand shot her a glare that said she was very close to stepping over the line. "Pass the peas, please."

"Certainly, dear." Handing the bowl to her son, she smiled. "I think we all know the reason Rand's remained a bachelor. He continues to believe in that silly story his father told him about the MacPherson men and their bad luck in love. I'm sure nothing as unusual as that has ever come up in your family, has it, Bill?"

Duke ignored Nancy's openmouthed stare as he cleared his throat. "Um . . . no, at least I don't think so. I've just been busy, I guess. I mean, with work and going to night school and everything—"

"You're going to night school?" Irene's face blossomed into a smile. "Good for you. And what are you studying?"

"So, Rand, I hope you don't mind if I bring the kids with me to the house this week," Nancy interrupted with a squeak. "They're on half-days because of Thanksgiving."

Just then, Princess trotted into the room carrying what looked to be the tattered remains of one of Melissa's precious storybooks.

"Princess, give me that," Nan snapped.

Melissa gave a shriek. Shooting from her chair, she started to chase the dog around the table while Robbie shouted encouragement.

Standing, Rand threw his nephew a laser glare. "Princess, sit!" he commanded.

Obediently, the dog dropped to its haunches and released the book. Melissa whipped it up from the floor. "You're a bad dog. You know you're not s'posed to touch my stuff."

Nancy guided the child to her chair and set the book on the sideboard. "That wouldn't have happened if you'd put your books away, like you were told. Now, eat your dinner."

Things settled down for a few minutes, and Rand thought they might actually get through the meal without incident ... until he heard Princess yip from somewhere in the room.

"Melissa, are you feeding that dog under the table?" Nancy asked.

"Nu-uh. I wasn't."

"Was too," Robbie chimed in much too cheerfully.

"Was not," the little girl repeated with a mutinous pout.

"Children, please. I'm still waiting for Mr. Dukovsky to answer my question. Now, Bill, tell us what it is you're taking in school."

"Maybe Duke doesn't want to talk about it, Mother," Rand warned. "I don't think Nancy invited him here to be interrogated."

"Oh, pooh." She gave a delicate sniff. "As if I'd do such a thing. I'm simply taking an interest, as I would in any friend of yours or my daughter's, that's all."

"Mom, Liss is feeding the dog again."

"Was not, you weenie—"

Nancy's flustered gaze shot from Rand to Irene to her children. "Melissa, that's enough. If you can't behave, you'll have to leave the room."

"Too bad we can't ask the same of Mother," Rand muttered, pouring an overflowing ladle of gravy onto his mashed potatoes.

Harry, who was sitting at the opposite end of the table from Rand, coughed into his napkin.

"Randall, that's not a bit funny," Irene scolded. "So, Bill, what did you say you were studying? And what college are you attending?"

"Irene," Harry finally interjected after taking a sip of his wine. "Leave the poor man alone."

Duke cleared his throat, his face only slightly red. "It's okay, Mr. Johnston, I don't mind answering. I went to William Patterson. But I'm finished. I graduated in June with a degree in accounting."

"You did?" Nancy's voice rose an octave. "Why didn't you tell me?"

"Did Rand know?" Irene interjected. "Because I'm sure he'd be willing to find a place for you in the management side of the company. It's a shame to be stuck in the field—"

"Mother." Rand raised his fork in the air.

"Thanks for the thought, Mrs. Johnston, but I like the construction end of the business. I got the degree just in case life threw me a curve one day and I had to do something else."

"Oh, my. You're not thinking of leaving MacPherson C&D, are you? Why, we've always considered you one of the family, haven't we, Nancy?"

"Yes, certainly. More rolls, anyone?"

"I hear you took Nancy and the children to the movies last night," Irene said pointedly.

Before Duke could answer the question, Melissa set her milk on the edge of her plate. The glass toppled in slow motion, sending a gush of liquid across the table, directly into his lap. In unison, he and Nancy jumped to their feet. Duke blotted the front of his pants with a napkin while Nan began to mop up the spill.

"Way to go, Liss," Robbie guffawed.

Melissa started to wail.

"It's okay, sweetie, it's only milk. And you, young man, had better calm down." Nan picked up the plate and dabbed at the puddle. "Bill, are you okay?"

Duke mumbled an affirmative and Robbie stared into his dinner, but Melissa continued to sob. Obviously distressed, she cried, "I miss my daddy. I want my daddy." A huge tear rolled down her cheek and landed on the soaked tablecloth. "Why doesn't Daddy live here anymore?"

Nan opened then closed her mouth as she patted the four-year-old's hand. "Come on, finish your dinner and you can help me serve dessert like a big girl. It's chocolate cream pie, your favorite."

"I gots a tummyache," Melissa moaned, sniffling loudly.

"Come here, darling." Irene slid her chair away from the table. "Sit on Grandma's lap and let me make it all better."

Nancy clutched at the napkin she'd used to sop up the milk. "She doesn't need to be babied, Mom. I've already explained to both children Warren won't be coming back here to live. They have to start accepting the idea—"

"I only want to help," insisted Irene, her lip thrust out in a perfect imitation of her granddaughter's pout. "Did you ever consider they may need counseling to help get them through this difficult time in their little lives?"

"Like you took us to counseling when you and Dad called it quits?" Rand prodded. When he got a chance to speak to his mother alone, he was going to lay down the law big-time.

"Well," Irene gasped.

Duke took his seat and rolled his eyes. "You about done there, Robbie?" he asked when the conversation mercifully stalled. "We men can clear the table for your mom if you're finished."

Robbie sat back and folded his arms. "I can take care of my mother just fine. She doesn't need your help."

Leaning into the table, Nancy ignored Melissa's next wail. "Robbie, that was rude. Apologize to Bill."

"Hey, Nan, it's no big deal, really. The boy just misses his father, that's all. I understand," Duke said, his face now a ruddy red.

Robbie stood and walked to Melissa. When he took his sister's hand, she immediately calmed. He tugged and she slid off the chair to stand by his side. "No one here gets it, do they? We don't need you, and we don't need a new dad. Come on, Liss."

"Robbie," Nancy sputtered, her eyes filling with tears.

"But I wants choc-a-let pie," Melissa blubbered softly.

Rand rose to his feet but sat back down when he felt a hand on his shoulder.

"No one is leaving this room," Duke said in a quiet but firm voice. "Robbie, sit and finish your dinner. You, too, Melissa."

After several tense seconds, Robbie walked to his chair and sat down with a huff. When Melissa saw that her brother had obeyed, she did the same.

"That's better." Duke took a sip of red wine as he surveyed the table. "If you kids want dessert, you have to clean your plates, right, Nan?"

Nancy threw him a grateful smile. "That's right. And when everyone is finished, Mother and I will bring out dessert."

"Irene, I think that's your cue to finish your own dinner as well," Harry said with a grin.

Rand waited until his mother gave an annoyed but subdued *hmmph,* then raised his glass to Duke. "So, Harry, what do you think of the wine. Duke brought it."

Harry held his goblet to the light. "It's quite appealing. Just dry enough to compliment the beef. An excellent choice, Duke. And please, call me Harry."

Looking unusually pleased with himself, the foreman nodded his thanks. Rand lifted his glass in a toast. "Here's to families, big and small. And the holidays. I can hardly wait."

Chapter Eighteen

Cassandra rubbed her burning eyes. She'd been reading for hours and was completely discouraged. As far as she could tell, not one of Madame Ragnar's or Irene's books would be of any help with her problem.

She reached over the side of her bed, pulled the final book from the sack, and held it to the light. Smaller than the others and decidedly ragged-looking, it was bound in dark burgundy leather. Though most of the books she'd perused had been newer, they all looked well used. The cracked binding and parchment-like pages of this one told her it might be the oldest of the lot, so she opened it carefully.

Flipping slowly to the title page, she blinked. Handwritten in ink, there was only one word: *Grimoire*.

The hair on her arms rippled and her heart beat like a drum. Knowing full well she shouldn't jump to conclusions, she closed her eyes and said a little prayer. Unless her memory was playing tricks on her, *Grimoire* had been the title of her grandmother's book of spells. Could this possibly be a copy?

But Gram's book had been typeset, with her own hand-penned notations decorating the margins. If the title page was any indication, this text was handwritten.

Slowly, Cassandra turned more blank pages, until she came to one headed The Beginning, exactly as the first chapter in Gram's book had begun. Scanning quickly, she saw that even though she'd been correct about the print, the handwritten words were slightly different and more dated than what she could remember from the other book.

Examining the cover from all angles, she searched for a printer's mark or something that might reveal the publication date. Finding none, her eyes widened at the enormity of what she had in her possession. Could this be the original *Grimoire* from which her grandmother's book had been taken? If so, it had to be very old, the spells possibly more precious and exacting than the ones she'd studied all those years ago.

She settled against the pillows, prepared to read each page thoroughly in order to compare what she remembered. But before she could begin her task, she heard the snick of the front door lock and the sound of a familiar whistle.

Springing from the mattress, she dropped to her knees, stuffed as many of the books as she could into the bag, and shoved the entire bundle under the bed and up against the wall. Rand's footsteps pounded up the steps, and she stood, haphazardly kicking the last few books from sight. The *Grimoire* was still sitting on the coverlet, so she snatched it up, raced across the room and tossed it into the shopping bag holding her underwear.

"Cassandra? You awake?" Rand's hesitant voice asked from the third-floor landing.

Pasting a smile of welcome on her lips, she spun around to greet him. He walked through the door, straight into her arms, and pulled her close. His embrace, almost desperate in intensity, sent a rush of warmth pulsing through her veins.

"God, what a night. It's so good to be home."

With her heart aflutter, she rested her head against his chest. The idea she'd been keeping secrets from him, the man with whom she was destined to share her life, had plagued her throughout the day. If only she could tell him of her miraculous find and all it implied. Knowing that was impossible, she snuggled closer. "I thought you loved being with your sister and her children?"

His chest quaked with silent laughter. "I do. But if you'd been there, you would have been appalled. My mother is amazing."

"Aye, that she is," Cassandra agreed, thinking of the book hidden in her lingerie.

He pulled back and gazed at her through questioning eyes. "First of all, you've never met the woman, so you can't possibly know what I'm getting at. Second of all, even if you had met her, there's no way to understand what I'm saying unless you see Irene in action. In today's jargon, she's what we politely call 'a piece of work.' "

"But everything's all right, isn't it? The dinner went well? Your sister and Duke were glad you came?"

He grinned down at her. "Oh, yeah. If for nothing else than to act as referee."

"There were fisticuffs?" she asked with a giggle.

"Ah, there's that bloodthirsty streak again," Rand teased. "Not a fistfight exactly, but there were enough verbal jabs thrown to put the presidential debates to shame. If I had to declare a winner, surprisingly, it would be Dukovsky. Not only did he manage Mother and Robbie like a veteran, he also calmed Melissa and Nancy and gave me a hand at seeing to it everyone got through dinner in one piece. I waited until Harry and Mother left before I made my exit. I figured Duke could help Nancy clear the debris and put the kids to bed. Looks like he's going to need practice before he gets used to navigating with the old ball and chain.''

"Practice? Ball and chain?'' Cassandra drew back to meet his gaze. ''I don't understand.''

Looking a bit smug, Rand said, ''I think in your day it might have been called leg-shackled. You know, when a poor slob is so smitten with a woman, he let's himself get caught.''

Poor slob? Caught? She furrowed her brow. Was Rand implying he pitied the Duke for being in love with his sister? Did he truly think the bond of matrimony was akin to wearing leg irons? Fearful the conversation was heading in a direction she did not want to pursue, she bit at her lower lip. Perhaps she was mistaken.

''Do you mean married?''

''Exactly.'' He dipped his head and planted a smacking kiss on her cheek. Still grinning, he headed toward the foyer. ''Did you eat dinner?''

Feeling as if she'd been struck with a caber, Cassandra fisted her hands while she let Rand's words sink in. All the while she'd been doing her best to get the man to tell her he loved her, he'd been thinking marriage was a trap to be avoided. Worse, any man who allowed himself to be caught was a fool. Incredible.

''Cassandra, you ate, right? And got some rest? Or did you spend the night watching television?''

''Hmm? Oh, I did both, actually. The reheated Chinese food was quite tasty.''

But I'd much rather have wiled away the time with you, you miserable cur!

''Come on, let's go to bed.'' He held out his hand, as if automatically assuming she would join him.

Resisting the urge to cosh him on the head, she grabbed her sleepshirt. Obviously, tonight was not the most opportune time to spill her heart. If Rand truly believed marriage was as bad as a prison sentence, perhaps the time would never be right.

"You don't need a nightgown," he remarked, his voice as dark and soothing as hot chocolate. Suddenly, he was behind her. His arms wrapped about her waist, then moved to cover her breasts. "I really missed you, sweetheart. Come to my room and I'll show you how much."

Rand pulled her into his chest, stealing her breath along with her common sense. She felt his arousal, hard and demanding when he shifted his hips against her bottom. His lips traced a line of kisses from the nape of her neck to her cheek, and she sighed as she turned in his arms. If she had half a brain, she would tell him to go find another woman to share his bed, someone who had no intention of robbing him of his precious freedom. She finally understood why he'd never said he loved her— he didn't want to get married. And from the sound of it, he never would.

But before she could get her bearings, he captured her mouth with his, and she turned into a quivering mass of longing. Lost in his touch, Cassandra barely noticed when Rand picked her up and carried her to his room.

Rand stared grimly into the bathroom mirror. Wiping at the steamy haze with one hand, he used the other to run a razor over his morning stubble. After a quick shower, he planned to get dressed and make his way downstairs as quietly as possible. He had a ton of stuff to do before the crew arrived for work, and it was too early for Cassandra to be up. Especially after the night they'd just shared.

Once in the shower, he let the warm water sluice over his head, hoping it would clear his brain. There was no glossing over one simple fact: He couldn't get enough of Cassandra Kinross. Sharing a bed with her and having her climax in his arms was better than anything he'd ever had the pleasure to experience. No woman in his memory, either recent or past, had ever exerted such an unexplainable pull on his senses.

But as much as the reality thrilled him, he knew he had to go slowly. He and Cassandra already had two strikes against them. Besides the fact he came from a long line of men who were batting zero in the marriage game, she was a transformed spirit with a tenuous hold on life. One stray step and the delicate balance they were walking could tip, tumbling them flat onto their butts.

The last thing he wanted was to screw it up and ruin both their lives.

Mulling over the path he needed to take to get them on track, he finished his shower and dressed. After tiptoeing to the door, he turned just in time to see Cassandra snuggle deeper under the covers. The sight of her, sleep-tussled and soft-looking, took his breath away. How he itched to go to her and run his fingers through her spun-gold hair, to kiss her awake and tell her how much he cared.

When she curled into his pillow and clutched it to her breasts, he simply stood and stared. Suddenly too dazed to move, his stomach did a weird little somersault. Seconds passed before he was able to run a shaking hand over his face.

How could he have been so blind? So stupid? Why hadn't he realized what the hell had been happening?

He may have been telling himself he wanted to protect Cassandra and find a way to make up to her all she'd suffered at his uncle's hands, but the truth was much more simple . . . and way more complicated.

He was in love with her!

Resisting the urge to bang his head against the wall, he backed onto the balcony and stuffed his hands into his pockets. Still reeling from what he now knew to be the truth, he walked down the stairs. Well, crap, he thought, shaking his head, this was definitely one predicament he hadn't bargained for.

Cassandra kept her eyes shut and her breathing even. She'd been awake from the moment Rand left the bed. Just now, as he stood in the doorway, she'd rolled over and pretended to snuggle deeper into sleep. After all, there was no reason for her to give the arrogant bonehead the upper hand by showing him she was completely besotted.

The least he could have done was touch her or kiss her, or speak a cheerful word of good morning, as he's done the past two days. Instead, he'd skulked to the bath like a thief.

And that's exactly what the blackguard was, she thought, holding back a sniff. For he had stolen her heart as surely as if he'd cut it from her chest. It was clear now, after the remarks he'd made last night about marriage and the men foolish enough to fall into the trap, that he never intended to be caught in such a stupid manner.

Tossing to her back, she stared at the ceiling. She needed to make a decision, and it had to be soon. Should she take her chances, bare her battered heart and hope he would take pity? Or should she play a game, force him to say he loved her by way of seduction or maybe another spell? Should she use the *Grimoire?* Though none of those ideas sounded palatable, she didn't think she had many choices.

She rose from the bed and fumbled into her clothes. The rattle of a truck coming up the drive—probably Duke, arriving to start the workday—jarred her into action. She washed her face and tidied her hair, then went to the door and peeked onto the balcony in time to see the *poor slob* head for the kitchen. If she hurried, she could make it to her bedroom before anyone noticed.

Once on the third floor, she walked straight to the paper

sack that held her lingerie, prepared to retrieve the book. A knock on the door startled her, and she turned.

"Sorry, I didn't mean to make you jump." Rand walked in carrying a tray laden with a steaming mug of what smelled like tea and a muffin. "This was the best I could do since Duke showed early. I stopped in my bedroom first, but when you weren't there—"

He set the tray on the foot of her bed. "You okay?"

Tongue-tied, she nodded. How dare the man bring her breakfast in bed when he didn't give two figs about making an honest woman of her? If she had an ounce of common sense, she'd pick up the bloody tray and—

Gathering her composure, she sucked in a breath. "I thought it might be best if I were gone from the room. It's on a level the men wander freely, and I'd hate to come face-to-face with one of them, or your sister."

Rand crossed his arms and walked closer. "You're right, especially Duke. He was there when we opened the closet and . . . um, you know. After yesterday, I wouldn't want to give him any more reasons for taking the next train out of town."

She ignored his pointed reference to Duke's pathetic condition and met him at the bottom of the bed. "This was very thoughtful. Thank you."

He reached out as if to touch her, then pulled back his hand. "Cassandra, I'm going to be out of the house for the next couple of days. I have to take care of a few things."

"You're leaving town?" she asked, trying her best to sound unconcerned.

"Just to go to company headquarters. Duke came early to inform me I was needed at the office. My secretary gave him orders to hog-tie me and drag me in if he had to. Seems some problems have come up and I have to go in and make like the president."

The man did have a business to run, she reminded

herself, and as far as the MacPherson knew, her troubles were almost certainly taken care of. Why should he stay here and hold her hand every hour of the day?

"I see. Well, then . . ."

"It's not a big deal. I figure I can bring you breakfast before I leave each morning, and a sandwich and soda for later."

And maybe, when you're finished with business, you'll bring me your heart? Nonsense, utter nonsense, she thought sadly.

Rand gazed around the room. "You want me to cart the television up from the kitchen? If you keep the sound low, I doubt anyone will notice."

"That would be nice," she answered. "I'm still learning about things . . . and I have my list."

"List?" His gaze followed hers to the paper and pencil lying on the bed. "Oh, yeah. For our shopping expedition. Maybe we can get to it later tonight."

In the distance a door slammed. The sound of male voices carried up the stairs, a signal the workmen were ready to begin the day. "Guess I'd better get going. I'll be back with a pot of tea and the television before I leave, okay?"

She smiled, unable to think of anything else to say that might keep him in the room. Rand backed away slowly, and went out the door. When his footsteps faded, she pulled the *Grimoire* from the sack and brought it to the bed. Placing it on the tray, she carried everything to the head of the bed and set it beside her. After propping herself against the pillows, she sipped the tea, opened the book and began to read.

Cassandra stared out the bedroom window, the *Grimoire* in her hand. After three days, she'd not found one incantation or spell she thought sensible enough or safe enough to try on her own. The only thing she'd been able to discover was this: in order to rescind a curse of such magnitude, one which had lasted a century and encompassed generations, both of the involved parties needed to voice the words out loud with great determination and profound passion that would break the curse. And they had to be said freely, without coercion or trickery.

Walking to her bed, she sat with a sigh. Every evening this week, Rand had come home late and they'd spent the night wrapped in each other's arms. When he awoke, he'd snuggled against her and asked about her health, then ordered her to do nothing more taxing than watch television.

Today, just as he'd done every morning before he left for the office, he'd carried up a tray holding a pot of tea and a bit of breakfast, as well as fresh fruit and a sandwich for later. Only this morning, he confessed he'd been mulling over an idea about how they could explain her presence.

An idea that would require her leaving the house.

What in the name of heaven was she supposed to do now? Pleading a headache had worked once, but she doubted the excuse would get past him a second time. Even if she knew how to work the phone, she didn't have Irene's number. She had no way to inform the woman of Rand's plans. The last thing they needed was for the MacPherson to find out she'd deceived him with his mother and her psychic friend.

Worse, if he learned she was a witch who had placed a curse on Colin, and that curse had directly affected his parents' marriage—his entire family—well, she didn't want to think about what would happen then.

Noisy shouts and the sound of running feet rose from the foyer, which led her to suspect Rand's niece and nephew were in the house again, as they'd been each day this week. She smiled at the memory of meeting Melissa and Princess in this very room on Monday morning. In the course of their first visit, she'd learned that Robbie had decided to supervise the electricians, but his sister had been bored. Even with Rand's makeshift barricade at the foot of the stairs, the child and her dog had found their way to the third floor.

Melissa was sweet and bright and loving, just like the children she'd hoped to one day mother. Unfortunately, as long as the MacPherson continued to hold his skewed views on matrimony and refused to fall in love with her, that dream seemed to shrink into a smaller and smaller bit of reality with each passing day.

She heard a scuffling noise and tucked the *Grimoire* under the bed, then slid to the floor to wait. The door popped open a few inches, and Princess pattered across the threshold, straight to her side. Before she knew it, Cassandra was in love. When she cuddled the dog to her chest, the wee thing stuck its nose into her sweater and began a chorus of soft doggie moans. A feeling of contentment filled her as the fluffy white poodle nestled peacefully in the valley of her thighs. Before long, she heard muffled steps on the stairs.

"Cassandra, you in there? I'm lookin' for Princess."

At the sound of the child-sized whisper, the dog perked its ears, its tiny head cocked at attention. Melissa peeked into the room. Dressed in jeans and a bright yellow sweater, her hair braided neatly at the back of her head, the little girl smiled pure sunshine when she spied her dog and her new friend.

"Hello. We've been waiting for you." Cassandra scooted over to make room.

"I brought lotsa books today, and my favorite game." Melissa snuggled down beside her and laid the backpack on her thighs. One by one, she pulled out a variety of books and a worn deck of old maid and set them in a pile.

"Princess, go someplace else, you piggy," Melissa scolded. Picking up the box holding the cards, she shoved the dog to the side and settled herself between Cassandra's outstretched legs. With her brow wrinkled in concentration, she made a little-girl attempt to shuffle and deal the cards.

Princess roamed from spot to spot, first sniffing a trash can, then nudging aside several of the storybooks before finally disappearing beneath the bed.

The afternoon passed quickly, with the dog leaving from time to time to explore the rest of the house and Melissa going downstairs to check in with her mother. For the remainder of the day, Cassandra and the little girl entertained each other with stories of make-believe and childlike games.

Finally, Nancy called out that it was time to leave. Melissa stood and gave Cassandra a hug. "When Mommy asked me what I was doin' upstairs, I told her I was reading. I decided you're gonna be *my* special friend, Cassandra. I don't want to share you, not even with Robbie."

"And you shall be mine, little darlin'," Cassandra answered as she smiled and waved good-bye.

Alone again, she paced the darkened house, microwaved her supper and watched for Rand's arrival. But she was careful to dress in her sleepshirt, just in case he offered to take her out somewhere. She would be up and waiting for him, so they could talk, but she felt certain he wouldn't insist she get dressed again.

The foyer door opened and she heard Rand's cheerful whistle. "I'm home, Cassandra. Where are you?"

He walked into the kitchen and set his briefcase and a bag on the floor. Suddenly overcome with a feeling of upheaval, she bolted around the island and jumped straight into his arms, hoping to dispel her fears. Rand caught her as she wrapped her legs around his hips. Praying they would find a way to be together, she hung on tight.

He raised her up and sat her on the island. "Well, to what do I owe the pleasure of this warm and fuzzy welcome?" he asked, nuzzling at her throat.

She placed her palms on his shoulders. "I've been lonely, MacPherson. It's time I had a bit of companionship, don't you think?"

He covered her hands with his and leaned close. Pressing his mouth to hers, he stole her breath with a long, stirring kiss. Gasping for air, they pulled apart and gazed longingly into each other's eyes.

He pecked at the tip of her nose. "I know it hasn't been fun for you these last few days, holed up in your third-floor cell, but it'll be over soon. It's too late to go out to dinner, so I stopped and bought some snack food and two of those pastries I was telling you about. I hope you're hungry."

"Definitely," she answered. "But not necessarily for food."

Waggling his eyebrows, he grinned. "Tomorrow is Thanksgiving, a major family holiday in the United States. I'm supposed to celebrate it at Irene and Harry's house. Nan and the kids will be there, and Duke's going to make an appearance after he spends some time with his own family."

"I understand," she said with a touch of sadness. "Family is very important in a person's life."

Stepping back, he took both her hands in his. "I want you to come with me."

She hopped off the island as the feeling of upheaval threatened to burst from her chest. "No, I couldn't. I mean, why can't everyone gather here?"

He grinned as he shook his head. "Nope, no can do. Mom's already got turkey and all the trimmings and Nan's made the pies and a bunch of other stuff. It's tradition. Besides, having you slave in a kitchen the first time you meet my family is the last thing you need to do.''

Her mouth grew dry as a ball of freshly rolled yarn. A fist of panic seized her and squeezed until she thought she might faint dead away. ''And how do you plan to introduce me? Who exactly will you tell them I am?''

He stepped close and set his hands on her shoulders. ''I've been thinking about it all week, and I've decided you're going to be Cassandra Kinross's great-great-niece. We can say you grew curious about the country your aunt emigrated to and decided to come for a vacation. You knocked on my door because you found this address when you went through some old family papers.''

Cassandra stepped back and clutched at her arms. ''And what about the documents you said I needed?''

''No problem. I'll just tell Harry you lost your handbag right after you got through customs. He flies to England all the time. Next visit he can make a stop in Scotland and work some legal magic. He'll find a way to get you a passport and birth certificate.''

Turning her back, she paced to the sink and stared out at the darkness. Black as pitch, it reminded her of the hope dying in her heart. ''I don't know enough of the modern world. I could never talk about current events or—''

''All you have to do is sit and smile and answer Mother's questions about Scotland. Believe me, they'll soak you up like a sponge. Irene is a real Anglophile, and Nan and the kids will adore you.''

Hiding the need to draw air into her lungs, she gripped the edge of the sink until her knuckles turned white. ''But they've seen me . . . my body. Surely the Duke or your mother will notice.''

She shuddered when she felt him stroke her hair. ''And that's going to work to our advantage. It can be another reason you had to come to America. Everyone in your family convinced you that you were so much like the first Cassandra, it was just natural you would want to find out what happened to her.''

Rand turned her into his arms and drew her near. ''After what Colin did, I doubt anyone will mention much about the *real* Cassandra.''

She nodded dumbly, unable to utter another word. He had an answer for every protest, every excuse she tossed his way. It was obvious he'd thought it all through. Only he didn't know the consequences . . . didn't realize that by taking her out of this house, he would destroy her all over again.

Rand moved back and raised her chin with his fingers. ''Hey, don't look so glum. After you've had a good night's sleep, you'll see I'm right about this. Why don't you bring the wine upstairs and climb into bed? I'll find a couple of glasses, set this stuff on a tray, and be right up.''

Rand watched her take the bottle and walk from the room. Jeez, he hadn't meant to make her so unhappy. Cassandra had every right to be nervous, but she had to know he'd protect her, and he'd damned sure keep his family from overwhelming her. For the past three days he'd done nothing but sit through meetings and listen to the expediters ramble about deadlines and budgets and estimates. And the entire while, he'd been distracted, unable to concentrate on the company or his work.

It had taken him all week to come up with a plan, then find the courage to say the hell with it and carry it out. Just when he thought he had the bases covered, she was acting like he'd invited her to a funeral. His uncle was the reason everything she'd ever had—her home, her family . . . her life—was gone. All he was trying to do was find a way to give it back.

Tomorrow, after she met his relatives and realized

things were going to be okay, he planned to confess that he loved her and wanted to spend the rest of his life with her.

Finally, he was going to make things right.

Chapter Nineteen

"Hey, sleepyhead." Rand nuzzled the back of Cassandra's ear. His hands cupped her breasts and fondled gently. "Time to wake up. We practically slept the morning away. It's almost time to go to Mother's."

Cassandra was up; she had been awake since the crack of dawn. Last night, after Rand drifted to sleep, she'd crept upstairs to hunt for the *Grimoire,* determined to take a final stab at freeing them of the curse. Instead, she'd been unable to find the book. Frantic, she'd returned to the bed and lain awake for hours.

Right now her eyes burned, her palms were damp, and her stomach felt like a swollen boil so filled with poison, it threatened to burst. Where was the book? How could she have misplaced it?

"Stay in bed and relax," Rand ordered. "I'll get cleaned up first. We can grab some fast food on the way to Irene's, to tide us over. Wait until you see the spread her housekeeper puts on." He climbed from the bed and headed to the bath. "If you thought Americans chowed down before, you won't believe what happens on Thanksgiving."

The second the bathroom door closed, Cassandra scrambled from the covers. Last night she'd had nothing but a lantern and a dim overhead fixture to light her bedroom. This morning, with the sunshine streaming through the windows, she would surely find the *Grimoire*.

Tugging on one of Rand's flannel shirts, she raced up the stairs. Once in her room, she scooped out the books and paper bag from under the bed and began tossing volumes, one after another, onto the coverlet.

She stared blankly at the pile while her heart pounded in her breast. Finally she stood and fisted her hands at her temples. *Think, Cassandra, think. What are you going to do?*

She walked to the landing, about to go back down the stairs, when she spied something through Rand's barely open office door. She slipped into the room, picked up a book from the pile strewn about the floor, and read the title. Though not the *Grimoire,* it was one of the volumes she'd received from Irene. How had it gotten here, into this room?

She scanned the office, her gaze drawn to the area around Rand's desk, and spotted more books scattered under his chair and in the cubbyhole. On her hands and knees, she raked them all out, or what was left of them. For each one was damaged, the leather bindings riddled with holes, the torn pages filled with what looked to be teeth marks.

Her breath clogged in her throat as she realized what had happened. So much for befriending that traitorous four-legged ball of fluff, she thought. For heaped around her like the plucked feathers of a goose lay the shredded remains of the *Grimoire*. Tentatively, her hand reached for a torn page, hand-penned with the first half of the word she'd been searching for.

Gone, she realized with a shiver of hopelessness. Her every dream for the future had been torn to bits. Gathering the yellowed scraps, she clutched them to her breast and struggled to her feet.

"So this is where you disappeared to," Rand's cheerful voice rang out, so normal, so carefree, and completely unaware. He had no idea that her very existence now lay solely in his hands. "What the heck happened in here? Looks like the paper shredder threw up."

She felt his fingers stroke her back. Afraid she would fall prey to his charms, Cassandra kept her eyes trained on a far wall. She couldn't allow herself to be swayed by the touch of his hands, his smiling eyes, or the way his crisp white shirt fit across his expansive chest. "I think 'twas your niece's dog, Princess. Melissa brought her to visit me this week."

"You mean that little imp had the nerve to cross my barrier? So what did you say when you met her? Who does she think you are?"

She cleared her throat and took a few steps toward the door. "She named me her special friend and decided to keep our meetings a secret. She seemed more interested in her storybooks than in trying to figure out who I was."

"That's great. One less person we need to worry about today. But why didn't you tell me?"

"I . . . um . . . it just didn't enter my mind."

He bent and picked up one of the mangled books. "Nan said she was going to bring the kids this week. She probably thought the dog would keep them occupied. That poodle is full of the devil. Chewed one of Melissa's—"

He raised the book to the light. *"Secrets of a Haunted House?"* He opened the cover and read the inscription. "This doesn't belong to me. It's one of Irene's."

Snapping up his head, he stared at her. "How did one of my mother's books find its way in here?"

Unwilling to answer, Cassandra sidled farther away while he retrieved a few more volumes. "These books are from Mother's library. How in the hell . . . ?"

She'd almost escaped in time to execute her plan—locking herself in her room until she could find the courage to tell him the truth—when she felt him grasp her shoulder.

"Cassandra. Has Irene been in this house? Up here with you? Have you met my mother?"

Shrugging off his hand, she stared straight ahead. Lies built upon lies, she acknowledged, were like a house constructed of cards. Eventually, they would come tumbling down to destroy the prevaricator.

"Yes, I have."

Rand swallowed hard. How . . . when had his mother been here, and why hadn't Cassandra told him? They'd talked often enough about what might happen if Irene found her, the dangers, the repercussions . . .

"What was my mother doing in this house? And what in God's name made you decide to talk to her?"

He watched her shoulders stiffen. Confused, he juggled the books in one hand and stayed at her heels as she raced into her room. So close, in fact, that when she tried to slam the door, it practically smacked him in the face. Rubbing at his nose, he shoved the door inward. "Cassandra, how long have you been lying to me? And why?"

The door hit the wall and she spun around. With her wide-open eyes and bright red cheeks, she looked frightened and angry at the same time.

"She showed up here one day and backed me into a corner. I couldn't very well ignore the woman, so I talked with her."

Rand's gaze narrowed. "After I warned you what might happen if she and that nutcase friend of hers found you? Were you out of your mind?"

Cassandra clutched the tattered pages to her breast. "Madame Ragnar is as sane as you or I, and she's a very nice woman. Besides, they only wanted to help."

"Help?" He couldn't believe his ears. All his mother

had yammered about was getting the woman to conduct a séance and exorcize the house. What had happened to change her mind? And when had the three of them had the opportunity to meet? "Please don't tell me they found you when you were still a ghost?"

Cassandra's militant gaze darted to the door. "And what if they did? Nothing happened. And they were kind enough to bring me those books to see if I could—" She slapped a hand to her open mouth.

"Could what? What were they trying to help you do?"

She walked to the bed and dumped the shredded bits of paper and binding on the mattress. Hands on her hips, she raised her chin a notch. "They were trying to help me find a way to break the curse."

Rand cocked his head and rapped the heel of his free hand against his ear, his shout deafening. "Excuse me? Run that one by me again?"

"I said they wanted to help me break the curse," she responded with an annoyed-sounding huff.

"Curse? *What* curse?"

"The one I placed on your uncle," came her subdued reply.

Cassandra made to step around him, but Rand blocked her escape. It took a second before he was finally able to grind out, "I assume you're talking about Colin?"

Incredibly, she had the nerve to glare. "Of course it was Colin. What other uncle of yours have I met?"

He waved one of the battered books at her. "How the hell should I know? I didn't think you were acquainted with my mother either, and now it sounds like she's become the official lending library for transformed spirits."

One at a time, he raised up a book, called out its title, and threw it on the bed. *"How to Cast Spells by Moonlight. The Truth About Modern Witchcraft. One Thousand Ways to Get What You Want Using Magic.*

Why the heck were you reading this kind of crap? Never mind a séance, sounds to me like you need a black cat and a freakin' broom.''

Pacing in an angry circle, he ran a hand over his hair. "Are you telling me I'm supposed to believe you're a witch and you put a curse on my uncle? Because people just don't do that unless—Cassandra, besides being stupid, the stuff you're talking about can be dangerous."

She folded her arms, her face still flushed. "Witchcraft is an art I learned from my grandmother."

He raised a brow and tried not to smirk. If he didn't know better, he'd think he was in one of those quirky teenage horror flicks—a weird mix of Casper, Sabrina, and Beetlejuice. Pieces of the puzzle he'd been mulling over since her transformation were now falling into place.

"Okay. I'm going to make a wild guess here, and I want you to tell me if I'm even close to getting it straight. You and your grandmother were witches back in Scotland. Your father found out, broke up the coven, and decided to sweep the scandal under the rug by marrying you off to some poor, unsuspecting slob in the States. Do I have it right so far?"

"There was no coven," Cassandra corrected him, her hands fisted at her sides. "It was just Grandmother and myself. And Colin MacPherson was no *poor, unsuspecting slob.*"

"All right, so I exaggerated, but I think I've got the picture pretty much in focus. Daddy managed to find some jerk desperate enough to marry you and he sent you here. Once you arrived, you decided you didn't want my uncle. When Colin got mad, he put you in the closet and you laid this so-called curse on him. Or did you threaten him with your hocus-pocus *first,* and then he decided to get rid of you?"

Cassandra marched near, until she stood a foot from his chest. "I already told you what happened. Your uncle wouldn't listen. He was trying to force me into a loveless marriage. I refused and he walled me up. I begged him not to, pleaded for my life . . . and then I cursed him."

She looked so earnest, so determined to get him to see her side of it, Rand silently admitted he was probably overreacting. Common sense told him she'd been a victim, but as for the rest . . . "All right. Then why did you lie to me about Irene? You know how I feel about her, and you know what she and that woman wanted to do to you. How could you take the chance?"

Cassandra seemed to crumple as she dropped to the bed. "I had no choice. When your mother and Madame Ragnar found me, I could no longer make myself invisible. They acted so concerned with my plight, I began to answer their questions and the story just bubbled out."

Rand began to circle the room. He needed to think. Hell, he needed to have his head examined for getting mixed up with the woman in the first place. "Look, how about you get dressed and come downstairs? I'll make coffee and we can talk. I need to absorb some of this before we go any further."

Without waiting for an answer, he headed out the door.

Cassandra dressed slowly. Anything, she decided, to delay the inevitable. The MacPherson had yet to ask the details of the curse, but when he did, it would be the true test of his understanding nature. Unfortunately, once he found out what it implied, the chance of him ever falling in love with her would become nonexistent.

Before her father had sent her to America, he'd told her she was an abomination, a demon creature so despicable, no one would ever love her. She'd tried to atone for her sins, but it was obvious the Good Lord didn't want her to find happiness in this lifetime or any other.

Dragging her feet, she made her way down the stairs

and into the kitchen. Rand was staring out the window, his back rigid, his hands folded across his chest. She shuffled into the room and he spoke without looking at her.

"Tea?"

"That would be nice."

She made her way to the table and waited until he walked over and handed her a steaming mug. "Thank you."

"No problem." He returned to the counter, poured coffee into an identical cup, and took a seat across from her. "I'm sorry I lost my temper. Everything you said was just such a surprise."

"I understand. And that's one of the reasons I didn't tell you right away. I knew you would be upset."

Finally, he looked her in the eye. "Okay. You've made your point." He set his coffee down and folded his hands. "Can I ask you a few more questions?"

She nodded. What else was she supposed to do?

"You think you're a witch, right?"

Wanting to be completely honest, she said, "I know I am."

He cleared his throat, his gaze riveted to hers. "All right. Do something."

"Do something?" She lifted a brow. "Like what, exactly?"

"I don't know." He picked up a paper tomato from the basket on the table and set it between them. "Make this disappear. Turn it into a mouse or something."

She refused to let his request rattle her. Though it was a fairly simple task, it would prove beyond a shadow of a doubt she was what she said she was. Could Rand deal with the reality, or would he run from her in fear? "You're sure?"

Setting his mouth in a thin line, he nodded.

Cassandra closed her eyes and concentrated, imagined

the tomato as a tiny, invisible puff of air that shrunk easily into itself. When she lifted her lids, the tomato was gone. And Rand's eyes were as big as pie plates.

"Holy shit!" He waved a hand through the space the tomato had once occupied, then raised his shocked gaze to hers. "The roofing shingles, the workmen's tools . . . ?"

"I'm afraid so," she admitted. "I was just so angry you were threatening my home—"

"Sure. Of course." He pushed from the table and walked across the kitchen. An eternity seemed to pass before he turned and rested his backside against the counter. Finally, he asked, "So what was it, this curse you laid on my uncle?"

Cassandra's heart seemed to stop beating. The time to tell the complete truth in the simplest way possible had arrived. And it was the most difficult thing she'd ever had to do. She folded her hands and took a fortifying breath. "I denied him true love for the remainder of his mortal existence."

Rand set his cup down hard on the island. "Well, that sure as hell happened, now, didn't it? After Colin closed up this house, I don't think he ever found a woman who'd agree to stay in the same room with him, never mind live with him. No wonder he went crazy."

She leaned forward in her chair. "There's more, Mac-Pherson. Much more."

"More? How much more? I'm sure someone in this family would have noticed if you'd turned him into a toad."

Her lips trembled as she held back a rueful grin. "I didn't have to do anything that extreme to the man. His madness was punishment enough."

"So?"

"I cursed his family as well."

"His family? *My* family?" One corner of his mouth twitched. "Funny, I don't recall a single story about any of my ancestors doing time on a lily pad or baying at the moon."

Thinking his attempt at humor had to be a positive sign, she asked, "Ah, but did any of the MacPherson men ever find their one true love?"

Rand started at the simple question. His uncles and their miserable marriages, the failure of his parents' relationship, his heartache over their divorce . . . Cassandra was admitting she was responsible for it all?

He fixed his gaze on hers. "Run that by me again, with a few more details."

She stood and walked toward him. "I didn't realize what I was doing. All I could think was that I had to find a way to punish the man, to make him sorry for what he was doing to me. He wanted a wife, so I thought a curse would be the best way to keep him from finding one. When I spoke the words, I damned not only Colin, but every MacPherson male who would be born. I decreed all of them incapable of finding their one true love, until—"

Somewhere inside of Rand, a red haze began to build. "You decreed?" he thundered. "You decided, in all your righteous judgment, that every male in our family be punished for the sins of one man?"

"Please let me finish."

She laid a palm on his arm and he shrugged it off. "Then the story Dad told me was true. The MacPherson men are cursed. And you're the cause of it."

She dropped her hand to her side. "Aye."

Feeling gut-punched, he hissed out the first string of words that didn't lodge sideways in his throat. "I think you'd better leave."

"You're throwing me out?"

Smugly, he noted, it was her turn to look poleaxed.

"Not out, exactly. I just think I . . . we need to put some distance between us. Since you and Irene seem to be so chummy, maybe you should visit her for a while."

A look of terror flickered across her face, but Rand refused to let himself feel any pity. Surprisingly, she took a warrior's stance.

"Since this house is rightfully mine, MacPherson, perhaps 'tis you who should find another place to live."

Rightfully hers? When she'd demanded every one of his male ancestors pay the price for his uncle's stupidity?

The red haze inched up to his heart. "Get your jacket and pack a bag. I'll drive you to my mother's."

She backed away. Bumping into the table, her gaze flashed defiance. "You don't know what you're saying— what you're asking of me."

Rand felt the crimson haze rise to his throat. Hell, of course he knew. Now that the quicksand of guilt he'd been mired in for the past month had firmed up, things were beginning to make sense. Cassandra had brought everything on herself. She'd been the reason Colin had turned into a bitter, lonely man. Not only was she the one responsible for his parents' divorce—she was the reason he'd never found a woman who wanted him.

He had to get her out of there before he did something they'd both be sorry for.

"Never mind." He headed for the hallway. "I'll throw some clothes in a suitcase for you. I'll even get your jacket. Go outside and get into the car."

"I canna," she said softly.

He stopped in his tracks. "Excuse me? I don't think I heard you right."

She'd worked her way into a corner of the breakfast nook. If he didn't know better, he'd suspect she was cowering. Retracing his steps, he stood in front of her, grasped one of her hands, and pulled. "Sure you can. Let's go."

Frantically, she tugged from his iron grip. "You don't understand. I canna leave this house. You canna make me go."

The crimson haze engulfed his brain. Coloring his vision, it blinded his self-control. "The hell I can't," he shot back, snagging her hand again. "Come on. It'll be better for both of us if you're out of here."

Together, they struggled from the kitchen into the hall. Cassandra dug in her heels, but Rand continued to pull until they arrived in the foyer. Just before they reached the front door she hit the marble tiles like a stone, but that only fueled his anger. Their battle had become more than one of wills. He needed to show her she'd been wrong, had to make her understand how dangerous it was when one person thought they had the right to mete out punishment to others.

And how in the hell could he ever come to terms with that other crap . . . the witchcraft stuff? What would he do if they had an argument one day and he suddenly found himself catching flies in the backyard pond?

Slowly, he drew air into his lungs. "I've carried you before, Cassandra. Don't think playing dead will stop me."

She rose to her knees and he hauled her to her feet. She opened her mouth to speak, but he refused to listen. Wrestling her to the door, he tugged until she was halfway across the threshold.

She screamed as her eyes darted to her arms. Or where her arms were supposed to be.

Rand tracked her gaze, saw the emptiness he was clinging to, and let go. "What the hell . . . !"

Falling to her backside, she stared up from the floor. Her face was pale, her mouth a thin line of pain, but her arms were back in view. "That's what I'm trying to tell you. I canna leave here. There's more I need to explain about the curse."

He took a half-step forward, then quickly changed his mind. She wasn't a flesh-and-blood woman. She was some kind of freak. Holy hell, he was as insane as Colin.

Cassandra struggled to her feet. "I'm real, but not completely. I won't be until I've taken care of my part of the curse."

"Your part?" God, could he sound any more pathetic?

"Before any future MacPherson males can ever find their own happiness, I have to admit I've found my one true love. And I have. I love you, Randall MacPherson, with all my heart."

Again she raised her hand to him, but he skittered out of reach. "Rand, please. The only way the spell can be broken is for you to acknowledge your feelings for me as well."

He took a step backward, then another, and another, until he was on the edge of the porch and she was a small form huddled on the other side of the door. Just before he turned away, Cassandra stretched out an arm and they both watched as it disappeared into the sunlight.

Incapable of speech, he opened then closed his mouth. After pounding down the stairs, he climbed into his Jeep and raced up the drive without a single look back.

Cassandra paced her room, unable to speak or even whisper a prayer. Over the past few hours her emotions had ranged from furious to miserable to resigned. She had lost the only man who could save her from her netherworld existence. The only man she would ever love.

The revulsion on the MacPherson's face when he'd seen her turn into nothingness had done more than shame her. It had made her physically ill. After emptying her belly of the little bit of tea she'd swallowed, she'd trudged to the third floor in a daze. A lifetime seemed to have passed before she'd felt well enough to rise from the bed.

Surely by now he'd finished his family celebration. What, she wondered, had he talked to them about? Had he confronted Irene or quizzed Melissa? Had he told them how much he despised her?

She would never forget the horror in his eyes, the disgust on his face when he'd seen her arms disappear. Not only would he never love her, he would most probably never look her in the eye again. Maybe he would even refuse to live here or set foot in the house, knowing she was in residence.

Worse, he might demand she leave and try to force her into the outside world one final time.

Shivering, she pulled the coverlet tighter around her shoulders. If she could see inside her heart, she was positive it would look as bleak as the night creeping in through the bedroom windows. She had nowhere to go. She was trapped here, doomed to live out her life with a man who hated her.

A chill rippled through her body, and she realized the house was frigid, almost as if the heating system had failed. Perhaps she needed to go to the main floor and fiddle with the temperature gauge. She might not be fully human, but it was certain she still needed all the comforts to survive.

Drawing a shaky breath, she rose to her feet. Once on the landing, she flipped the switch, but the area remained in darkness. Making her way down to the balcony, she sniffed at the acrid smell that seemed to permeate the air, almost as if something were burning.

She gasped when a burst of light caught her eye. Gazing from the balcony, she spied a brief shimmer of flame dance from the hall that led to the kitchen. As she made her way down the stairs, the smell intensified, as did the cloud of smoke billowing from the pantry.

Suddenly a shaft of fire writhed from the hallway into

the foyer. The roar of an explosion filled the crackling
air.

Smoke coated her throat, and Cassandra pressed a hand
to her mouth. She stared in stunned horror as a sheet of
flame shot toward her from the hall.

Chapter Twenty

Rand drove the streets in a daze. At first, he couldn't think straight . . . hell, he couldn't think at all. The only thing he could envision was Cassandra, struggling against him in the doorway, staring in horror as pieces of her body disappeared from view.

He couldn't describe the experience properly. One second he'd been dragging her across the threshold, the next he was holding what felt like the same unset Jell-O he'd touched when they'd first met. Only he hadn't been able to *see* anything. Cassandra was there, but she wasn't.

He slammed a palm against the steering wheel. None of it made any sense. Who in the heck would believe him if he tried to explain it? Not a damned soul, except maybe his mother and her partner in crime, that Ragweed woman. And Irene was the last person he wanted to talk to right now.

Cassandra might not be a spirit in the strictest sense of the word, but she surely wasn't human. And it was obvious from the way she held back, then agonized over telling him the story, that she'd been pretty certain of his reaction once he learned the truth.

What had she wanted him to do? Mutter that he forgave her for ruining his parents' lives? Tell her it was perfectly okay to continue practicing her own special brand of medieval voodoo? How was he supposed to tell people he was in love with a woman who couldn't leave the house? Did she actually expect them to live together as if they were a normal everyday couple—with him going about his daily business while she toiled over a boiling cauldron in the bowels of the basement?

Did witches get sick? What if Cassandra needed medical attention that couldn't be provided for in the house? Could she get pregnant? If so, what would their children be like? Would she, as they'd feared, disappear completely one day and leave him to spend his life alone, maybe go crazy like his uncle?

The questions were mounting and he didn't have the patience to wait for answers. He'd been duped, played for a fool. Cassandra and his mother had known about each other for weeks, and neither had said a word. He'd just spent the past few days making love to an enigma. A woman who was a spirit and a spirit who was a woman—not totally one or the other. What kind of idiot did she think he was?

Would she ever be real?

She'd lied to him about so many things, he wasn't sure where the fantasy left off and reality began.

Cassandra said she loved him, but she'd also confessed she needed his help. Her impassioned plea sounded just a bit too desperate to be anything more than a pathetic attempt to get him to utter those three little words. Could he ever trust her to tell him the truth?

Hours late for dinner, Rand arrived in the neighborhood where he'd grown up. He'd never noticed how quiet the street was until then. Of course, most everyone was inside, recuperating from the feast, probably watching a football game or snoozing away the traditional Thanksgiving meal. Living like normal people in a normal world—something he hadn't done for weeks.

Something he would probably never be able to do again.

He pulled into the drive and parked behind Nancy's SUV. He doubted anyone had missed him, except his sister, of course. His mother wouldn't have worried, because she knew he was playing house with a woman who'd ruined the life of every MacPherson male for the past one hundred years. Leave it to Irene to be kind to Cassandra even after she realized what the little witch . . . aw, crap, what *Cassandra* had done.

He sat and stared at the house without a clue as to whether or not he should go inside. How was he supposed to act? How could he sit at the table and pretend things were fine and dandy when he'd been thrown a curve so daunting, it was a miracle he hadn't driven off the side of the road on his way over here?

Commotion erupted on the porch. The brightly painted front door swung open and Princess charged out, dragging Robbie behind on the leash. The boy's eyes lit up when he spied Rand and he barreled straight for the Jeep.

"Hey, Uncle Rand, where ya been? Dinner's over. Grandma's going to cut the pies."

Rand didn't answer right away. He wasn't even sure he could get out of his car.

"Uncle Rand? You okay? Where have you been?"

"Hmm? Oh, hey, sport. How you doin'?"

"I'm stuffed. Mom and Melissa are playing a card game and Grandpa Harry is asleep on the sofa. Mom was worried about you, but Grandma said you were probably busy and you'd get here when you got here. She's acting really goofy today."

Rand rested his forehead on the steering wheel. Just

as he suspected, everything was perfectly normal with *his* family. So now what was he supposed to do? Go inside and confront his mother? Or go home to Cassandra and tell her she had to find her way out of his life?

Unhappy with both choices, he rubbed a hand across his jaw. Cassandra had turned his uncle into a raving lunatic. She'd wrecked his parents' marriage and, without realizing it, played havoc with the relationship he had with his mother. True, Colin had deserved his fate, but his mom and dad hadn't needed a curse to help muck up the mess they'd been in.

"Uncle Rand? You coming inside?" Princess had pulled Robbie three feet from the driveway and was now daintily doing her doggie business on the manicured lawn.

Rand had just about decided to turn around and drive straight back to the house, when Nancy shot from the front door and ran down the stairs, shouting at the top of her lungs. "Thank God you're here. Bill called. You have to go back home!"

She skidded to a stop inches from the Jeep. Panting, she held her hand to her chest. "I asked him to stop and find out what was keeping you. He's there right now, hosing down the rear of the house."

Hosing down the house?

Irene, Harry, and Melissa stepped onto the porch. "I'll take the children next door to the Gilberts. We'll meet you over there," his mother called, shuffling his niece down the steps.

Rand stared blankly at his sister. "What the heck are you talking about?"

Nancy was already climbing into her car. "Get going! Your house is on fire!"

Cassandra crouched in a far corner of her bedroom. The acrid smell of burning chemicals and charred wood stung her nose and clawed at her throat. The air in the room seemed blurry, and she was having a hard time drawing breath into her lungs.

When she'd first come upon the fire, she'd tried to put it out with wet towels she'd carried from the master bath, but the towels had dried almost before she'd thrown them on the flames. After a second series of small explosions echoed from the hall leading to the kitchen, the smoke had begun to billow in earnest, so she'd taken one of Rand's shirts and doused it in water, then wrapped it around her head and face and made her way up the stairs into her room.

Now, through the crackle of flames, she thought she heard the wail of a fire engine. She stumbled to her feet and peered out a back window. In the glow cast by the flames she could see Duke struggling with some kind of pump and hose equipment he'd dragged to the pond. Finally, he managed to carry the hose to the house and raise it to his shoulder.

A wave of water hit the window, then another and another. But the fanning arc of wetness didn't seem to be having much effect. Cassandra could hear the house's century-old beams scream in protest as they were devoured by the fire.

Sagging against the window, she knew her life was over . . . again. If she didn't burn to death, the smoke would kill her, or she would be exposed to the elements and disappear.

Worse, she would never see the MacPherson again.

Another blast of water hit the house and she started. Suddenly, she recalled the conversation she and Rand had shared before he left. She'd told him she believed she was a witch, had even made a tomato disappear to prove it. Didn't that mean she was still capable of calling on the elements to aid her?

She raced to the door and laid her palms on the wood.

The door was warm to the touch, as was the metal knob, but she could still grasp it in her hand. She rearranged the damp cloth around her head and mouth and stepped onto the landing. Smoke filled the air, but the flames had yet to reach the third floor.

She followed the stairs to the balcony. Somewhere she had heard that people caught in a burning building should stay low to the ground. Dropping to her knees, she crawled to the lip of the landing. The downstairs foyer walls were ablaze, the front windows blown out, but thanks to the marble tiles the stairway was still intact.

Kneeling, she raised her arms over her head as she called on the element of water to do her bidding. With her eyes closed, she imagined a gentle rain drizzling from the ceiling into the foyer, the kitchen, the library. The vision built until she saw the water soak the wallpaper, curtains, floor.

A screaming sound joined with the hissing all around her. Snapping open her eyes, she saw a heavy mist trying to permeate the smoke-filled air. But as fast as the damp spray melded into the downstairs, it turned to steam. In despair, Cassandra rose to her feet as a sheet of flame roared up the staircase, catching the bottom step and banister on fire.

The screech of sirens grew deafening, then came a barrage of noise, pounding footsteps, the sound of metal hitting wood as an ax shattered the front door. Men dressed in raincoats and fire-fighting gear charged through the archway. Dragging equipment in their wake, they ran through the house, swamping everything in their path.

Instinctively, Cassandra cowered against the balcony wall. If the firemen carried her outside, she would disappear. It would be better, she decided, to be consumed by the flames than cast to the unknown nothingness.

She heard a racket on the lawn. The MacPherson flew through the door. One of the firemen grabbed him and hauled him to a stop. Another pinned his arms from behind. "You can't be here," the first man shouted. "This place is a tinderbox."

Rand's gaze darted to the second floor. "I've got to find her!"

"Rand!" Cassandra cried. "Listen to them. Get out of here!"

Rand saw Cassandra through the sheet of fire engulfing the staircase. She'd backed herself against the wall and was shouting, but he couldn't make out her words over the roar.

The fireman at his back jerked him toward the door. "Go outside—let us do our job!"

"You don't understand." Rand shook off both men and headed for the stairs. "I've got to get to the balcony. I've got to save her."

A trio of firefighters bolted past them to the rear of the house. Another yelled in his ear. "Who's up there? Is someone upstairs?"

Rand stared at Cassandra's wavering form, barely visible through the smoke and flames. Holy God, she was disappearing before his very eyes!

He inhaled a breath, his lungs filling with smoke. Just as he pushed the fireman aside, he was grabbed from behind and half lifted in the air.

"No way, boss man," Duke shouted, whirling them both around to the front door. "There's nothing up there more important than your life."

Rand struggled, tore from the foreman's grip, and lunged toward the steps. "Get the hell out of my way. She's up there. Cassandra! I'm coming!"

Streaming jets of water arced around him, but they had no affect on the fire. Smoke blew through the second floor, flames licked the upper landing walls. Duke's soot-streaked hands dragged him back again, but Rand managed to break free.

"Cassandra! Hang on!" he cried, vaulting to the middle of the staircase.

He saw her then, standing like a Viking princess against the flames. Her hair was a halo of sparks dancing around her head, yet there was a resigned, almost serene look on her smoke-blackened face. Like a warrior on her funeral barge, she seemed to embrace the fire as it consumed her.

"Cassandra! I'm coming!"

She shook her head, smiled at him through the wall of smoke and flames. Dreamlike, she held out her arms. "Save yourself, MacPherson, but always remember that I loved you. Now and forever!"

The sound of her voice stopped him in his tracks. Even after he had left her to be burned alive, she still loved him. And all it would have taken to save her were three little words.

Rand staggered up the stairs, heard the groan of wood, the frantic shouts as the staircase swayed. He grabbed at the burning banister, prepared to hoist himself up the final steps. He would save her or die trying.

A ceiling beam dropped in front of him, shearing the charred stairway from the second-floor landing.

Raising his gaze to the balcony, he saw her tear-streaked face as she reached out to him.

"Cassandra, I love you!"

In slow motion, the wood beneath his feet fell away. The last thing he heard was her scream as he dropped into the flames.

"How is he today?"

"Better," a hushed voice answered. "He even asked for water a little while ago. I'm afraid it's going to be a bit longer before his lungs and throat are back to normal."

"I know. I just wish . . ."

"His hands are healing nicely. Dr. Wayne said he'd remove the bandages in a day or two."

"Do you think he'll talk to me today?"

"It's possible. We've lowered the dosage on his pain medication and the monitor says he's awake. His brain activity is fine and his vitals are good. The best thing you and your daughter can do is visit him every day, so he knows his loved ones are near."

Rand heard the whispered conversation from a distance, as though he were floating on a cresting wave of water. Familiar noises welled around him, and he pictured the scenario in his mind. The squeaking of rubber-soled shoes and the swish of the door meant the nurse had left the room. The sound of scraping metal told him his mother was pulling up a chair. The rustle of fabric when she sat down and the movement of his mattress said she was leaning near.

"Randall, I'm here. How are you feeling today?"

Irene's voice was shaky and filled with tears. Vaguely, he remembered hearing it this same way for the past several days. He licked his tongue across his cracked lower lip and worked the muscles in his throat, but all he could manage was a thick rasp of breath.

"Would you like some water?"

He heard a gentle splash, envisioned her pouring the crystal liquid into a glass, felt the straw as she threaded it carefully through his lips. Slowly, painfully, he sucked until the cool water soothed his aching throat.

He heard more movement, then the clink of the glass as it hit his beside table. "I brought the latest Tom Clancy. Would you like me to read to you?"

Rand knew it would annoy her, so he shrugged out a no.

"All right, if you don't want me to read, then you'll simply have to listen to what I have to say."

Vehemently, he whipped his head back and forth, wincing at the pain. Cassandra was gone. There was nothing left for them to talk about. Not today. Not ever.

"It's been three weeks since the fire. I realize you're still in pain, but I'm certain you've been coherent for a few days now. It's time we had a talk about Cass—"

He fluttered his eyelids open and glared against the bright hospital lights. It was obvious from her expression of surprise that he'd shocked her.

"I knew that would do it," she said with a smug tilt of her chin. "You're being stubborn and difficult—an unbecoming trait, even for you. You have to listen to my news."

Wearily, he closed his eyes. "Go way, Moth-er."

"You spoke!" Irene squeezed the little finger of his right hand, the only place on his upper body that had survived the ravages of the fire.

Every muscle ached, and Rand imagined he was bruised in places too private to talk about in mixed company. Then again, how else should he expect to feel when he'd fallen fifteen feet and landed in the middle of a burning staircase? In answer, he pulled his hand away. Through the silence, he heard her sniffle.

"Don't," he muttered, though the effort almost made him pass out. "Just go."

He heard the rustle of her handbag, a heaving sigh. Irene blew her nose, then there was a moment of resigned silence.

"If you won't allow me to speak of Cassandra, perhaps you'd like to hear about Bill. He helped the firemen drag you out of the house, you know. His throat is sore and his hands had some superficial burns, but they're almost healed. Best of all, Robbie thinks he's a hero."

He turned up his lips in a half-smile. "Go-od for Duke."

He heard her sigh, so forceful the rush of air feathered his face. "If you won't let me talk to you about . . . her, then believe me when I tell you how sorry I am that all of this happened. I should have told you the truth from the moment I met the girl. I understand what you've been going through.''

The urge to scream overwhelmed him. *You don't know! You can't know!* he wanted to shout, but the very thought of making an effort wore him out.

All he wanted was to sleep, because when he slept he dreamed. And when he dreamed, it was always about Cassandra. In his dreams, she was alive and well. Sometimes, she was standing in the circle of his arms, other times she was pacing their bedroom, her hands on her hips while she dared him to see her side of things. But the best dreams were the ones where she was in his bed, loving him the way he didn't deserve to be loved.

''Rand, I'm not leaving you.'' Irene's voice trembled with unspoken resolve. ''But we are going to talk about her . . . someday soon.''

Crap, he thought when he felt a tear slip from the corner of his eye. His mother dabbed at it with a tissue and he turned his head in embarrassment.

''Why don't you take a nap? If I'm not here when you wake up, Nancy will be.''

Good idea, Rand thought, because he really needed to see Cassandra.

Rand rolled to his back and heaved a sigh. He'd been home from the hospital for less than a week and he was feeling almost normal. The respiratory therapy had done its job. The clawing rawness in his lungs and throat was gone; physically, at least, he was going to be fine.

He heard the click of the lock on his apartment door and checked the clock on his nightstand. Jeez, it was barely nine A.M. What a time for his sister or his mother to come see how he was doing.

Tap . . . tap . . . tap . . .

Well, that took care of the mystery. Irene had either brought him breakfast or planned to rearrange his furniture for the umpteenth time. Since the fire, she couldn't seem to stay away.

She had become the ideal doting mother. She'd refurnished his apartment from top to bottom, bought him a closet full of new clothes and restocked his kitchen. She'd even slept on his sofa the first night he was home. Over the past week, they'd managed to air a lot of old laundry, including her take on the divorce. Even though he continued to refuse to let her speak Cassandra's name, they'd grown close.

A wave of misery swept through him, as it did every morning, and he welcomed it, clinging to the ache constricting his heart. It had been over a month since the fire, and his memory of it was just as sharp, just as vivid, just as painful. But he was learning to cope.

The day he'd left the hospital, he'd driven to the house and searched the rubble. Duke had dragged him away because no one, not even the investigators, had found a trace of a body in the remains. According to the fire marshal, the flames had been fueled by the paint, liquid sealants, and other construction materials stacked inside. Coupled with the hundred-year-old wood, the house had burned as hot as a crematorium.

Of course, no one believed him when he'd insisted there'd been a woman trapped inside. They'd chalked up his obsessive concern to delirium or post-traumatic shock and advised him to seek help if he couldn't get a handle on his depression. When Irene's irreverent comment about how much he was acting like Colin made him chuckle, he realized she really did know how he felt. That had drawn them even closer.

Rising from the bed, he walked to the dresser, opened a drawer and tugged on a new pair of jeans. His burns had healed, but it was going to take a hell of a lot longer to cure his guilty conscience . . . and he didn't think his heart would ever return to normal. He was going to make damn sure he didn't go mad like his uncle, but he was prepared to live a solitary life.

He'd lost the one thing in the world that truly mattered, and it wasn't a charred pile of wood and mortar. He'd lost the only woman he would ever love. If he couldn't have Cassandra, he would have no one.

He heard a whisper of voices, then the quick tapping of Irene's heels. Drawing a breath, he sat on the edge of the mattress and put on his socks and shoes. Seconds later, a soft knock hit the bedroom door.

"Come on in, Mom. I'm dressed."

The door inched open a crack. "Hello, dear. How are you feeling?"

He stood and walked to the door. "Better, thanks. I thought you were going to stay home and get ready for tonight? You know how you love Christmas Eve."

She smiled as she slipped into the room. "True, but I had to bring over your present first."

He saw the sparkle in her eyes and groaned, wondering what more she could give him. The only thing he wanted was completely out of reach, and she knew it as well as he did.

"Mom, you've done enough. The furniture, the clothes, the baby-sitting. I can take care of myself. Honest."

"I'm sure you can," she said with a knowing smile. "It's just that my surprise—well, it's Harry's surprise too—has been ready for a while now, and I couldn't wait a minute longer to give it to you. It's a bit large, so we decided you should open . . . unwrap . . . um, you needed to see it here first."

"I thought I heard voices. Is Harry in the living room?"

"No. He's at home making his world-famous eggnog."

"Then who were you talking to?" Rand went to the mirror and ran his hands through his newly grown hair.

Instead of answering, she stood next to him and locked her gaze with his in the mirror. "I'm leaving. I just needed to say something to you before you came to the house tonight."

Rand turned and gave her a hug. "And what would that be?"

They stood close for a few seconds, then she backed up and stared at him with a strange smile on her face. "I just need for you to know that all I've ever wanted is your happiness."

Before he could reply, she was gone. The noisy staccato of her heels faded, and he shrugged. What, he wondered, was that all about?

He stepped from the bedroom into the foyer, prepared to head for the kitchen, when movement in the living room caught his attention. Framed in the morning sunshine streaming through the window was a woman gazing at the softly falling snow.

Her hair was short, curly as a lamb's, and as golden as the sunrise. She wore gray tailored slacks and a bright red sweater, and someone had taken a white satin ribbon, wrapped it around the woman's waist and tied it into a huge bow at her back.

His heart did a stutter step and he gasped. At the sound of his indrawn breath, the figure spun on her heel. Tear-filled eyes the color of wet amethysts stared at him for a half-second before she spoke.

"Merry Christmas, MacPherson. I hope you're happy with your present."

Rand's jaw dropped to his chest. Positive he was in the midst of another of his crazy dreams, he stood rooted in place. "Cassandra? How in the . . . ?"

"It was you." She wiped her cheeks as she whispered, "You saved me. When you told me you loved me, you broke the curse. At that moment, the whole world heard how much you cared. I became real.''

God, she was even more beautiful than he remembered. But she had to hate him. It was because of him that she'd almost burned to death. "How did you get away?"

With her palms open, she held her arms at her sides. "Truly, I'm not sure. I heard you say the words, watched you fall, and it was like the house just spat me out onto the back lawn. Your mother found me wandering and whisked me away before anyone realized it."

Fearful she'd disappear if he moved, he asked, "Why did you stay away? Why didn't you come to me sooner?"

"I wanted to." She fluttered her hands through her hair. "But you were so sick, and I was a bit of a mess myself. Harry said it was important I stay hidden until he got the paperwork done. Then your mother told me you didn't want to discuss what had happened. She tended to my burns and nursed me whenever she wasn't with you at the hospital. She's been a saint."

"Mother," he said with a grimace. "I don't know whether I should kiss her or kill her for putting me through all this." He tucked his hands into his pockets. "I guess I deserve the misery I've been going through for being such a jerk, for not believing you."

"Not another word." Her eyes twinkled through the tears. "It's time to move on with our lives . . . if you'll have me."

If he'd have her! "Jeez, Cassandra, how can you ask me that? I'm the one who should be begging your forgiveness. I've been such a fool."

She took a step toward him, her sweet face a mask of amused patience. "True. But I hear you've reformed."

Finally, his feet came to life. Walking toward her, he expelled a breath. "You're all right, then? You're not going to disappear? You're here to stay?"

"Why don't you unwrap me and find out for yourself?" She twirled flirtatiously, then gave him a teasing grin.

Rand uttered a small prayer of thanks. Opening his arms, he caught her as she took a flying leap at his chest. Stumbling backward into his bedroom, they tumbled together onto the bed.

"I was a jerk. A total idiot," he muttered, kissing her eyes, her nose, her chin. "I don't deserve you . . . this . . . us."

She set her palms on his cheeks. "But you love me?"

He barked out a laugh. "Baby, I think I loved you *before* I even saw you."

"Then I'll be a reasonable woman. I'll let you spend the rest of our lives making it up to me . . . now and forever."

In answer, Rand managed to say again the words Cassandra had been waiting a century to hear.

Epilogue

Cassandra gazed out the kitchen window, her mind drifting to the past year. So many wonderful things had happened, all of them culminating in this one perfect afternoon. She and Rand would be celebrating their first wedding anniversary in less than a week. They had moved into their new home just yesterday, and amazingly, she was nine months pregnant with their child.

She would be the first to admit they'd had hurdles along the way. On that first Christmas Eve, when Rand had brought her to his mother's, Nancy and Duke had asked a hundred questions. Though they had stuck to his original idea of introducing her as the great-great-niece of Cassandra Kinross, it had still been a trial for her to act and speak the lie. Then Harry had tackled a mountain of red tape in order to obtain the papers for her citizenship. And if people raised their eyebrows at the hasty way she and the MacPherson had married, well, the speculation had passed quickly enough.

Now, blissfully happy, Cassandra made it a daily practice to thank the Lord for granting her a second chance at life.

She peered into the oven to check on the roast and felt a growing ache in her lower back. She'd been having mild contractions on and off for most of the morning, but this one was more severe than the others. At first she'd thought they were only Braxton-Hicks contractions. Now she wasn't so sure. From the feel of it, this bairn was going to be born on the very day they were christening their new home.

"Cassandra," Rand called from the front of the house. "What's taking so long? Everybody's waiting."

"I'll be right there!" she answered as she pictured her family gathered on the porch.

Irene and Harry were probably fussing over Robbie and Melissa, while Duke and Nancy were holding hands and casting each other calf-eyed looks like a typical engaged couple. Knowing Rand, he was pacing with a bottle of champagne in his hands, counting the seconds it took for her to join them.

This home was situated farther back on the property and sat sideways to the refurbished pond, so they had a wonderful view of the woodland creatures who often came to visit. The new Victorian was almost exactly like the one Colin had built, except that everything in it was of Cassandra's own choosing. Rand had allowed her free rein with the design and decorating. With Nancy's help, the mansion had turned into a true showcase.

"Cass. Don't make me come get you," Rand yelled, his voice only half threatening. Since she'd grown so large, the great bonehead had taken to carrying her from room to room, just to show everyone how precious she and their soon-to-be-born child were to him.

She took a deep breath and relaxed as the pain passed. Surely the contractions were mild enough that she had time to finish their celebration? Rand had told her he wanted the ceremony to resemble the christening of a battleship before its maiden voyage. Afterward, they were supposed to have their first family dinner in the dining room.

Just as she decided it was time to warn everyone of the impending birth, Rand strode into the kitchen. Setting the champagne bottle on the center island, he walked directly in front of her. Placing his hands on her belly, he gave her a loud smacking kiss on her lips.

"What the heck have you been doing? You're holding up the main event."

The next contraction took her unaware, and she clutched at him until her knuckles turned white. "Don't look at me, MacPherson. It's your child who plans to ruin this party."

"The baby. It's the baby?" He caught her in his arms as she staggered. "Isn't it too early? It can't be the baby."

She grinned against the pain. Lifting her hand, she patted his pale cheek. "Tell that to the wee one, please, for I fear he or she will be here soon enough."

"Aw, crap. Aw, jeez." Rand scooped her up in his arms. "Do you think everything's okay? You know, because you were a . . . a . . . well, you remember."

She giggled as she uttered a tiny white lie. "Have I done one thing to make you think my powers are still intact? Now, put me down. I'm perfectly capable of walking to the car."

"Unh-unh, not on a bet." He carried her through the hall and into the foyer. "Duke, get Cassandra's bag, would you? It's in the front closet."

Duke's shocked gaze skittered to her bulging stomach. "The baby's here?"

Nancy shoved at his shoulder. "Not yet. It's her first, so it's probably going to be a while."

Harry and Irene each took one of the kids in tow. "Come along," Irene ordered mustering the troops. "Everyone can follow us to the hospital."

One by one, they marched down the stairs. Rand

brought Cassandra to the car and set her on her feet. Another wave of pain hit, and she clung to his arms. As soon as the contraction passed, she softened against his chest.

"I'm so flustered, I'm not sure I can drive," he said with a shaky laugh, helping her into the car. "Have we taken care of everything? Is the oven off?"

Cassandra wrinkled her nose. "Aye."

Rand scrambled to the driver's side, climbed in, and started the engine. "What about the front door?"

Turning toward the porch, she blinked. "Done," she managed to say through smiling lips.

"Well then, I guess there's nothing left but to get this show on the road." Rand headed the car up the drive. Once they reached the highway, he grabbed one of her hands and squeezed. "Have I told you lately how much I love you?"

Another contraction took hold. Drawing comfort from the feel of their joined hands, Cassandra exhaled a breath. "Aye, MacPherson, every day, in every way. Never doubt for a moment we are each other's one true love."

ABOUT THE AUTHOR

JUDI MCCOY has been writing for seven years. An elite level women's gymnastic judge, she lives in North Texas with her husband, Dennis, and two lively little dogs named Rudy and Buckley. She raised two beautiful daughters, Sara and Carey, and is now living her dream as a full-time author of romance. Please visit her website at www.judimccoy.com

To find out what happens when an eighteenth-
century treasure hunting pirate helps a
present-day, savvy single mom save a floundering
town of senior citizens in the Florida Keys

... read ...

SAY YOU'RE MINE

by

Judi McCoy

COMING IN SEPTEMBER 2002